The Sunshine Chronicles: Forgotten Flare

Kelsey Leign

All artwork by Kelsey Leign.

Women's handwriting by Alyssa Ruiz.

Men's handwriting by Kelsey Leign.

Copyright © 2024 Kelsey Leign

All rights reserved.

To the teacher who encouraged me to keep writing at seventeen.
This one's for you, Ms. Kelley.

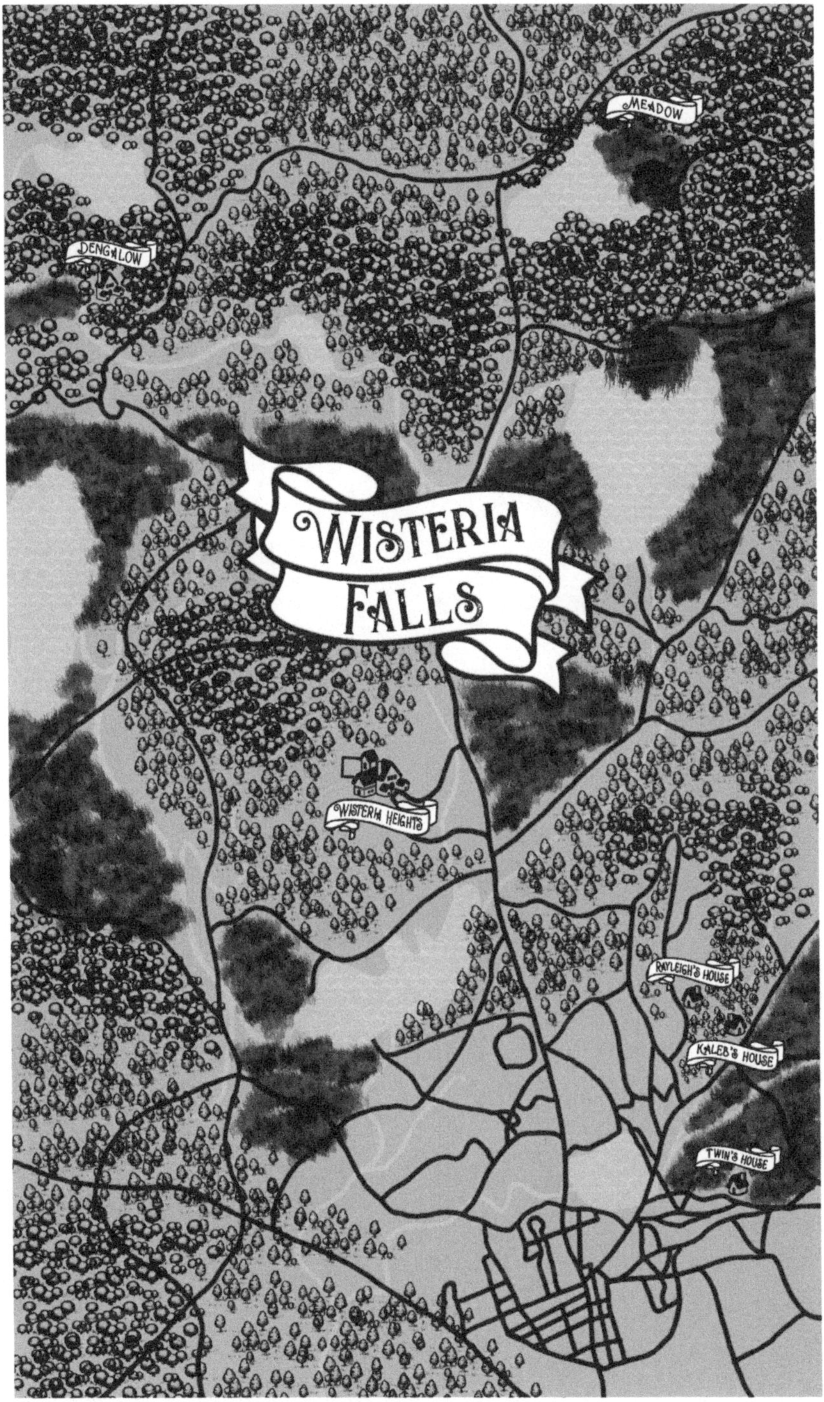
MEADOW
DENGALOW
WISTERIA FALLS
WISTERIA HEIGHTS
RAYLEIGH'S HOUSE
KALEB'S HOUSE
TWIN'S HOUSE

Prologue

The first night I escaped death was the night I wish it had taken me.

Arabella and I were driving back from a Taylor Swift concert, listening to our favorite album and scream-singing every song at the top of our lungs. It was pouring outside, but it only encouraged us to sing louder to drown out the sound of the rain pelting the car.

She was fully immersed in the song, her face scrunched up as she sang our favorite part of "Bad Blood."

There was no traffic on the road when I started to make that fatal left turn.

But then I saw the headlights of a truck.

They were visible right past her head, growing bigger far too quickly to be slowing down.

There was nothing I could have done to stop what happened next.

The headlights flared brighter.

A horn honked.

The world went white.

A scream echoed by a roar of thunder.

Then everything went black.

Silence.

I woke up in a white room—back stiff, neck in a brace, and pain radiating down my left side—probably a broken rib. I recognized the familiar sounds of an emergency room, if only because of my clumsiness as a child.

The room came into focus around me. I became aware of all the people surrounding me. Hands were everywhere. It was hard to tell who was doing what. Someone checked my vitals while others picked out pieces of glass and rocks embedded in my arm. After some time, the debris was removed, the bleeding slowed, and the wounds were cleansed before being covered in salve and bandages. I couldn't see past the arm they tended to because none of my muscles wanted to cooperate. I only assumed they had more to do based on the pain I could feel throughout the rest of my body.

The person taking my vitals noticed my eyes were open and turned his attention to me, pulling a small flashlight out to check my pupils for responsiveness. After blinking harshly at the sudden bright light and wincing from the pain it caused, he took away the flashlight. I opened my eyes again, trying to focus on his face. His mouth was moving, but I couldn't hear his voice. That seemed odd since the other noises in the room were clear as day. I focused on his moving mouth and willed myself to hear his voice, using my lip-reading skills as a backup.

He asked me to squeeze his hand. But I couldn't even feel my hand, let alone move it. He understood and switched tactics, asking me to blink if I could hear him. I did, wincing again at the pain that shot through my head. He nodded and asked me to answer his questions with one blink for "no" and two for "yes."

"Does anything hurt?" He asked.

I blinked twice.

"Can you move any part of your body?"

One blink.

He pressed lightly just above my brow, and pain radiated down my temple. "Can you feel this?"

Two blinks, wincing through both.

"Can you tell me your name?" He asked.

I concentrated on moving my lips and felt them open. I tried to voice my name, but only a gurgling sound came out. Liquid filled my mouth, a strange taste of metal and salt. I blinked once.

He nodded and turned away to ask one of the others to clear the blood and extra saliva out of my mouth. Then he turned to the man who had just entered the room. The doctor wore familiar smiley face scrubs, and the lines of concern on his face deepened as he took me in. Something the nurse said made him shift his focus to something beyond me. He was nodding at whatever the man beside him said, his eyebrows growing closer with each nod. But when I strained to hear what was said, someone blocked my view and placed a suction hose in my mouth. On my other side, a nurse with a water hose went to work rinsing my mouth of blood.

I closed my eyes to avoid the slight spray of water and tried to remember how I'd gotten there.

Bright lights.

A scream.

Thunder.

My eyes shot open, and my heart sank to my stomach.

Something was missing. Something important.

A little voice in my head told me it was in the direction of Dr. Smiles's worried expression.

I tried turning my head to look around the room, but it wouldn't budge. The nurse with the water hose in my mouth made it impossible to see past her. I coughed, causing a burst of pain to rush through my chest, which confirmed my theory of a broken rib. The lady noticed my distress, told the other nurse to halt the suction, and walked around the bed to speak with the men by the door, still engaged in an intense conversation from what I could see.

Her absence created an opening. I mustered my strength and pushed myself to move. I needed to know. I forced my neck to turn my head. To search for what I was missing. Agonizing pain kicked in as my head finally cooperated, and my view of the room changed to include the bed next to mine.

Horror ran through my body as I took in what I saw. A sheet that could have once been white or blue—but was no longer—covered a mass on the bed. It had been stained red from the amount of blood on it.

She lay motionless underneath it.

She can't be gone, I thought to myself.

But I had to make sure... My eyes fell to her chest, and as I stared at the unmoving sheets, I knew.

My heart didn't want to believe it, though. There was only one way to confirm it.

Only *one thing* would tell me.

My eyes traveled to the forearm hanging off the gurney.

Tears stung my eyes as I saw the moon tattoo with the familiar words "to the moon and back."

It matched the one on mine.

I
You'll Be in My Heart

October 24th. A year since the crash. I didn't know if the tears would let me out of bed. How did I survive an entire year without my other half? She was the only one who could have brought a smile to my face, yet I woke to find her bed still empty. The unmoved sheets mocked me from across the room. My eyes burned as tears fell to join the stains on my pillow from the night before.

The memory of the night that changed my life forever flashed through my mind as my emotions consumed me. The truck hit the passenger side, causing our car to flip in the intersection. The impact had killed Arabella instantly. But I walked away. Granted, I had three broken ribs, a broken arm, a cracked hip bone, and stitches in my head and down the length of my forearm where our matching tattoos were. It left a scar across the moon that never faded.

Arabella was brought to the hospital in hopes of revival, but in the end, we could only say goodbye.

I heard a knock at my door. "Come in." I didn't think my gravelly voice was loud enough for the person on the other side of the door to hear, but my dad peeked his head in as I swung my feet to the ground.

"Morning, Daddy." I gave him a small smile as he walked in to sit beside me on my bed. He reached his hand up to wipe some of the tears from my face, and I noticed he was fighting back his own.

"Good morning, my little Ray of sunshine." He put his arm around my shoulder and squeezed as he kissed my head. "It's supposed to rain today. Would you like to go to the meadow after I get off work?" He smiled.

A meadow not too far from our house ran alongside a small lake. Wildflowers and tall grass grew freely in the surrounding clearing. A massive tree sat at the center with a twisted trunk and long leafy branches—a perfect place to enjoy the shade. Dad usually sat there with his journal or guitar, writing lyrics or learning the chords of new songs. He brought Arabella and me along if we weren't in school, and we danced to his music. Sometimes, he attempted to teach us to play guitar. Whenever he brought Mitch along, though, the day's activities would turn into tag or hide and seek, and eventually, someone would get pushed into the lake for a swim. There was a cave nearby that Arabella and I had made use of for hide-and-seek with Mitch—He hated that cave.

Jordin, our mom, came along to paint sometimes, too. She always disappeared into the surrounding trees when we were all distracted and reappeared with a fully painted canvas when it was almost time to go. She told us painting from different views of the area helped her better capture the beauty.

Today, though, I knew Dad wanted to go to the meadow in memory of Arabella. One of her favorite things to do was dance in the rain, and it seemed to be fate that it was raining today—the anniversary of her death. I'd only gone to the meadow one other time since she died.

"That sounds great, Dad." I leaned into his hug, breathing in his warm, earthy scent. My dad's hugs were the best. His arms were the one place I always knew I was safe. He squeezed a little harder as I rested my head on his shoulder, my hot tears soaking through his shirt. I pulled away and saw tears collecting in the stubble around his jaw. I smiled weakly. My gaze dropped to the ground where several books lay scattered. I stood, picking up a well-worn one, and turned it over to read the title of the first Harry Potter book. The corner of my lip pulled up as a memory flashed across my mind.

Arabella was sitting cross-legged on her bed. She'd been begging me to read the books, knowing I'd love the adventure in them, but I always shrugged her off. One day, I said if she wanted me to read it so badly, she could read it to me. She didn't hesitate. She made me sit and dove right in, using her best British accent and silly voices for all the characters. I laughed through most of it, but it was one of my favorite memories.

"I wish I could curl up and read one of Arabella's favorite books. Skip school. Get lost in a world of fantasy. Forget all my responsibilities." I hugged the book to my chest as I looked down at Dad. "You could skip work too…?" I said hopefully.

He stood up next to me. "That sounds like a marvelous idea for you, Sunshine. But I told Brinkley I'd be in by eleven this morning." He said his last words with regret. "Your mother called the school and told them you wouldn't be in. Besides," he gestured toward the clock, "it's past nine already."

How had I slept so late? Classes would have started over an hour ago, and I already missed the first block. "I'll have to thank Jordin for that," I said. Dad made a slight face when I called her by her first name, but I went on before he could address it. "I couldn't fall asleep last night," I confessed.

Every time I closed my eyes, flashes of the accident made me jerk them open again. When I finally managed to fall asleep, I woke up thrashing in bed, terrified of the monster that came to claim my twin sister. Or I was dragged away by the same monster only to wake up from the sensation of falling from its clutches. It was one of the recurring nightmares that kept me up most nights over the past year. No one knew about the night terrors. I didn't want them to know I still suffered. I knew I could tell Dad; he'd only want to help. But that was precisely why I didn't tell him, because there was nothing he *could* do.

Something he said made me ask, "How did you get time off this morning?" It was almost impossible for him to get away from work, or so he said.

"Well, being the CEO of the company has its perks." I raised an eyebrow at him, knowing that never made a difference. He shrugged, "Brinkley can handle things for a few hours." His wink and soft smile told me to drop it. I had no idea what my dad did for work, but it was such a well-kept secret that I didn't even know his company's name or if he had an office. He claimed it had something to do with the government. We were left to trust that it wasn't something illegal. Sometimes, I wondered if he was part of a mafia because the only person we knew he worked with was Brinkley, and he wouldn't, or couldn't, tell us anything else. "Besides, I wanted to make you breakfast this morning. Your favorite!"

All thoughts of his mysterious job vanished, and my eyes widened, "Really? You even made th-"

"Everything. Come on!" He led me out the door to the spiral staircase, which I carefully maneuvered—seeing as I've fallen down the stairs more times than I cared to admit. It was the curse of having two left feet.

When we reached the landing, I turned to the dining room windows and watched the rain fall on the trees in our backyard grove. The flowers were blooming brightly, and the green trees were dripping rain. They seemed to be crying, in a way. The day matched the mood I was in.

Dad pulled a chair out at the head of the table, where a small array of food sat waiting for us, including my absolute favorite: French toast with strawberries and powdered sugar on top. I filled my plate with food and quickly devoured each bite of deliciousness. Dad and I usually cooked together, which was part of the reason I wanted to go to school to be a chef. There were so many foods in the world, and I wanted to learn to make them all. Dad knew his way around the kitchen and taught me everything he knew, but my cooking class at school helped, too. He and Kaleb referred to me as Chef Foster, knowing I could make a meal from anything; give me a spice cabinet and a stove.

"I should get ready for work," Dad said, downing the rest of his orange juice before setting his napkin on the table and crossing over to me. "You okay with doing the dishes?"

I nodded as I finished off my coffee.

"Thanks, Sunshine." He kissed my head as he passed, heading for the stairs. But he stopped at the bottom and turned toward me. "Which dress will it be today?"

A sad smile crossed my face. Arabella and I used to wear different colored dresses that matched Dad's two-toned ties to dance in the meadow, knowing the rain would soak us to the bone in our fancy attire but not caring at all. Today felt different; it was the first time he'd suggested going since she…died. It would be a solid-colored tie today. Only one option made sense to me: Her favorite dress. "Red," I finally said.

"Perfect," Dad said, and he was up the stairs and out of sight before I could stand.

I gathered all the dishes and headed for the sink. After putting them down, I turned on the ball of my foot to grab the juice. Unfortunately, my big toe found the edge of the rug I was standing on, and when I lifted my foot to take a step, I fell straight toward the counter. I reached for the ledge but caught the runner instead, pulling that and the vase full of marble rocks down with me. My head hit the corner as I fell, and I heard glass shattering before my left arm broke my fall, landing on the shards and rocks.

"Ow…" I groaned loudly, raising my uninjured hand slowly to where I'd hit my head. Liquid warmth immediately started running through my fingers. Great.

I heard Dad running down the stairs before I had time to sit up. My left arm was throbbing, and pain shot up my shoulder when I tried to use it to push myself up. Switching my other hand from the gash on my head to the floor, I moved myself into a sitting position, replacing my hand immediately on my forehead when dizziness set in. My eyes had closed of their own accord, and when I opened them to examine my surroundings, there was a lot of red among the broken pieces of the vase. Cursing my lack of coordination, I reached for the countertop with my bloody hand and tried pulling myself up, but my vision flickered. My ass slammed back down to the ground, and I leaned against the cupboards instead.

"Rayleigh?" I heard Dad say. "Rayleigh, are you alright? I heard a ruckus, and I ca-" He must have walked around the corner and stopped short, taking in the scene. Glass crunched under his slippered feet. My vision slowly recovered to find his ghostly face in front of mine. "Oh my..." He reached his arms under my shoulders and helped me to stand slowly. I wobbled slightly, but he immediately noticed and scooped me up in his arms, carrying me to a chair in the dining room for better examination. It wasn't a small feat for him to lift me, but he made it seem like I was light as a feather. I mentally added bodybuilder to the list of his possible jobs.

Dad asked what caused my newest Oscar-winning special effect makeup look, and I recalled the events of the fall, gesturing to my injuries as I went. He grabbed a couple of warm washcloths and returned, pulling my hand away from the wound on my head to put a washcloth there. Then he started wiping the blood from my arm. I winced at the sharp pain. Removing the cloth, he pursed his lips and pinched something from my arm, holding up the glass for me to see. I gave him a wince of a smile.

"Well," he chuckled, "I'm sure Dr. Smiles will enjoy this one. Let me take a look here." His hand gently covered the one on my head, lifting it to examine the damage. "It looks to be in the same spot as the scar from the tree that jumped out at you while you were roller skating." He winked. I knew he was trying to make me laugh, which worked—until it hurt. "What is this, trip number three to the ER this year? Or is it four?" He chuckled, wiping the still-warm blood from my face and arm. He handed me another clean towel for my head and took the soiled one away. "Put some pressure on there. It should hold the bleeding off until we get to the hospital. The cut isn't too deep, but head injuries bleed forever. The cut on your arm isn't too bad, but I'm not about to make it worse by removing more of that glass myself. I'll leave that to Smiles."

"Thanks." I gave him a weak smile and then replied to his rhetorical question. "And it's five, Dad."

He laughed, "Come on, let's get you to the car." I nodded, knowing the drill.

He got me to the garage without breaking a sweat, making that body-building theory more realistic, even at forty. When he opened the door to his car, I took one look at the nice beige interior and practically yelled, "I'm going to get blood all over your car!"

He chuckled, setting me down anyway, "Wouldn't be the first time. I'm pretty sure there's still a stain from when you thought your finger was a carrot you were slicing." He pulled the seatbelt out to examine it, "Ah yes, just as I suspected." He flashed the dark, stained seatbelt my way, and I rolled my eyes, wondering how he could stand to have such damage to the interior of his Jaguar. He finished extending the seatbelt and buckled me in.

I pulled the washcloth away to adjust it, looking him over head to toe. He was still wearing his blue plaid pajama pants, a fuzzy black robe, and matching slippers. "Um, Dad? You aren't even dressed."

Before closing the door, he bent down, "You looked in the mirror lately?" He asked, gesturing towards my outfit. "Blood-stained bathrobe, white and red polka-dotted pants, blood-covered face. You're starting to look like a zombie!" He made a mock, scared face and then winked. "We're going to the hospital. You think all those people in gowns that hardly cover their asses are going to care?"

"Touché," I smirked, one eyebrow raised.

When he closed the door, I saw my Honda Civic sitting on the other side of the garage. After the accident, I never wanted to drive again. It caused all sorts of triggers that led to panic attacks and became more dangerous than it was worth. But after a few months, I had to overcome that fear because driving became necessary unless I wanted my parents to drive me everywhere. The car totaled in the crash was a gift for Arabella and me for our sixteenth birthday—a ruby red Mustang GT Fastback. We were obsessed with fast cars, and our parents knew that all too well. But after the accident, I didn't want to go anywhere near them again, not without Arabella to do it with me. Nothing could replace what I truly lost in that accident.

So I went for something simple. Something that got the job done without being flashy. Hence Chitty.

Dad opened the garage and backed out, saying, "Remember your first trip to the hospital?" My long-term memory wasn't the best, so I shook my head in answer. "You broke your leg jumping off a swing. The only way to calm you down was by singing to you. Remember?"

He asked, heading toward the road.

"That I remember," I said, easing the pressure on my throbbing head. "You sing the same song every time we go to the ER." I looked at him expectantly.

He obliged immediately, singing the sweet song from Tarzan. It always seemed to stop the pain and tears.

I closed my eyes, breathing in the lyrics, which brought back memories of past trips to the ER. That song calmed me down, no matter the situation. Right now, for example, I was well accustomed to getting hurt, but the pain was still there. The sound of him singing brought a sense of calm I hardly felt anymore. The tone of his voice and the smiles at just the right moments made the pain disappear. It was almost magical.

I was Daddy's little girl, no doubt about it. If he weren't around when I got hurt, Jordin would have to call him to meet us at the hospital because she could never calm me down for the doctors.

There was only one time his singing didn't work. I had dropped a huge glob of hot glue on my leg. It burned the skin and dried on top, adhering to the burn. Dr. Smiles informed me the only way to remove the glue was to rip it off, which would hurt. Bad.

Three nurses were called in. My dad held my head while Ma and the nurses each grabbed a limb. When Smiles started the process, Dad tried singing, but my screams drowned him out, along with every other thought in my head besides pain. When the glue finally came free, Smiles turned to me and said, "You did much better than I expected you to." And walked out as the nurses tended to my freshly opened burn wound. Dad didn't stop singing until the wound was wrapped, and my sobs subsided.

Smiles later told me he'd expected me to pass out from the pain, but my strength surprised him. He always seemed impressed by my pain tolerance.

Dad turned on the music in his car, drumming along on the steering wheel to Phil Collins. I chuckled softly, knowing my legs would be his drums if I weren't in pain.

The throbbing in my head turned to a steady headache, and my arm tingled. I wasn't sure if it was from being elevated or because the glass pieces were still embedded in my flesh.

I leaned forward, bringing the towel away from my head, and pulled down the visor to look at the gash in the mirror. I cringed at the sight of my blood-matted hair and oozing cut. The bleeding wasn't as bad as it had been, but it was still pretty bad. I closed the mirror and replaced the washcloth over the cut. What a great way to start the week…

"Nice to see you again, Rayleigh." Dr. Smiles said, walking in with his infamous smiley-face scrubs on. I had asked before, so I knew he wore those scrubs for two reasons: it made kids giggle, distracting them from any pain they might have been feeling, but also because his last name was, in fact, Smiles. "So tell me," he started, grabbing his swivel chair to straddle. "What's the tale of your cuts and bruises this time?" His tone was slightly sarcastic, only because he'd seen me in the hospital too many times in my seventeen years, and I always made up the most ridiculous stories for my injuries. Sometimes, it seemed like he was the only doctor who worked in the emergency room because I couldn't recall ever seeing another doctor. He was in every memory I had of the ER. He was even there when I was brought in from the car crash last year. But perhaps it was just a happy accident. Pun intended.

"Well," I said dramatically, "I was running to jump off a cliff, but before I made it to the edge, that one rock—you know, the one that always gets me—jumped out of nowhere, throwing me straight into a tree," I pointed at my head, "and I fell into a big bush." I finished, lifting my torn-up arm.

"Cliff jumping this early in the morning?" Smiles shook his head and chuckled, grabbing some gauze and tweezers before returning to tend to my arm. "What really happened? Because I've never heard of a bush growing glass." He held up a long, thin shard he pulled from my arm. My arm must have been numb because I'd forgotten all about the glass. No wonder my shirt was soaked in blood. He continued pulling glass from my arm as I told the boring version of my fall.

When he pulled the final piece of glass from my arm, he stitched up the deeper cuts and the gash on my head before sending me to the x-ray room. I had broken my arm just below the elbow. They cast me up before sending me home with pain meds, a waterproof arm sleeve, and instructions to take it easy.

We pulled into the garage as the clock turned to one. "You should get going," I said, unbuckling. "You're two hours late." When I opened my door, he was already there to help me.

"How can you be so concerned about me going to work when you can barely stand on your own?" I shrugged in answer, knowing he would have to go to work either way. Besides, I could handle being alone for a few hours until Mitch or my mom got home. Dad sighed, "If you must know, I called Brinkley while you were getting your x-ray. She said she was fine until after lunch." He opened the door to the house and guided me in. "Do you still want to go to the meadow today?"

I looked down at my arm, wrapped in a blue cast. "Well. If I can manage to get that waterproof thing over this monstrosity, I should be able to shower."

"I'll take that as a yes." He nudged me in the ribs and shut the door behind us. After depositing me in a chair, he took in his appearance, scrunching his face at the filth my accident caused him, "Looks like I need a shower myself. Holler if you need anything, okay?"

I nodded as he bound up the stairs. The pain started creeping up on me, so I fished out the pain meds I'd been given and took one before slowly heading upstairs with the goodies Dr. Smiles sent me home with.

When I walked into my room, I was reminded of how the day started, and I couldn't help but laugh at how drastically it changed. Typical of me, honestly. Arabella would have laughed silly at the irony of visiting the hospital on the anniversary of her death. She had such a twisted sense of humor. Instead of letting myself go back to wallowing, I stuck my tongue out at her empty bed as if she were sitting there mocking me. "You were just as clumsy, so don't even start."

I rummaged through my closet until I found Arabella's favorite dress, pulling it out to lay on the bed. Red was certainly the color of the day. I found the waterproof arm sleeve in the bag and ripped open the package. It looked like a giant orange oven mitt. The opening was barely big enough to fit my fist, let alone my cast.

Determined to get the sleeve on, I sat on the bed and took a deep breath before sticking my big toe in the opening and using my un-cast hand to pull the opening wider. That made it look like the opening of a mail slot. I sighed. It looked like I'd have to use both feet *and* my hand to make the hole big enough. With sweat starting at my hairline, I stuck my tongue out in concentration, brought my other foot to the rubber mitt, and got my big toe in before a knock came at my door.

"Yes?" I said, struggling to keep my balance on the edge of the bed.

"Are you decent? Can I come in?" A muffled voice said.

"Double yes," I grunted, pulling on the sleeve to open it wider.

My big toe slipped out of the opening and slammed onto the floor just as Dad peeked his head in. "Do you think—" He noticed my dilemma and cocked his eyebrow at me. "Ray..." He opened the door fully, crossing the room. "I said to holler if you needed anything."

An eye roll wasn't enough for my stubbornness, so I dramatically rolled my head. "I know! But you're already late!"

"What's a couple more minutes, Sunshine?" He gave a weak smile and reached for the rubber mitt, grabbing the edges of the opening and holding the other side out for me to grasp. We struggled for the better part of five minutes to get it over my cast. When it was finally on, we both had sweat glistening on our brows. It was a good thing neither of us had showered yet. Who knows how long it would have taken me if he hadn't knocked on my door?

He looked at me pointedly, and I gave him my best mock-innocence smile. "Ray, it's okay to ask for help." I opened my mouth to retort, but he held up a finger to stop me. "Even if you are *certain* you can do it yourself, asking someone for help will not only make it easier but more efficient." He raised his eyebrows at me, waiting for me to argue, but I just lowered my head in defeat.

"I just don't want to be a burden," I mumbled. "It makes me feel...

I don't know… weak."

He lifted my chin with a single finger, "You've never been a burden, and you never will be. Asking for help doesn't make you weak; it makes you courageous." The finger that lifted my chin touched the tip of my nose for emphasis.

I scrunched my nose and said, "Asking for help to put on a rubber glove is courageous?" I scoffed. "More like desperate."

He looked at me skeptically and stepped back to lean on the wall. "Do you think you can drive with that on your arm?"

I looked at my arm but gestured to my head as I said, "I don't think Smiles would approve." He pursed his lips, likely having forgotten about the head injury. I dropped my hand heavily into my lap, "Why?"

He sighed, pulling out his phone to type something out. "Well, your mother has a meeting at four, and I won't be home until dinner."

"Jordin always has meetings…" I said, more to myself than him. My head dropped to study my fingers as they twiddled in my lap.

I heard his sigh of frustration, "Why are you referring to your mother by her first name all of a sudden?"

I gave him a sidelong glance. "She barely treats me like a daughter." Shrugging my shoulders, I returned my gaze to my hands and mumbled, "I don't see why I should call her mom if she doesn't act like one."

When he said nothing, I looked back up to him. His eyebrows were scrunched together. He knew there was more to it than that, but he also understood where I came from. Since Arabella's death, Jordin had been distant, gone most of the time, and barely showed me affection. She became stricter and less involved in my life, leaving me with responsibilities she should have taken on herself or shared with Dad.

"I'll talk to her." Dad sighed, knowing today wasn't the day to continue arguing about it. He returned to his original question. "Any way you could convince one of your friends to take you to pick Mitch up from practice?"

Thankful for the change of subject, I smiled. "Probably." I cocked a brow at him, raising my gloved arm. "Boy, he's in for a treat, huh?"

"He sure is." He pushed off the wall and took a step toward me. "Be safe. And no more accidents, okay?" The smile faded a little from his face as I chuckled, and his face turned more solemn. "I'm serious. Promise me no more accidents." He tilted his head back and forth as a smile crept onto his face. "At least until I get home."

I suppressed another laugh, "Of course, I'll wait until you get home to get injured again." I winked.

He laughed, pulling me into a hug. "I love you, Sunshine."

"I love you more, Daddy." I went on my toes to kiss his cheek. "See you after work for our date to the meadow!"

"I can't wait," he said. Then he left the room, leaving me to shower.

Washing my hair with one hand wasn't easy. It took twice as long as usual between the length and the stitches I had to avoid. I had asked Kendall if she could skip the last few classes of the day to help me with Mitch, but she reminded me she had a final in her last class. So I texted the one person who would drop everything for me: Kaleb. I typed out my message as quickly as I could with one hand.

The waterproof sleeve was just as challenging to take off as it was to put on, but I managed to get it over the lip of the cast and roll it down. I was breathless, sitting on the edge of the bed, when Kaleb replied, saying he was on his way. I wouldn't be driving for a while, so I headed downstairs to grab my school bag and umbrella out of my car.

When I walked into the garage, Dad's Jaguar was still there. He was sitting in the front seat studying something on his laptop. He must not have seen me because he jumped when I knocked on his window. He sighed and rolled his window down when he realized it was just me.

"What's up?" He asked, but I could tell he was still distracted by whatever was on his laptop, his eyes shifting between me and the screen quickly.

"What are you still doing here? You were supposed to leave an hour ago." I rested my good arm on the roof of his car, dipping my head to get a better look at his face.

"Oh. Chief Bass stopped by." That might seem odd, but the town police chief stopped by many times over the last year to check in. "He dropped off some dinner and asked how you were doing today." Of course, he knew what today was. He'd been one of the first on the scene of the accident.

I nodded, tucking the information away to thank him the next time I saw him. I nodded to his laptop, "And what of that?" I couldn't distinguish what was on the screen, but soft words from the radio finally reached my ears, and I recognized the announcer's voice, who usually gave traffic reports.

Dad reached to turn off the radio, which was talking about an accident somewhere out of town. "I was, uh, listening to the accident report on the interstate. I wanted to avoid the traffic from it and was looking for a better way on Google." My eyes traveled to his laptop again, sensing his lie, but he shut it before I could get a good look at what he was doing. He sat straight, placed the laptop on the passenger seat, and pushed a button above his head to open the garage door. "I'll see you later, Sunshine." He forced a smile.

I stood quickly, twisting my face up in confusion, but let his weird behavior slide, seeing as his job was, well, whatever it was. "Don't forget to buckle!" I shouted as I watched him back out of the garage and turn onto the driveway. It was pouring rain like he said it would be all day. It didn't rain too often in Wisteria Falls, but when it did, it poured. Before taking off down the never-ending driveway, he showed me he was buckling and blew me a kiss through the window. I caught it and placed it against my heart with a smile.

That was the last time I saw my father alive.

II
Oracle

A loud pounding roused me from sleep.

"Rayleigh?" Jordin yelled through my bedroom door, pounding again to ensure I was awake. "Mitch's practice was canceled, so he's riding with you." I was barely awake, my eyes slowly drifting open and closed a few times before registering what she said. She pounded again.

"Yeah! Okay!" I yelled, pushing myself up in bed while gripping my pillow to my chest. I looked at the clock—6:47 a.m. April 24th, 2017.

The last six months had been different around the house. Jordin was always going somewhere, and I had taken on most of the responsibilities with Mitch, getting him to and from school or practice. He was quiet most of the time but recently started opening up to me with all the time we'd spent together. He would tell me about his school life, ask for advice on things he should have been able to talk to our parents about, and even tell me about the girls in his life, asking for advice on what to do.

He said recently that I was great at giving advice but terrible at taking my own, teasing me about my best friend Kaleb every chance he got. I reminded him every time I wasn't interested in Kaleb like that. He always rolled his eyes.

Our bond went beyond that, though. We hung out after school and played video and board games with Kaleb and my twin best friends, Kendall and Leighton. I bought him a new pack of Nerf guns for his birthday last week, and we had already put them to good use in a couple of battles in the backyard. He never missed a chance to tell me how terrible I was, which always earned him a bullet in the face.

The other three brought their own Nerf guns whenever they came over, knowing there was always a chance for an all-out war to break out. Sometimes, Kaleb would show up on the front porch, aimed and ready for whoever answered when he rang the bell. He hadn't done that since Jordin answered the door, and he shot her straight between the eyes. The horror that crossed his face before his apologies set in was priceless. Mitch and I watched it happen from the stairs behind her and were in fits of laughter as Kaleb groveled at her feet for forgiveness. Jordin, thankfully, shrugged it off and left us to enjoy ourselves.

Several other moments like that made me giggle, and as I sat in bed thinking about the time I shot Mitch in the ear, heavy footsteps thudded down the hall. Knowing what was coming, I smiled and prepared my pillow as a shield. Mornings in this house were rarely quiet, and I knew better than to think this would be one of them. Mitch knew I hadn't had my coffee yet, but he didn't seem to think that would be an issue today. He was probably right. It was almost impossible for me to be mad at him.

His footsteps grew closer, and I had difficulty keeping myself from laughing. I didn't want him to realize I knew he was coming.

He stopped outside my room, his shadow visible in the crack under the door. My smile grew. There was a moment of silence before the door flew open, and Nerf bullets came flying in. Mitch shot round after round, and I started laughing behind my makeshift shield.

The firing stopped, and Mitch's deep voice cracked as he whined, "Hey! That's cheating!" He stepped into my room and turned on the lights as I cautiously put down my guard. "How did you even know I was coming?"

I squinted at the sudden bright lights but took in my not-so-little

little brother's face, and the mock shock there sent me into another fit of giggles. "Mitch, you know I have impeccable hearing, and you walk a lot louder than you think, *Big Foot.*" I chucked the pillow at him, but he ducked just in time, following the flight of the pillow into the hallway beyond.

I forgot that was my shield until he turned slowly back to me, revealing a wicked grin as he lifted his gun again. "Big mistake, *Little Foot.*" I yelped as the bullets started flying my way again, lifting my arms to use them as a shield for my face, but they weren't very effective.

Why didn't I get him something else for his birthday? I could have gotten the comic books or the video games he wanted, but no—I got him the freaking rapid-fire Nerf gun.

My hands found the comforter, and I yanked it over my head as a new shield too quickly because I hit the shelf above my bed, and pain shot up my arm at the impact. Several items crashed to the ground, but the shattering glass made my heart drop. There was only one breakable thing on that shelf. The bullets stopped, and I lowered my guard, afraid of what I was about to see.

On the ground were several of Arabella's favorite books, my water cup, and a family photo lying within the shattered pieces of my snow globe. The trees were in one piece, but the fragments of the crystal ball, water, and sparkling raindrops had disappeared into the rug. I looked up to see regret in Mitch's eyes, mine starting to burn as I tried to hold back the tears.

"I— I'll go get a towel." He said and darted out the door.

I slowly slid off my bed and kneeled before the mess, careful not to put my knees in the glass. I picked up the still intact base, checking the handcrafted piece for damage. Dad had gone to a shop where they made custom snow globes and showed them a picture of our meadow. He told them my favorite view was when it was raining and the flowers were in full bloom. They crafted it perfectly. He gave it to me for my birthday the year after Arabella died. Besides the box of letters under my bed, the snow globe was the only memory I had left. I'm sure I could have brought it to the shop to get fixed, but staring at the shattered remains cracked open the vault of emotions I'd created when I lost him six months ago.

It felt like losing Arabella all over again, but this was much worse. Everything around his death was so hard to think about. Those first few days, I didn't leave my room. Jordin was gone most of the time, and even when she was home, she never tried to comfort me. Mitch was just as destroyed as I was, but he at least came to me when he felt overwhelmed with grief. The first week, he and I ended up in each other's rooms at least once a day, seeking comfort in being around each other, even if we couldn't find the words to express our feelings. More than once, I found him with silent tears tracking down his face as he stared at nothing in particular and sat beside him, pulling him into a hug without saying a word.

He recovered far better than I, putting his emotions into swimming and school work.

Eventually, the pain that tore through me every time I thought of my dad became too much. I couldn't handle it anymore. I didn't want to feel anything. So, one day, I curled up on my bed, not planning to get up.

That was the first day Kaleb came to check on me.

When I saw his head poke through my door, I broke down. He knew how Arabella's death affected me and was worried I'd be worse off. He was right. But just like with her death, he walked me through the pain of my dad's. When I told him how I felt before he got there, he said he would never let me do that to myself. He promised to check on me every day and stay with me if I needed him to. Once or twice, I fell asleep while he held and comforted me, but he was always gone by the time I woke up.

But the pain and sorrow always returned. It seemed like it would never go away.

Then, one morning, I woke up feeling drowned by my emotions but decided it was time to take control. Dad's death wasn't going to control my life, and neither was Arabella's. I gathered all my emotions and pushed them deep down into the bottomless chasm within myself —so far that I couldn't feel them even if I wanted to—and they hadn't resurfaced.

Until now.

I stared at the broken snow globe through tears. I took a shaky breath and held it, taking the eight seconds to shove every emotion back from where it came. When I released it, residual emotions seeped through, and I went through the breathing method again to push them down. Little by little, they retreated to that chasm.

Tears were sliding down my face when Mitchell returned and knelt beside me. He started dabbing up the water with the towel and reached to pull me into a side hug with his free hand. It felt so similar to Dad's hugs that it almost made those emotions I was trying to keep down sneak out again. So I pulled out of his reach and started picking up the visible pieces of glass, setting them on the towel Mitch had set down, and continued pushing down my grief. He picked up the other items that fell off the shelf, wiping them off as best he could before placing them on my nightstand.

"I'm so sorry, Ray." His shoulders slumped forward as he turned back to me.

"It's not your fault," I sniffed. "I hit the shelf, trying to defend myself." I wiped my tears and placed the last pieces of glass in the towel, picking it up by the four corners and carefully placing it on the nightstand.

"Yeah, but you wouldn't have had to if I hadn't continued shooting." He set the cracked picture frame next to the towel full of glass and turned towards me. "Ray, look at me." He put his hands on my shoulders and turned me toward him. "I know how much this snow globe means to you. I promise I'll find a way to make it up to you."

He looked so much like Dad, and after breaking the last gift I ever received from him... I leaned into a hug, reminding myself it was Mitch. He had a tall, muscular frame, angular contours on a fading baby face, and eyes that sparkled a pale green under his wavy brown hair. Jordin's eyes, but everything else was Dad. Looking at him now and seeing Dad so clearly in his teenage frame was wild. Losing loved ones really did make you grow up faster.

Mitch squeezed me tight and apologized again, this time into my hair. My usual alarm went off, and I pulled away from him, finding tears had formed in his eyes. I gave him a tight smile and told him I was okay, wiping my tears as he did the same.

"We should get ready for school." I switched off my alarm and grabbed the books he'd set on the nightstand to replace them on the shelf. He snatched the towel full of glass and headed out of my room, swiping up his Nerf gun from where he'd dropped it near the door on his way out.

I took a deep breath to clear the last of my tears and went to my closet, grabbing my favorite ripped jeans and pink crop top before heading to the bathroom to get ready for school.

One look in the mirror had me turning on the cold water to splash my face. I didn't want to rock the puffy eyes and tear tracks today. When I found my blue eyes in the mirror again, they shone brightly from the tears, and my hair was a frizzy mess. I used to tell Arabella I hated looking in the mirror because I didn't like what I saw. She reminded me every time that if I didn't like how I looked, I was insulting her, too, since we were identical. It hit me harder as we got older because I thought she was beautiful whenever I looked at her. I started to view myself differently shortly before she died.

Now, I could *only* see her.

I hated my reflection the first few months because it brought emotions bubbling to the surface. But after a while, I started looking to remind myself what she looked like, which served as a reminder that she was always with me. Some people didn't have that luxury after losing someone they loved.

Studying my reflection, I took in my five foot eight, muscular yet thicker frame and smiled. I tanned like Dad, with blue eyes similar to his, but my smile and dark hair were Jordin's. Both Arabella and I put blonde highlights in our hair, though. The only difference between us now would be the scars on my neck, arms, and collarbone from the accident and all the other accidents throughout my life. She had her own scars, but I could no longer remember where they were. I took more risks than she did, leading to more ER visits while her injuries were quickly healed at home.

After my last promise to Dad, though, I had made a serious commitment to prevent any more accidents as best as possible.

The Sunshine Chronicles : Forgotten Flare

I was slipping on my sparkly, rose-colored tennis shoes when my phone started ringing. I grabbed my earrings and put them in as I rushed to my nightstand and picked up the music source. The name on the screen made me answer the phone with a knowing smile. "What's up, Ken?"

The calm and collected one of the friend group let out a long, exasperated sigh before saying, "We need a ride."

I held back a laugh and said, "Again?"

"Yes, *again*," She huffed.

"No worries, girl. I'll be there in ten." She thanked me and hung up. I shook my head with a small smile. This wasn't the first time this year their car had broken down, and I knew it annoyed Ken more than she let on, but she would never complain. It wasn't like her.

I snatched my backpack and ran down the stairs, setting it down on the table on my way to the kitchen. Jordin was there, messing with something on the stove. I ignored her, finding my travel coffee mug and filling it to the brim with the bitter liquid. I opened the fridge and topped off my coffee with creamer, taking a sip before screwing on the lid. I let out an audible noise of satisfaction. That snagged Jordin's attention.

"I made breakfast," she said a bit timidly.

I glanced at the sorry excuse for an omelet and said, "No thanks." Reaching, instead, for the muffins I'd made the night before.

Jordin's shoulders sagged slightly as I grabbed a second muffin for Mitch. She turned and dropped the pan—omelet and all—into the sink before snatching her bag off the counter and rushing out the garage door without another word.

I shook my head as I watched her run away—again—then reached for my backpack and headed for the garage door. "Mitch!" I yelled. "Chitty leaves in T-minus two minutes!" I heard his thunderous footsteps coming down the stairs. He beat me to the door, holding it open like he'd been there the whole time. I tossed his muffin at him while taking a bite of mine. "Here's your tip," I said through my mouthful.

He caught it and rolled his eyes with a smile as I walked out the door to the car.

"We have to pick up Ken and Leigh on the way. Would you mind hopping in the back when we get to their house?" I asked nicely, even though I knew his legs barely fit in the backseat.

He rolled his eyes again. "Yeah, I guess…" He slid into the front, throwing his backpack onto the back seat.

"Thanks!" I jumped in, tossing my backpack to join his, and buckled before turning the key. Chitty choked and made a funny noise but started on the first try. I sighed, not knowing how much longer he would last me. Lately, he'd been getting harder to bring to life.

I backed out of the open garage door and turned onto the never-ending driveway toward the highway into town. "Ready for your swim meet this weekend?" I asked casually, knowing Mitch's silence was likely due to this morning's events.

Mitch nodded. "Coach has me on the four-by-two relay. Says my time has improved drastically."

I raised my eyebrows at his tone and gave him a quick, sideways glance. "You're surprised by this?"

He shrugged, "Kinda. I've only ever done the long races. Endurance over speed has always been my thing."

"Well, with how often I drive you to and from the pool, I'm not surprised," I said. He'd been putting in more effort than he was letting on, spending all his free time swimming laps. Knowing precisely what would pull him out of his funk from our morning fiasco, I smirked and asked, "Will Lily be there?"

He turned toward the window to hide the small smile that appeared there. "Yeah, she's always there," he said quietly.

She was becoming one of my favorite people. I'd never seen Mitch so giddy about something. She made him nervous, which made me laugh. "Good, I can finally meet her then!"

He turned back to me, his eyes wide in horror. "You can*not* talk to her about me. At all. Ever," he practically begged.

I laughed, "I would never embarrass you, *Mitchy*."

"Ugh." He threw his head back against the headrest. "You're the worst." But he was smiling. I knew he wanted me to meet her. He was just nervous that I *could* embarrass him, not necessarily that I *would*.

"I'll take any chance I get to see you flustered like that," I grinned.

He sighed loudly. "Can't wait to do the same to you one day."

"You know you love me."

He muttered, "Yeah, yeah, more than the sun."

I laughed to myself at the memory he brought up. When we were kids, he and I were in the back seat fighting about leg space or something stupid. It turned into a shouting match, yelling about how much we hated each other. He would say, "I hate you more than baths." And I'd return it with, "I hate you more than spiders." Back and forth until I finally yelled, "I hate you more than the sun!" Jordin couldn't stop herself from laughing in the front seat. She told us the story when we were older, and we started using it in fights to make each other laugh. But it slowly became a more loving statement over the years, changing the hate to love.

Ken was waiting on the doorstep under the awning when we pulled into their driveway. Mitch gave me a look of mock disdain and transferred to the backseat without another word. Kendall jumped up off the step and yelled for her sister before heading to the car. Leighton appeared shortly after, carefully navigating her way down the steps in heels I would break my ankle in. Her curls bounced with each step, and her floral dress flowed in the breeze. Kendall wore a bright blue hoodie, boyfriend jeans, high-tops, and her strawberry hair in a high ponytail—identical twins who couldn't be more different. But I admired that about them because it reminded me so much of how Arabella and I used to be.

"I owe you for this one," Kendall said as she plopped into the front seat. "How was your weekend?"

"Alright, I guess," I said, trying not to bring up this morning's events to dampen the mood. I waited for Leighton to get her long legs in the back seat before backing down the drive. "Jordin asked me to go with her to find new drapes for the living room. She's almost done redecorating." I pulled onto the road and headed for school.

"Really?" I heard Leighton's excited tone from the backseat. "I want to see it! When can I come over?"

I shrugged, looking at her in the mirror. "Not sure. I'll let you know when I get home tonight."

"Okay!" She started fixing her curls. "Thanks again for picking us up today. Our car was making funny noises. Something's wrong with the transmansion or whatever." She said, transferring her attention to her nails.

I glanced at Ken sideways, "So what's wrong with the bug this time?"

She smiled, "The *transmission* busted last night when she was driving. Tom took it in this morning. Hopefully, it'll be fixed before school gets out." Tom was their adoptive dad, but they hadn't been able to call him dad just yet. Their parents died just over a year ago on a business trip when their train went off the tracks in Germany. The girls were old enough to do a lot independently but didn't want to be put in a group home. Tom was listed as the girls' official guardian in their parents' will. When he showed up, we were all shocked. He didn't seem like the type of guy ready to take on the responsibilities of two teenagers. He was in his late twenties and looked like he was on his way to model for board shorts in California. Ken and Leigh were skeptical, unsure why their parents didn't introduce them to their young godparent, but they had no choice but to accept it. He hadn't officially adopted them, but the twins knew he wanted to. They just needed time.

"That sounds expensive," I said, wondering why she wanted it done before school was out. I looked at the smile she was trying to hide on her face and knew she was waiting for me to ask. I obliged, "What's after school?"

"Well," she looked out the window, "Leighton and I are going shopping for prom dresses."

It took me one whole second to realize why that was a big deal. "Roshan asked you to the dance?!" She and I both screamed in celebration. Roshan and Kendall had been seeing each other since school started in the fall. Her first boyfriend and now her first official date to a dance. "Spill it, Ken!"

She was grinning ear to ear before she started her story. "Well, when I got home last night, after the catastrophe of the car incident, I walked in to find chocolate kisses leading to my bedroom. There was a note at the end of the trail. I picked it up, and it said, 'Now that I've kissed the ground you walk on, will you accompany me to the Prom?'" She and I squealed, and she let out a long sigh before melting into her seat with the biggest grin. When she spoke again, it sounded like hushed happiness, "And when I called him, I was so excited that I couldn't even get any words out, but he knew why I called and said, 'Can I take that as a yes?' After the giggles subsided, I barely whispered yes." She smiled brightly and sat up. She had been dreaming about this day since Leighton had her first date, so it wasn't hard to celebrate with her. Having an identical twin was hard sometimes, especially when they got all the attention from the boys. I had the same trouble with Arabella and wondered why, if we looked the same, didn't any boys like me? Kendall's situation was similar until she met Roshan.

"I'm so happy for you, Ken. You get to go to your first dance our senior year!" She squealed again as I smiled and looked at Leighton in the mirror. "What about you? Do you have a date yet?"

She didn't smile when she said, "Charlie Knott asked me last weekend after the football game." Her not-so-thrilled tone made me wonder if she even said yes to him. Or maybe she wanted someone else to ask. She hadn't brought up any boys at our latest sleepovers, except the ones that were always drooling over her. I wondered if something else was happening with her, and I made a mental note to ask her later.

"Where are you guys going to get your dresses?" I asked, looking back at the road.

"Donna Marie's. Obviously." Kendall said, referring to the store within the city mall closest to our small town.

Leighton leaned up from the back seat so fast that I jumped, "You wanna come with us? We could always use your opinion!" She smiled. They loved dragging me along to these types of things.

"Obviously." I grinned. "What time do you want to go?"

"We were hoping to go right after school," Ken said, bummed. "But with the bug in the shop..."

Picking up on what Kendall was lying down, I looked at Mitch in the mirror, who was silently watching the world go by out the window. "Mitch, you think you could walk to Grams' house after practice today?"

He continued staring out the window as if I hadn't said anything. Was he ignoring me? Leighton tapped him on the shoulder, and he turned to her, pulling out the headphones concealed under his hair. *Oh.* "Yeah?"

Leighton took over, "You think you could walk to your grandma's house after practice? Rayleigh's going to take us shopping." She smiled.

He gave her a tight-lipped smile. "Yeah, sure."

Leighton did her cute little happy dance in the backseat. "Yay!"

Mitch turned to look at me in the mirror. "Make sure you let Mom know." He put his headphones back in and returned to looking out the window.

"Right. Jordin." I handed Kendall my phone, who opened Jordin's thread and typed out my message to her. It wasn't more than a thirty-minute drive to the city, but she always insisted on knowing exactly where I was going if I wasn't going to be home.

"Uh, Ray?" I heard Mitch from the backseat. "You missed the entrance."

"Whoops!" Spacing out was normal for me, always missing turns on the road if I was even the slightest bit distracted. I pulled a U-turn at the next intersection and went to where I dropped Mitch off for English. "There ya go, bud. Good luck on your test!" I said as he opened the door quickly.

"Thanks, Ray! I love you!" He said and slammed the door.

"More than the sun," I said, more to myself than him. He was already running through the doors, but we always said I love you when one of us was leaving. We never knew if it would be the last time we saw each other. With Arabella and Dad both gone within a year of each other, those words meant everything to us. Even on quick phone calls or leaving the house for a walk, we would always say, "I love you," just in case.

Ken, Leigh, and I all had our first class together, so they stayed in the car while I searched for parking.

"Isn't there a new guy in Chem today?" Leighton asked absentmindedly.

"Yeah." Kendall said, facing her, "His name is Conor or something, isn't it?"

"Yeah, something like that," Leighton mumbled.

"I remember hearing something about him," I said. "Kaleb said he's from a school almost three times the size of ours." I heard a faint bell from inside the building, and there was no parking in sight. "I don't want you guys to be late." I pulled up to the science hall entrance, and they hopped out, leaving me to circle the lot again.

I drove up and down every aisle and only saw one open spot, but I could barely even call it that with what little space there was. It was next to a brand new, black Audi R8. Thanks to my dad, I knew the specs of many cars. This one wasn't cheap and definitely didn't belong in our small town's high school parking lot. Every other car in the lot resembled Chitty or was a little newer—but a brand new Audi? That stuck out.

Parking next to it proved difficult because, as I said, I could barely call it a spot, considering the Audi decided to take up part of the spot next to it. They also reversed into the spot to prove themselves a *douche*.

After squeezing into the tight space between the Audi and the curb on the other side, I was forced to crawl out the passenger side, which was just as graceful as it sounds. I hit my head crawling out, and slammed my passenger door, grabbing my backpack from the back seat.

No matter how much I hated its driver, I had to take a minute to admire the car's beauty. I couldn't deny they had good taste: the custom rims, perfect shiny black paint job, and detailed work on the body. There was only one explanation for this car being on the lot today: the new student.

New guy already comes off as an entitled asshole, and I haven't even met him yet, I thought to myself. I locked my car and ran towards the school.

I rushed through the doors four minutes past the start of class and stopped dead as every head turned and looked straight at me. Apparently, they were waiting for me. I forced a smile and walked to my seat with my head held high. The usually empty seat beside mine had the only head that wasn't turned toward me.

Great. I have to sit next to the douche with the fancy car.

III
Unfamiliar

"Excellent timing, Ms. Foster," Mr. Blake said. "Please, take your seat." He gestured to the stool I was standing next to, staring at the back of the new guy's head.

Red in the face, both from anger and embarrassment, I sat down heavily next to him. He hadn't watched my embarrassing entrance, probably because he didn't care, or maybe he was feeling that way, being the new guy and all.

Mr. Blake started his lecture, and I put my stuff on the ground. Pulling out my chemistry binder, I opened it to the work he assigned yesterday and was reaching for a pencil when the hairs on the back of my neck stood up. I turned slowly to find my lab partner's deep green eyes staring back at me.

They were mesmerizing.

I tried to find the words to introduce myself, but they got lost somewhere between my brain and mouth. Before I could figure out why my mouth wasn't working, his eyes darted back to the front of the classroom.

I sat there, unable to move for a minute. It felt like he bared his soul to me, which was anything but harmless. But I also felt like he'd seen my soul and turned away, unsatisfied, as if whatever he was searching for wasn't there.

Mr. Blake started explaining the lab for the day, but my head was spinning, and I couldn't focus on his words.

I turned to the front just in time to hear him say, "You may begin."

My partner shot out of his seat as if something had poked him in the ass, swiftly making his way to the storage supply. I searched the room for Ken and Leigh, noticing both were getting their supplies while openly staring at the new guy with their mouths gaping. Of course, they were preoccupied with staring at the could-be model. Why was I surprised? All I could see was an asshole with a fancy car. It seemed I would have to inform them if they didn't stop staring at him like that. After failing to get their attention, I put my head in my hands on the table.

I reached for my phone, but my lab partner had returned with the supplies and dumped them on his side of the table. I left my phone in its place and reached out to lend a hand.

Before I could grab anything, my partner slapped my hand away.

My jaw dropped. *Excuse me*. He *slapped* my hand. Like I was a child. Like it was a normal thing for him to do. I stared at the hand that hit me, which was now working on starting the bunsen burner. There was no way he slapped my hand like that without some joking manner behind it. Looking up at his emotionless face, I realized that he did, in fact, do just that. There was no humor on his unfortunately beautiful face.

I scoffed, then turned to see if I could get Ken's attention again, but she was busy setting up her station and whispering frantically to Leigh.

"Pssst." I heard from directly behind me. It was Kaleb—who apparently saw my distress. "We're supposed to be making smoke bombs." My helpless look must have told him I had no idea what was happening.

"Thanks," I said with a big sigh of relief.

He smiled, "No worries. I could tell you were... *preoccupied*." He looked at my partner and then back to me before waggling both eyebrows suggestively. I rolled my eyes and shivered with disgust, hoping to relay that it would be a hard pass from me.

I returned my attention to my table to find my partner mixing the ingredients in the pan over the small fire. I looked around the room and noticed everyone else still measuring the ingredients. I squinted at him, "Are you sure you measured those out correctly?" *Dumbass* is what I didn't add.

He continued silently stirring the sugar and potassium nitrate as if I didn't exist. This guy was acting as if my help would destroy his work. But *my* perfect grade was on the line. If he had measured those ingredients wrong... I couldn't let that happen.

I stood, intending to ask Mr. Blake if I could work alone, but then I heard it.

The deepest, gravelly-sounding voice.

"It doesn't have to be exact," he said, "as long as you're close in measurements, it'll work." He was still concentrating on stirring as though he hadn't spoken. I narrowed my eyes at him, not wanting to trust this process he made up, but something about how he said it made any thoughts of him being a lousy lab partner dissipate. I let him do his thing with the lab, sitting back in my seat to watch him stir the ingredients.

He didn't look up once. Didn't continue the conversation. And I sure as hell wasn't going to with how he had treated me thus far. I stared at him, trying to decipher what on earth could be possessing him. His concentration didn't falter, even though I knew he could feel my gaze burning a hole through his thick skull. I'm not sure if it bothered me more that he was ignoring me or the fact that I wanted him to acknowledge me even after he acted like an asshole.

When Mr. Blake came around to check on everyone's progress, I held a piece of bowled aluminum open while my partner spooned the last of our mixture onto the foil. That seemed to be the only way I was allowed to help. Truthfully, I had grabbed the aluminum, started making the makeshift bowls before he could stop me, and held them hostage until the mixture was ready. Even then, he didn't say a word to me, nor did he look at me as I held it out for him to scoop the ingredients into. Everyone else was still trying to melt the mixture or just starting on their aluminum bowls.

Mr. Blake stopped at our table, looked at us with his "you shouldn't be done yet" face, raised his eyebrows a little, but then moved on without a word.

Once back at his desk, Mr. Blake announced, "There will be a contest for the longest-lasting smoke bomb. Whoever wins can have these." He held up a pair of King Size Snickers bars and set them back on his desk. *Why is it always chocolate?* "Five more minutes."

Everyone started rushing to finish. I sat back and wondered how badly we would lose the contest.

I didn't like how hostile this new partnership had started, so I turned to my partner again and stuck my hand out. "I'm Rayleigh, but everyone calls me Ray."

He sat deathly still, looking straight ahead, clenching his jaw, once again acting like I didn't exist. But I saw a sparkle of defiance in his eyes. I waited with my arm extended longer than I should have, expecting him to do *something* in reaction to my introduction. Instead, I held my hand there for what felt like forever before letting it fall and making a face at him for ignoring me.

Hearing a snicker behind me, I whipped around to find Kaleb seemingly concentrating on his experiment with his partner. But he couldn't hide the smile playing on his mouth. He locked eyes with me, pursing his lips to keep from laughing. I knew then he'd seen the whole interaction, so I gave him a vulgar gesture before dropping my shoulders in defeat and giving him a pleading look. He had the nerve to shrug at me, point his chin at the new guy with a suggestive look, and return to his experiment without a word.

I shook my head slowly at his betrayal, turning back toward the front and crossing my arms in disgust. The last two months of school were going to suck if my lab partner continued to act like this, especially if Kaleb was going to ignore me, too. I almost pulled my phone out to text the twins when that deep, rich voice spoke again.

"Didn't your parents ever tell you not to talk to strangers?" I looked over to find those bright green eyes trained on me. There wasn't a hint of sarcasm in his voice, but his mouth twitched.

I squinted at him. "They did." My eyes trailed over him slowly, giving him a show. Then I placed my elbow on the table and my chin in my hand as I leaned toward him and whispered, "But I'm curious enough to eat the candy you're selling." I tried not to smile, but my facial muscles threatened to betray me.

He shifted and looked at me with slightly squinting eyes, then whispered, "I'm not the one holding the candy." He put his elbow on the table and placed his temple to his fist, mirroring me. Again, no hint of a smile, but his eyes sparkled with mischief. "Mr. Blake up there has the candy." He pointed with his eyes to the front of the class, where I knew the teacher was standing, holding the candy and ready to head outside.

My head started spinning when his eyes fell back to mine, and the whole class disappeared from my vision. Was looking at him making me dizzy? Ignoring that question, I turned to reach for the smoke bombs he'd piled on our tray and said, "Then we better win that candy."

Before I even touched the tray, his hand tapped mine away. *Again?* I looked at him sideways with fire in my eyes.

The corner of his mouth lifted, and my stupid stomach flipped. I scolded myself for that tiny feeling. Using one finger, he dragged the tray of smoke bombs to his side of the table, out of my reach. That stupid smirk aimed my way the whole time. I took half a second to admire the beauty around the gaze piercing my soul. The dark, messy hair tousled to perfection, curls hitting his face on either side of his chiseled cheekbones. His golden brown skin was darkened by a five o'clock shadow, enhancing his sharp jawline. His thick, dark lashes highlighted his sparkling blue eyes.

Wait. Weren't his eyes green a minute ago?

Shaking my head slightly, I blinked and opened my eyes to see his green eyes shining. I cocked my head to the side, stared for a second too long, then shook my head again. I must have imagined it. Despite my mind playing tricks on me, he looked like a model out of uniform.

Something flashed across his eyes, but I couldn't figure it out before he spoke again. "My name is Kyler, but everyone calls me Ky." His mocking tone wasn't missed, even though there was still no hint of a smile on his face.

I dropped my tense shoulders and made a face at him. "Do they really call you Ky, or did you just make that up because I said it?" I cocked my eyebrow at him, letting him know I wouldn't let it slide.

The corner of his mouth lifted again, "Guess you'll never know." He whispered, then turned back to the front in time to see Mr. Blake ring the bell on his desk, signaling time was up.

It was time to head outside, so everyone gathered their smoke bombs and headed toward the back door. It took me a minute to compose myself after his intense gaze again left me feeling light-headed and dizzy, but I shook myself out of the trance and grabbed the lighter. Kyler grabbed the small tray of smoke bombs he created and headed out the door. I followed him but heard the quick, shuffling footsteps of four feet rushing up behind me. I smirked, knowing exactly who it was.

"What's the new guy like?" I heard Ken whisper in one ear while Leigh simultaneously breathed in the other, "How'd you end up with the hottest partner?"

"His name is Kyler. I can't decide if he's sarcastic, an asshole, or a sarcastic asshole, but I'll fill you in later." The way his head was angled slightly toward us made me think he was listening in. I caught up to him at the patch of grass surrounding the flagpole in front of the school.

Mr. Blake positioned himself on the cement part directly attached to the flagpole and told us to spread out. He held up a stopwatch. "There will be five rounds. The overall longest smoke trail will win the Snickers." He straightened the cuffs of his crisp, clean shirt. The no-bullshit look on his face found the usual troublemakers in the class as he said, "If *anything* but the smoke bombs starts on fire, there will be consequences." He locked eyes with Sera and Tate before looking up to the rest of the class again and holding up the stopwatch.

Kyler set down our first smoke bomb, still keeping the tray out of my reach, and I knelt next to it, readying the lighter. He eyed my hand with the lighter, and I cocked my eyebrow at him, "What are you gonna do, snatch the lighter out of my hand?"

He mirrored my look, "I was thinking about it."

Before he got the chance, I clicked the lighter and brought the flame to life as Mr. Blake said, "Go!" I moved the fire to the fuse on our bomb, and everyone else's went off simultaneously. I smirked at him, even as something like rage boiled in his eyes. He didn't bother snatching the lighter but turned back to the smoke bomb.

It smelt like burning candy, which was disgusting but not at the same time. I coughed, backing out of the smoke trails, and watched as they curled up and away from the group. A cloud of smoke surrounded the entire class. I watched through squinting eyes, hoping silently that whatever Kyler did with the mixture in class didn't cost us. My competitive side tensed, hoping for a win, even though chocolate made me sick.

The smoke started dissipating as some of the other bombs had stopped producing smoke, but ours was still going strong even after the last of the other ones went out. Shocked at how long the first smoke bomb lasted, I glanced at Kyler with wide eyes. He was staring at the last of the smoke as it sputtered out of our bomb, and when it fully stopped, he replaced it with a new one. I shook my head in disbelief. Mr. Blake announced ours as the winner, and I readied myself to light the next bomb.

Four rounds later, Kyler and I not only won the candy bars but also one of Mr. Blake's rare smiles. Our smoke bombs had lasted the longest every single round.

When we were announced the winners, I jumped up and down and, before thinking about it, gave Kyler an excited hug.

He froze. Didn't move a muscle. Tense under my embrace. I let go immediately, backing away as heat flooded my cheeks. I'm sure my face was ten shades of red and hot to the touch because, while I was definitely a hugger, I'd never hugged someone I barely knew with so much excitement. Especially one who had been nothing but rude to me from the moment we met.

Humiliation washed over me, and I started stumbling to get words out when I finally settled with, "Sorry. Didn't mean to invade your space." As if it was the most casual thing ever. I shrugged, trying to act like it wasn't a big deal. Not knowing what else to say, I gave him a weird smile and *finger guns*. I mentally facepalmed. The look he gave me was unreadable. I took a deep breath, trying to ignore mortification setting in, and pushed past him in an attempt to run away as fast as I could.

But of course, my foot caught on the curb right behind him, and I flew toward the ground. My brain went empty as I watched the ground fly toward my face. I didn't even have time to bring my hands up to catch myself before I accepted my fate of hitting the pavement face-first.

Miraculously, though, I didn't faceplant. Something stopped me. I was relieved to know someone was nice enough to do so. But my relief was short-lived. There was only one person close enough to catch me so quickly. The arm holding me several inches from the ground was flat against my exposed midriff. How he was supporting me with just one arm at this angle was beyond me. But it wasn't exactly a hero's rescue. My skin felt like it was burning where his hand lay against my ribs. A sharp inhale and hiss told me he felt it, too. But what caused it?

Kyler suddenly released me, and I fell the remaining few inches to the ground with an "Oof."

I had enough sense to bring my hands up to catch myself before my face slammed into the asphalt, but that didn't make it any less embarrassing. I pushed myself up in time to see Kyler walking in the opposite direction, flexing his hand by his side as he went.

Heat crawled up my neck, replaying what just happened in my head.

He'd caught me. Sure.

And who knows why he went through the trouble? He *dropped* me anyway.

Jackass.

With an obscene gesture aimed at his back, I got up, fixed my jeans, and pulled my shirt down as much as possible, which wasn't as much as I'd liked, seeing as it was a crop top. I stepped *over* the curb and walked away as fast as my shaking legs could carry me, cursing myself the whole way.

I had been so good at controlling my clumsiness over the last several months, but the minute that guy appeared, all that training went down the drain.

Mentally scolding myself, I saw Ken and Leigh heading back to class arm-in-arm. I picked up my pace to catch them, trying to block out the laughter that was coming from behind me.

I felt a hand on my shoulder and inhaled sharply. Turning slowly, I let out my breath as I realized it wasn't who I expected. "Kaleb!" I melted into the hug he offered, realizing I needed it more than I thought. "What's up?"

As I pulled away, he started to say something, but my gaze traveled behind him to see who Kyler had found to laugh with about my awkward and clumsy moments. He wasn't there. It was Sera and Tate laughing at something one of them said. My eyes scanned the rest of the class, but I didn't see Kyler anywhere.

Before I could turn around to see where he'd gone, a hand waved in front of my face, and I focused on Kaleb again. "Hello? Earth to Rayleigh!" He put his hand down, and I noticed a red tint in his cheeks like he'd been a part of the embarrassing events I experienced moments ago.

"I'm sorry! I was... distracted when you grabbed me." I rubbed a hand down my face to try and clear the redness I knew was still there. "What did you say?" I felt terrible for ignoring him, but I could still feel the heat of the arm wrapped around my waist. My hand traveled to where he caught me, and I found the skin to be a bit warmer, even through the material of my shirt. It must have been the blood rushing to the surface at the pressure of his hand catching me. I fell hard, after all...

Kaleb cleared his throat, "I asked if you had a date for the prom yet. And if not, I— well... I'd like to take you." He pursed his lips and wrung his hands while waiting for my answer.

The rosy cheeks made sense now. I wondered why the question caused him to blush, but then remembered the last time he asked me to a dance. It was Homecoming. I said no—mostly because I had two left feet and didn't want to step on anybody's toes. He must have taken that no as an "I don't want to go with *you*" instead of an "I don't want to *go*."

I studied my best friend, who was running his fingers through his curly brown locks, his honey-brown eyes shining with hope, and I asked myself how I never realized how attractive he was. *Huh.* I decided he wouldn't be the worst date for senior prom. At least he wouldn't make it awkward, right? I sighed and smiled at him, "I'd love to go with you, Kaleb."

His eyes sparkled with joy, and his mouth widened to show off his winning smile as it spread ear to ear. "Really?"

I nodded, a laugh escaping as I said, "I'm going dress shopping with the twins tonight. I'll let you know how it goes." I turned to walk away, but he stepped in my path and hugged me again. It surprised me, but I returned the hug with a chuckle. "It's just a dance, Kaleb!"

He pulled away, and the smile was still there, brighter than could be. "Let me know what color your dress is!" He said as he backed away, then turned around and yelled over his shoulder, "I'll make dinner plans!" On his way back to the chemistry building, he ran to catch his other friends, doing a little jump and heel click that he often did to show his excitement.

I shook my head and laughed, taking slow, careful steps back to class, my legs still shaking from the disaster of an almost-face plant. I took in the space around me, realizing I was alone. Everyone must have made it back while Kaleb and I were talking. I picked up my pace, trying to catch the last students walking back, thinking about what I had just gotten myself into.

He'd been the girls' and my best friend for years—part of the group that hung out after school with Mitch and me. He made us watch his favorite superhero movies while we made him watch our favorite rom-com. He'd somehow talk us into playing some crazy board game every once in a while. During free periods, he joined the girls and me to do homework or read one of his favorite novels about knights and dragons or magic and other realms, always saying I should give them a shot. I reminded him that reading was Arabella's thing. Those two exchanged books weekly and talked about them when they finished.

He and I had to talk a while back because some people thought we were dating, and it felt like he was starting to lean that way. I didn't want to lead him on because I only saw him as a friend, but I also wanted to clear the air on where we stood with each other. Thankfully, he said he only saw me as his best friend, promising me it was nothing more.

After the way he reacted to my "yes" for the dance, though, it seemed I might have to check in with him again.

When I entered the classroom, Kyler sat at our table, studying his Chemistry book. The Snickers from our prize-winning smoke bombs were sitting on my side of the table, untouched. I approached nonchalantly, the place where he had caught me still hot under my shirt. Sliding onto my stool, I barely sat on the part of the seat farthest away from him. Not looking up, I started pushing one of the candy bars across the table to him.

He quickly reached out a hand to stop me, careful not to touch me again, but gave me a sideways glance. "I got the only prize I need." He gave me a devilish smirk, and my heart almost stopped at his insinuation. "Besides," he shut his Chemistry book, put it in his backpack, stood up, and started toward the door. He stopped, leaning to whisper in my ear as he passed. "I don't like chocolate."

Chills ran down my spine, sending a shiver down my back at his proximity. I turned to watch him walk out the classroom door right as the bell rang, my mouth gaping.

Kaleb caught my eye and raised an eyebrow, "Close your mouth, girlie, or you'll start catching flies." He chuckled and grabbed his things while I shut my mouth and did the same.

My mind was still reeling from what had happened in the last ten minutes, but I chose to focus on how the hell Kyler knew it was time to go. After all, it was only his first day.

IV
R U Crazy?

When I sat down in Spanish, there was a note on my side of the table. According to Senora Rodriguez's rules, we couldn't speak English in her class. Any conversation had to be in Spanish… or in secret. While Kendall was decent with her Spanish, I once told someone I was pregnant instead of embarrassed. I never made that mistake again, but there were plenty of other ways to fail Spanish. That's why Ken and I stuck to notes.

I sighed heavily as I shrugged my backpack off, knowing precisely what Ken's note was about. I pulled out my binder and placed it in front of me before opening up the scrap of paper.

> 1- tell me everything about the new guy!
> 2- what did Kaleb say after smoke bombs?

I rolled my eyes before putting my pen to the paper with my response. It barely landed in front of Ken before she swiped it from the table to read. Then she scribbled a quick reply before it landed in front of me again. I unfolded it and let out a huff through my nose, smiling slightly.

> *that's it?*
> *he's an ass?*
> *and prom with Kaleb?*

My one-word reply didn't go over well. After reading it, she crumpled up the note and tossed it in the trash near us. All I wrote was 'later' because I didn't feel like writing it all on paper. Aside from that, it prevented me from trying to understand Senora Rodriguez. With my attention entirely on her, I tried to catch what she said, but my ears were not tuned to the language. I let out a frustrated sigh and leaned back in my chair. All I could gather from her chatter were the words 'test' and 'today,' and I, of course, hadn't studied.

After failing that test, I moved on to Trig. My singled-out desk was perfect for this class. Thank goodness I didn't have anyone to distract me. It was the one class I couldn't afford it, as I was practically failing as it was.

None of my math classes would be helpful to me outside of school, so it didn't make sense why I had to take it. High school made us believe that the world needed everyone to know what tangent, sine, and cosine were and how they measured a triangle. But I knew that no such thing would be required in the line of work I wanted to go into. Being a chef didn't require knowledge of triangles and their angles. We measured in dashes and sprinkles and occasionally cups and tablespoons. The only pie we talked about was the kind we can eat.

Why couldn't I take more cooking classes or learn how to run a restaurant? This class made me feel like nails were scratching my brain. The teacher didn't make it any better. Her monotone voice turned my brain to mush as she went on about our semester final and how important it would be to our grade. *Great. I'm definitely going to fail,* I thought to myself. She started passing out review packets, and as the thirteen-page novella landed on my desk, my phone buzzed in my pocket.

Mrs. Glass had already passed my desk, making it easier to sneak my phone out of my pocket and read Leighton's message.

Meet me outside French after class.

I replied with a thumbs up, pocketing my phone again. I knew what she wanted to talk about. The girls were notorious for bugging me when any guy was involved. I'd been single my entire life, and the girls always complained about how picky I was, but it was one of the few things I prided myself on. Settling for someone because they're available and cute isn't something I ever saw myself doing, even if they were the nicest person on earth. I wanted someone who knew everything about me, even my little quirks, and loved me even more for them.

Sometimes, I felt so comfortable around guys that I overlooked when they started to catch feelings for me until it was too late. One guy confessed his feelings to me, thinking I felt the same, and it caught me off guard. I had to tell him he read the situation wrong. He had the audacity to tell me to pull back on the flirty touching, so I put him in a chokehold and said, "Do you prefer this?" He could only sputter his answer. I pushed him away from me before I let any more anger out on him, and he ran to tell a teacher. Unfortunately for him, Mr. Piper shrugged and told him to run a lap around the gym.

Leigh probably wanted to know the same things Ken asked, and I knew I'd have to tell them both of my encounters during Chemistry were innocent. Kaleb's my best friend. That's it. They knew that, but with him and I hanging out more regularly after school and all last summer, it didn't surprise me that they questioned our relationship. That one would be easy to explain.

Kyler, on the other hand… I knew he caught their attention the moment they saw him. So, it was no surprise that they saw every encounter between us as something more than it was: the awkward hug, his saving me from nearly falling on my face, and then his whispering in my ear before he left the classroom.

My hand smacked my forehead as I recalled the awkward moments. Sure, I hugged my friends often, but I had no idea what possessed me to hug Kyler. What a terrible idea.

I hated to blame my clumsiness for the almost-face plant because I'd been working hard to improve my coordination and balance. But there was no way I could tell her why he saved but didn't save me from falling. It made no sense.

The whisper… That wasn't something I could explain. And who

knew what that looked like to anyone else who'd seen it? I'm pretty sure I shuddered from the chills that ran down my spine. Not to mention, my ears turned red. I can't imagine what people thought he said to get that reaction out of me.

Shaking my head, I tried concentrating on the review packet in front of me. The numbers and words ran together as brain fog started taking over. This morning, sitting next to Kyler was incredibly distracting. The heat radiating from him and his eye contact made me dizzy. I got lost in the beauty of his green eyes more than once. Or were they blue?

In my mental image of him, I studied his features, trying to remember his eyes, but the color kept changing in my brain. My eyes fell to the mental picture of his curved nose. To his lips, wondering if they felt as soft as they looked, imagining what they would feel like—

Something clattered on the floor, breaking me from my stupor. I checked the clock—two minutes left in class. I slammed my math book closed a little too loud, earning a glare from Mrs. Glass over her glasses, and placed the review packet inside the front cover before putting them both in my backpack.

The bell rang, and I jumped to my feet, hustling out the door. The French hallway was near my next class, but Leigh would likely keep me as long as possible, badgering me with questions. Leighton was waiting right where she said she'd be, facing the other direction with her head down, likely on her phone.

"What's up?" I asked when I reached her side.

She turned quickly to face me, a knowing smile on her face. "I saw Kyler outside Government." She paused, waiting for some reaction that I wouldn't have. She went on, "He was on the phone with someone." She definitely wanted me to ask for elaboration.

"Okay." I dragged out the word. "Why are you acting like I should care?"

Her eyebrows raised. "He was whispering, so I couldn't hear it all. But…" She leaned in to whisper, "I heard him say *your name.*" Her elbow nudged me playfully, the smile on her face spreading wider.

My ears heated, and my stomach filled with acid. "Why would he be talking about me? He just met me."

Leigh shrugged, "I dunno." Her smile turned devious, "Maybe he likes you?"

My cheeks turned the color of my ears. "Again, he *just* met me." An idea of why he might be talking about me crossed my mind, and I clenched my jaw, saying, "He was probably retelling the tale of my face plant or the awkward hug to someone he knows so he could have someone to laugh about it with." Rolling my eyes, I turned toward Government.

Leigh grabbed my elbow before I could take a step, "I didn't hear him laughing." Her face had become more stern at my apparent dismissal. "You never know, Ray. You could have charmed him like you do with everyone else."

"Doubtful. Besides, he's a jerk. He left me to fall on my face." Thinking back to his reaction in the classroom, I said, "*And* he smacked my hand when I tried to help with the smoke bombs. *Twice*."

She shrugged again, "Give it a chance, Ray. You always push guys away. Maybe it's time for a change." She clearly wasn't listening to anything I told her. It was starting to piss me off.

"But *that guy*? He's an *ass*, Leigh!" She had to see that. She stared at me with an eyebrow raised, so I switched to offense. "What about you, huh? Why'd you get all weird this morning when we were talking about Prom?"

Her face went white, but she straightened and crossed her arms before saying, "I have no idea what you're talking about."

"Oh, come off it!" I said playfully, lightly smacking her shoulder. "You acted like going with Charlie Knott is the worst decision you've ever made." Leigh avoided looking at me. A thought occurred to me, and I lowered my voice, stepping closer to whisper, "Leigh, did he do something?"

Her gaze finally snapped to mine. "What? No!" She shrieked, then realized her mistake and sighed, "No." She repeated. "Charlie's really nice, it's just—"

The warning bell chimed, and Leigh didn't waste time. She whipped around and hurried off before I could say anything else, her curls bouncing as she stalked away. There wasn't much time to get to Government, so I hurried around the corner, thinking about what

Leighton said... and didn't say.

Unfortunately, as I sat down in Mr. Douglas's class, thoughts about Kyler filled my head. Why did he treat me the way he did? Did he smack my hand because he thought I would mess up the experiment? Why did he catch me after I tripped, only to drop me and let me fall the rest of the way? He basically assisted me in saving myself. He had a quick and effective reflex to save me. What made him change his mind halfway through the save? Did his instinct kick in before his brain? And when it finally caught up, he just... dropped me? Or did it have to do with the burn I felt with the skin-to-skin contact? I'd never experienced anything like that. If he felt it, too, perhaps he released me because of the pain. But it wasn't *that* painful. It was more uncomfortable than anything.

It didn't matter. He still dropped me. He could have easily hoisted me up before releasing me.

Mr. Douglas cleared his throat, returning me to his lecture, which I was supposed to take notes on. I cursed silently at the notebook page I'd been doodling on. I scribbled out the doodle and wrote jackass with an arrow pointing to Kyler's mostly indecipherable name. I hastily turned the page and focused back on Mr. Douglas, mentally judging myself for having such lousy taste in men.

१ के स र

After class, I was in the cafeteria line, searching the tables for my friends, when I felt a presence behind me. I turned slowly to find Kyler directly behind me, grinning. I jumped a little, swearing quietly at his proximity, and took a significant step away from him.

"Sorry," he said roughly, smirking like he'd enjoyed scaring the shit out of me. It made that stupid, funny feeling make another appearance in my stomach. I faced the front of the line, not caring what else he had to say. "Done talking to strangers?" His breath caressed the back of my neck, and I could feel every inch of space between us fill with heat.

It dispersed quickly as I said, "Why would I want to talk to someone who let me fall face-first onto the pavement?" I grabbed food from the display case and put it on my lunch tray.

"Pfft," I could almost hear his eyes roll, "I caught you."

I raised my eyebrows but didn't turn around as I said, "I caught myself. After you *dropped me.*"

His whispered reply tickled my neck again, and I refused to let myself shiver in response. "Still caught you, though." He was definitely smirking.

I fought the urge to throw my head back against his face to wipe the look off his face, electing to grab a cookie from the basket near the register instead. "And what's your excuse for not letting me help with the smoke bombs?"

He didn't laugh as he said, "I didn't want you to mess them up."

I whirled on him, anger rising at his insinuation, even though I'd guessed that on my own. "I was doing perfectly fine on my own in Chemistry before you came along." I shoved a finger into his sternum, which made him retreat slightly in surprise. "Perfect, actually. So what, pray tell, made you think that I would 'mess them up'?" I hoped my eyes reflected the fire I felt inside, but I bet I looked more like an angry kitten.

He raised his hands in mock surrender, a smile playing at his lips. "You're right. My fault for assuming." He dropped his hands and cocked a brow at me, reaching around me to grab a cookie from the basket and causing me to move and my finger to fall from his chest. "You're just a little ray of sunshine, aren't you?"

I ignored him, clenching my jaw and turning toward the table where Ken, Leigh, and Kaleb waited. Kyler stepped in front of me before I could take a step towards them. "Come on. Give me a chance."

I squinted at his words. They resembled Leighton's so closely. My gaze went from him to the table where my friends waited, eyeing me expectantly. Leigh's eyes caught mine, and her words echoed through my head again. I closed my eyes, took a deep breath, and opened them to face Kyler. "Don't make me regret this."

The way he smirked at me, I knew he would do just that. But I walked toward the table anyway, knowing he'd follow.

I sat heavily between Ken and Kaleb, making sure not to leave a seat next to me. I realized my mistake right before he sat directly across from me.

Great. Now I have to look at him.

I didn't want to fall into that dizzying gaze again, so I turned to my friends, "Guys, this is Kyler. But everyone calls him Ky." My mocking tone did not go unnoticed by Kyler. I could tell because of the small breath of laughter he let slip before gaining his composure all too quickly. The girls didn't seem to be affected by my mocking tone at all. No. They were ogling Kyler like he was the most gorgeous thing they had ever seen. This didn't surprise me until I remembered Kendall's boyfriend would be there any minute, and I shot her with a death glare. She didn't notice, though.

"Hi, Ky." The girls sighed in sync, sounding like they were melting into the table. My eyes rolled so far back into my head that I almost gave myself a headache. I ripped a chunk of my pizza off with my teeth and studied my plate, not wanting to deal with this.

"What shall I call you two *lovely* ladies?" *Barf. Who says that?*

The girls talked over each other, starting but never finishing their introductions. When they couldn't decide who would speak first, I took over the duty.

I sighed, "That's Kendall, and that's Leighton," I pointed respectively. "They are two of my best friends." They smiled again, lost in the blue eyes that weren't even looking at them. *Wait. Blue again?* I checked. *Nope. They are green.* "And this," I slapped my hand onto Kaleb's shoulder, "Is my other best friend. Kaleb."

Kaleb failed to hide a smile as he eyed me. I ignored him and tore another chunk off my pizza, sliding my hand down to hold onto his arm for emotional support. His hand found mine in the crook of his elbow and gave me a reassuring squeeze. The simple gesture relaxed my rigid body, and he returned to eating with his left hand.

"How long have you all been friends?" Kyler asked. Thank goodness he was taking charge of the conversation because I didn't want to say anything more than I had to—to any of them, especially him. Shoving another bite of pizza in my mouth, I realized I had no idea how hungry I was.

Leighton answered immediately, "Oh, we've been friends since

Kindergarten!" She smiled sweetly, and Kyler nodded, chewing on his pizza and waiting for the next part of the conversation. I closed my eyes at the uncomfortable silence, knowing the girls were staring at him expectantly.

Roshan finally showed up and plopped down next to Kendall, drawing her attention from Kyler momentarily as she gave him a peck on the cheek. I thought she turned back to Kyler too quickly, and apparently, Roshan felt the same. He grabbed her by the chin almost immediately, turned her back to face him, and gave her a proper kiss. She melted into him like syrup, which had the rest of us looking away momentarily to avoid the awkwardness.

Kaleb, thankfully, cleared his throat, causing them to break apart, and said, "What brought you to Wisteria Heights, Kyler?" I casually looked up, acknowledging my curiosity about his answer.

He took a deep breath, his eyes locked on mine like I had asked the question, and whispered, "That's top-secret information." His eyes sparkled in the light, mischief dancing among them. I turned away. There was no way I was getting caught in that again. He addressed Kaleb with the rest of his answer. "My father is from the area. We come back this way quite often. He wanted to put some roots down and decided this was the best place. He has a lot of business here."

The way he said business told me he would definitely not answer Kaleb's next question, "What kind of business?"

He chuckled softly, the sound making my stomach do weird things. I mentally scolded myself at my body's inability to recognize all the red flags from this guy. "He works in the medical field. Works with different hospitals around the area." The answer seemed normal enough. "What do your parents do?" He seemed to be asking all of us, but his eyes were on me again, like he knew something I didn't.

My heart sank at the question, and I shoved another bite in my mouth to avoid answering. The pizza tasted like ash on my tongue.

I heard Kaleb answer, but the words jumbled in my brain. Kyler's gaze was burning a hole in my head. I should have sat next to him. He wouldn't have been able to stare without making it awkward.

Kendall's hand found my bouncing leg under the table, and she squeezed lightly. I saw the question in her eyes but shook my head, barely noticeable to anyone else.

Everyone else answered Kyler's question, and I thought for a moment he wouldn't press the subject, but I had no such luck.

His gaze was still on me as he said, "And your parents?"

I squared my shoulder, refusing to let him affect me more than he already had. "My mom does interior design and architecture stuff." The rest of that answer was too raw for me to recite. Before he could pry further, I stood, grabbed my empty tray, and walked to the trash cans. I saved the cookie but dumped everything else before going to the courtyard to spend the rest of my lunch alone.

V
Everything's Okay

It hadn't occurred to me that I wouldn't be allowed to have alone time. But when the door opened behind me, I took a deep breath in preparation to tell Kendall I was fine. But it wasn't Kendall jogging to catch up to me.

It was Kaleb. "Everything okay, Ray?"

I shook the surprise from my face and let him catch me before continuing on the path that ran a large circle around the courtyard. He fell into step beside me, matching my stride like he had on all our strolls around the courtyard.

"I didn't want to tell him about my dad." Kaleb nodded, offering me his elbow, sensing I was on the verge of a breakdown. I took it gratefully and wrapped both arms around his elbow as we kept walking, leaning into him a little as we went.

"Tell me what's really going on, girlie." He nudged me. "That can't be the only reason you stomped out of the cafeteria."

"I didn't stomp out!" I snapped, but the grin on his face told me he was teasing, and I pursed my lips at my outburst. He led the way around the path, allowing me time to find the right words. Something caught in my throat when I tried to talk, but I cleared it and started again. "He wasn't nice to me in class. I mean, you saw what happened.

He ignored me completely when I introduced myself to him, smacked my hand like a child, and then he almost snatched the lighter from my hands when we were starting smoke bombs. Not to mention, he let me fall face-first onto the pavement when I tripped over the curb."

"I thought he caught you. With one hand no less." Kaleb had been nearby, so it made sense that he'd know that, but how had he not seen him drop me?

"Well, technically, yes," I admitted, but quickly continued, "but he didn't help me back up. He let go, and I fell the rest of the way!"

Kaleb tried and failed to hold back a chuckle, which earned him an elbow to the gut. He grunted, "Sorry." His suppressed smile told me enough about his apology. "I must have missed that part."

"The point is," I pressed on, "He acted like an entitled asshole." I thought about the other feelings that had come up when I was around him, which reminded me of the moments before Chemistry class. "And I'm pretty sure he's the douchebag who took up two parking spaces. I had to crawl through the passenger door to get out of my car!"

This time, Kaleb didn't try to hide his laugh, "You crawled out the passenger door?" When I nodded, biting my lip to hold back my smile at his contagious laughter, he let out a full belly laugh, throwing his head back and everything. "Oh, I would have *paid* to see that!"

His full laugh made my smile break through, and I rolled my eyes, "Well, I'm sure if you want the show, I'll probably have to do it again if he's still parked there after school." I hated that possibility, but at least I got out of class earlier than everyone else, so no one would see me making the climb back in.

Kaleb's laugh subsided as he nudged me with the elbow I held. "Don't let him get to you." His eyes were bright with laughter as it faded. "Maybe he did those things because he thought he was protecting you. Or maybe he thought it would turn you on." He waggled his eyebrows suggestively like he knew he was right.

I shook my head, turning back to the path ahead. "Why does everyone think he's acting that way because I'm irresistible? He *literally* just met me." I didn't feel the need to mention that being mean was not the best way to let someone know you like them.

Kaleb lifted one shoulder. "Well, he'd be blind if he didn't think you were cute." My eyes shot to him at the blatant tone, but he winked and turned away. "Besides, you ever heard of love at first sight, Ray?"

"Ha!" The laugh echoed loudly throughout the courtyard. "That is a myth. There's no such thing—except in fairytales."

He touched his heart in mock hurt, mouth gaping. "I'll have you know that my parents met on a blind date and have been happily married for over twenty-three years. So pardon me if I disagree with your assessment." He tapped my nose like I was being silly, smirking while returning his focus to the path ahead.

His previous comment gave me pause, and I opened and closed my mouth, feeling like a fish out of water. Was now the best time to ensure we were still on the same page with… us?

I loosened my grip on his arm, but his other hand stopped me, his gaze meeting mine and holding it earnestly. "I know what you're going to say."

"How could you possibly—"

He placed a finger on my lips, and I raised my eyebrows, but he pressed on. "Don't worry about us, Ray." Damn. He really did follow my thoughts well. "You're my best friend. I'm not gonna mess that up by confessing my love to you. You're too important to me." My jaw dropped slightly, and he touched my chin to close my mouth before continuing. "Besides, we already had this talk." He tucked my hair behind my ear and returned to lead us around the courtyard, smiling. "I'm honestly just looking forward to watching you make a fool of yourself on the dance floor." He caught my gaze with a sideways look of his own, winking. "And dancing with you at your first and last dance."

A weight lifted off my chest. I wasn't aware it was there, but something deeper stirred in my stomach. I chose to ignore that feeling in the moment, though. "Thanks," was all I could say. We stayed silent for a minute while I processed what he said, wondering if we cleared the air or if things had gotten messier. "You could have danced with me even if we went separately, you know."

Before he spoke, I knew what he was going to say. And it was one hundred percent correct. "Ray, you wouldn't be going if I hadn't asked you."

He *was* right, but I didn't *want* him to be. And he knew that I didn't want him to be. "You don't know that," I said casually, shrugging. "Maybe Kyler would have asked me," I mocked, trying to hide the shudder that rolled through me at the thought. Kaleb laughed at my reaction to my own suggestion. I released a sigh, "You're right. I probably wouldn't go if you hadn't asked." Another thought occurred to me as we made our way back to the cafeteria doors. "You're important to me too, Kaleb. You've been there for me through... everything that's happened over the past few years. When I needed you most, you dropped whatever you were doing to be there, and I... I don't want to lose this either." I squeezed his arm for emphasis, knowing he knew it was more than this conversation. "Besides," I looked at him through my lashes, "Who would shoot a Nerf gun at Jordin's face if you weren't around?" A huge grin covered my face before I finished the sentence, and Kaleb pulled out of my grasp so quickly that I keeled over from laughter.

The shock on his face alone would have kept me laughing, but he voiced his thoughts, making my fits of laughter worse. "Whyyy would you bring that up right now?!" His voice cracked, taking in the betrayal I'd thrown at him. "You know that was an accident!" I was in hysterics, laughing so hard I had to grip my stomach. "She looked like she was going to *kill* me that day." His shocked face slowly broke into a smile as my giggling became contagious. He pointed straight at my face, holding back his laugh, "If I never shoot another Nerf gun in that house again, don't be surprised."

He turned away dramatically, but I hugged him around the waist from behind playfully, trapping his arms and making it impossible to walk away. "Nooo! You have to! We have such fun Nerf wars at the house!" He stopped trying to walk and tried turning in my grasp instead. I let him, and his winning smile was spread from ear to ear. "We can battle in the backyard next time, just like when we were younger. Build forts and everything. Like that one tim—"

"Can I join in on that war?" The deep voice came from the cafeteria doors behind me, and I stood up straight, all laughter melting from my face as I turned around. Kyler leaned on the wall outside the door like he'd been standing there a while.

"No." My dead-toned answer surprised even me, and as Kaleb stepped into my peripherals, I could tell his face turned into something unreadable. Clearing my throat, I clarified, "Uh, no. The Nerf wars are for family and friends only."

Something like hurt flashed in his eyes before it disappeared, and he cleared his own throat, "Fair enough." He took in Kaleb before his eyes found mine again. "Can I talk to you for a minute?"

Kaleb gave me a sideways glance. I knew he was giving me the option to walk away with him as he offered his arm, subtle enough that Kyler wouldn't have noticed. But I remembered his comment from earlier, Leighton's echoing through my head again, too. I took a deep breath and said, "One minute." I nodded to Kaleb, who took the hint and walked through the cafeteria doors.

Kyler didn't move from the wall but watched Kaleb leave with a predator's gaze. He let the door shut before turning back to me. "I wanted to apologize."

Surprise rushed through me as his tone suggested he might be sincere. But I wasn't going to let him off that easily. "For what, exactly?" I crossed my arms, tapping my finger to count the seconds.

He pushed off the wall, closing the distance between us in a few strides, hands in his pockets as he said, "For whatever I did that upset you in there." I raised my eyebrows at the lack of specifics, but he ignored that. "You seemed pretty upset when you left the table."

Oh. So this wasn't about his actions during Chemistry, but what happened at the lunch table? "The reason I left the table... It wasn't because of you." There wasn't anything else I could say about that without giving away too much. "And that's a pretty lame apology for how you treated me in Chemistry." He let his head fall back and let out a long sigh. His chin dropped back down with the words on his tongue, but I didn't give him a chance. "Your minute is up." And like magic, the bell rang. "Apology not accepted." I shouldered past him and walked through the cafeteria doors, bee-lining to Kaleb, Ken, and Leigh, who were waiting on the other side of the room. I hooked arms with the twins and didn't glance backward, knowing I would find

Kyler watching me run away if I did. But I didn't care. If he didn't realize what he did was awful, I would ignore him until he did.

१ को श द

Creative writing was my favorite class, and the teacher was even better. Seeing her standing in the doorway returned the joy I'd lost after this morning's events. Ms. Kelley was handing out candy as everyone was walking in. I sidled up next to her and said, "What's the occasion?" I took the strawberry lollipop she held out to me.

She looked at me and giggled. "Ah, well, you see, there is this annual thing for a lot of people called a birthday. Today just so happens to be mine." She winked, pulling out a piece of candy for the student behind me.

"Well, Happy Birthday!" I gave her a side hug. She smiled and held the bucket out to me again.

After grabbing some pieces of fruity candy, I headed to my desk next to Leighton.

Noticing the dumb grin on her face, I raised my eyebrow at her, "What?"

"Oh, nothing... I heard you said yes to Kaleb, though." The teasing tone made me roll my eyes. I'd done that a lot today, making the headache I developed over the last few hours make sense.

I set my backpack down and dug for my class notebook. "I'm surprised you didn't bring it up before now," I mumbled, not knowing how to answer the question in her statement. I sighed loudly and said, "I guess I just wanted to go to senior prom and going with Kaleb... I don't know. I feel comfortable knowing I won't have to worry about the night getting ruined somehow."

Leighton raised a brow, "Uh huh... Well, he sounded *very* excited when he told me." She pulled out her notebook and a set of blank notecards we were told to bring to class.

How she said 'very' made me think the conversation in the courtyard hadn't gone how I thought it had. He said he wouldn't ruin our friendship by *confessing* his love for me, but did that mean he *did* have feelings for me and he wasn't going to tell me? Or that he wouldn't entertain the idea of liking me? Or is it possible he really didn't have feelings for me?

I sighed. I wasn't sure I wanted to bring it up with Kaleb again because I might not like his answer.

"Ray," Leigh pulled me from my thoughts. "What's going on? Why the long sigh?"

I shook the thoughts from my head. "I dunno. He and I talked at lunch, and it seemed like he had more than friendship on his mind. He assured me he didn't, but…"

"Ahh…" She nodded as if she knew something I didn't. "Let me guess, he called you cute and flirted with you?" I balked at her, and she just laughed, leaning in again, "I'm nosey, remember?" She nudged me with her elbow.

I stuck my tongue out and said, "Yes, he's flirty and goofy with me, but it's always been like that, hasn't it?"

Leigh's eyebrows shot up as she pursed her lips. "Even when Bell was around?"

"Yes! I—" But she had a point. It wasn't until this last summer that I noticed he was more flirty and touchy. I hadn't thought anything of it because, to me, it was just a best friend thing. We were all like that with each other. At least, I thought we were. But looking back on it now, he only acted that way with me.

Leigh leaned in, seeing Ms. Kelley walking around to collect homework, and whispered, "Are you sure *you* don't have feelings for *him*?" Before I could protest, she reached across me to hand Ms. Kelley her notebook, and I did the same before Leigh continued. "You forget, I hang out with you guys all the time. It doesn't really seem one-sided, Ray."

And here I thought Ken was the blunt one. My cheeks flushed. "Well, I—" I took a deep breath and cleared my throat, whispering, "It's not on purpose."

Leigh raised her eyebrows, but the look I gave her made her sigh. "Well, then…you have to accept that you can't control how people interpret your words or actions. Believe me." She turned to the front of the class to listen to Ms. Kelley give instructions on our project, due next week.

I mulled over her words, wondering what experience made her say that. My mind went straight to her date for prom and how weird she had acted earlier. When Ms. Kelley dismissed us to start designing our project—something that could never exist in real life—I asked Leigh quietly, "What happened between you and Charlie?"

She took a deep breath, releasing it slowly before she said, "Nothing happened, Ray. I just…" She avoided my eyes but said, "There was someone else I wanted to go to prom with, but they already have a date."

"Oh," I said, thinking back on all our recent conversations for a mention of someone she liked. None came to mind, so I asked, "Who?"

"It doesn't matter," she said quickly. Before I could press her, she asked, "Are you and Kaleb joining Braxton at Wisteria Creek for dinner?"

Taken aback by her change of subject, I shook my head. "I dunno. We haven't talked about that yet." Thinking she couldn't possibly want to go with Brax, I squinted, "Does *he* have a date?"

"Yeah." Her cheeks turned a slight pink. "Anyway, Charlie wants to have dinner there too, so I figured we could make a group out of it. Ken said she would ask Roshan."

There was something she wasn't saying, but it didn't look like I would get it out of her. "I'll ask Kaleb. Although knowing him, he's probably already got it all planned out." I grinned, but it faded as I thought about Kaleb's words in the courtyard again.

Leigh grabbed my hand. "Hey, if Kaleb said he doesn't have feelings for you, you'll just have to trust him." I sighed, unsure how she followed my thoughts, but I knew she was right. "You've been best friends for years. I can't imagine him ruining that. He would never force anything on you, even if he did like you. That's not who he is."

I nodded, then put my free hand on top of hers. "Are you sure you're okay going to dinner with Braxton and his date?"

"Yeah," she said as if it were no big deal, although her cheeks tinted red again.

I squinted at her. "Do you like him now? Is that what this is about? Because, correct me if I'm wrong, you're the one that turned him down."

Her eyes got big. "No! No, gosh, no. He and I are… well, we're on okay terms."

"Okay…" I dragged out the word but softened my tone as I said, "Whatever it is you're not telling me, I hope you know I'm all ears when you're ready."

A line of silver appeared in her eyes as she smiled. "Thanks, Ray." I hugged her arm, and we got to work designing the Snurgleform pen.

VI
Red Flag

As usual, Mr. Piper let me leave gym class early. Ever since he found out about my training sessions outside of school, he would give me a task halfway through class as an excuse to let me leave and never expected me back. He claimed it was because I was getting the exercise I needed in my training without participating in his class.

Today was no different. He sent me to his office with some kettlebells that needed returning and said he'd see me Wednesday. After dropping them off, I headed to my car to wait for Ken and Leigh, texting Kaleb on the way.

>did u make dinner plans for prom?

He replied almost immediately:
>Yeah. Wisteria Creek with Brax and Amariel.

I scratched my head as I walked through the parking lot, not knowing of anyone by that name.

>who's amariel?

>New girl. Started a few weeks ago.

There was no way I missed a new student in this school. It was too small.

My phone buzzed again.

> **Are you telling me you don't know someone at this school?**

A laugh filtered through my nose at the shocked face emoji. I sent one back with its tongue sticking out.

I had forgotten about the Audi until I saw it still parked beside my car. I shook my head, snapping a picture to send to Kaleb.

> **see? kyler = asshole.**

He only sent the laughing face emoji before I pocketed my phone. Hopefully, he didn't request a video of me crawling through because that would be too embarrassing.

As I passed the Audi, I kicked the front bumper—not hard, but enough to let some of my anger out—and cursed its owner. I rounded the back of my car to the passenger side, threw my bag in the back, and prepared myself for the crawl through.

Opening the front door, I hiked my jeans to make moving easier, but nothing could have made the crouch and crawl any less humiliating. Sitting down and scooting might have been a better choice than the one I made, but it was too late to change tactics. With my foot planted on the passenger seat and the other landing on the driver's seat, I cursed aloud at my stupidity. I grabbed the steering wheel and hauled myself over the console. My knee hit the horn when my foot got stuck under the emergency brake, blaring and grabbing the single person's attention in the parking lot. Another spew of curses left my mouth as I readjusted to pull my foot from its trapped position and lifted my knee off the horn. I slid my leg under the steering wheel and plopped onto the seat before lowering the other. I gave an awkward wave to the student, who was still staring at me from a distance. I hoped they hadn't seen the entire debacle.

I threw my head back against the headrest and let out a hefty sigh. Kyler was going to get one hell of an earful tomorrow.

Movement outside my window grabbed my attention.

Heat crawled slowly up my neck as the tinted window of the Audi rolled down, and I saw a phone facing my direction. I had no doubt the person holding that phone recorded the whole fiasco.

The phone lowered to reveal dark shades on that perfectly angular face, now holding the world's douchiest smirk as he gave me a two-fingered salute. I clenched my jaw, facing forward again, and turned the key one click to roll the window down. "How long, exactly, were you sitting there watching me struggle?" I asked as the window lowered, not daring to look at him again.

"Me?" The mock innocence was heavy in his tone. I raised my eyebrows, not saying a word. Waiting. The savage smirk returned when I eyed him sideways. He held up his phone and confessed, "Oh, I saw it all, Sunshine." A shiver ran down my spine at how that nickname rolled off his tongue, causing something within me to stir unpleasantly. Sorrow crept in— *Not now!* I suppressed the feelings and tried to grab the phone, but he moved it out of reach before I could get my hands on it. "Don't worry, I'll keep it to myself." He held it close to his chest and whispered, "My own personal entertainment." He winked and pocketed the phone, keeping his eyes on me.

"Delete it," I snarled, swallowing the lump in my throat. I tried my best to sneer, knowing it wouldn't do much, but I wanted to be clear I didn't care for his charades. I wasn't used to being mean to people, but this guy was getting under my skin like no one else could.

He leaned out his window, resting his chin on his forearms, which lay on the frame. His shades slid down his nose as he raised his eyebrows enough for me to see his mischievous green eyes. "Make me." Heat boiled in my stomach as I thought about punching him. He *was* within arms reach. I could have done it. He was parked so close that if I leaned out the window like he was, our noses would touch, and if I leaned a little farther—

I banished the thought and could have sworn heat flashed in his eyes, but it disappeared quickly. He was still waiting for my reply. "What do you want me to do? Reach over and take the phone out of your pocket?" His cocky smirk at this distance made me realize something. "Hang on. How did you get into *your* car?" His two-door car was backward in the parking spot. He would have had to do what I did to get into the driver's seat.

He held up a tiny remote key. "Car has a self-parking feature. Push this button, and it'll park itself, or pull out of a parking spot for me." Amusement shined in his eyes as he let that information sink in.

"You mean to tell me," I licked my lips, trying to control my temper, "that you remotely pulled the car out, got in, and *re-parked the car*?" His expression didn't change. He didn't drop his gaze. He held my stare as anger started seeping off me. My nostrils flared, my voice strained as I said, "You are—"

"Charming. Delightful. *Gorgeous.*" His eyes sparkled.

"An entitled asshole!" There wasn't a better way to describe him. No other label would fit his vibe. Nope. "How did you even know this was my car?"

He finally sat back in his seat, leaning against the headrest, and chuckled softly. "I didn't. Just lucky, I guess." I crossed my arms, glaring at him and trying not to acknowledge that his chuckle made my insides squirm. He glanced at me sideways, taking me in, and seemed to come to some decision as he said, "I'm waiting for my sister."

Surprise crossed my face before I could stop it. Fixing my face back to a glare, something clicked. "Amariel?" I asked.

His head snapped towards me. "How do you know her name?"

"Lucky guess." I shook my head, letting it fall back on the headrest. "God, I hope she's nothing like you," I muttered. Going on a double date with a girl version of Kyler sounded awful. Not my idea of a good time.

Kyler had gone quiet, likely not understanding why I would say that. When I glanced at him, he was studying me closely. "She's more like you than me." He practically scowled his comment, but I couldn't bring myself to ask why that would be a bad thing. "Why does it matter?" He asked.

I sighed, not knowing if he was worth having this conversation with, but decided I had time to kill and gave in. "My date for prom is best friends with her date. We're all going to dinner before the dance." He didn't need any more details, so I stopped there.

"Kaleb and Braxton are best friends?" It was my turn to whip my head towards him. His eyes were bright with amusement. How did he know Kaleb asked me to the dance? He disappeared after the incident in Chemistry. I squinted at him and opened my mouth to ask, but he cut me off. "Why isn't he part of your friend group?"

The question caught me off guard, mainly because the topic had already been brought up today, but I wasn't about to tell him that. "It's... complicated." Brax had stopped hanging out with us shortly after he asked Leigh out, being too self-conscious about the situation and wanting to give Leighton her space. I respected his decision but sometimes missed having him around the group. He used to give the wildest dares and always had embarrassing stories about Kaleb.

Kyler was mulling over my short response before arriving at his next question. "How did you and Kaleb become friends?" He flexed his jaw ever so slightly.

I scrunched my brows, studying Kyler for a moment. Was he jealous? "He and I—" I paused, realizing that if I told him this story, I'd have to give him information about me that I wasn't sure I was ready to share. I met his gaze, seeing the intensity there, the patience to see if I would continue. "We met in kindergarten. He was friends with my twin first." Shock flashed in his eyes, as I knew it would. He furrowed his brow, struggling to unpack that particular statement.

"Your twin?" He finally said, making me regret saying anything. He was still staring at me intensely, waiting. But what was I supposed to say to that?

Mercifully, I wouldn't have to say anything.

The bell rang.

I cleared my throat of the emotion that got stuck there and reached to start my car. Chitty didn't even make a sound when I turned the key. Heat crawled up my neck and onto my ears. Of course, this would happen right now. *Come on, Chitty! Please don't embarrass me like this...* I turned the key again, and it sputtered a little, giving out after a couple of seconds. "C'mon, *start!*" I yelled through clenched teeth, trying again. He purred to life as if he hadn't just embarrassed me in the worst way.

My shoulders sagged in relief, and ignoring Kyler's stare, I rolled my window up to block him out. Before it closed, a chuckle caressed my ears right before his engine roared to life. Literally. Roared. I almost jumped out of my seat. It was the loudest engine I'd ever heard. How incredibly obnoxious.

I clenched my jaw but continued staring straight ahead, keeping my eyes on the doors I knew Ken and Leigh would emerge from at any moment. Kyler was making a spectacle out of it. He was probably laughing to himself about my car not starting. It added to the list of reasons I couldn't and wouldn't entertain any of the ideas that had flooded my mind about him. He was conceited and controlling, two of the biggest red flags I knew to avoid.

Not wanting to stay parked next to him anymore, I threw my car into reverse and started pulling out of the parking spot to pick the girls up at the door. Mid-reverse, a horn blared, and I slammed on my brakes, whipping around to check the lot behind me. When I saw no cars, I closed my eyes and took a deep breath, realizing who honked. With a vulgar gesture in Kyler's direction, I backed up faster and went to door two. I swear I could hear his laughter through my window as I drove off. Ken and Leigh walked out as I pulled up, hopping in, and I took off before either of them could ask why my face was so red.

"I still don't understand why you said yes to Kaleb," Ken said as we pulled into the mall thirty minutes later.

I had sped off so fast from the school parking lot that poor Chitty's tires squealed. It wasn't until halfway to town that Leigh's whispered request to slow down came from the backseat. Only then was Ken bold enough to ask what happened. I wasn't clear-headed enough to address the answer yet, so instead, I told them everything about Kaleb asking me to prom. Leigh knew most of the details already, but Ken was still surprised.

"You've told us so many times you don't like him, and yet you're going to *senior prom* with him?" She paused, turning toward me with a huge grin. "I mean, what about Kyler?"

We hadn't touched on *that* subject the entire ride, which meant she had yet to hear all my complaints about him. I avoided bringing him up because I was still so embarrassed by the situation in the parking lot that I knew I'd get flustered, and they'd see it as something completely different than what it was. Ken only remembered the pretty face she saw, the looks he'd given me, and that he'd found me outside the cafeteria to talk. There didn't seem to be an easy way to break it to her that the new guy was worse than Draco Malfoy.

When I pulled into a parking spot, I released a loud sigh. "Look, I don't expect you to understand why I told Kaleb yes. Like I told Leigh earlier, I want to go with someone who would make the night fun, and I don't need another reason." Frustration made me look away, but I took a deep breath and voiced the real reason I felt frustrated, "Kyler may be hot, but he has no redeeming qualities aside from that. He's an arrogant ass with a pretty face. That's it." I bit out, hoping to get my point across. When Kendall said nothing, I realized it might have been too harsh. Her mouth hung open as she stared at me. She had hardly ever seen me angry. No one had. "Sorry. I shouldn't have snapped at you. Kyler really got under my skin today."

Ken shut her gaping mouth and swallowed, "Yeah— no, it's okay." She peered at Leigh in the back, whose face mirrored Ken's. They both smirked. "Who knew you could get so spicy, Ray? We've known you for, what, twelve years?" I let out a chuckle, and they both joined me. "What did he *do*?"

I scoffed and relayed the day's events involving him, knowing it sounded like a lot of whiny bullshit, but they didn't call me out for it. No. Instead, they both held back a grin as Leighton said, "Sounds a lot like he's flirting with you."

Ken nodded in agreement, "Yeah, he's giving off real Damon Salvatore vibes." She made a face like she was drooling, which made Leighton laugh, but I snapped.

"Ugh, enough! I don't want to talk about him right now!" Even though she was right, he gave off hot enemy vampire vibes. I told myself I wasn't going to entertain those thoughts, and I was going to stick to it. Perhaps if I pretended he was a vicious monster, that would help. Right? It seemed the girls weren't buying the act, so I changed the subject. "Come on! We *all* need to find dresses in," I glanced at the clock, "less than two hours. Remember that lovely curfew of mine?" I pulled myself out of the car, the girls following quickly.

"You have to get that changed," Leigh said in her miss-know-it-all voice, slamming her car door for emphasis. "I mean, honestly, eight PM?? You're a senior in high school! You need more privileges."

We made our way to the front of the mall, and I rolled my eyes as I locked the car. "You know why Jordin won't extend it. She's worr—"

"She's worried she'll lose you to a drunk driver or something terrible." Ken mocked, finishing my usual excuse for that statement. I knew she understood, but she still pressed on. "But it's been a year and a half. Can't she at least extend it til ten?"

"I doubt it." I opened the door to the mall, letting the girls file in first. When I went to follow them through the door, a guy came out of nowhere and shoulder-checked me as he pushed his way through the door I was holding. I whipped around, "Watch it, asshole!" I yelled at his retreating back, adding a vulgar gesture to the mix even though he never saw it. The hooded figure kept walking, and I turned to find the girls staring at me with their brows raised.

"You good?" Ken asked.

I huffed but nodded, "Yeah. Why do men always think they have the right of way?" I asked rhetorically and walked between them into the mall. We emerged into the center circle before I turned to them and asked, "Okay, so food or dress shopping first?"

"Like you have to ask." They said in sync, and we headed to our favorite dress shop.

The twins went crazy, grabbing several dresses to try on for themselves and even throwing a couple my way. Only one caught my eye, though—a lavender dress with glitter cascading down from the empire waist.

I took all five dresses over my arm to the dressing rooms to appease the girls. Something caught my eye in the mirror when I pulled off my shirt to try on the first dress. Right along my ribcage was a slight red mark, warm to the touch. Odd. What could have caused—

My breath caught. Only one thing came to mind: Kyler catching me. The memory of the burning sensation crowded my thoughts. But why would it still be red so many hours later? There was no explanation except maybe he caught me rougher than I remembered. I continued trying on dresses, mulling over what it could mean.

I ended up choosing the lavender dress. Ken ended up with a green, blue, and yellow one that resembled watercolor flowers on the skirt. Leigh picked a pink dress with a ruffled bottom and little flowers at the top of the waist. Together, we had a rainbow of colors.

I thought finding matching shoes would be difficult since I couldn't wear heels, but when we got to the shoe section, I saw the perfect pair—silver, sparkly Converse high tops.

The girls were searching for their heels when my mind traveled ahead in time, playing out the night of prom. My imagined scenario snagged on who was sitting next to Braxton. I turned to Ken, "Do you know the name Amariel?"

She scrunched her brows, searching for the name, but shook her head. "No, why?"

"Apparently, Brax is taking her to Prom. Kaleb and I are joining them for dinner." I shrugged.

"I thought I told you that!" Leigh piped up from the next aisle, popping around the corner a second later. "She started a couple of weeks ago. Brax and I are in French with her!" Her slight smile grew as she tried on the two pairs of shoes she found. "She's lovely. I think you'll like her."

I narrowed my eyes, but she didn't look up at me. "Why didn't you tell me you knew her earlier?"

She kept her eyes on her feet, and her hair fell in her face as she bent over to strap on the heels. "I thought it was obvious," she mumbled.

Ken and I exchanged glances, but she just shrugged, returning to strapping on her heels.

I let the subject drop, seeing as it still wasn't the right moment for Leigh to tell me what was going on in that brain of hers. She stood to test the heels she had on, turning from us to check the mirror in front of her. "Which ones?"

Her change of subject added to my curiosity, but I pointed to her left shoe—white, strappy heels. Ken agreed and then asked the same of her choices. She ended up with black ones with blue accents.

I'd finished checking out when I asked Ken, "Do you think Kaleb has feelings for me?"

She whipped her head to me, apparently shocked by my question. "What makes you think that?" Something in her voice made me think she knew exactly why I would ask.

I narrowed my eyes but tried to explain my thought process, giving her the spark notes version of the courtyard conversation.

Ken was paying now but said over her shoulder, "I've always thought he secretly liked you but valued your friendship too much to act on it." Leigh shot Ken a look, communicating something with her eyes, to which Ken shrugged innocently.

"Uh-uh. What was that?" My finger went back and forth between the girls, waiting for one of them to fess up. When neither of them did, I threw my hands up with a sigh. "What is going on? You guys never keep secrets from me! Neither does Kaleb."

Ken sighed heavily and switched spots with Leigh. "Ray, Kaleb had a thing for Bell, remember?" Hearing the nickname for my twin struck a chord, and a twinge of pain crossed my face. When I said nothing, she went on, "Your *identical* twin. It wouldn't surprise me if he started to like you since… well, since she's been gone. Plus, you guys have spent a ton of time together over the last year."

My gaze fell to the floor. I didn't want what she said to be true, but it made sense. The way Kaleb so carefully worded his confession became more apparent, too. Maybe he didn't want to confess feelings for me because he thought they were still feelings for Bell, and he didn't want to confuse the two and make a mistake.

He and I were in a precarious situation. Bell and Kaleb had barely acknowledged their feelings for each other before she was gone, so Kaleb hadn't gotten to take her to a dance. It occurred to me that this dance could mean something entirely different to him than I initially thought.

Leighton was handing her card to the cashier when I saw him.

A man. Standing nearby. Staring straight at me.

His face wasn't visible under the black hoodie, and I couldn't tell if it was because of the shadows or if he was wearing a mask. The clenched fists. The tilt of his head. The way his shoulders tensed. The rage seeped off him. I could *feel* his piercing stare. Like his anger was meant for me.

My eyes widened, and I whipped around to Kendall, who was looking at something on her phone. I grabbed her hand to get her attention as subtly as I could. "Seven o'clock," I whispered frantically.

Kendall slowly turned her eyes in that direction. Then her muscles loosened, and her whole head turned. "What's at seven o'clock?"

I snapped my head so quickly in that direction that my neck popped. Rubbing my now sore neck, I scanned where he'd been, but he was gone. Ken had a worried expression on her face, but I quickly defended myself. "There was a man," I said between quick breaths, "He wore a dark hoodie. He was staring at me. He seemed... angry. Like he knew me, and he *hated* me. But I couldn't see his face to know whether or not I recognized him." I checked again in case he was back, but he wasn't. Ken still looked worried, but I ignored it and turned to ask Leighton if she saw him.

But she wasn't at the counter anymore.

I turned in a full circle but didn't see her anywhere. "Ken... Where's Leighton?"

Kendall made a tight circle, too, but it only confirmed what I already knew: Leighton was gone. Ken ran up to the cashier and asked her which way Leighton had gone. The cashier either didn't hear her or ignored Kendall because she continued folding the clothes on the counter as if neither of us existed.

Ken and I tried everything to get her attention: waving our arms, yelling loudly, hitting the counter— Ken even tried shaking the lady's arm, but it was useless. She didn't respond to any of it. Ken turned to me with a look of panic in her eyes.

"What's going on, Ken?" I asked, a slight trembling in my voice.

She grabbed my shaking hands, "Take a deep breath. We— we'll figure this out." Her voice shook, too, but she had always been calm in high-stress situations, so she searched for some explanation, scanning the store as if the answer were there somewhere.

I closed my eyes briefly and took a few deep breaths.

A hand landed on my shoulder, making me scream and jump away from the source and straight into a rack of clothing. Leighton grabbed my arm to save me from falling, but not in time to stop the clothing rack from tumbling down.

When I regained my footing again, Leighton gave me a weird look. "Why so jumpy, Ray?"

My jaw dropped. *Where did she come from?* No words came out of my mouth, though. I was speechless.

But the cashier wasn't. "What in the sam heck is going on over here?" She snapped, walking over to the fallen rack, pointing at it but looking at me. "Pick up this mess immediately, or I'm calling security." I nodded nervously, and she returned to folding the clothes on her desk.

Kendall addressed Leighton while my shaking hands picked up the rack and started hanging the clothes in their places. "Leigh, you disappeared." Leighton seemed unfazed by the comment as Kendall studied her. "There was a creepy guy, I guess, staring at Ray, and then you were gone, and the cashier couldn't even see us." She whispered the last part, but the lady looked up in a way that said she could see us now. "Where were you?" Ken demanded from Leighton.

Leighton stared at her like she was crazy. "I've been standing here the whole time. We just bought our stuff, remember?" She held up her bag and smiled excitedly as if she hadn't heard anything Kendall said. "Now come on! I'm starving." And she sauntered off, out the department store doors and into the mall.

I placed the last clothes on the rack, staring after Leighton with wide eyes. Kendall's face mirrored my own. Her jaw was slack. How could Leigh act like everything was just fine? There was no way Ken and I just imagined all of that happening. And yet...

Kendall shook the shock from her face, shrugged her shoulders, and followed Leighton out the door. I closed my still-open mouth and watched Ken disappear into the crowd behind Leighton with a bit of surprise.

Making a choice, I closed my eyes, took a deep breath, and pushed the creepy situation from my mind. Perhaps my hunger was making me see things.

I tracked the girls through the mall but couldn't shake the feeling that someone was following me. I glanced over my shoulders several times between the dress shop and the food court. The hairs on my neck stood up when we were standing in line for food. It felt like someone was breathing fire down my back. I shivered and glanced behind me, only to find a couple of pre-teen girls there. They looked disgusted when I made eye contact as if they thought I'd been listening to their conversation. My eyes must have looked a little crazy. I *felt* a little crazy. I shook my head, intending to turn back to the front of the line when something caught my eye behind the girls.

There, just under the stairs, it was him—the man in the hoodie. He stared at me again, though I couldn't see his eyes.

I blinked.

He was gone.

I had to be imagining it. No one could disappear that quickly.

I didn't mention the second sighting to the girls. Instead, I tried to clear my mind and enjoy dinner. The thought of the hooded man lingered, but I wanted to ignore it, seeing as there was no way to prove he existed.

After dinner, Leighton begged to go to the arcade to play DDR. Ken and I agreed that it would distract us from our thoughts. We lost track of time, and when I finally checked the clock in the arcade, it was 8:45.

"Uh, guys! Curfew!" I pointed at the clock. "Jordin is going to kill me! Come on!!" I grabbed my bags and sprinted out of the arcade towards the exit. It took half an hour to get home on a good day. I was almost an hour late already, plus I still had to drop off the girls. When I reached the car, the girls were several paces behind me, clearly not understanding the importance of being quick. "Hurry! I'm already late!" I jumped into the car, turning the key before the door shut. Thankfully, it started on the first try, and the girls hadn't even closed their doors before the car was moving.

"Geez, Ray, slow down!" Leighton yelled from the backseat. "Just call your mom and tell her we lost track of time. She'll understand!" She jammed her seatbelt into the buckle as I pulled onto the road.

"That would be a great idea if I wasn't driving!" I pulled out my phone anyway and handed it to Kendall. "Call Jordin and put it on speaker."

Ken unlocked my phone, but she didn't dial anything. She stared at the screen. "Ray. When was the last time you checked your phone?"

My brow creased, "I dunno before we got to the mall? Why?"

She held up the phone, "You have thirteen missed calls, eight voicemails, and a ton of texts. Who has that much anything in three hours?" She opened the phone app to see who was desperately trying to get ahold of me and whispered, "They're mostly from Jordin, except the first few from Mitch." Instead of dialing Jordin, she clicked through the voicemails from Jordin, and my blood ran cold when I heard her panicked voice through the speaker.

"Rayleigh, where are you?" "Ray, I need you home NOW!" "Please tell me you're still alive." "Rayleigh, why aren't you answering your phone?" "Ray, I'm getting worried. Please call me back! I need you here." "Rayleigh," her sobs were quiet, "please come home safe…" Her voice trailed off. My face had gone pale. Tears formed in my eyes. I pulled the car over, ripped the phone from Kendall's hand, and dialed Jordin myself. She answered halfway through the first ring.

"Rayleigh?" She was still crying, but there was no mistaking the relief in her voice when she said, "Are you okay?"

"Yeah, mom, I'm fine," I sighed. "Wh—what's wrong? Is everything okay?" I asked quietly, trying not to let my emotions come through.

She wasn't telling me something when she said, "I'm just glad you're alright. But I need you to come home right away." She sniffled, "Mitch is in the hospital."

VII
In My Blood

My stomach dropped. The phone slipped from my hands, landing in the console. This couldn't be happening. First Arabella, then Dad, now Mitch? Was my family cursed? How could this be happening again?

Ken picked up the phone and finished the conversation with Jordin, letting her know we were on our way and giving her our ETA. I don't remember switching to the backseat or laying my head in Leighton's lap. Kendall sped as fast as she dared down the highway. My head was spinning, and silent tears fell from my eyes. One thought went through my head over and over— I couldn't lose Mitch. I wouldn't be able to handle it. He had to be okay. He had to.

At one point, Leighton whispered, "He's okay, Ray. He's alive. He's still with us." She rubbed my shoulder and ran her fingers through my hair, keeping it out of my face. I nodded, letting her know I heard her, and she continued, "The doctors don't have any answers yet, but they should have some when we get there."

Ken reached her hand back to grab mine. I let her. "We're here with you, Ray. It's gonna be okay."

Was it, though? Mitch was hurt, somehow, and I had no answers. How could it be okay?

I listened to their soothing words as we hurried down the highway, but in my mind, I couldn't stop the horrible thoughts pouring in—how everything that's happened with my family had been my fault. *I* was driving the night Arabella died. Dad went in late to work because of *me*. And Mitch… I don't know what happened, but I know if I had taken him home from practice instead of selfishly going dress shopping, nothing would have happened to him.

It was all my fault. It's always been my fault.

The tears came faster as we raced toward home.

Ken pulled up to the house, where Jordin told us to meet her. However, as I suspected, she wasn't waiting outside to go to the hospital. So the girls helped me into the house, where a couple of officers, including the police chief, were milling about.

Chief Bass had been close to my parents for years, but since Bell's death, he occasionally stopped by to check on things. As a small-town Chief, it was customary for him to check in on the families who had lost loved ones, but when Dad passed, Chief took it upon himself to stop by more often. He said he wanted to ensure we felt safe, even though I sometimes felt far from it with the night terrors I had.

One of the cops was hunched over a laptop in the kitchen, clicking through frame by frame of what looked like a traffic cam. Was Mitch involved in a car crash? Why was it always a car crash? But Mitch didn't have a car—

The officer sat up quickly and turned to where Chief was talking to Jordin at the counter. "We got a still on the driver, sir. He looks to be wearing a mask of some sort. No discernible features."

I went up behind Chief as he looked over the shoulder of the officer. He studied the blurry frame momentarily, then pointed to a section near the steering wheel where the suspect's hand was. "See if you can get this part a little clearer. It looks like a tattoo." That part of the picture was so blurry that I wasn't sure how Chief even saw it. There was no way they were going to get clarity on that image. I studied the rest of the image and noticed the face had been distorted, too, like the man said, but it didn't seem like a mask. It seemed familiar, but I couldn't think of why. Before I could sift through the muddied thoughts in my brain for the answer, Chief stood up, bumping into me as I was still leaning over his shoulder. "Ah, Rayleigh, I'm so glad you made it here safely." He reached to embrace me, and I let him for a moment before backing away to find Jordin.

She was sitting at the counter with her back to me, but when Chief said my name, she whipped around to find me, tears rolling down her face. She slid off the stool and wrapped me in her arms. Her muffled voice spoke against my head, "Rayleigh." She pulled away, grabbing my face and examining my tear-filled eyes. Her hands were trembling. "I was so worried about you." The embrace and words felt strange. She never acted this way toward me. Barely ever showed me affection. It's the main reason I resorted to calling her Jordin.

That may have deepened the chasm between us, but I couldn't forgive her so easily. Couldn't let her forget who she wished she could be embracing. I grabbed her face, a bit rougher than she did to me, and held her gaze. "Everything's gonna be fine. I'm here now." I sounded confident for her, but on the inside, I didn't believe my own words. It felt like my body was going to give out any minute. I tried to hide my shaking bones, but the longer it took to get to Mitch, the worse it got. I grabbed her hand and pulled her towards the front door. "Come on. Let's go check on the Little Monster."

Jordin followed quickly, smiling at the nickname. Mitch was a terrible toddler, always getting into things he shouldn't, pulling everything off the shelves minutes after Jordin put everything away. He caused her more trouble than Arabella and I combined, earning him that nickname before age two.

He solidified it when he got older, hiding around corners and jumping out to scare anyone coming with a tiny roar. Jordin and Dad had to hide their laughter and pretend to be scared. But Little Monster stuck.

Chief assigned one of his officers to take the twins home, and I hugged them both before climbing into the back of his cruiser. We'd get there faster if he drove. Jordin climbed in next to me. Chief turned his lights on and sped off toward the hospital.

Every chair in the waiting room was empty except for three. Chief, Jordin, and I sat nervously for over an hour after we arrived. Mitch was in surgery, reconstructing the bones in his left leg. That's the side the car hit. The impact shattered his femur. On top of that, his left arm had a clean break in both forearm bones, his hip and three ribs were cracked, and he had twelve stitches in his head.

The car ran a red light and struck him in the crosswalk. The doctors were surprised the car wasn't damaged by the force it hit Mitch. They said the car was going about forty-five miles an hour. Mitch flipped several times in the air and hit the ground, only to continue rolling across the cement. Everyone said he should have died from the impact, but Mitch was stronger than that.

According to Chief, the car didn't have any plates or remarkable features that could help differentiate it from any other black vehicle. Even the car's logo was removed to make identification more challenging. The street lights in the area weren't on at the time of the incident, and the sun had just set, meaning the darkness made things that much harder to determine. Mitch's swim practice must have run late because he should have been out before the sunset. Or perhaps he stayed late to keep practicing. Chief said he put his best agents on it but seemed less than hopeful about finding the culprit.

When we were finally called back to see Mitch, Jordin and I had to hold back sobs at the sight of him. He had a cast almost head to toe on his left side, and there were bruises and scrapes on the skin that weren't covered. His face looked as if someone had punched him with a brass knuckle several times. I took the chair beside his unbroken arm and wrapped my hand gingerly around his. Jordin sat at the end of the bed with her head in her hands, crying.

Dr. Smiles stood in the doorway and told us that Mitchell had been in a coma since he arrived and wasn't sure if he'd be waking up anytime soon. After telling us where to get breakfast in the morning, he left the room with a sad smile.

Neither of us slept that night. We stayed awake, hoping and praying that Mitch would miraculously wake up. But he didn't.

The next day came with a few visitors: Chief had breakfast, the twins brought my homework during their free period, and Grams and Gramps came with some hot soup for lunch. Grams said she didn't want us eating the hospital food because that's what put her in the hospital after Gramps's hip surgery.

By the time the afternoon rolled around and all the visitors were gone, I had pulled out my homework on the rolling table next to Mitch. I hadn't left his side. As I started on the review packet for the Chemistry test the next day, my thoughts wandered.

The first one to roll through my head was from Chem class when Kyler slapped my hand away. I tried to remember if his hand had felt hot in those moments but only remembered how much it stung—the slap itself and a bit of my ego. Maybe the sting of the slap was because of the heat, but he hadn't touched me in any other way before or after he caught me. He'd been careful to avoid it if I remembered correctly. My hand idly rubbed my ribs, where the skin was still oddly tender.

Kaleb's face flashed across my mind, and the walk in the courtyard started replaying. I was still wary of his intentions, but they didn't bother me as much as they originally had.

Thinking of prom led me to dress shopping and the man in the hoodie. It might have all been in my imagination, but Ken and I were practically invisible to the cashier. While she didn't ever see the man in the hoodie, she seemed to believe that I did. Plus, Ken experienced Leigh disappearing and reappearing suddenly, which I know neither of us imagined. The man appearing again under the staircase. According to the reports I overheard, Mitch got hit around that time—

Hold on.

What if the man in the hoodie at the mall was related to Mitch's accident? The traffic cam caught a visual of the driver, but they were wearing a mask, just like the man at the mall... What if they were both following us? *That's not possible.* Unless someone was following Mitch *and* me, there was no way the mysterious man in the mall could have had anything to do with Mitch's accident back in Wisteria Falls, *right?*

I closed my eyes, shaking the thought from my head. Now was no time to pretend I was the main character in one of Arabella's mystery books.

I peered out the window to see a cloudless sky and the sun shining bright. It was such a beautiful day. I almost wished I could go to the meadow. The flowers would bloom brightly, reaching toward the sun to get their daily dose of Vitamin D. The grass would be glistening from last night's fresh rainfall. The spot under the tree would be calling my name— the perfect place to sit, listening to the sounds of nature around me.

My gaze traveled back to Mitch. He was more important. The meadow would still be there when he was awake. I was right where I belonged.

Smiling a little at Mitch's relaxed face, I hoped his dreams were filled with Nerf gun wars and nervous laughter with Lily instead of nightmares filled with car accidents or monsters like mine usually were.

I brushed a piece of hair from his face, and his eyes shot open, making me jump back. He stared at me wide-eyed, and before I could say anything, he whispered, "They're coming."

He looked straight past me, and I turned to see what he was looking at, but someone grabbed me from behind and yanked me out of my chair. I started kicking and screaming, trying to break their hold on me, but they wouldn't let go. My blood ran cold as something covered my mouth, and the world slipped away.

A voice in my head whispered, *This isn't real.* But it didn't sound like the usual voice in my head. It was deeper. Calm. Someone else. *Wake up! This isn't real!*

The voice in my head repeated that phrase over and over, but all I felt were the strong arms holding me as I thrashed in their grasp, still trying to break free. By the time I remembered my training, it was too late.

A sharp pain shot through my right arm, and my body reacted immediately. I slid to the ground, paralyzed within seconds.

Minutes—or hours—later, a bright light shone in my eyes. A blurry room came into focus around me. A surgical lamp hovered over me, and everything became clearer as the seconds passed. I began screaming and thrashing again because something was wrong. I could feel it. Hands pushed me down against the table, and I felt a sharp pain in my arm again.

Again, within seconds, I lay paralyzed on the table, but I could see everything around me still. Voices became apparent, and one in particular stood out. He was talking to me.

"Rayleigh." Doctor Smiles leaned over me on the table, blocking the surgical lamp's light. "Can you hear me?" Knowing I wouldn't be able to speak, I blinked twice. "I have given you a paralytic shot that works temporarily. You had a nightmare that caused you to react wildly, and you weren't waking up." *My night terrors.* I didn't even remember falling asleep. "The paralysis will wear off in about three minutes, and then we will discuss your situation. Please don't try to move. I have to check on your brother. I'll be back soon." I blinked twice, and he left my field of vision. The bright surgical lamp caused me to squint.

For the next few minutes, I wracked my brain for what went wrong. Smiles said I fell asleep, but I never even laid down. Mitch woke up and said something… I tried to ask the nurses if he was awake. One of them heard my moan, the only noise I could produce, and leaned over me. "Rayleigh, try not to talk, okay? The paralysis will wear off soon, and we'll get you up." I blinked twice, willing the paralysis to go away faster as she stepped away.

If Mitch woke up, why was everyone focused on me? Shouldn't they be in his room checking on him? I guess that's what Smiles said he was doing… I closed my eyes and thought for a moment, then remembered that his eyes had opened right before I was grabbed from behind. That meant it was part of my nightmare.

The nurse came back, leaning over the table again. My fingers twitched. "I'm going to remove these straps now. Wait until I have them all off before trying to move. We don't want you getting hurt." She started undoing the straps along the table, starting with my ankles. The four straps were thick and tight against my body. It felt like forever before I could sit up on the edge of the bed. Dizziness set in, so I sat there for a minute to clear my head.

I heard footsteps and lifted my head to see Smiles walking in the door, a grim look on his face. "Smiles—" My voice was raspy, and my throat was dry, so I took the cup of water the nurse offered, swallowed it, and tried again. "What happened?"

He looked up from the clipboard he was holding and handed it to a nurse, crossing the distance between us to crouch in front of me. "You fell asleep in the chair next to Mitchell. About five minutes later, you started to scream and thrash around. You were holding Mitchell's hand when you fell asleep and gripped it as a lifeline. It took us a minute to get you to let go, but you got a couple of good pulls on his arm before we decided to use the tranquilizer." He grimaced before he continued, "You dislocated his shoulder."

I deflated at his words. What was happening to me? How had I fallen asleep without realizing it?

"You were in here for about twenty minutes before you woke up and started panicking again." He sighed.

I put my head in my hands, shaking with disbelief as I held back tears. I knew I had night terrors, but they'd never caused me to injure someone before. Then again, I'd never been around someone when I had them. No one knew about them. Until now.

Smiles' hand landed on my shoulder. "Rayleigh, don't worry about it. The coma your brother is in—" He paused, choosing his words carefully, "he most likely didn't feel anything." That didn't make it any better. "They're resetting his shoulder right now. He's going to be fine." He stood from his crouched position and grabbed the clipboard from the nurse again. "I called Chief Bass. He's sending someone to pick you up and take you home. I had a prescription brought to your mother for you to take home so you don't have any more night terrors."

His words settled in, and I gave him a panicked look. "No… No! I need to stay here! With Mitch!" I screeched, falling forward off the table and barely catching myself. "I need to be here when he wakes up. He *needs* me!" My voice cracked as a sob escaped.

Smiles gave me a sad smile. "Your brother will be fine. What you need is to go home and get some rest. Come back in a few days. Your mother will stay with Mitchell and keep you updated." He reached out a hand to help me stand. "I'm sure you'll be back before Mitch wakes up, but he needs time to heal. Come." He started walking me towards the door. "You need to gather your things before your friend arrives."

I hung my head as he escorted me back to Mitch's room. This was not how I wanted this day to go. The last thing I wanted to do was leave Mitch, but I knew I would only be hurting myself if I stayed here. Sleep wouldn't be as important to me as watching Mitch for any signs of consciousness. I could accidentally fall asleep again, and who knows what I'd do to him then...

When we returned to Mitch's room, Smiles led me through the door and waited patiently just inside it as I crossed the room to retrieve my backpack. Jordin was sitting in the chair in the corner of the room but jumped up when she saw me, rushing to pull me into a hug, and started crying on my shoulder. Her embrace was still foreign to me, but I leaned into it anyway, feeling numb from everything that happened.

"Are you okay?" She whispered in my ear. "I was so scared for you. I didn't know what to do." She pulled away, holding onto my shoulders as she looked me over head to toe.

A single tear rolled down my face as I stared at the spot in the room where Mitch's bed had been. "I'm so sorry. I didn't mean to hurt him..." I trailed off, not knowing what else I could say.

Jordin wiped the tear from my face and tucked my hair behind my ears. "I know, sweetheart, I know. This has all been very traumatic. I can't imagine what you're going through." She kissed me on the head and pulled me in for another hug. Her words seemed odd, but I didn't have the brainpower to process them.

"Doctor Smiles." The nurse who stood in the doorway was jarringly loud for a hospital. "The car for Rayleigh has arrived." I pulled away from Jordin and swung my backpack over my shoulder, but the nurse wasn't done with her announcements. "Mitchell's arm has been set, and he is on his way back." She left without waiting for a response.

Jordin put her hands on either side of my face and kissed my forehead before finally letting me go. Her sudden affection bothered me, but I wasn't about to call her out in the hospital. She held out a small bottle to me, shaking its contents with her movements. "Please remember to take these before you go to sleep." She pursed her lips as I took them from her. "I don't want to hear about nightmare tantrums while I'm not around, understand?" There she was. This firm tone and rigid posture were more familiar to me. I nodded at her instructions and put the pills in my backpack. Jordin tried to give me another hug, but with the look I gave her, she let her hands fall to her sides as I stepped into the hallway and out of reach.

Mitchell's bed rolled down the hallway. Smiles put a hand out to stop me from walking in that direction to exit. Tears welled in my eyes when the bed rolled past, but I blinked them back. There was no new cast, but a sling held his arm in place across his chest. I was used to hospitals and being cast up myself, but seeing someone else I loved in a hospital bed for an extended time was new and more challenging to deal with.

I closed my eyes, turned to the hospital exit, and tried to picture Mitch as he was the day before, aiming a Nerf gun at me from my bedroom door. How was that only yesterday?

A loud car engine roared to life as soon as I stepped outside. Before I could turn to find the culprit, someone called my name from the opposite direction. Following the sound of my name, I saw a familiar SUV with its passenger door open, the driver patiently waiting next to it.

VIII
Gentle

Kaleb gave me a weak smile like he had no idea if he should be happy to see me or sorry that my brother was in a coma. I tried to smile back, but my lips started to tremble as tears built up in my eyes again at the sight of him waiting for me. I held them back as I walked up to him.

"So you got stuck being my caretaker, huh?" My voice was weak and raspy from screaming, but his smile grew.

"I guess you could say that, yeah." He held out his arms, and I walked into his embrace. He pulled me close, and I buried my face in his chest, squeezing him back. I couldn't hold the tears back anymore, so I let myself cry as he rubbed my back, soothing the tears away as the minutes passed.

When I finally caught my breath, I pulled away to wipe the tears from my face. He led me into the passenger seat and closed my door before walking around the car. I buckled my seatbelt, and he hopped in, doing the same. Aside from my sniffles, the first few minutes of the car ride were quiet, but I didn't like the silence once we were on the main road home. It made my thoughts go too dark. "Why did Chief Bass call you, of all people?"

Kaleb glanced at me sideways and smiled a little. "I went to your house during my free period since you hadn't shown up in Chemistry and weren't answering your phone. Ken and Leigh told me something had happened to Mitch, and I knew I had to check on you. Chief was at your house when I pulled up. He said he was getting something for your mom. I asked where you were, and he told me you hadn't left Mitch's side." He gave me a knowing smile. He was one of the few people who knew how close Mitch and I were and knew I wouldn't willingly leave his side, considering his state. "I gave him my number and asked him to update me on everything. He called me thirty minutes ago and asked if I'd be willing to care for you for the next couple of days. I was already in the car and on my way here before I hung up." He gently grabbed my hand, rubbing his thumb against mine.

I stared at our hands and briefly considered pulling mine away, but the comforting contact felt like it kept me from completely breaking down again. The gesture made things a little murky between us, but the way he made me feel safe with such a simple act... It wasn't the first time he'd done something like that. As I thought of the times he was there for me, it reminded me how vulnerable I was with him—allowing him to see the broken parts of me. He never shied away. He kept coming back. Always gentle. Always patient.

So I let him hold my hand and gazed back up at him again. He clenched his jaw as if he were restraining from saying something. The act defined his face, making his cheekbones pop and his nose flare. His curly brown hair fell just above his eyes, shining like a rich copper in the sunlight. My insides started to churn as I stared at him, not seeing the boy I grew up with but *a man*.

He was watching the road but glanced my way when he felt my eyes on him. I averted my gaze to the road but asked myself how I never realized how attractive Kaleb was— and how no other girls had seen it. Aside from Bell, I hadn't seen or heard about any girls approaching him. Or maybe he didn't tell me if they did...

Self-consciously, I removed my hand from his and pretended it was to turn the radio on. The music helped fill my head with something other than the confusing thoughts mingling around there. His mention of my phone had me reaching for it in my backpack, if only to keep me from grabbing his hand again. I pulled it out to find it dead. Of course. It made sense. I'd been at the hospital all night and hadn't thought of anything outside of Mitch, including my friends.

"Do you have a charger?" I asked, holding up my dead phone for him to see. He opened the center console and pulled a cord from inside, plugging it into the car before handing me the other end. "Thanks."

As my phone started, I noticed several messages from the twins and Kaleb. Ken had texted me to let me know she and Leigh were dropping off my homework and to tell me Kaleb had been asking about me. After reading that, I gave a nervous glance toward him, unsure what to think.

Leighton decided it was necessary to tell me Kyler asked about me in Chemistry, then disappeared for the rest of the school day. I mentally rolled my eyes, not understanding why he would even care after his actions yesterday.

Kaleb's texts started last night, inquiring how dress shopping was going, asking about the rest of my night, and then turned into asking if I was okay and if I needed anything. My stomach flipped again, and I tried to ignore it, scrolling to the following missed messages, realizing they were the ones from Mitch last night. My throat constricted as I clicked on his thread. The first one said he passed his English test, which he gave me credit for helping him study the night before. The second was asking if I could get him something from the mall. The third was where it got strange. It came around the time he would have been walking to Gram's house.

> I have this weird feeling that I'm being followed. Can I call you, just in case?

The blood drained from my face. I switched to my voicemail to check the time of his last call. It came shortly after the text. I found the voicemail he left and put the phone to my ear.

"Hey, Ray!" His voice was chipper but laced with panic. "What're you doing?" He paused. With confusion, I waited for him to go on. "Oh right, I forgot you were going to the mall…" He trailed off. He was trying to make it sound like a conversation instead of a voicemail.

"Well, since you're there, do you mind getting me a few of those cookies from that one place? I've been craving them since the last time we went." Again, he paused, chuckled as if I said something funny, and said, "Yeah, well, coach can deal with it because I'm not giving up sugar for swimming." He laughed again, and in the background, I heard a loud engine quiet to an idle. Faintly, I heard a man ask him which way the falls were. "Just follow this road for about a mile, and on the right, you'll see a rock with 'Wisteria Falls' painted on it with an arrow. Turn there. You can't miss them." The guy responded with a thanks, and the sound of the car engine trailed off. "Well, that was weird." Mitch's voice addressed the phone again. "I could have sworn that was the guy following me," he whispered.

Chills ran down my spine. Had the person who hit Mitch talked to him moments before they ran him over?

"Anyway," Mitch was back to his conversational cadence, "Have fun at the mall with the girls. I'll probably end up playing Scrabble with Grams until Mom gets there. See you tonight. Love you-" He cut off as the roar of an engine blared through the phone. My hand flew to my mouth as I heard him yell something that was instantly cut off by the sounds of the car slamming into Mitch. The cracking of bones echoed in my ear as the crunch of his phone hitting the pavement followed. The voicemail ended with the car engine disappearing in the background and a sudden silence to end the call.

Shaking, I pulled the phone from my ear and looked at Kaleb, who had been eyeing me from the driver's seat. "Ray. What's wrong?" He could see the panic in my eyes. The horror of what I'd just listened to. My eyes felt like they were bulging out of my head, tears flooding my vision. My breathing was coming too quickly. I felt my heartbeat against my chest. My head felt light as dizziness set in.

Kaleb turned the wheel sharply, pulling onto the side of the two-lane highway. He jumped out of the car, rounding the car impossibly fast, and wrenched my door open. He knelt in the ditch outside my door, unbuckled my seatbelt, and twisted my legs to be outside the car. When I fully faced him, he straightened on his knees to make his face level with mine and said, "Rayleigh, I need you to look at me." My eyes were unfocused. I couldn't think past the noises of the car slamming into Mitch. "Rayleigh!" Kaleb grabbed my face, turning me towards him. His nose was inches from mine. "I'm with you." His thumb caressed my cheek. The crunch of bones echoed in my head. "Right here." The feeling of his thumb made me focus on his words as the echo of a car engine roared in my mind. "You're safe." His eyes came into focus—warm, honey-brown eyes. Mitch's last I love you whispered in my head. "Breathe," Kaleb instructed as he noticed my eyes focus on his. Tears had formed in his pretty eyes. "In." He demonstrated for me, and I followed his lead, the panic slightly leaving his voice as he heard me take a staggering breath in. "Out." I did as he did, and he walked me through it several more times. Each time I breathed in, the sounds from the voicemail faded. I listened to our synced breathing, focusing on his eyes as I did. It grounded me.

Kaleb kept his hold on my face, and our breaths mixed between us as I inhaled again, this time through my nose. A mix of spearmint and cedar filled my nose. I closed my eyes, leaning my forehead against his, breathing in his scent as I relaxed my shoulders with an exhale. "Thank you…"

His head moved slightly against mine as he let out his breath. "You haven't had a panic attack like that since the weeks following your dad's accident." He pulled back to look at my face, eyes darting back and forth between mine to see that I was still with him. "What were you listening to?"

I took another deep breath, reaching up to pull his hands away from my face. My eyes followed as I laid our joined hands in my lap. "It was a voicemail." I swallowed the lump in my throat. "From Mitch." Kaleb took another long breath, squeezing my hand to urge me on. "He called because he thought he was being followed."

Kaleb sensed it before I could, "Breathe, Ray. In." We did it together. "Out."

When I released my breath, I continued, "He pretended to converse with me when some guy pulled up and asked him for directions. When he drove off, Mitch said he thought that was the guy following him, but went back to his fake conversation and then…" I choked back a tiny sob and followed Kaleb's silent lead into another deep breath. "Then all I could hear was the accident." I sniffled before taking another deep breath.

Kaleb squeezed my hands again, cursing under his breath. "That's not something anyone should ever have to hear." He lifted my chin with a single finger. His eyes darted between mine again, and his hand traveled to cup my face. "I'm so sorry you had to listen to that, Rayleigh." He used that hand to pull me into a hug. My body shook, but I didn't realize how bad it was until he wrapped his arms around me in a bear hug. He didn't say anything else. He just held me until the trembling slowed. I pulled back a little, giving him the sign to sit back on his heels, and moved his hands to my knees. His eyes were full of determination. "Let's get back to my place, and we can send that voicemail to Chief." When I scrunched my eyebrows together, he clarified, "It could help with the investigation."

I nodded, and he pushed back from my knees, intending, I'm sure, to stand up, but he must have forgotten we were next to a ditch. The force of his little push made him lose his balance, and he fell back into the small ditch, doing an awkward backward somersault, landing with his legs in a v-shape in front of him. He threw himself back, laughing, not embarrassed in the slightest, causing me to let out a little laugh, too. The event was ridiculous enough to pull me from my panicked moment. Kaleb met my eyes as I laughed, and a sparkle shone within the rich brown, making my stomach flip as he gazed at me.

He stood and walked back up the small, steep hill toward me. "Well, that was unexpected. I'm glad it made you smile, though." He smirked and nudged my legs to push them back into the car before shutting the door. He slid into the driver's seat a moment later and resumed our drive back to his house.

I stared at him, taking in what he had just done for me, and said, "Thank you."

"You don't have to thank me for that." His eyes showed such understanding, and I didn't want to acknowledge how it made me feel, so I pressed on.

"No one else has been around to witness my panic attacks. But you have. Where did you learn… that?" He'd helped me through so many after Arabella and Dad, but I never thought to ask him that until now.

He sucked in a breath, "Honestly?" I nodded, and he let the breath out. "The first time you ever experienced it." Those first few times after Arabella's death were brutal. He went on, "You probably don't even remember me being there... but I came to visit you when you were in the hospital after your accident with Bell."

I couldn't hide the shock. The slight pink in his cheeks made me turn and watch out the window as he spoke because he was right. I didn't remember. Everything around her death blurred together or disappeared from my memory altogether.

He took a deep breath, turned back to the road, and went on, "The day I visited, you were sort of out of it with all the medication. Everyone else had gone to get something to eat or some coffee. While I was alone with you, you woke up in a panic and started screaming Arabella's name. It scared me so bad I almost ran to get someone else. But you looked so terrified..." he trailed off, lost in the memory. "You weren't looking at anyone. Your eyes were wide with terror at whatever you were seeing. You stared at a wall but weren't focused on anything. You were seeing things that weren't there. So I did the only thing I thought would help you—I jumped on the bed, careful to avoid your injuries, and grabbed your face, making you focus on me like I did just now. Only that time, I was straddling you on the hospital bed with our faces very close together." He paused long enough that I turned to look at him and saw his cheeks had turned a deeper shade of red, but the smirk on his face told a different story. "Your heart monitor went off, beeping loudly because of your elevated heart rate. How the nurses heard that but not your screams never made sense to me, but one of them rushed in to see what the problem was. I knew what it looked like at that point. You had calmed down, you were looking at me dazed, and your heart rate had gone up." He pursed his lips briefly before continuing, "I climbed off that bed so fast and ran out of the room with my tail between my legs." I suppressed a chuckle as I pictured Kaleb straddling me on a bed and a nurse finding us. Kaleb laughed at my expression. "Luckily, I didn't have to explain what happened to anyone, and no one ever brought it up again, but boy, was I red when I left that hospital room."

His laughter made me break into a genuine smile, and a weight lifted off my chest. I had no idea he was at the hospital after the accident. The thought of him seeing me in that state, so vulnerable, was scary, but hearing that he hadn't hesitated to bring me back from wherever my mind had taken me cracked something open deep inside me. I focused on him again, taking in the soft smile that played on his lips while he focused on the road. "Why didn't you ever tell me you were there?"

The smile slowly faded. He didn't look at me when he said, "Because I didn't think you would care." The blow hit low. I sagged in my seat. "Or maybe you would think I wasn't there for you." The second blow was worse than the first.

"Kaleb…" My hand found his forearm, which rested on the console between us. "Why on earth would you think I wouldn't care?"

His eyes fell to where my hand was on his arm, but he still couldn't meet my gaze. Instead, he lifted his eyes back to the road. "We were just buddies. Friends." When he realized his wording, he quickly said, "We still are! But it's… It's different now. We're closer. I didn't think we could have that before without someone thinking there was… more." His voice lowered slightly, and I rubbed my thumb on his arm for encouragement. "So I didn't tell you I came to visit because it didn't matter that I had. You didn't remember it, and obviously, no one else cared to tell you, and I just… didn't feel like it needed to be known." He shrugged again and finally met my gaze.

The look on his face was vulnerable. Open. I tried to mirror it as I spoke. "Honestly, Kaleb, knowing you did that then would have made it way less awkward when you grabbed my face the next time I hyperventilated." He couldn't stop the bark of laughter that escaped as I smirked at him. "Seriously, though. It means the world to me that you were there. Especially knowing losing Arabella affected you, too." The smile on his face faded but didn't disappear. It turned into more of a sad smile. "I know how you felt about her before she died. I only see her when I look in the mirror, and that's hard enough. But you see her whenever you look at me, don't you?"

"Not anymore." His quick response surprised me, but he hurried on before I could comment. "I'll admit that's how it was at first. Those quiet moments before you woke in the hospital room were—" He searched for a word, "difficult. But as soon as you started panicking and needed me, I knew it was you, not her. She probably would have smacked my hands away if I tried to do that to her." I smiled at the truth in that. I'd seen her do just that when she didn't want to be touched. That brought up the memory of someone slapping *my* hand, but I shoved it down. I did not need to think about that right now. Kaleb said, "Bell was feistier than you, but I think you've picked up on the slack a bit in the last year. Probably hanging around me too much." He elbowed me with the arm my hand rested on, and I brought my hand back to my lap.

"Well, either way. Thank you for telling me." I said sincerely. "What you did that day and every day since doesn't go unnoticed, just so you know."

IX
Hesitate

Kaleb pulled into his driveway, and only then did I realize how little I'd been to his house. Only one time came to mind, and I could almost guarantee it was why we weren't allowed back. My house was the usual gathering spot, but Kaleb invited us all to his one day, claiming his parents were out of town. They didn't enjoy the sound of rowdy teenagers, and calling our group rowdy was the understatement of the century. With the house to ourselves, we decided to do a cheap remake of one of Kendall's favorite Arnold Schwarzenegger movies.

The sound effects were made with pots and pans, and the lines were yelled because there were no microphones. Kendall insisted on playing Arnold herself. That alone made the film a comedy because she was still in a boot from her foot surgery the month before, meaning we had to move her on and off camera anytime Arnold was supposed to be on screen. In the entire film, you can hear anyone off-screen cackling at the absurdity of it.

Later, we learned Kaleb was severely punished because we broke a vase while dragging Ken across the entrance hall. We were never invited over again.

I laughed out loud at the memory, and Kaleb raised his eyebrow as he parked the car. I shook my head, "I was just thinking about when we remade the entire Terminator film. It was one of the only times I've been allowed at your house."

He laughed through his nose but couldn't hide the way his jaw clenched or the steel in his eyes as he said, "Well, I didn't exactly ask my parents' permission for you to stay here this time." The words seemed harsh, but he never spoke too fondly of his parents. I'd never met them, seeing as he was usually at my place, and he never brought up introducing me to them. "They're not in town." Typical. They traveled a lot for work. When they were home, Kaleb was usually at my house more. He never said why, and I never asked, but he knew my house was always open to him.

We got out of the car, and he grabbed a duffle from the trunk before walking to the front door. He held the door for me, and I stepped into the foyer of the vaguely familiar house.

"We don't have an extra bedroom, so I'll sleep on the floor, and you can have my bed." The thought of sleeping in the same room as him made my heartbeat quicken, but I couldn't tell what that meant, so I ignored it as best I could. "Mom would tell me to sleep on the couch, but with what Jordin told me happened at the hospital..." He trailed off, giving me a wary look. "I don't want you to be alone," he confessed, giving me a weak smile, which I returned and followed as he led me upstairs.

I wondered briefly why we were staying at his house and not my own, but I remembered the stalker from the mall and decided I'd rather be at Kaleb's house than mine. What if they knew where I lived? I didn't want to stay there.

I pulled my backpack off and set it just inside the door. He threw his duffle in the corner of his room and stripped his unmade bed, tossing the dirty sheets in the hamper before grabbing fresh ones from the closet and proceeding to make the bed. I walked over to the shelves in his room to look at his display of books, pictures, and, to my surprise, trophies. His books consisted of fantasy novels with knights, dragons, and elves on the covers. The images of our group of friends were similar to some on my shelf at home, plus a few of him and his parents. The trophies, I realized, were for tae kwon do.

"Since when do you do martial arts?" I asked, trying to sound nonchalant.

He looked at me with a smirk. "I used to compete when I was younger. Now it's just a hobby."

The most recent trophy was dated last year. First place. "Just a hobby?" I said, holding up the gold trophy. He shrugged. "Why haven't you invited me to your competitions?"

"You don't do mornings," he said, spreading a fresh blanket on the bed. I opened my mouth to respond, but he cut me off. "Especially on the weekends," he winked. I closed my mouth. Sometimes, I thought he knew me a little too well.

I replaced the trophy on the shelf and said, "I'm coming to your next match." Giving him no room to argue. He grinned at me as he threw the pillows back on the bed.

While scanning his shelf for more exciting things about his life, I saw a photo strip tucked behind one of his books. I reached to bring it closer for inspection and heard Kaleb inhale sharply. When I saw the pictures more clearly, I realized why.

It was him and Arabella from their first date at the fair. It was the first time Dad allowed Bell to go out alone with him. The pictures were innocent enough: smiling, laughing, and kissing each other on the cheek. The last one showed them smiling at each other. I hadn't seen those pictures before.

Kaleb came up behind me, stepping so close that I could feel his body heat through my clothes. He reached around me, slowly pulling the photo strip out of my hand. I reluctantly let him. He glanced at it briefly and replaced it behind the book. "I like to remember her like that," he whispered. "Smiling. *Happy*." He didn't have to voice the rest of his thoughts. I knew what he meant. The last visual I had of her was in the hospital. Stiff. Covered in blood. Her body broken. The nightmares never let me forget.

"She wasn't always *happy* and smiling." I tried to make my voice more lilting, but it faltered instead. I cleared my throat. "She was usually smirking at her own snarky comments." I sighed heavily, stepping out from where he'd trapped me between him and the bookshelf, and walked to the bed. I was about to sit when I realized I hadn't showered or changed clothes in over thirty-six hours. "Any chance we can go to my house and get some stuff?"

Kaleb's eyebrows knitted together, no doubt wondering why I'd changed the subject. But after a moment, he nodded. "Yeah, we can walk through the grove if you want."

The grove was the only thing separating our backyards. It was common ground during our younger years when we would play with sticks as swords, pretending to be knights locked in a battle over a princess. Several years ago, we had built a treehouse to escape when our lives seemed too chaotic. None of us had been there in years, but Kaleb walked through the grove constantly to get to our house. The drive around it seemed pointless when the walk was only five minutes.

Kaleb led the way out the back door. I hadn't ever made the trek from his house to mine, but the tall grass was familiar because it lined my side of the grove, too. I ran my fingers along the top of the grass, reminding myself of the meadow. The trees were blooming their usual flowers this time of year. Some were orange trees on the edge of his property, but most trees within the grove were big oak trees, providing tons of shade and climbing spots. We came to the creek, and I was surprised that the homemade bridge was still standing from years ago. Kaleb made his way nimbly across the fallen trunk and turned to offer me a hand, but I waved him away. He raised his brows in surprise. I gave him a look that I hoped portrayed my self-confidence and stepped onto the log, pulling all my training from the past few months to the surface. I was across in four easy steps, not a wobble in sight. I jumped down on the other side of the creek and continued walking right past Kaleb's gawking face.

No one I know would have confidence in my making it across that log without help, especially with my record amount of ER visits. A few of those visits were from me trying to cross that creek alone. It didn't seem like it was going to be a problem anymore.

Kaleb caught up with me, matching my stride as we exited the grove into my backyard. "Seems like you've been keeping secrets of your own." He eyed me suspiciously, and when my only answer was a shrug, he playfully punched my shoulder, "Come on, Ray! You can't tell me you're suddenly as graceful as a gazelle. What aren't you telling me?"

I shrugged again, keeping my eyes ahead as we walked up to my back door. "Guess I've finally gotten used to my height." I couldn't say anything else because it would give up the one thing I'd been able to keep for myself. Aside from Mr. Piper and Mr. Hood, no one else knew about my training. I wasn't about to confess to that now, even if I was starting to notice differences when I looked in the mirror recently. My friends were bound to notice at some point...

Kaleb narrowed his eyes but thankfully didn't push on the subject. I pulled the loose brick from the back wall of my house and tipped its contents into my hand. After using the spare key to unlock the door, I replaced it in the hollow brick and put it back in the wall. I headed for my room, Kaleb following close behind.

The house was eerily quiet. When I walked past Mitch's door, I had to push down the unwelcome thoughts that crept in. I didn't want to succumb to them right now. I'd already cried enough in the last twenty-four hours.

I grabbed a duffle from my closet and started throwing clothes into it, packing enough for a few days. I didn't know how long I'd be at Kaleb's, but I knew I could always return for more if it were longer. I threw in my favorite pair of chucks and patched jean jacket, then headed for the bathroom to grab what I needed.

When I went to grab my phone charger from the nightstand, I saw my snow globe still sitting there, broken. Had that been only yesterday? It felt like a lifetime ago. I ran my fingers down the carefully crafted trees now exposed and sighed heavily.

"What happened to your snow globe?" Kaleb's voice was soft, but my heart skipped a beat. I forgot he was there. He was leaning on the doorframe, hands in his pockets, studying me. He looked so comfortable. Relaxed. *Attractive*, even.

Before he could accuse me of staring or see the blush that had risen to my cheeks, I turned and grabbed my pillow from the bed. "Mitch woke me up with a Nerf gun yesterday. It got a little crazy, and I accidentally knocked it off my shelf." I said softly, turning back to him and pulling the duffle strap onto my shoulder, hugging my pillow loosely. "I'm gonna see if I can fix it when he's back home."

Kaleb's sad eyes reflected my own. He knew who got me that snow globe. He knew practically everything about me, especially the hard things I'd been through in the last few years. Not just the accidents but the moments when things got so hard that I broke. Rarely was I alone in those moments. He was usually right there to talk me through it or hold me while sobs wracked my entire body. He never once shied away from any of it.

Sometimes, he would fill the time by telling stories to make me laugh, pulling me out of my darkest moments. Other times, he knew I just needed to cry and would rub my back until I could take a deep breath. He was so gentle and thoughtful in those moments.

There was no doubt in my mind why Arabella felt the way she did about him. They had very little time to explore their feelings for each other. She barely realized she was falling for him by the time we turned sixteen. Several months later, she finally told him how she felt, and they had gone on their first date. She came home that night and fell into bed with a big grin. We pillow talked into the wee hours of the night about it, reliving every moment.

Two weeks later, she was gone.

As I studied Kaleb leaning on the doorframe, I wondered briefly what it would be like if it had been me rather than Bell, who confessed feelings for him, but I shoved those thoughts away before they got too far. It was weird enough that he had been my best friend for so long, but throw in the mix that he had been interested in my twin, which made things *extra* weird. Clearing the air between us yesterday was intended to make him let go of the idea. But now I thought we needed to clear it again to shove the idea from *my* head. Whatever this was between us, it shouldn't be acted on. It would make things far too complicated.

He pushed off the doorframe and walked towards me. My breath caught as he stopped inches from me. But he just reached out to lift the duffle from my shoulder, a question in his eyes. I let him take it and walked out the door. Being that close to him made me want to change my mind—no use tempting the beast, now awake and pacing in my stomach.

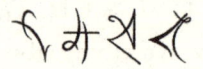

Kaleb recruited me to make dinner with the few ingredients in his kitchen, reminding me I could make magic out of two ingredients if I had the right spices. He wasn't wrong. I had my dad to thank for that—and the extra culinary class I had added to my syllabus this year. Kaleb's kitchen was very low stocked on spices and food, but I made do with what he had. His parents didn't buy groceries because neither of them liked to cook. Their budget included eating out most of the time.

I found crushed tomatoes and garlic in the pantry, then pulled onion powder, dried basil, salt, and sugar from the spice cabinet. I pulsed the tomatoes and garlic in the blender before pouring them into the skillet on the stove and adding the rest of the spices with a splash of water. Kaleb put the pasta in the boiling water and toasted some bread that was pretty stale but edible. I instructed him to butter the toast and add garlic salt when it popped, but he accidentally shook it too hard the first time. He laughed but didn't argue when I said I wouldn't eat that one. He agreed to suffer through the salty toast.

I tasted the sauce as it simmered and smacked my lips, trying to figure out what was missing. Opening the spice cupboard again, I rummaged until I found what I was looking for at the very back. I sprinkled the red pepper flakes into the sauce, catching Kaleb's skeptical stare, and added a few more shakes with a pointed look.

"You recruited me. Gotta trust me." I winked and stirred the sauce, letting it absorb the flavors a little longer before testing it and sounding my approval. I touched the spoon to the sauce again and raised it to Kaleb's lips. He opened hesitantly, but as soon as the flavors hit his tongue, I knew he was pleasantly surprised by how his eyebrows rose. "Ye of little faith," I scolded playfully.

He chuckled and turned the stove off, grabbing the pasta to drain in the sink. I grabbed plates from the cupboard, and he heaped the noodles on while I covered them with my perfect sauce. He placed the overly seasoned toast on my plate, but with the look I gave him, he grinned and quickly switched it with the good one. We ate in silence, hunger consuming us both.

As we sat there, I wondered if this was what a relationship would be like with someone. Easy, fun, and carefree. Despite everything in my life, I felt those things with Kaleb. Knowing he wasn't judging me for needing to let go of the hard stuff for a little while. He'd still be there for me when I inevitably broke down again. But he was also there when I felt at peace and happy. I liked feeling like I could be both of those things with Kaleb.

When we finished, Kaleb grabbed our plates and took them to the kitchen. "You can jump in the shower now if you want. I'll do the dishes and then take one myself."

The thought of showering in his bathroom made my cheeks heat, but I tried not to let it show as I grabbed the washcloth from the sink to wipe down the table. "Okay." I hadn't showered all day and suddenly felt self-conscious as I stepped close to Kaleb to replace the washcloth.

With one last look at him cleaning up, I hurried up the stairs to the bathroom. I spun my hair into a tight bun and peeled off my clothes. They felt sticky after wearing them all day yesterday and today. I scrubbed my body to remove the residue from the hospital and sweat from my panic attacks and night terrors. When the washcloth passed over my ribs on my right side. I jerked away at the slight pain and tenderness, glancing down to see what it—

No...

A red mark. From yesterday? Or was it the restraints at the hospital? There *was* one around my abdomen... There was also one around my shoulders and both ankles. I looked down at my ankles to see if there was any mark there.

Nothing.

A little concerned, I rinsed off and got out of the shower, wrapping a towel around myself and wiping the fog from the mirror to check my shoulders.

Nothing.

I examined the mark on my ribs more closely in the mirror. I hadn't realized how clearly the mark resembled a handprint—in the exact spot Kyler had caught me. I stared at the branding in the mirror, tracing it with my finger to see how tender it was. It didn't hurt, but it felt like a fresh layer of skin—extra sensitive and tender, baby smooth and pink.

How could his hand have left this mark?

A knock at the door made me jump away from the mirror. "Ray? Everything okay in there?" Kaleb's muffled voice didn't sound worried, just curious.

"Yeah!" I quickly pulled on my pajamas and yanked the door open, revealing him leaning against the doorframe on the other side. My heartbeat thumped against my chest. "Sorry, I just…" I trailed off, unsure if I should tell him about the mark. The situation was already strange. "I have a weird mark on my stomach. Probably from the restraints at the hospital." The lie slipped out too easily. I'm not sure why I felt like I couldn't tell him the truth, but it seemed like the type of thing he would think was too crazy to believe. I shrugged it off. "I was just making sure it didn't need bacitracin or something."

He chuckled, cocking his brow. "Bacitracin? Really?"

I smacked his shoulder and walked past him. "Baymax taught me everything I need to know."

He rolled his eyes and walked into the bathroom. "I'll be out in a few," he said, shutting the door.

I heard the shower start and decided to occupy my mind with other thoughts than the one that immediately popped into my head at the sound of the shower. In the silence, I released my hair from the tight bun and braided it in pigtails. After finishing the second braid, I pulled my phone charger out and plugged in my phone for the night. I turned on my vampire playlist, mainly consisting of songs from The Vampire Diaries and Twilight. I laid back on the bed and stared at the ceiling, listening to Plumb sing a ballad, wondering what it would be like to have a vampire for a boyfriend. I shivered at the thought of teeth sinking into my skin and drinking my blood. Blech. Disgusting.

I closed my eyes and heard the shower turn off as the song changed. Moments later, the door opened, and I didn't think about it before opening my eyes and looking toward the bathroom door.

Kaleb appeared, chest bare and a towel wrapped around his waist. I diverted my eyes too quickly and said, "Ew... put some clothes on."

He laughed. "What's wrong, Ray? Never seen a guy without a shirt on?"

I made a face, sticking my tongue out. "Of course, I've seen guys without a shirt on. But they usually wear trunks, not a towel with nothing underneath it."

"Oh, I promise there's something underneath this towel." That comment and the smirk that accompanied it earned him a pillow to the face. He just chuckled and disappeared into his closet.

"Why do you always have to make dirty jokes?" I yelled loud enough for him to hear.

"Because if I didn't, you wouldn't make that scrunched-up face I love." He peeked his head out the closet door and pointed his finger at me. "Yep, that's the one!" His full smile spread across his face as my disgust deepened, but my insides churned at the sight of his happiness. He disappeared again, reappearing with sleep pants instead of a towel, but still no shirt. "Want to flip the lamp on?" He gestured to said lamp next to my phone and went to turn the main light off as I switched it on.

He pulled a sleeping bag from his closet and rolled it out before crawling into it. He turned on his side and propped his head up with his hand, that cocky grin on his face.

"What?" I asked, less snarky than I intended.

"Nothing. Just find it funny that we're having a sleepover."

I chuckled softly and rolled onto my back to look at the ceiling to avoid the look he gave me. I also didn't want to think about what he said about the faces I made at his crude comments. "Sleepover implies sleeping. We also have school tomorrow." Another thought occurred to me, and I couldn't believe it had taken me this long to think about it again. Kaleb was a good distraction, that was for sure. I turned to him again, catching his gaze still on me. "And I want to go see Mitch after school."

He nodded, like that had already been a part of the plan. "Anything else, girlie?"

I narrowed my eyes. I hated it when he called me that. He knew I hated it—which is why he continued to use the nickname. "Yes, actually. If I'm going to be stuck in this house for a few days, then we need to get some groceries. I need proper food, not just a half-assed meal from the stale ingredients in your cupboard."

His eyebrows raised, changing from surprise as he blinked in confirmation. "Alright, we'll add it to the to-do list. For now, try to get some sleep." He pointed his chin at the lamp and rolled onto his back, his hands behind his head.

I flicked off the lamp and pulled the covers up to my shoulders. My eyes found Kaleb again in the dark, and I couldn't help but stare as sleep consumed me. The last thing I saw before I closed my eyes was Kaleb illuminated by the moon, his arms behind his head, bare torso half covered with the sleeping bag, and a small smile playing at his lips, eyes closed.

X
Trapped in a Dream

It made sense that my dream featured a shirtless Kaleb. At first, it seemed like an ordinary dream. He was sitting across from me at the table with food between us, and while his words were jumbled, the conversation seemed casual.

The scene around us changed to the cafeteria at school. I blinked, and the figure changed.

Kyler now sat before me. Shirtless. His eyes started flickering between blue and green. A smile spread slowly across his face. He had fangs that sparkled in the light. My stomach dropped.

The scene changed again. We were standing in the hospital. My eyes widened when I noticed the sharp canines growing longer and sharper. Kyler started stalking towards me—a predator's gleam in his eyes.

I tried to turn and run but felt something preventing me. I looked down to see I was strapped to a table by my ankles and across my waist and shoulders. I struggled against the restraints, my attempt becoming more and more frantic with each step he took. His face started transforming, and his canines elongated even more, seemingly turning into something else entirely.

His attention snapped to something on my left. I followed his gaze. A new frantic energy took over at what I saw, and I started screaming and thrashing. I needed to distract him from what lay on the table next to me.

Arabella's limp body lay there, her eyes locked on mine with a plea on her lips. *Help*. The creature Kyler had turned into closed in on her and started tearing into her with his teeth. I let out an ear-shattering scream.

Suddenly, it wasn't Arabella anymore. It was Dad—the same look in his dead eyes and a plea to help him.

Then it was Mitch.

I pulled and struggled against the restraints, screaming for mercy from the monster tearing my family apart. The image kept switching between the three of them, and hot tears rolled down my face as I continued the fight to get free.

I felt my skin tearing where the belts cut into me, the pain of the breakage so real. My muscles were tired from restrained use when the monster suddenly lifted his face to mine. A fresh wave of panic washed over me as he pinned me to the table.

His rows of sharp teeth were dripping with blood. His hot breath washed over my face. I started screaming again as he transformed, taking the shape of something I'd never seen before.

Claws—no *talons*— popped out of his fingers and sliced through the restraints on my left shoulder, cutting straight through my skin. A new scream ripped out of me at the pain that coursed through me. The cut burned. Bad. My voice echoed in the room, and suddenly, he was on top of me, his mouth full of sharp teeth so close to my face. Its mouth was moving like it was trying to say something.

Saying... *My name*. The creature was saying my name.

"Rayleigh. You need to wake up." The calm voice sounded strange from the terrifying creature now towering over me.

The monster had stopped his advance on me. He was straddling me. His face was morphing back again. Kyler's green eyes reappeared.

"Wake up, Rayleigh," his tone was gentle. "This isn't real."

The voice repeated those words and slowly faded, replaced by someone else yelling.

Kaleb.

Kaleb was yelling outside the dream.

When the monster's words sank in that it was all a dream, my eyes snapped open to find Kaleb straddling me, hands on either shoulder. Panic laced his voice as he repeatedly yelled my name, shaking my shoulders, clearly unsure if I could see him.

"Rayleigh!" I blinked rapidly, which I think gave him the indication that I could see and hear him because his face changed from panic to relief, and his voice dropped to a whisper. "I'm with you," his voice shook, and one of his trembling hands moved to my face, cupping my cheek. "Right here." His eyes searched mine. "You're *safe*." His thumb brushed my cheek, eyes darting between mine. "Breathe," he instructed.

I hadn't realized I wasn't. I sucked in a sharp, deep breath, and he gently walked me through a few calmer breaths until my heart settled.

"Are you with me?" His voice was less panicked, but his eyes still reflected it.

My throat was raw, indicating that the screams from my dream were vocalized externally. No wonder Kaleb looked so worried. I nodded, unable to speak.

He sighed, his shoulders relaxed, and his head hung in relief, his forehead momentarily brushing mine. He pulled back to look at me again, panic mostly gone from his eyes, and he moved his legs from straddling me to sitting next to me on the bed. "You scared the hell out of me," he whispered, taking another deep breath, and I joined him, even though I was slightly paralyzed in my spot on the bed. His eyes found mine, and he seemed to make the connection at the same time I did. "You forgot to take your medicine."

Yep. I closed my eyes. I hadn't taken it from my backpack since Ma put it there at the hospital. When I shook my head, he climbed off the bed and grabbed my bag, fishing out the little bottle and opening it to hand me one of the tiny pills as I slowly pushed myself to a sitting position. He disappeared into the bathroom, returning with a small cup of water for me to swallow the pill. He waited until I'd finished to take the cup from me, setting it on the nightstand. Without another word, he turned to go back to his bed on the floor.

I didn't think. I just moved and grabbed his arm to stop him. Even with the water, my throat was still too raw from screaming, and the words to ask for what I wanted would probably come out wrong anyway. So, with a plea in my eyes, I scooted myself over on the bed and pushed the covers back on the spot I had just occupied.

Something unreadable flashed in his sleepy eyes before understanding settled in its place. He crawled onto the bed and pulled the covers over his legs. He reached his arm out for me. I hesitated momentarily, knowing I had asked for this, but I was unsure if it was the right choice. He waited patiently, seeing my inner battle. Finally, I laid myself down beside him and gingerly put my head on his chest with my hand close by. He wrapped his arm around my shoulder, and his other hand found mine on his chest, covering it lightly.

He let out a long breath through his nose, which I felt on the top of my head. My body started shaking uncontrollably, and he just pulled me tighter and whispered into my hair, "I'm here. You're safe." I didn't know how much I needed to hear those words until the tears formed in my eyes. I didn't let them fall but slowly nodded my head against his chest. "Sleep, Ray."

The trembling subsided after a few minutes, and exhaustion overwhelmed me. I finally closed my eyes and fell into a dreamless sleep.

My eyes fluttered open to sunlight peeking in the window. Kaleb's breaths were steadily hitting the top of my head. Neither of us had moved during the night, aside from my arm slipping around his torso completely and his hand lightly holding my arm where it lay across his bare chest. I lay there, unmoving for a moment, trying to decide if I wanted to risk waking him by getting up or relishing in the safety I felt with his arms around me.

Before I could decide, he shifted under me, yawning and stretching as much as he could without moving me. Figuring he thought I was still asleep, I tilted my head to his face from where it lay on his chest, his tired eyes finding mine through several blinks. He smiled softly at me. I returned it but pushed myself up slowly, not wanting the moment to be more intimate than it already was.

Pain shot through my shoulder, and my skin felt stiff and sore as I stretched. Sitting up, I crossed my legs and buried my hands in my lap. Kaleb didn't seem to notice the pain I was trying to hide. He was up and off the bed so quickly that I thought maybe I had scared him away. He headed straight for the bathroom.

I stayed on the bed and mentally checked the pain coursing through my body, stretching this way and that, questioning how so much pain could come from being restrained during a night terror by straps or a person. Kaleb was quite a bit taller than me and packed on some muscle, but I couldn't imagine I'd been fighting against his hold for too long.

Taking in my injuries, I wondered if I gave Kaleb any like I had Mitch. The fact that I dislocated Mitch's shoulder made me want to vomit, and I made a deal with myself not to go near him today when I visited—no use putting him in danger. Standing in the doorway to his room would be enough to ensure he was okay.

Kaleb emerged from the bathroom, hair tousled in a carefree yet perfect mess, and grumbled something about coffee as he headed downstairs. I stared after him, jaw slightly slack. I guess I hadn't been around him enough in the morning to know he didn't fare well without his coffee. We were more alike in that sense than I thought.

On the plus side, he didn't seem injured at all from last night's incident.

I unfolded myself from my position on the bed, joints screaming as I stretched out their stiffness and skin pulling taut in some places. Thrashing against real restraints on a hospital bed and fake ones in a dream used more muscles than I thought because the short walk to the bathroom proved difficult.

Even removing my pajamas was painful. I gasped at what I found when I checked myself in the mirror. Purple bruises on my shoulders and stomach, burn marks where the straps had rubbed my skin raw, and a deep gash on my left shoulder that hadn't left any blood on my shirt but was freshly scabbed over.

I didn't remember seeing those injuries after my shower last night. The gash on my shoulder made the least sense because I didn't remember getting cut by any—

The talon. The gash on my shoulder was right where it had sliced through the strap in my dream.

My hand flew to my mouth, blood running cold as a shiver went down my spine. I hadn't noticed the injuries last night because they *hadn't been there*. They were from my dream.

Panic crept up on me, stealing my breath away. I found my eyes in the mirror, wide and shining with fear. Speaking to my reflection in the mirror, I said, "Breathe."

A shaky breath followed, and I let it out slowly.

The nightmare wasn't real. But the injuries were.

"Breathe in," I whispered to myself.

How is this possible? Is there any explanation? Am I going crazy?

"Breath out."

My thoughts wandered to another time when things didn't seem real. Kendall was there. She witnessed it.

"Breathe in." My voice was shaky but persistent.

Should I tell Ken? What if she doesn't believe me?

"Breathe. Out."

No. She would listen and try to help me understand. She was the one person who *might* not think I was crazy. I should tell her.

But until I saw her, I had to cover up the evidence of my injuries. Pretend like they didn't exist. There wasn't any excess blood from the scratches, but I wiped them clean with a wet washcloth anyway. I pulled on my outfit for school, careful not to open any of the wounds, and headed downstairs with my backpack slung over my uninjured shoulder.

When I rounded the corner into the kitchen, Kaleb's hand extended toward me, holding a mug full of coffee. He wore his favorite shirt, a sage green tee, with jeans and chucks—typical Kaleb fashion. But I'd never noticed how nicely the clothes fit his muscular figure. I shook that thought from my head and took the coffee wordlessly. He leaned back against the counter, watching me closely as I sipped.

My eyebrows rose in surprise as the flavors hit my tongue. "How did you know how I like my coffee?"

He gave a short, breathy laugh into his cup before taking a sip. "Because you steal sips of mine often enough."

"Ah, touché." I sat at the counter, sipping more coffee to avoid making faces at the pain shooting through my entire body.

He stayed where he was, leaning on the counter, but eyed me warily. At first, I thought he noticed the stiff movements and was about to ask me about it, but instead, he sighed and closed his eyes. "We don't have anything here for breakfast."

I shrugged, realizing it was a bad idea too late. The pain caused my face to twitch slightly. I tried to cover it up by wrinkling my nose and saying, "I don't usually eat much in the morning anyway."

Kaleb didn't miss a thing, though. Squinting at me, he said, "Ray," dragging out my name. "Are you okay?"

Deciding a version of the truth was best, I said, "Yeah. Turns out thrashing against restraints in a bed makes for sore muscles the next day." I held up my coffee in fake cheers before taking another big gulp.

"Well, remind me not to straddle you and pin you down to a bed again." I choked on my coffee, sputtering it back into the cup while he laughed into his own and took an innocent sip.

Wiping the coffee from my mouth, I set my mug down forcefully and made a face at him. "You're so charming, Kaleb." The sarcasm dripped heavily as he winked at me over his cup. I got up to dump the rest of my coffee in the sink, telling myself it wasn't to hide the pink that flushed my cheeks. "I was talking about the hospital bed I'd been strapped to, with *actual* restraints."

"Ah, well, I'll make sure to have the proper materials next time." He chuckled as my fist slammed into his shoulder—a little harder than I intended. "Ow! Hey! No need for violence, girlie!" His mock pain turned into real, albeit surprised, pain as he rubbed his shoulder. "That *actually* hurt."

"Good." I crossed my arms, ignoring the slight pain the punch sent through my shoulder. The minute my arm lay against my torso, a burning sensation made me lift it away, but only slightly.

He watched me over the rim of his mug as he finished his coffee and placed the mug in the sink. "First, you cross the log without hurting yourself. Now, you're strong enough that a single punch can leave a bruise. Not to mention, you almost threw me off of you several times while I was trying to wake you last night…"

"You must be getting weaker." The snarky comment was similar to something Arabella would have said to him in a moment like this. If the look that flashed across his face told me anything, he realized that, too.

He ignored it, though, stepping into my personal space while his eyes searched mine. "Or you're getting *stronger*." He gave me a knowing look, obviously expecting me to confess something, but I had no intention of doing so.

I shrugged. "Either way, you would still lose in a fight." His jaw dropped, but I suppressed a smirk as I situated my backpack. "Come on." I turned on my heel toward the front door. "We're going to be late."

He sighed loudly but followed me out the door. I knew he wouldn't let me off that easily and would bring it up again at some point, but I wasn't quite ready to tell him about my training. Not yet.

Arriving back at school felt out of place and time. I forgot I missed an entire day, but no one else had.

Jordin had kindly requested that Chief keep the story out of the news and not tell the school any details of Mitch's accident.

So, naturally, the whole school knew.

They knew Mitch was in a coma, that he'd been hit by a car, and that I had been with him at the hospital when I missed school yesterday.

The minute I stepped into Chemistry class, Ken and Leigh pushed through the crowd around me to pull me away from the frenzy of questions. "Will your brother wake up?" or "Have they found the person who hit him?" or, as Sera and Tate asked, "How much blood was there?" That earned them several weird looks and made me want to ask them why they were the way they were.

Once I was seated, Kaleb, Ken, and Leighton surrounded me, leaving no room for anyone to get close enough to ask me anything else. They struck up a conversation among themselves, but I didn't have the brain power to keep up with what they were saying. They knew what they were doing, and I'd have to thank them later. It wasn't often one found a friend who knew being there for someone didn't always require conversation. I was lucky enough to have found three.

It took me a minute to realize Kaleb was telling them about the night terrors—the one that occurred at the hospital and the one from last night. He seemed to know it would be difficult for me to talk about. He relayed the details of my nightmare to them that I'd told him on the way to school.

I hadn't given him all the details, but he got the gist of it. I said something about the scratches feeling real, but not that I woke up to find that they *were* real. I waited for him to comment on him being shirtless in my dream, but he seemed too focused on the part about him turning into the monster that attacked me.

Oh... I guess I left the part out where his shirtless form turned into Kyler before turning into the monster... *That* would have earned a comment, which is why I left it out. And the part where I heard Kyler's monstrous form saying I needed to wake up... and him telling me that the dream wasn't real... I gave the essential details, okay?

The warning bell rang, dispersing everyone back to their seats. The twins each squeezed my hand gently before leaving my table, letting me know they were there if they needed me.

Kaleb touched his lips to my head as he walked to his spot behind me. The gesture was simple and sweet, but it gave me giddy goosebumps.

Realizing I hadn't been able to say anything to Kendall, I twisted in my seat and caught her eye, giving her the hand signal we used when we needed to talk to each other in private. She gave a slight nod, and I turned back to the front.

I felt, rather than saw, Kyler sit down next to me as the final bell rang. He barely made a sound as he sat, his bag slinking to the floor between us. I caught a whiff of smoke, but not like cigarettes. It was different, almost like a campfire with something more, but I couldn't put my finger on it. Before I could sniff again to try and place it, the smokiness was replaced by the sweet scent of strawberries. Out of the corner of my eye, I saw a lollipop stick poking out of his mouth.

Clenching my teeth together, I whispered, "Mr. Blake doesn't allow candy in his class." I don't know what made me tell him. He would have found out on his own. He could have gotten in trouble, and I would have had a good laugh about it.

He turned his head slowly, *so slowly,* toward me, sliding the lollipop from his mouth and clicking his tongue. He leaned closer, but I leaned away because I could only see the monster he became in my dream last night. And the fact that he'd *spoken* to me in that dream. Maybe I'd imagined that part and didn't hear his voice. He chuckled at my actions and whispered, "You gonna tattle on me, Sunshine?"

"Don't call me that." I snapped before I knew what I was saying. Anger started boiling under the surface. I swallowed the feeling and clenched a fist on the table. That nickname didn't belong to him. I didn't care what feelings ran through my body as his deep voice rumbled. My body was not on my team right now. I hadn't looked at him yet. I didn't want to experience the dizziness from his eye contact again. The way I clenched my jaw and spit the words at him, I knew he could tell how mad it made me when he used that nickname, but I didn't care. Mad wasn't even the right word. When he called me Sunshine the other day, the sorrow deep within me threatened to crack open the box I shoved it in. But with everything over the last two days, that sorrow pushed harder on that box, proving harder to keep at bay.

He released a breath, and a fresh wave of strawberry scent washed over me. It took everything in me not to inhale deeply at the smell. The small sniff I allowed myself to take was utterly intoxicating, and I tried not to let it go to my head. Within the strawberry and smoky scent he was trying to cover was something else I couldn't place. It was vaguely familiar, though, like something I smelled often.

His hand landed on the table between us and pushed back to balance on the chair's back legs. "What should I call you then, *Sunshine?*"

Suddenly, the pencil in front of me was in my hand, hovering millimeters above his hand, where it still lay on the edge of the table. The sorrow pushing on the box quickly turned to rage, and I had trouble reigning it back in. Kyler watched me with rapt attention, eyes darting to the sharp pencil before lifting back to mine. His chair dropped to the ground, and his jaw clenched in anticipation of my next move.

"Not that. Anything else. But *not that*." Our eyes were locked. The dizziness hadn't started, so I wasn't about to back down.

He worked his jaw, making me wonder why he was so upset when it should be me. But he still looked at me like I was the one who'd done something terrible. Perhaps he didn't like it when people surprised him. Maybe I'd caught him off guard.

His gaze gave something away. Like he was fighting something. There was conflict in his eyes. But I wouldn't give him the satisfaction of showing him the same. I threw every ounce of hatred into the glare I gave him because if he saw one ounce of what lay directly beneath that hate, a simple glance into the box full of emotions I've trapped inside, he would see the hurt. He would know the pain that nickname caused. I couldn't allow that vulnerability. Not with him.

Someone cleared their throat behind us, breaking our staring contest, and I relaxed my grip on the pencil, letting the sharpened tip drop as I righted myself in my seat. I heard his hiss of pain as the pencil hit its mark and fought to keep the grin from my face.

Kaleb must have given the warning because not a second after the pencil fell into place on the table, Mr. Blake stepped up next to me and handed us a test.

The color drained from my face. I forgot to study. The girls had brought my things to study yesterday, but with my night terrors and Kaleb picking me up—

I knew Chemistry well enough. I paid attention in class. I could remember what I needed to do for this test, right?

Wrong. The words on the page melted together, and everything I thought I knew about the subject vanished from my brain. Was it because of what happened with Mitch? Or was it the charged energy that still lingered between Kyler and me, making me hyper-aware of every little movement in his chair?

After staring at the words on the paper for several minutes, I felt the sudden urge to pee. Perhaps that would help me break through the brain fog. I walked up and asked for the hall pass, hoping that splashing cold water on my face would snap me out of this funk, and I'd come back with plenty of time to finish the test.

XI
Trying My Best

I was washing my hands when the bathroom door opened. Kendall stepped in, leaning on the door as it closed behind her. Her eyes locked on mine. "You good?"

Furrowing my brow, I responded a bit snarkily, "Yeah. Just... using the bathroom?" I grabbed a few paper towels to dry my dripping hands. Kendall's eyes fixated on the water as the droplets hit the floor.

She shook her head from the trance and crossed her arms over her chest. "It took you thirty minutes to go to the bathroom?"

"Thirty minutes? I left three minutes ago." I felt the blood drain from my face as she slowly shook her head.

"Ray, class is almost over." Her voice seemed far away. The bell rang, signaling the end of Chemistry, and Ken pointed at the bell above the door, "See? Mr. Blake sent me to see if you were okay."

My breathing became shallow. My heart beat wildly. I rubbed at my chest where it tried to escape, and my fingers brushed the tender cut on my shoulder, causing me to wince. The pain pulled me from the panic.

Kendall tilted her head, staring at the spot I'd touched. "What was that?" She closed the distance between us, my mind still reeling about the missing time. I didn't try to stop her as she slid my shirt aside to reveal the gash there. "Rayleigh, *what happened?*" My full name brought her face into focus, eyes wide and forehead taut.

The nightmare. She hadn't heard the whole thing. I hoped what I was about to tell her would wipe away the crazy look in her eyes. She was the only other person with me when time changed around me before. I took a deep breath and settled on a small portion of the truth. "Remember what happened at the mall?" She nodded. I swallowed the lump in my throat. "I *swear* I just left for the bathroom three minutes ago." I trod carefully with my next words, not wanting to pour it all on her at once. "Something's happening to me, Ken. I feel— I feel like I'm going crazy." The last word barely squeaked out as my throat constricted.

Ken dropped her tense shoulders and moved to wrap her arms around me, squeezing too tight. I hissed in pain, and she loosened her hold, pulling back to look me dead in the eyes. "You're not going crazy. What happened at the mall was weird, and even though I didn't see the guy in the hoodie, I believe *you* did." When I said nothing, her hands moved from my shoulders to my face, eyes searching mine. "You're not crazy, Ray, but you have to tell me what's going on."

Her hazel eyes shone with sincerity as she searched mine for the answers she needed. She would wait for me to tell her, though. She wouldn't break eye contact until I did. That calm, cool, and collected demeanor was all I needed before deciding to tell her everything.

So I did.

The night terrors, the voicemail, the second sighting of the man in the hoodie, the panic attacks. All of it. Or as much as I could in three minutes.

As I was about to tell her about Kyler's involvement, if I could call it that, the warning bell rang. "There's one more thing." I gripped her arm so she couldn't leave. It was the only thing I was still hesitant to tell her. If only because it didn't make sense. It didn't fit. Kyler was the one thing that felt out of place in all of it. But maybe that's why I needed to tell her. Perhaps that would help her piece things together with me. Maybe speaking the words out loud would make it make sense. The voice in my dreams, the mark on my ribcage… but we had to get to class. "Can you come to Kaleb's after school?"

The wheels of her mind were turning, processing everything. She wasn't looking at me like I was crazy. Not yet. There was still time for that. She shook her head, clearing the thoughts racing through. "Yeah, uh... I can come over for dinner?"

"Bring Leighton." The thought of relaying all the information again seemed daunting, but I couldn't tell one without telling the other. Even if she did disappear that night at the mall, Leighton had a knack for knowing things and might be able to help me decipher Kyler's involvement in it all. Kaleb probably should know, too, mainly the part about the man in the mall. It seemed like whatever was happening around me was only beginning, and I would need other people to know in case I needed their help. Making another quick decision, I added, "I've got something right after school for a few hours. Let's say six?"

Ken nodded and pulled me into a tight hug. Pain shot through my shoulder, but I ignored it this time, squeezing her right back. She pulled away, catching and holding my gaze, and said, "We'll figure this out, Ray. Together."

I gave her a weak smile, knowing there was no possible way we could figure this out on our own, but I followed her out the bathroom door anyway. Kaleb stood there with our bags, a question in his eyes. I grabbed my bag from him and said, "Later," as an answer. He grabbed my arm before I could walk away and opened his mouth to protest, but I put a hand on his chest. "I promise."

His brown eyes shone with concern as he looked down at me. They closed for a moment while he took a deep breath, and when he opened them, he said, "Okay. Later." I pushed on his chest to turn him toward his class while Ken and I hurried off to Spanish, texting Jordin on the way there.

The rest of the day was uneventful. Some people asked about Mitch, but I could keep them away if I let the tears shine in my eyes. People my age hated emotions like that.

In creative writing, Leigh and I only talked about her progress with the Snurgleform pen and didn't allow anyone else to bring up Mitch. She had written down all the characteristics of it, how it worked, and why it would never be possible. She said she left the design to me. So, I drew up the most obnoxious-looking pen I could think of during class. No one would ever mistake it for an ordinary writing utensil, which was good because no one would want to draw something only to have it come to life accidentally.

When class was over, Leigh grabbed my elbow before I could walk away. "Ken said you wanted to hang tonight. Are you planning a game night?" She beamed at me.

"Uh... No?" I said, matching her smile and wondering where she got that idea.

She noted my confusion and said, "Oh. Kaleb had said something about planning one so you could meet Amariel."

"Right." I dragged out the word, forgetting I was to spend prom night in the presence of a girl related to the one person on this earth who made me want to breathe fire. I couldn't hide the glower on my face as I said, "Sounds fun."

Leigh gave me a weird smile, "You don't seem excited to meet her... Did I miss something?"

"No..." I let out a breath. "It's just...she's Kyler's sister." At my statement, her other eyebrow joined the first. I raised my hands in defense. "I'm sure she's nothing like him."

"She's really not," Leigh said, crossing her arms. "Don't judge her based on him."

"But he's the *worst*. Arrogant. Rude. Condescending." I could have listed several more colorful adjectives, but the look on Leighton's face made me stop. "Again, I'm sure Amariel is nothing like him."

She shook her head, a slow smile spreading across her face, "She's not. I promise. She's actually, like, the complete opposite of him." Her words reminded me of how Kyler described her. I shook the thought from my head and focused on Leigh, whose small smile slowly faded. "Do you really think Brax would ask someone like that to prom?"

I sighed, relaxing my shoulders. "You're right. I'm excited to meet her. Maybe we can do game night this weekend?" Tonight was not the night to meet new people.

She beamed at me. "I'll run it by them. You check with Kaleb?"

"Deal." I gave her a quick hug before she headed off to her last class.

I turned to head to the parking lot but ran directly into something hard.

Ouch. I stepped back and looked up to the wall—

Nope. Not a wall.

It felt like one, but it wasn't.

No.

It was an asshole, clenching his teeth with his shoulders tensed. The glare he aimed at me could have pierced my soul. I stepped back, masking my fear by crossing my arms, trying not to stumble out of his shadow.

"Better watch where you're going, *Sunshine*," he growled at me.

Whatever fear I felt at the look on his face vanished, replaced with boiling rage at the sound of that nickname coming from his mouth yet again. I uncrossed one arm and shoved my finger into his chest, stepping into him. "What don't you understand about the words 'don't call me that'?"

The corner of his mouth lifted slightly, making him look pure evil. His voice lowered with his head, "From what I just heard, I'm arrogant, rude, and condescending." My blood ran cold. He looked down at the finger still poking his chest and slowly grabbed my entire hand to remove it. He returned his gaze to mine, his eyes cutting through me. "Be a shame if I didn't live up to that."

Heat ran up my neck. He'd heard everything. How long had he been standing there? It didn't matter. The heat of his hand holding mine made me rip it out of his grasp. "You know, most people would try to prove they're *not* those things instead of just proving that they *are*."

"Oh, but Sunshine…" He stepped toward me, leaving only inches between us, and I felt his hot breath on my ear as he whispered, "Where's the fun in that?" A shiver ran through me as he shoulder-checked me on his way down the hall and out the door leading to the courtyard.

The fact that I considered him attractive made me want to scream. I admit saying those things wasn't very nice, but they weren't wrong. He confirmed it himself.

Letting out a noise of frustration, I whipped back toward the exit and made my way to my car. I needed to let off some steam, and I needed to do it *now*.

As Jordin promised, Chitty was in the parking lot with the key above the tire. She and Chief Bass had made sure it got here so I could do what I needed without asking Kaleb to take me. I still wasn't ready for him to know.

I slammed the door to my car harder than necessary and jammed the key into the ignition, only to have Chitty choke when I turned the key. That straw broke the dam.

The box I'd been holding closed within me burst open, and the emotions poured out of me. I couldn't stop the flow. I screamed into the empty void of my car, not caring if anyone was around to hear me. I punched the steering wheel several times before feeling hot tears spill down my face.

Kyler overhearing what I said sealed the fate of our back-and-forth. It was no longer fun and games, as it started. I had no doubt he would do anything to tear me down now, starting with using that nickname whenever he wanted, as often as he wanted. There's nothing I could do to stop him.

I'll see you later, Sunshine.

Those were the last words my dad ever spoke to me, which is why they hurt so much. Hearing someone else call me that was jarring enough, but Kyler's use of it was more of a taunt than anything. It *hurt* to hear it used that way.

My overflow of emotions brought the memory of my dad's accident crashing down on me.

Kaleb was driving Mitch and me home after picking him up from practice. The traffic was stopped on the two-lane highway. After sitting for a few minutes, several people in front of us got out of their parked cars to investigate.

Mitch pointed ahead, seeing smoke trail up into the sky. We all got out of the car and walked toward the accident. We reached a point where we could see a vehicle had crashed into a tree, flames climbing up the tree and spreading to the grass surrounding it.

The fire should have been our warning to stay back, but Mitch and I continued to creep forward, even as Kaleb tried to drag us back to his car. We felt pulled to the fire. As we got closer, I knew why. As soon as I recognized the car, I started running, screaming. The highway was blocked by several fire trucks, an ambulance, and police cars. I headed straight for the ambulance, Mitch hot on my heels.

A scream that wasn't my own pierced the sky, making me stop.

It hadn't come from the ambulance.

Everything around me faded away.

The sounds.

The people.

The fire.

My focus narrowed in on the car.

Panic crept up in me as I shifted my sprint toward the car.

Toward the scream coming from inside.

Someone grabbed me around the waist from behind, pulling me back against their chest before I made it anywhere near the car. My dad was screaming for help as fire licked toward the sky. The first responders were all just standing there. Watching. Faces somber. Doing nothing as the flames took his life away.

The officer who'd grabbed me had to adjust his grip because I started fighting him, trying to pry his hands off me. "That's my dad!!" I screamed at the officer. "That's my dad! He's still alive! Get him out of there!" I directed the last scream at the firefighters whose attention I'd finally grabbed. They didn't move, though. Their sad eyes just fell to the ground. But I couldn't accept that. I wouldn't. "What are you doing?! He needs help! Can't you see that? HELP HIM!"

The officer had a good grip on me now, pinning my arms to my chest from behind, and his mouth was next to my ear. He whispered, "There's nothing we can do." The words were like a gut punch. "The steering wheel trapped him against his seat. We can't get him out. It's too dangerous. The car could explode with any movement." My body had lost its fight. I stopped struggling in his grip. He released me slowly, ensuring I could support myself, as sobs were making my entire body shake.

The sounds around me returned, and I heard Mitchell yelling behind me as my knees gave out. Strong arms caught me. Kaleb lowered us to the ground, my eyes finding Mitch. The firefighter holding him back released him when he'd stopped *struggling, and Mitch rushed to where I collapsed on the ground with Kaleb, tears streaming down both of our faces.*

We shouldn't have stayed. Kaleb begged us to get up and get back to the car, but we couldn't. We held each other until the screams stopped.

We listened to our dad die.

His screams of pain and anguish echoed in my mind for days after his death. It took me weeks to recover. I pushed all my emotions deep down inside that box, fighting against them anytime they tried to break out and resurface. The first few days, I couldn't even get out of bed. Kaleb was there those mornings, like he knew which ones I would wake up and be unable to function. He tried coaxing me to sit up, drink water, and eat something. Sometimes, it worked; others, it didn't, and he would sit on the floor next to the bed and talk to me until the feelings passed, and I would finally sit up. I couldn't remember feeling that way when Bell died, but I was also heavily medicated then.

Jordin had disappeared. Again. I didn't know if it was to her room or to work, but I didn't see her for several days. When I did, she ignored me, staring at nothing and talking to no one. Mitch and I had to be there for each other because she never was.

I never truly acknowledged the emotions after he died. There were nights I'd wake up from night terrors, screaming, but muffled my cries so Mitch and Jordin wouldn't hear. I cried myself to sleep almost every night for weeks.

It was the most devastating time of my life.

As the waves of the emotional dam subsided, I took some staggering breaths, trying to compose myself in the parking lot. I carefully pushed all the emotions back into the box. I gently caressed my steering wheel to apologize to Chitty for taking it out on him, and then I turned the key. He purred to life, and I wiped my tears away.

With the crying out of the way, I zoned in on the anger I'd been holding onto and hoped my instructor would let me go to town during training.

XII
Overwhelmed

Sweat dripped down my nose onto the mat. I stayed there for a minute, trying to catch my breath. As suspected, Mr. Hood didn't take it easy on me, but I'd asked him not to. He reached down his hand to help me up. I gladly took it after he just made me do ten-minute solo drills.

He bid me goodbye, and I headed to my car, texting Kaleb that I'd meet him at his house. I needed a shower before we did anything else today. I stretched my sore muscles, finding the skin around my shoulder tight from the deep scratch. But when I checked it before my session, it seemed to have healed most of the way. The bruises were a bit tender, but I barely felt the injuries as I went through the motions of the lesson. The release of the emotions I had in my car earlier had helped, but with Mr. Hood's encouragement, I honed in on the anger and released it as I moved. He told me it was the best I'd performed in a while, and whatever I used as my motivation was working.

When I stepped into the parking lot, a loud car engine revved nearby, the tires squealing as it sped out of the parking lot next door. When I turned toward the noise to see who felt the need to be so obnoxious, the car was already gone and disappeared behind the buildings down the street. I could still hear the engine growl as it faded into the distance. I shook my head, muttering to myself.

I turned back to my car and froze.

A figure stood just beyond it. In a dark hoodie.

My blood ran cold despite the rigorous training I'd just finished.

They stood, unmoving, on the sidewalk. Staring in my direction. I didn't take my eyes off them. My car was equidistant from either of us.

My body was tired, but my mind was clear. I'd been trained well and knew how to defend myself if it came to that. If that was the same person from the mall—

I moved toward my car, covering the distance quickly. The figure hesitated. They weren't expecting me to walk toward them, but when they realized I was heading to the car, they started walking, too. I got there first, unlocking just my door and throwing myself in. There was traffic on the main road, so I wasn't sure what this person thought they would do if they reached me.

The figure was fifteen feet from my car when I locked my door. I gave Chitty a strong word of encouragement, hoping he would start on the first try. I turned the key. They were ten feet away. Chitty purred to life. Five feet. I jammed the car into drive and hit the gas.

Their fingers grazed the handle, but I peeled out of the parking lot and into traffic before they could grip it.

In the rearview mirror, I saw the figure standing in the parking lot, watching as I drove away. Someone beside me laid on their horn, and I swerved back into my lane. When I checked the mirror again, they were gone.

I sank into the driver's seat with a deep breath. My heartbeat was erratic in my ears, but I escaped. From whoever that stalker was.

Accepting something was happening in my life and confirming it were two completely different things. The adrenaline coursing through me was something I'd never felt before. Thinking back, maybe I should have done something else. Shouted at them. Asked what they wanted. Why were they following me? But it probably wouldn't have done anything. They would have ignored the questions, and my momentary distraction would have led to them catching me.

Obviously, I would have fought back, but getting away felt more important than figuring out who they were. While some would consider it brave to stand up to your stalker alone, others might think it foolish. It was better to wait until someone was with me to help.

Mentally adding that incident to the list of things to tell everyone, I accepted that this evening might go from info dumping to making a plan. The four of us were notorious for being ridiculous, but I knew they would want to help me figure everything out. And make a plan to corner the person following me. Knowing that about them was comforting, but this whole situation was getting a little dangerous.

The idea to tell Chief popped into my head, but I quickly squashed it. I knew he'd bring Jordin into this, and she'd never let me leave the house again.

The drive to Kaleb's calmed me down, helping me focus on what I had to do. Halfway there, the silence became overwhelming, so I blasted some old-school Jonas Brothers to bring me out of my funk.

Kaleb wasn't home when I arrived, so I let myself in with the key under the small potted tree out front. After a quick shower, I wiped the mirror off to investigate my scars and bruises again. My jaw dropped at my reflection.

The scratches were gone. Healed. Faint white scars replaced them. The big one on my shoulder was pink, the flesh of newly healed skin. The bruises had turned a greenish yellow and weren't tender at all. There was no way I should have healed that quickly... right?

The only thing that was still obvious was the handprint. It had faded along the edges, but as I ran my finger along the slightly darker skin, I noticed it wasn't tender anymore. Sensitive, yes, but that could have been because of where it was.

The fact that I was about to tell my friends about this... It wasn't going to be easy. Who knew how they would react? I already thought it was ridiculous. They'd likely feel the same. Worse, they'd see the mark and confront Kyler about it, which is the furthest thing from what I wanted. I didn't want anything to do with him. If I never had to see him again, I would thank whatever higher being I needed to because it would be the best thing that's happened this week.

A car door slammed outside. Kaleb. I threw on my clothes, ignoring the questions that were building up in my head, and went downstairs.

When I rounded the corner into the kitchen, he had just set his backpack down. He crossed his arms like an upset parent and said, "Where were you?"

The tone gave me chills. Shit. I forgot to text him. "Oh— There was something I had to do." Omitting the truth was easy. I wasn't sure why I didn't just tell him about my training, but this was one thing I just wanted to keep to myself. The look on his face told me he knew I wasn't telling him something.

"Something you *had* to do?" His voice was louder this time, and his eyebrows raised. "Rayleigh, I'm supposed to be looking after you!" He threw his arm out in a gesture like I'd run in that direction. "You can't just disappear like that." The worry that laced his words had guilt rising in my stomach.

"I didn't think you'd care..." I mumbled. By the look in his eyes, I could see that my words struck a nerve. Putting myself in his shoes momentarily, I thought about how I would feel if the roles were reversed and knew he was right. I should have texted him. I'd been too distracted by what happened with Kyler. It didn't matter that I meant to. I hadn't. "You're right." I dropped my shoulders in defeat and gave him my sincere puppy dog eyes. "I forgot to text you, but that's no excuse. I'm sorry."

His gaze softened, and he dropped his arms to his side, closing the distance between us. He tucked a piece of hair behind my ear and tilted my chin to meet his gaze. "Just try to remember that people are worried about you. *I'm* worried about you." At this distance, his eyes sparkled as he searched mine. For what, I didn't know. "Don't tell yourself that no one cares. You have no idea just how much so many people do. How much *I* do."

I stared at him, his finger still holding my chin, and something went taut between us. I knew he was waiting for me to acknowledge his words with my own, but I could only nod. His finger dropped from my chin, and I stepped back, clearing my throat from the emotions he stirred, before changing the subject. "Ken and Leigh are coming over for dinner." If he was surprised, he didn't show it. He just stepped back to lean against the counter and crossed his arms, waiting for me to go on. "I have something I need to tell you guys. It'll be better to do it all at once." He blinked. "I'll tell you what they already know on the way to the store."

He took a deep breath and pinched the bridge of his nose, shaking his head as if clearing his mind of whatever he'd imagined I had to tell him. "On our way where?"

"The store," I said pointedly. He blinked at me again. "Gah, Kaleb! Groceries. Remember?"

He threw his head back in exaggerated realization, "Ah, right. Grocery store." He grabbed the car keys and swept his hand in front of him toward the front door. "After you."

I squinted at him, "What store did you think I meant?"

He sighed loudly behind me, "Honestly, no idea. I was lost in thought." We walked out the door, and he locked it behind us.

"Are you sure that lady wasn't just ignoring you?" Kaleb asked after I told him about the mall.

"Yes! Both Ken and I tried to get her attention. We shook her arm, Kaleb. She didn't even try to yank it away from us." This was one of the many things I'd thought through because it *was* possible, but how could she ignore someone grabbing her?

"And you're sure that you looked everywhere for Leighton?"

I rolled my eyes. "*Yes!* We both shouted her name. She wasn't there. But then, when I closed my eyes for a second, she suddenly appeared, and the lady could magically see us again as I knocked the rack over."

He nodded, contemplating everything I said. He was skeptical, which was understandable. "And this guy in the hoodie." He pursed his lips. "You're sure it wasn't just a mannequin?"

That question made me pause for a moment. Only a moment, though. "I'm sure. Because I saw him again under the stairs in the food court." Kaleb shook his head slowly, clearly having trouble believing me. "All of this happened around the same time Mitch got hit." I reminded him. Where I thought my emotions would come up again, I found the strength and determination to puzzle this out. "You heard what he said in the voicemail. He felt like he was being followed." I almost told him about the incident after my training but stopped myself. I only wanted to say it once. It could wait.

Kaleb was silent. Processing. He took a deep breath and let it out extra slowly. "Yep. Something's definitely happening."

I stared at him. Dumbfounded. After everything I just told him—"Wow."

"What?"

"That's all you have to say?"

His voice went high on the defense, "What am I supposed to say? 'It looks like we've got ourselves a mystery! Let me get Scooby and the gang!'" I knew he was trying to be funny, to bring me back from the cliff I was on, but I was already wobbling precariously on the edge.

"I don't know! Maybe just tell me I'm not crazy! That you'll help me figure it out!" I surprised myself with my raised voice.

His teasing eyes softened, and he reached for my hand in my lap. "Of course, I don't think you're crazy, Ray." He rubbed his thumb along my knuckles, calming me enough to take a deep breath. "You know I'll do what I can to help, but it's a lot to take in. *You're* not crazy, but the situation is."

He was right. It was crazy. He still didn't know just how crazy it was, though. Who knew what he would—or wouldn't—say when he found out about Kyler? "Yeah, I know." I gently pulled my hand from his grasp and placed both of mine under my thighs, telling myself it was because of the nerves. Not because holding his hand was making me *feel* things.

He brought his hand back to the steering wheel, and I couldn't help but notice he seemed a little hurt by my actions. But I didn't want to explore anything between us until I knew what was happening to me. There's no reason to possibly put him in danger, too, right? Although, if I was honest with myself, he was probably already at risk. The people I cared about always ended up hurt. Or dead.

Perhaps I should stop caring so much. Stop loving people. That way, no one could get hurt, including me.

But I knew that wasn't the solution. There's no telling the answer yet, but it's not that. If anything, I needed those closest to me to help me get through this. The people I cared about, they cared about me, too. That's why I was going to tell them everything. Even the things that seemed so strange they couldn't be possible. Like someone leaving a permanent handprint on me when they tried to stop me from face-planting. Just thinking about saying that out loud made my stomach churn. But I knew if I were to trust them to help me figure this out, they would need all the details. Of course, they already knew he saved me. They'd all seen that.

I rubbed the spot on my ribs absentmindedly, still wondering how it was possible, but came up blank. We wouldn't get answers without going straight to the source, but I wasn't willing to do that alone.

Kaleb parked the car, which brought me back to my senses. We got out and walked across the parking lot to Trader Joe's. He slung his arm around my shoulders as we walked. "Where'd you go just now?"

I comfortably wrapped my arm around his waist, giving him a slight squeeze. "I'm just trying to compile my thoughts about everything I have to tell you guys."

He nodded. "Does it include telling us where you snuck out today?"

My eyes widened. I hadn't thought about that. Should I tell them about my lessons? The girls would be surprised. Maybe Kaleb would, too. Perhaps it was time they knew what I was up to, though. "Maybe," I shrugged, trying not to make a big deal of it.

"Is this something you do often? Sneak off when you think no one will notice?" He raised an eyebrow at me as he grabbed a basket from the stack inside the door. I mirrored his look and snatched the basket from him, putting it back and grabbing a cart instead. He rolled his eyes.

"Guess you'll just have to wait and see, won't you?" I pushed past him with the cart toward the fresh produce aisle.

He caught up to me quickly and cleared his throat before saying louder than necessary, "You're not taking pole dancing classes, are you?"

The back of my hand smacked into his chest, and he coughed from the surprise impact. I pointed my finger in his face, "You—" But I couldn't help the giggle that escaped when I saw the shit-eating grin on his face. He threw back his head and laughed much louder than I had, and I knew then what he'd done. I squinted at him. "I hate you," I said, biting my lip to keep from laughing again. I turned back to the selection of produce, scanning the shelves for things to bring back to his house.

When his laugh quieted, I felt him step up behind me and lean down to whisper, "I'd come watch your shows if you were."

I whipped around to face him, "Kaleb!" I lowered my voice as heat crept into my cheeks, unsure why this time felt different from any other time he made a dirty joke. "That's so inappropriate." I forced myself to keep my scrunched-up face as I bit back a smile. I scanned the people around us, wondering if they heard what he said.

But Kaleb pointed at my face like he expected my nose to be crinkled and my lips to scrunch up, concealing that smile. "There it is. My favorite face." He winked, flicking my nose as I stuck my tongue out at him.

Unable to say anything without sounding flustered, I turned and started throwing stuff to snack on in the cart. We were in the protein section when I finally felt like the heat left my cheeks. I cleared my throat and asked, "What will you eat?"

"Anything you make." He grinned, grabbing some chicken and steak off the shelf and holding them up for me. "What would the ever-so-talented Chef Foster make with these?"

I bit my lip, tilting my head to consider the question. "Stir fry with the beef and alfredo with the chicken."

He thought about that momentarily before dropping both in the cart and pointing a finger at me. "You get whatever you need for the stir-fry, and I'll get the alfredo ingredients. We'll meet at the front." He spun on his heel and skipped away before I could say anything.

I yelled after him anyway, "You don't even know what to get!"

He waved me away over his head as if what I said was crazy, and he did his little hop-and-heel-click before disappearing around the corner. I shook my head as I tried to hide the grin on my face. He made me crazy sometimes, but he sure knew how to distract me and make me smile. I returned to the produce section to collect the ingredients for stir fry.

Several more people filled the area when I returned to the veggie aisle. Not surprising, though. It was always crowded in Trader Joe's. I waited until there was a small opening and reached in for a bag of sugar snap peas.

Someone else grabbed it at the same time.

My eyes followed the arm back to the person gripping the bag, and I released it, stepping out of the crowd. The most beautiful man I'd ever seen stepped back with me, his piercing blue eyes following my every move.

He still had the bag of peas in his hand as he stepped toward me, smiling brightly. He held the bag out to me, "Sorry, love." His accent was heavy, from somewhere in Europe. "Did you need these?"

My jaw dropped at the sight of his smile. I snapped it shut the moment I realized I looked like an idiot. Words weren't coming, so I just shook my head.

"You're sure?" He tilted his head like he knew I was lying. "It's the last bag." He gestured to the shelf with his head.

I couldn't stop staring to check if his statement was true. He extended the bag to me again. I glanced from the peas to him and back too many times. I shook my head and gave him a weird smile. Words sputtered out something like, "I'll jus— there are oth— I can grab— find some— different." Wow. How embarrassing. I smacked my hand to my forehead. It's just a guy with blue eyes. Nothing more. Why was he making me so flustered?

I dragged my hand slowly down my face to find him staring at me. "That was adorable." He smiled fully. It took my breath away. I tried to take a deep breath as he said, "What would you make?"

The question caught me off guard. I opened my mouth, moving my lips, but no words came out. *Come on, Rayleigh, speak!* "What makes you think I'm the cook?" *Sarcasm? Really?*

He held his hands up in defense. "Fair enough." He smiled and tossed the bag into my cart.

I pursed my lips, nodding my thanks. "Stir fry. With— with the beef." I pointed to the food already in the cart.

"Sounds delicious." He turned back to the shelf, mostly clear of people now. "I guess you'll probably need some of these, too, huh?"

He held up some bell peppers and a bag of broccoli.

I bit my lip, hiding my smile, and nodded. He dropped them into my cart. "You must be the chef in your house." He looked young but not quite as young as me. Maybe eighteen or nineteen. His blonde hair was cropped short, a little longer on top. His features were soft but defined. His skin was tan, and full lips surrounded his bright smile that he aimed my way again. I was staring. I dropped my gaze quickly, color blooming in my cheeks *again*.

He held out his hand. "I'm Aaidan."

I blinked.

His outstretched hand reminded me of the last time someone introduced themselves to me—how that hand later caught me and left a mark.

There was also someone following me.

Slowly, my eyes returned to Aaidan's face, and I tried to keep my shy smile from faltering. He didn't seem phased by my hesitation. Instead, he retracted his hand to where he was holding his basket and nodded as if he understood.

Doing a quick scan from head to toe, I looked for anything similar to a dark hoodie but found clothes that a college kid would wear. He didn't seem like a stalker type. In fact, he came off as genuinely nice. I bowed my head a little and said, "I'm Rayleigh." My first name wouldn't give him too much to go on if he *was* the person following me. "Sorry, I've just never seen someone this gorgeous in a grocery store." The words flew out of my mouth before I could stop them. *Did I really say that out loud?* I was trying to get away from this guy, not draw him in!

He laughed through his nose, a slight color popping into his cheeks as it was his turn to look away. "I could say the same." His blue eyes peered at me through his lashes.

The laugh that escaped me sounded more like a bark, and I slapped my hand over my mouth to prevent it from happening again. "Okay… I think I'm going to go now," I said behind my hand and started to walk away, but he stepped into my path a little—not completely blocking me, but enough to stop me.

"Was it something I said?" His smile faltered a little.

I pursed my lips. How could I tell him I think someone is stalking me, and I'm unsure who they are or what they want? And because of that, I don't know if I can trust anyone, especially a gorgeous man who happens to be reaching for the same bag of sugar snap peas at the grocery store, knows how to cook, and tells me that I am gorgeous. "No..." I took a deep breath. "I'm just—someone's waiting for me."

The tightened muscles in his face relaxed, and he nodded. "Ah. Well, then, you mustn't keep them waiting." He stepped out of my way and watched as I walked past him with a nod.

I dared a look over my shoulder to see him continuing to watch me walk away with a slight sadness in his eyes. He quickly went back to browsing the produce when I caught his gaze.

Continuing to the front of the store, I couldn't help but wonder if I'd just messed that up. And what for? Because I'm paranoid? What if Aaidan was a nice guy, and we just had our meet cute, only for me to ruin it?

The mixed feelings churned inside me as I searched the registers for Kaleb. I couldn't see him in any of the lines, so I hopped in one to wait for him. He shouldn't take too much longer. I was almost to the front of the line, and he still hadn't shown. I stood on my tiptoes to try and spot his curly brown hair, but he was nowhere to be found. My heart beat faster. *He's probably fine.* Maybe he's already in the car... I did talk to Aaidan for a bit. Perhaps he thought *I* was waiting by the car.

That was the only thing that made sense, so I checked out and headed outside.

But he wasn't there.

Okay...

Seeing as I didn't have the key, I left the groceries next to the car and headed back in to see if I'd missed him. My heart was racing.

I wasn't two steps from the car before someone grabbed me from behind. They wrapped both arms around me, trapping my own, and whispered into my ear, "You were right to hesitate." Chills ran down my spine.

Aaidan.

I pushed the panic down and set my jaw, calling on my training.

I dropped my weight, bent my knees, and followed the basic steps to escape his hold. It was the first maneuver my instructor ever taught me. I took him down in three moves and slid out of his grasp, standing back up in a crouch.

He quickly righted himself, a deadly smirk replacing the momentary look of surprise.

I wasn't running away this time. Kaleb was somewhere nearby, and I felt this guy had something to do with him missing.

Aaidan stalked towards me, "You really shouldn't have done that." He gave me a wicked grin, but I watched his steps, readying myself for his next move.

"I'm not scared of you," I said through gritted teeth.

But he wasn't looking at me anymore. I realized too late there was someone behind me. Another set of arms wrapped around me. This time, one covered my mouth with a cloth. *Shit!*

The last thing I saw before my vision faded to black was Aaidan's smiling face lowering with me as I fell.

XIII
Bones

The world was dark.

No, wait— there were little specks of light, like stars.

My head throbbed. I blinked slowly several times, willing the ache to go away. A faint light flickered through the covering on my head. It smelled musty, the fabric rough against my skin— a burlap sack.

Where am I?

The memories of how I got there were foggy... Kaleb and I were getting groceries. He made a dirty joke. I met a beautiful man—

Aaidan.

He took me from the parking lot. Drugged me. And Kaleb disappeared shortly before. Was he in danger, too? Panic fluttered in my chest at the thought.

I couldn't succumb to it, though. I had to focus and figure out where I was and what was going on. Everything else could wait until I got out of here—because I *was* getting out.

I assessed myself. I was bound to a chair by both ankles and a rope around my midsection. My hands were tied behind my back. All the ropes were tight enough that I could barely move. The one around my ribcage burned with every breath.

Wherever they brought me, it was warm and sticky. Through the musty smell of the sack, I could smell burning wood. A fire must be the source of flickering light. There was a steady drip of water nearby, and—

Voices. There were voices. But they were distant. Not in the same area as me.

The ropes stung, but I started wiggling my hands to reach the knot that held them together. When I found it, I groaned. There was more than one knot—at least three. Whoever tied me up expected me to try to escape. I fiddled with the rope enough to get the knot between my fingers and began working to undo it.

The voices grew louder— an argument seemed to break out. Steadying my breathing, I strained my ears to listen. There were two voices. Men. One sounded more authoritative than the other. If one was Aaidan, he faked the accent at the store. Clever.

My mind began clearing as the drugs wore off, even though the headache deepened. The muffled conversation became clearer, too, words piercing through whatever barrier separated us. While I could hear them, I still had a hard time understanding. Mainly because what I *could* hear didn't make sense.

"—but then what? Won't Gustav come here? Do we take her to him anyway?" Even without the accent, I knew that was Aaidan. My instinct in the store was correct. The charm and beautiful face could fool anyone. Yes, I'd listened to my gut, but mentally, I kicked myself for not thinking there could be more than one person stalking me.

"No, Adarachi," the other man said. His voice was oddly familiar, but I couldn't place where I'd heard it before. "First, we must ensure her Omada cannot interfere."

Aaidan scoffed, "I'm not scared of a few Kidemos. I was raised on their training grounds." The confidence that dripped from that statement made me roll my eyes. He couldn't even keep hold of me in the parking lot.

"She not only has some of the highest-ranking Kidemos but at least one Councilor assigned to her," the other man said. "I wouldn't be surprised if Mitera herself had a personal hand in her protection." That comment sounded a bit off-hand.

"Again," Aaidan sounded bored, "They don't scare—"

"Regardless," the man cut him off sternly, "Extracting her from this world has already proven difficult. I can't imagine it will suddenly be easier because you're here." *Ooo burn!*

There was so much to unpack in that tiny tidbit of conversation. First, what the hell was an Omada, and how did I have one without knowing it? Kidemos? A councilor? Who is Mitera? *This world?* I needed to figure out what those words meant—as soon as I got out of there.

The first knot around my wrist came loose, and I shoved my finger through to undo it completely. The second knot was harder to reach and somehow tighter. I focused back on the voices.

Aaidan spoke again, "So what do we do?"

Silence. Neither of them spoke for a few minutes. I took the time to take in more of my surroundings as best as I could without my vision. I turned my head this way and that, noticing that there was no other light source than the fire directly ahead of me. It had to be nighttime. How long had I been knocked out? An owl hooted, crickets chirped, and tiny squeaking noises joined the chorus of the crackling fire. The lack of car noises made it clear we were far from town and any roads.

"We will have to lure out her Omada," the other man finally said. "They will know we've captured her soon, especially if the nilatís is in place." I added the new word to my list of things to look up. My list of questions was growing longer with every word he said. I wondered if anyone I knew would have the answers. A lot of the terms they used sounded made up. "That buffoon of a boy was easy enough to take down, but her Omada will not be such easy opponents."

Was he talking about Kaleb? I knew it. They *were* the reason I couldn't find him at the store. I didn't want to think about what "take down" meant, but the idea of him being hurt made my blood run cold. I should have told him about seeing the hooded man again today. He wouldn't have left my side if he'd known. I had to get out of here. I had to find him.

My fingertips were becoming raw from the harsh rope material, making it impossible to tell if the second knot had loosened.

"She's awake," Aaidan said. *How could he possibly know that?* "I'm going to *talk* to her." My fingers froze on the rope as footsteps echoed closer.

"Aidi," the footsteps paused. There was silence for a moment. "Do not taunt her. Your tactics will make things worse."

The footsteps resumed, and the clicking of too-nice shoes echoed louder, becoming sharper with every step. The minute they were right next to me, the sack was yanked from my head, ripping some hairs out with it, and I bared my teeth at the prick before me. The fire was in front of me, just like I thought, but the room was not what I expected it to be. It was a cave, one that looked oddly familiar...

Aaidan towered over me with a sneer on his face. Those piercing blue eyes shone with hatred. "So. You're the one all the fuss is about, huh?" He grabbed my chin, forcing me to look up, and turned it side to side. "Well, you are quite the beauty, I said so in the store. But you aren't very bright, are you? Weren't you taught not to talk to strangers?" The familiar line struck a chord somewhere deep inside me. "They could be stalkers... or worse." His devilish smile made me snarl at him. "Was it my killer smile?" He flashed his full smile; the one that took my breath away hours ago now made me want to vomit.

My snarl deepened as I glared at him, which made him chuckle. He didn't care to look anywhere but at my face, so I continued working on the knots behind my back. I had no clue what to do once my hands were free, but it was better than sitting here doing nothing.

"Not going to talk now? No incoherent sentences or sassy remarks?" I hated that he saw that. That he now used it against me. Jackass. "Pity." He leaned into my ear and whispered, "I know how to make people talk, princess." I gagged dramatically, and he pulled back laughing. He placed his hands on my knees and squatted in front of me. The feeling of his hands on me made me want to throw myself into the fire. It felt disgusting. He gritted his teeth as he whispered, "My superiors won't give me any information, so that leaves me to question you. So tell me," he leaned in to spit the words in my face, "What makes you so important that the strongest members of the Kidemos were sent to protect *you?*" His finger punched my sternum on the last word, forcing me to grunt. He paused, waiting for an answer to his question. But I wouldn't give him the satisfaction, even if I did know what he was talking about.

When he realized I wasn't going to say anything, he stood and started pacing in front of me. "When Gustav found out where they had been assigned, he tracked their movements but could not, for the life of him, figure out why a *human girl* would need such protection."

He said "human" like a curse word. This man just told me there are more than humans in this world, and the idea made me nauseous.

He stopped before me, placing both hands on the back of my chair above my shoulders. "What did you do to earn their loyalty?" He yelled in my face, tipping the chair back a bit. I only held his stare, pursing my lips. "Answer me!" His face was twisted in... anger? Jealousy? When I didn't do as he said, he pushed my chair back fully, releasing it. I hit the ground so hard that a sharp cry of pain left me involuntarily. My arms hit first, smashed by my weight and the chair. It was possible that I wouldn't be able to use them if I managed to escape. My head hit the stone floor last, causing my vision to blur. The fall knocked the wind out of me, and my coughs sputtered. Finally, air reached my lungs, but even that wasn't a full breath due to the tight rope digging into my ribs.

Aaidan placed his foot on my chest and pushed. There was no way oxygen was getting in now. My arms screamed in pain as his weight forced them further into the rocky floor. The burning sensation on my torso increased. I wouldn't scream, though. That was what he wanted. I wouldn't give him the satisfaction of showing him the pain he was causing. "The entirety of the Kidemos is under my father's control." He leaned in close, adding more pressure on my chest. A strained gasp left me at the loss of air and the burning sensation. He spat the next words in my face, "To think a human whore like yo—"

"Adarachi!" The other man's voice echoed in the cave. "Watch your tongue, or I will have it cut out."

Aaidan sneered but removed his foot from my chest, allowing me to breathe fully. "Yes, Lochi." Aaidan grabbed my feet and pulled, tipping the chair back upright again.

The blood rushed from my already throbbing head, causing my vision to go black momentarily. My arms and hands radiated pain, but I didn't feel the familiar sharp pain of a broken bone. Watching

Aaidan closely, I returned to fumbling with the knot in my hands.

He stepped back, grasped his hands behind his back like a soldier, and started pacing before me. He lowered his voice, "Once you are back in Niccodra, we will take you straight to Gustav to figure out exactly who was trying to hide you and how they overpowered the Dikitís."

More names to add to the list. Shit, the list was getting long. What was this place they were taking me? Nicola? Was it a foreign country? No, he had said something about worlds. Another world? Oh my... There didn't seem to be a way out of this. Nothing was stopping them from taking me if I didn't escape. Aside from this group he kept mentioning. Armada? But no one was coming to rescue me. No one knew I was with Kaleb at the grocery store. If he wasn't hurt right now, I have no doubt he would be trying to find me and rush through that door with some dramatic "save the day" vibe he no doubt stole from one of his books.

The second knot at my wrists finally gave way, and I slowly pulled apart the knot, keeping one eye on Aaidan to be sure he didn't see. There was one more—the tightest one. I could do this.

"But the question remains." Aaidan hadn't stopped monologuing. He was in my face again, hands braced on my legs. I tried not to make it evident that my hands were working behind my back and gave him a disgusted look at his touch. "What makes you so special?" He worked his jaw, squinting at me. Studying me. "Only one person could override my father's control of the Kidemos." His eyes searched mine, narrowed, and slowly widened as his jaw dropped a little. "Could it be?" He stepped back, his gaze crawling down my body, making me cringe. An evil smile spread across his face. His whispered words were laced with cunning, "Of course, if that's the case, I'll bring you back and claim you myself. We will become the most powerful duo in all the realms." He bent down, his mouth by my ear again. "Doesn't that sound exciting?"

"UGH, NO!" I couldn't help my outburst. I pulled as far away from him as possible, but the chair and restraints kept me in place. The last knot was tight, but I couldn't give up now. I was so close. I had to keep him distracted.

"It speaks! Lovely." He started to pull away, but before he could get far, I slammed my head into his so hard that he stumbled back. Not as much as I expected him to, unfortunately, because that blow would have made an average man's nose shatter. My head, on the other hand, started spinning from the impact. Head butts weren't the best defense, but I—

His backhand followed so quickly I didn't even see it coming. My jaw took most of the blow, and my already blurry vision went black completely for longer this time. For a moment, I thought he knocked me out. The pain that radiated down my neck said otherwise. It traveled up to my temple and then settled back into the spot where his hand had met my face. Slowly, my vision restored, and I lifted my head, shooting daggers with my eyes. I tilted my head and spat. The blood that had pooled in my mouth landed at his feet, and I licked my lip where a cut opened from his strike.

Aaidan briefly regarded the blood, straightened himself, and rounded the chair to stand behind me. I wrapped the almost-done knot in my hand to hide my progress. "You'd better watch it," his mouth was right against my ear again. His breath was *hot*. "Or I'll make you scream so loud Gustav himself will hear you from Niccodra."

"Do I look like I care?" The words were more challenging to form, with my jaw throbbing, but I pushed through the pain anyway. "I'll scream if that's what you want." My mouth opened in preparation, but Aaidan's hand clamped over it just in time to muffle the scream. He jerked my head back violently. The motion made my neck pop, and another cry of pain ripped through me, muffled by his fingers. It made me look at the cave ceiling. It was so familiar, but I couldn't figure out *why*. It was like an itch I couldn't scratch.

"Adarachi!" The other man's clipped tone confirmed that he disapproved of what was happening. But he didn't show himself, which meant he wasn't about to make him stop either. "Hands off. Now."

My eyes followed Aaidan's hand as he removed it from my mouth and walked in front of me again. "I see you're trained to take orders like a little *bitch*," I said, unable to stop myself.

His backhand was so strong this time that the chair tipped over again but to the side. I landed straight on my arm. The snap I heard as I hit the ground was unmistakable and confirmed a broken arm before the pain set in. The only sound I let out was a grunt, and it blew a slew of dirt and pebbles away from my mouth that I was sure now dribbled blood onto the floor. My eyes watered profusely from the pain radiating through my entire body. The rope around my ribs pulled taut once more, and the burning sensation increased tenfold.

Aaidan crouched down in front of me, tilting his head to look straight at me with a rage of fire in his eyes. "Don't. Insult me. Again. Or this," he gestured to my tortured body on the ground, "is going to feel like a spa day compared to what I'll do." I glared at him through the tears in my eyes with as much rage as I could muster. He stood back up, jaw clenched and eyes unfocused. "Koladon is my Lochi, and I will respect him." His eyes focused on me again before he went on. "Now, what was I saying…" He started pacing in front of my prone body, not bothering to set me back up. He opened his mouth—

The sound of his voice cut off. As did every other sound in the room.

Another voice spoke, but it wasn't in my ears… it was *in my head*.

Rayleigh. The voice was unfamiliar but masculine and friendly. *If you can hear me, give me a slight cough. Slight.*

I hesitated. There was no way this was happening. It had to be an illusion I created. Aside from my inner voice, I never heard other voices in my head.

Scanning the room again, I saw Aaidan's mouth moving, but the sound didn't reach my ears. In fact, I couldn't hear anything. Not even the fire crackling feet away from me. It could be the result of a concussion. I wouldn't be surprised due to how many times my head hit the ground.

The men who kidnapped me were using words I'd never heard before, insinuating that there was an entirely different realm out there. If all of this was real…

Man, if I thought I was going crazy before, now I really had a list of reasons to believe it.

She can't hear me. You try. The voice was quirky and upbeat, even in this dire situation. Interesting. Perhaps this was one of my nightmares, and I was more active than usual. But if this was real, the voice in my head could be someone trying to help me. In either case, what would be the harm in playing along?

I coughed a little, as instructed, drawing Aaidan's attention momentarily as his mouth continued to move. He disregarded the noise, likely relating it to the injuries he had caused, and went back to monologuing without a voice.

Rayleigh! Right. Good. Okay. It is imperative not to let Adarachi know you have this line of communication. This was definitely a delusion. Who speaks like that? *We are nearing your location and closing in.*

Watching Aaidan for any hint that he was waiting for me to answer, I decided that he didn't necessarily like conversation and instead liked to hold an audience so he could run his foul, pretty mouth. I tried speaking to the voice in my head by answering with my inner voice. *Who are you? And how are you talking to me right now?*

A short silence. Maybe he hadn't heard me. But his reply came a second later: *Unimportant. Have you managed to untie your bonds yet?*

How had he known I was doing that? I answered anyway, *No. The last knot on my hands is too tight. There's also rope around my chest and one on my ankles.*

Focus on your hands.

With my right arm still pinned and broken, moving the muscles to work the knot was difficult and painful. I held it with my injured hand and used my other fingers to loosen the knot. It finally gave way. I stuck a finger in and pulled. *Done,* I said to the stranger, wrapping my hand around the undone rope to hide it, just in case.

Aaidan had stopped pacing but was facing the cave entrance. He must have been listening to the other man. What did he call him? Kool-Aid man?

The voice in my head returned, *Good. Now, we've blocked your audio sensors, but you must close your eyes when I give the signal. Is Adarachi looking in your direction?*

I shook my head, then realized they might not be able to tell I'd done that. *No, he's focused on something else.*

Okay. Okay. I need you to try and wiggle out of that rope around your midsection. It's disrupting your location. Were they tracking me? How? And how could a rope be blocking the signal? Then again, how was any of this happening... I decided not to question it and slowly moved my left hand from behind the chair. I bit down on a hiss of pain from the movement. Aaidan's back was to me now, so he couldn't see me in his peripherals. A mercy, honestly. The rope around my arms had loosened quite a bit from being thrown to the ground attached to the chair. It made it easier to shift my arm enough to pull the rope over my shoulder. It was lying across my chest when I noticed Aaidan starting to turn around.

Shit. The man's voice echoed my inner voice. He yelled, *Close your eyes!*

Aaidan had turned fully toward me, and his eyes traveled to my chest and arm, which were now primarily free. He took a step toward me, but I closed my eyes.

A great, hot wind hit me where I lay, causing pain down my trapped arm as it pushed me back slightly. Pebbles and rocks pelted my face. The floor shook violently. I squeezed my eyes shut tighter, not wanting any debris in them. I pursed my lips as best I could with one swollen and a throbbing jaw. A bright light flashed behind my eyelids, and something hit my leg, which was still tied to the chair. It took everything in me not to scream at the pain as my leg started to burn. I didn't dare open my eyes to see what happened. There were still things flying at me, slicing and pelting my exposed skin as I lay there, unable to move.

Then there were hands on me. I almost opened my eyes, scared that it was Aaidan, but the touch was soft. Feminine. They were removing the rope around my chest. She then gently pushed the chair I was on, turning me on my back and helping me carefully pull my trapped arm from under it.

Another set of hands worked on the rope at my ankles. It felt like they were sawing instead of untying.

My auditory sense came back. The crackle of the fire had intensified, and there was loud shouting from somewhere else in the cave. The smell of smoke filled my nose, and suddenly, my lungs and I started coughing violently.

"Shit!" The feminine voice near my head hissed. "Her body can't handle the smoke!"

There was a grunt, followed by a splash of water. A wet cloth slapped against my chest. The feminine hands grappled for it, taking my left hand and placing it over my nose and mouth before putting the damp cloth on it. I gasped in the smoke-free oxygen and squeezed my eyes shut tighter. The smoke was making them burn.

The hands at my ankles resumed sawing the ropes, and they finally broke free. An arm slid under my knees. The other tried to slide under my shoulder blades. The chair's structure made it difficult, so the feminine hands lifted my shoulders, allowing the other person to reach under me completely. Their hand clamped down on my injured arm, and I cried out in pain before they could lift me.

The hands under me halted, loosening tightly as the feminine voice at my head spoke again. "Rayleigh, he has to carry you out of here."

"My arm. I think it's broken." My voice sounded like a frog.

The feminine hands gently lifted my right arm away from my body and laid it across my chest. Her hands avoided the break, but pain still shot through my arm, causing me to whimper. Once my arm was settled, the man gripped my ribcage instead and lifted me off the ground. He tilted me toward him slightly to keep my right arm from flopping off my chest.

"Keep your eyes closed." The woman said.

I had no idea who these people were, but I had to trust they were there to help me. To save me.

The man started moving. The heat dissipated. He must have been running because a breeze whipped my hair across my face. I didn't have time to think about how he could move quickly while carrying my weight. I wasn't even helping to hold myself up.

The cloth over my mouth became hot, making breathing difficult, so I pulled it away to see if we'd reached fresh air. The cool breeze that met my face was most welcome, and I took a big gulp of air. It still smelled like smoke, though. Based on how much I just inhaled, I figured we all must have carried the scent out of the cave.

I rubbed my eyes to see if I could unstick them, but they wouldn't budge.

We stopped moving.

"Oh, thank Mitera!" A masculine voice said. I recognized it as the one I heard in my head. It came from near my feet. "Here. Put her here." A vehicle door opened. The man holding me maneuvered me to lie down on the seat, and then the door slammed.

Three people rescued me. One hadn't uttered a word— the one who carried me. I wondered why. I tried opening my eyes again, but they were stuck. They must have been drier than I thought. The other doors to the car opened, and my three rescuers must have climbed in all at once, the car shifting under all their weight. The feminine hands lifted my head from the seat and slid into the empty spot, laying my head in her lap before closing the door. Before I could protest, a sudden wave of exhaustion hit me, and I couldn't fight it. My consciousness slipped away as the car started to move.

XIV
Ease My Mind

The sound of birds chirping greeted me as I woke. My eyes were sticky and dry, but I pried them open as far as possible. Sunlight filtered through a curtained window. My body felt stiff and sore, but I pushed myself into a sitting position anyway, arms protesting the weight I put on them.

The bed I was in was *huge* and unfamiliar. It was covered in a fluffy white comforter and surrounded by a canopy of curtains tied off on the poles. Looking around the room, I saw a wardrobe, a small nightstand with what looked like a hand-crafted lamp, and a desk with a chair next to the window.

Two doors sat on adjoining walls, one open and one shut. The open one led to a bathroom, where a light glowed from inside, and the closed door must open to a central room or hallway. Twin glass doors led outside to what appeared to be a patio or balcony.

I ran my hands along the soft sheets and blankets around me, trying to remember how I got to this strange, beautiful room. My hands were clean, not a scratch on them. Following the path up, I examined my arms. A faint green bruise lay just above my elbow. What caused that?

A crack echoed in my head.

Everything came rushing in.

Aaidan.

Kidnapped.

Abused.

Tortured.

Strange names and words.

Rescued by… someone.

I mentally assessed my body, recalling every injury I felt the night before. My right arm had snapped but now only had a slight bruise. I looked for the burns on my wrists I knew I'd gotten while trying to undo the bonds, but there were none. My hand flew to my face, my jaw. Where it should have been swollen, I just felt soft, clean skin. My fingers trailed along my lips, where I remember tasting blood, but they were smooth and unharmed.

Moving slowly, I lifted the fluffy white comforter from my legs and took in the sight of them. Where I was sure I'd be covered in blood, dirt, and bruises, I only saw clean, bare legs. A long scar bisected my calf. It wasn't from any of my previous accidents, and I have no idea what caused it.

No other signs of injury. Anywhere. *What the hell…*

I looked down at the silky nightgown I wore. I'd never seen it before, nor would I have bought it for myself under any circumstances. While it was relatively comfortable, it seemed a bit too skimpy and revealing for pajamas. For a brief moment, I wondered how I'd gotten into the gown but realized the people who saved me must have cleaned me up and changed me. I wasn't sure whether to be mortified or thankful, but I chose the latter. I was alive.

I racked my brain, trying to think of any details to help me determine who saved me from Aaidan and the Kool-Aid Man. Had I just been saved from those monsters to be captured by new ones? I was in an unfamiliar place, taken by unfamiliar people. Sure, they saved me, but where had they *taken* me?

I scooted to the edge of the bed, my body protesting at the movements. The stiff muscles didn't feel like they were from the injuries I acquired but more like I hadn't used them in a while. I suddenly wondered if the incident had only happened last night. I could have been knocked out for days, for all I knew.

When my feet hit the ground, a pair of slippers sat there waiting. Squinting at them, I elected to ignore them and go barefoot. They looked like they would be hard to run in if needed, and I was highly considering it.

Pushing myself to stand proved difficult as my legs threatened to give out, but I held firmly to the bed until they got used to bearing my weight again. I attempted to take a step, but my knee gave way as I transferred my weight. I hit the ground. Hard.

Footsteps outside my door and a knock broke the silence before a soft feminine voice said, "Rayleigh? Are you okay?"

The voice. She was the one who saved me.

My throat strained as I tried to speak, "Yes." I managed to get out. Then, clearing my throat, I changed my answer. "Not really." I rolled my body to sit and slowly pulled my knees to my chest.

"Can I come in?" The voice was light and warm—sweet, even. I didn't know who she was, why she saved me, or what was planned for me here. I hesitated momentarily before deciding I couldn't sit on the floor forever. Plus, I needed help and answers. Maybe she would give them to me.

"Yes." I tried to arrange my nightgown so it wasn't indecent and heard the door open.

A pair of blue-green eyes peered in with a curtain of brown hair. She smiled sweetly and fully entered the room, closing the door behind her. She immediately came to my side and offered her hands to help me, not saying a single word about me being on the floor. "Do you want to sit in the chair or back on the bed?"

I took her hands, releasing the nightgown, making it slide up my thighs, but she focused on my face, waiting for my answer. If someone bathed and clothed me, it was probably her. At least, I hoped it was. She tugged on my hands, and I used what muscle I could to help her without them protesting too much. "Chair, please." She quickly pulled me to my feet, letting go with one arm to slide it around my waist. She used her other to hook my arm around her shoulders. Taking most of my weight, she walked me over to the chair at the desk.

I plopped down heavily, and she walked over to the nightstand, grabbed the glass of water I had overlooked, and brought it to me. "Drink this. It'll help you recover faster." I grabbed the glass, squinting at her choice of words, but took a sip. It was water, but it had a sweet taste to it. It didn't hurt, so I took a bigger gulp and instantly felt my body sigh in relief. I finished the glass, and she refilled it with a pitcher that I had also, apparently, overlooked. When the second glass was gone, she watched me set it down on the desk and asked with a knowing but cautious smile, "Better?" I nodded. She sighed with relief and sat on the floor in front of me. Casual. Comfortable. Like she'd known me for years. "You must have a lot of questions."

I blinked. That was... easy. I regarded her with quiet curiosity. She looked back with an open expression, seemingly hiding nothing and everything within that gaze. She didn't push me. She didn't say anything else. She simply waited for me to respond. Odd behavior for someone if they were holding me captive. I squinted at her. "I'm not sure where to start." She smiled as if she knew that was what I would say first. But then, I couldn't stop the words that spilled out, "I guess... who are you? Where am I? Who were the other two men? Why was I kidnapped? What is going on?"

She gave a light laugh, holding up her hands to slow me down. "There they are." She put her hands down to rest in her lap and took a deep breath. "My name is uh—" She stopped short, cleared her throat, and continued. "Mari. You can call me Mari. You're at a safe house. The other two men are my partners. There are a lot more details to go with why you were kidnapped, but I don't think I am the best person to relay those. My partner Theo will have more information to give you when you're ready."

My breathing was much steadier than it should have been then, but I assumed it was due to Mari's calm responses. I geared up to ask more questions when it hit me. No one knew where I was. I'd been kidnapped, saved, then brought here. The last person I'd been with was... *Kaleb.*

My gaze shot to Mari, "I was at the store with my friend when I was taken." My voice shook, and my hands joined. I squeezed them between my thighs. The words 'take down' echoed through my head, and my vision blurred, but I blinked the tears away. "The men who kidnapped me said— said that they took him down?" The last word barely choked out past the lump in my throat.

Mari reached out a hand to comfort me, hesitated when I flinched away and decided to put it back in her lap. "He's okay," she reassured me, and I felt like I could finally take a deep breath, albeit shaky. "What's his name?" she asked gently.

"Kaleb," I squeaked out. Something inside me told me she already knew that but wanted me to say it—to hear it myself. Tears welled up again, and I dropped my gaze to my hands. I didn't know what I would do if Kaleb were hurt, especially if it were my fault. I'd already lost too many people. I couldn't lose him, too.

Mari's voice was soft when she spoke again, a level of understanding that made me meet her gaze again. "Kaleb is fine. He was knocked out just like you were, but he is safe." She stood up suddenly and went into the bathroom, immediately returning with a tissue box. I grabbed one and wiped away the tears that managed to escape. She set the box down on the desk behind me and resumed her seat on the floor. "The rest of your family is safe, too." My head shot up at that. I didn't even think they would be in trouble. She continued before I could ask her to elaborate. "We have them under our protection. They know what happened and that we have you here."

Jordin probably freaked out and refused to leave Mitch. Chief would have kept her company, assigning himself as her personal guard. And if Mari sent someone else to assist him, they were probably in good hands. Depending on what Mari told them exactly, Chief probably insisted that he had it covered anyway. He was close with Jordin, making me wonder if anything else had ever happened between the two— this was not the time to think about that. The point was, she was safe.

Kaleb and the twins, however... They were family, too. I hoped that when Mari said 'the rest of your family,' she also meant them. If they were smart, they would send someone to the school. The thought brought up more questions, but my brain couldn't process them quickly enough, so I focused on where I was and decided to start there.

I adjusted myself in the chair, folding one of my stiff legs under me, "How long have I been here?"

She looked to the door, silent momentarily, as if she were listening to something, then turned back to me. "You've been asleep for almost three days."

"*Three days??*" My jaw dropped. Three days. So much could happen in that amount of time. Kaleb was probably worried because he had been there when I was kidnapped. Jordin was perhaps too preoccupied with Mitch and keeping him company in the— My gaze shot to Mari. "My— my brother! He was in a co— he was hurt. He —"

"Rayleigh." Mari was on her knees in front of me, careful not to touch me, but held her hands up to get me to calm down. "Mitchell is fine." The sound of his name made my heart lurch. How did she know my family? "Remember? I said your family is *safe*." Her eyes darted between mine, worry shining through her blue-green gaze.

"What does *safe* mean?" My voice cracked. "These last few days, I have felt anything *but* safe. The man in the hoodie, Mitch being hit by a car, the nightmares, the kidnapping—" My heart was racing. Breathing became difficult. The room started spinning.

Mari placed her hands on the arms of the chair; her mouth was moving, but the words were silent. The noises in my head drowned her out. She sat back on her heels and disappeared from my vision.

I couldn't get oxygen to my lungs.

My vision started to fade.

Something pressed against my ear.

A voice broke through the noise in my head.

"Rayleigh?"

A sob tore through me.

Kaleb.

"I'm here." His voice was distant. "Right here. You're safe." He let out a breath. "Breathe in."

It took everything in me to focus on that breath through the sobs.

He did it with me. "Breathe out."

When I did, the blackness in my vision started to fade, and Mari came into focus in front of me. She was kneeling and holding a phone to my ear. She gestured to the phone as if she wanted me to take it.

"Are you with me?" Kaleb's voice came through the phone.

I put my shaking hand on the phone, taking it from Mari, and said, "Yes." My voice was quiet, eyes filled with tears.

Mari stood and backed up to the door, "I'll be right back." At my nod, she opened the door and disappeared, closing it behind her.

Kaleb's sigh of relief brought my attention back to the phone. "Are you okay?" I choked out.

"You're asking me if I'm okay? Are you serious?" His low chuckle made me smile through a sob. "You were kidnapped by some maniacs who *tortured you,* and you're worried about me?" I could almost hear his head shaking through the phone. "You are unbelievable." I could hear the smile, too.

I gave a breathy laugh. "Well, I *know* I'm okay. At least, I think I am." I took in the unfamiliar room again, hoping to learn more about my situation soon. "But I didn't know what happened to you after—" I couldn't bring myself to finish the sentence. I didn't know what he knew, and I didn't know what I was willing to tell him yet. I needed to learn more about why I was kidnapped. And why I was being held in a safe house. I needed to know what those men were talking about. The list of strange words and names still in my head. I needed to put it on paper so I could get some answers.

"I know, Ray." Kaleb sighed loudly. "I don't remember anything either. I woke up on the bathroom floor to some store employee banging on the door. It was like I lost time or blacked out. I don't even remember going to the bathroom." As he spoke, I realized they must not have told him he was attacked. A full breath hit my lungs, knowing he hadn't been hurt. "When I went looking through the store for you, I ran into, uh, that girl— Mari? She seemed calm but told me someone had kidnapped you. I immediately started trying to fight past her and ask her what she meant and how she knew. She just walked me out of the store and told me she would save you." He laughed a short, sharp chuckle. "I didn't believe her until I saw who she was with." He paused at this, letting out a loud sigh. Clearly, he wasn't saying something. It made me wonder who this Theo person was. Or was it her other partner? When he spoke again, it seemed like he was clenching his teeth. "They told me to go home and stay there. That I would only get in the way. Before I could protest, they took off. I tried to follow them, but I was too slow. I couldn't keep up. So I did what they said. I went home and waited." He paused again, letting out a frustrated sigh. "Her *partner*," he bit that word out, "knocked on my door a few hours later to inform me you were at a safe house. He told me you were healing, needed time, and would keep me updated. Then left before I could ask any questions." This time, his sigh seemed to release deeper emotions he hadn't addressed fully. His voice was low when he spoke again. "When he knocked on my door just now, he thrust the phone in my hand and walked away. I knew it was you before I put the phone to my ear." He sniffled. "I was so worried about you, Rayleigh." He went quiet, but I heard his breathing hitch in the silence.

The tears flowed freely down my face, but I let them fall. I don't know what Kaleb would have done if he had found me or how he could have helped. But the fact that he tried to get there… "I don't deserve you."

"Says the person who was just kidnapped and tortured and had the audacity to ask if *I* was okay." He laughed.

I echoed his laugh with a small one of my own. They'd told him I was kidnapped and tortured, and I was in a safe house, but did they tell him why? Did he know any of the details of who captured me? Did he know who the people who saved me were? I carefully worded my next question, "Have they told you anything else?" I still wasn't sure what I wanted him to know, wondering if keeping him in the dark was better than telling him everything I heard when I was captured.

"Nothing." He clicked his tongue. "Just that you'll be back to school on Monday."

"School?" The thought seemed absurd. After everything that had happened to me, how was I supposed to return to school? To a normal life? I figured Kaleb wouldn't know the answer, so I filed it away in the questions to ask Mari when she returned. "I guess that makes sense."

A knock at my door made me jump, but it was just Mari. "My

partners will be returning soon." She came in and closed the door. "We should get you cleaned up." While I didn't feel dirty, a hot bath sounded lovely. Maybe it would help my sore muscles.

Kaleb spoke again, "I'll try to call you later."

I nodded to Mari but said to Kaleb. "Thank you. For always being there for me. And making me feel safe."

He was quiet momentarily, then spoke softly, "You will always be safe with me, Rayleigh." The call cut off, and I pulled the phone away from my ear, placing it in Mari's outstretched hand.

She transferred the phone to her pocket and reached her hand out to me again. I looked up to her sweet, smiling face. She was waiting to help if I wanted it.

Nodding, I took her hand, and she gently pulled me off the chair. My legs wobbled, but they were stronger than earlier.

"I drew a bath for you before you woke up. It should still be hot." I had no idea how she knew I'd like a bath. But I was thankful and let her lead me to the bathroom.

A giant tub filled with steaming water sat in the middle of the bathroom. Various soaps and shampoos lined the edge. She slowly released my hand to let me walk on my own while she retrieved a towel from a cupboard under the sink and set it on a stool near the tub.

"I'll just be in the other room if you need anything. When you're done, you can put that on." She pointed to a robe hanging on the wall. "I will find you something to wear while you bathe and leave it on your bed."

She turned to leave. "Mari." She stopped in the doorway, her hand on the frame, and looked back over her shoulder. "How did you know to call Kaleb?"

She sighed. "Kaleb told my partner you suffer from panic attacks. He said he could help if needed. He thought you might not be doing so well after... well after you woke up."

My heart did something funny, but I tried to ignore it. "Thank you. For that." Thinking there was much more to thank her for, I added, "And for... everything else."

She gave a shy smile, "Anytime." Then she was gone.

I stripped off the nightgown and slid into the steaming hot water, hissing as it climbed up my legs and covered my whole body. It was a welcomed pain. The questions started running through my head as my body absorbed the liquid heat and my muscles relaxed.

It seemed everything I knew was about to change, so I relished in these last few moments of calmness. I closed my eyes and blocked out all thoughts and questions to enjoy the warm bath.

XV
As It Was

Mari had left a note on my bed, saying there were some choices for clothes in the wardrobe. I swung it open and stepped back in awe. There were definitely options. Ranging from a midnight blue, floor-length gown that looked like the stars had been sewn into it to oversized sweats to more of those silky nightgowns. At the bottom was a range of shoes and a basket of socks and undergarments. The question of how she knew what size I was in all these things crossed my mind, but I just added it to my mental list. I needed a notebook. I settled on leggings and a Wisteria Heights crewneck and grabbed some thick, fuzzy socks for my cold toes.

Once dressed, I sat on the edge of the bed, wondering if Mari would know to get me or if I should open the door and call for her. I was about to do just that when a knock came at the door. I stood, "Come in." Mari peeked her head in, but when she saw I was standing and ready, she opened the door fully. She leaned against the doorframe, making it possible to see the long, endless hallway behind her. How big was this place?

"I've prepared some food. We could only get you to drink the gl—" she cleared her throat, "the sweet water while you recovered. You must be starving." My stomach growled in response, and her mouth twitched as I tried to cover the source of the noise with crossed arms. "It's waiting in the kitchen—if you're ready?"

My feet didn't immediately move toward the promised food. I realized why a moment later, "Are your... friends back?" For some reason, the way Kaleb reacted to whoever Mari's partner was made me not want to interact with them just yet.

I wasn't sure whether the bodily shakes were from hunger, weakness, or nervousness. My anxiety was keeping me on edge. There was so much out of my control. Everything was still unknown. It was like floating down a river with a waterfall at the end. I couldn't see the waterfall or where it led. I'd probably survive the fall, but who knew what would happen when I was on the other side? Only time would tell. I didn't think I could keep food down while meeting new people simultaneously. My life was about to change. Drastically. I just wanted to eat in peace before everything flipped on its head.

"Not yet," Mari said. "Theo got held up at the hospital. Niko should be here soon, though." Nodding, I stepped into the hall, and she led me to the kitchen.

Through the winding hallways, I took in everything I could. The house was enormous, with so many doors to so many rooms. Some were open, but most were closed. One of the open doors revealed a piano with windows from floor to ceiling, looking out to the forest directly outside. It was beautiful. I only caught a small glimpse of it before we turned down a different hallway.

These walls held paintings and other decor on built-in shelves for display. Some paintings were of intricately detailed flowers. Others were mythical creatures like unicorns grazing in a pasture, wolves the size of bears, and dragons among the clouds or on top of mountains. Some paintings depicted human-like creatures with features that defined them as something non-human, such as pointed ears, wings like fairies, or textured skin, but all of them were otherworldly beautiful.

Perhaps this other world those men mentioned the other night did exist, and these were some of the creatures that inhabited it. Either that or whoever chose these paintings *really* liked mythical creatures.

A painting we passed caught my eye enough to make me pause. It was stunning. I couldn't tear my eyes away. It was a male and a female, both very human-like, but their features were sharper. More defined. That otherworldly beauty seemed to make them come alive. She was effortlessly beautiful, with light brown skin that shimmered along her cheeks, long black hair that shone like a raven's wings, and bright green eyes that bore into my soul, even through the painting. With an arm wrapped possessively around her waist from behind, the male stood a foot above her, black hair framing his face in waves, and his dark brown eyes focused on her. He had tattoos wrapped around his arms and coming up the side of his neck. They both wore elegant clothing. Her dress was midnight blue, low cut, hugging her in all the right places. The fabric seemed to glow and sparkle in several spots. It seemed oddly familiar to the one in my wardrobe. He wore a matching dark button-up unbuttoned enough to show off some of his tattoos on his chest, and the sleeves were rolled up to the elbows. On their heads, propped just above slightly pointed ears, were small circlets of white gold. Crowns. They stood on a dais, an intricately detailed throne behind them. The room was painted black with a silver trim, matching the throne.

Before I could step closer to examine the details, Mari stepped up beside me, "Beautiful, aren't they?"

They really were. "Who are they?"

She was silent for a moment and then looked at me with something like admiration. "You have so much to learn," she said. Her gaze fell, and she bowed her head slightly. "But again, I'm not the one to tell you," she looked back at the painting. "But these two are some of the most important people where you come from. They're also the reason you're alive."

My gaze shot to hers, my jaw slack and eyes wide. I couldn't form the words buzzing in my head into a coherent sentence, so I shifted my gaze back to the painting. To those beautiful creatures and gawked at them. Why did they save me? Who were they? How did they know who I was? Their features and beauty alone told me they weren't from this world. Which would confirm what that man— the Kool-Aid man — said about another world. I swallowed thickly. I wondered how I could be a part of this other realm if the standard for the folks who lived there looked like that.

"Come on," Mari spoke softly from next to me, lightly touching my back to lead me away from the painting. "Let's get some food in you before Niko gets here." As we walked away from the picture, I promised to return and study it when I had more time.

The hallway opened to a vast room lined with bookshelves, each filled with books from floor to ceiling. Before I could stop to admire the collection, Mari nudged me again into the kitchen. I filed it away as a room I'd have to come back and explore if only to wonder how many of the books Arabella would pick up if she were the one here instead.

My jaw hit the floor when we walked into the kitchen. "I wasn't sure what you'd be hungry for, so I put some of everything out." She wasn't kidding. When she said she prepared some food, I wasn't expecting the assortment I found on the island counter. It was like a charcuterie board but included the entire kitchen pantry. There was pasta, pizza, cereal, meats and cheeses, crackers, a veggie tray, and a fruit bowl. I think there was even some sushi on one end of the counter.

"I don't think I can eat all of this," I said, walking up to the counter and grabbing a plate to fill to appease the growl in my stomach.

Mari shrugged, "Whatever you don't eat, the boys and I will."

I glanced over my shoulder, narrowed my eyes, looked her up and down, and said, "Please tell me there's more than just the two of them."

She barked a laugh, the sound beautiful and happy. "You don't know the boys. They can eat *a lot*." She shook her head at something, perhaps a memory I had no idea about, and took a plate for herself. "Eat whatever you want, though. Niko is about ten minutes away. Theo will be here shortly after." She piled some food on her plate, rounded the island, and jumped to sit on the counter by the sink, stuffing a bite of pizza in her mouth as she said, "Are you feeling better after your bath?"

Grabbing myself some pizza, along with some veggies, I nodded. "My muscles seemed sore after—" Visions reeled through my mind of all the reasons my body could have been sore: the nightmares, training, fighting, being tortured— "Well, everything." I thought about my injuries from the incidents and sat heavily on a stool at the end of the island. "Wasn't I injured when you... saved me?" I did another assessment in the bath, and knowing how long I'd been asleep made me wonder how I healed from such injuries so quickly. She answered most of my questions earlier, and I figured this one was innocent enough. She didn't respond immediately, leaving me time to eat some of the food I'd grabbed as I waited for her answer. The minute that first bite hit my tongue, my body turned ravenous, like it hadn't been fed in a few days. Which, I suppose, it hadn't. I devoured everything on my plate, barely breathing in between bites as Mari took her time answering, finishing her slice of pizza.

"You were," she paused. It was almost like she wouldn't say anything else, but she continued quietly, watching me cautiously. "Over the last few months, your body has developed special abilities that help you heal faster."

I slowed my chewing, contemplating her words, realizing they kind of made sense. Ever since Dad's death and the promise I made him, I'd been more committed to not getting hurt. But when it did happen, the injuries seemed to heal far quicker than they should have. The scratch on my shoulder from the nightmare had healed by that evening, leaving only a scar as evidence that it had even happened. The same could be said for other minor scratches or bruises. Whatever injuries I got from my time tied to that chair had healed, too. But didn't I have a broken arm? That surprised me the most. And just because it made sense didn't mean I couldn't be weirded out by it. *And I was.* But the whole reality of the situation hadn't settled in yet, so I tucked away the information, deciding to process it later.

I returned to the counter, piling more food on my plate, and found a pouch of pop-tarts hiding behind the bowl of pasta. There were also flaming hot Cheetos in the mix, so I snatched those and some cream cheese before sitting down again.

Mari was gaping at me from her spot on the counter with a hint of a smile in her eyes. She closed her mouth as she slowly shook her head, trying and failing to hide her smile. I gave her half a grin and shrugged, shoving a spoonful of pasta in my mouth.

She jumped off the counter to rummage through the food again herself and stepped back to lean on the counter with several slices of cheese and crackers in her hand. "When Theo gets here, he'll probably want to take you to his study to talk."

Being alone in a room with someone I didn't know made me freeze mid-bite. My eyes must have shown the fear I suddenly felt because she walked over and sat at my feet.

"Don't worry. I'll be there too. So will Niko." I wasn't sure if another person being there made it worse or better. I was just held hostage in a cave by two men I didn't know. I closed my eyes, reminding myself that these people saved me from that torture. Probably saved my life. They took me from an unknown, scary situation and brought me to another unknown but not-so-scary situation. But they said I could go back to school on Monday. Although that was something Kaleb told me, so I still wasn't sure if that was true. "We won't hold you here against your will, Rayleigh."

My eyes popped open as my eye twitched at her. How could she have known that was where my train of thought ended up? What she said settled something inside me, though—calmed me. I was safe. For now. I took a deep breath and finished off my pasta. My stomach was bursting at the seams. Before anything else could grab my attention from the piles of food, I stood and took my plate to the sink. I'd save the Pop-Tarts and Cheetos for later.

As I was washing the plate, I asked, "If I go back to my normal life, will you guys still be…" I trailed off, not knowing what word to use, but settled on, "Guarding me?" I wasn't sure what that meant, but I was confident things would look completely different come Monday.

"Yes, but— Well… you see—" Her stumbling over her words reminded me so much of myself that I peered over my shoulder to see her fidgeting with her hands in her lap. Her cheeks had turned a shade of pink.

I took a deep breath and quietly said, "I can handle it."

She glanced at me through her lashes to see my eyebrows raised expectantly. When she let out the breath she'd been holding, the words spilled out so fast that I made her repeat it. "We've already inserted ourselves into your daily routine."

I blinked at her. Tilting my head to the side, I tried to get myself under control and turned back to the sink. The sponge was squeezed tightly in my hand, covering it with suds. I placed my hand and the plate under the running water, contemplating her words. "What, exactly, do you mean?"

Before she could answer, a door opened and closed. I glanced at where the noise came from at the other end of the kitchen.

My grip on the plate tightened, but the soapy suds made it slip from my hands. I heard it clatter in the sink and felt something slice my hand, but I ignored the pain.

My heart rate kicked up, but not because I was panicking.

No. This was something else entirely.

Red clouded my vision.

Leaning back against the door frame, the familiar figure pulled a lollipop from his mouth and smirked. "Hey, Sunshine."

XVI
Play With Fire

No.

This couldn't be happening.

Kyler pushed off the doorframe and stalked toward me with a smug smile.

Mari was next to me instantly, grabbing my arm and trying to pull me away from the sink. Her mouth was moving, but I couldn't hear her. The buzzing in my head was drowning out all sounds. Anger surged through my veins as I glared at Kyler.

Why him? Why did it have to be him?

Pain radiated up my arm, making me inhale sharply and pulling my attention to my hand. Blood dripped on the floor from a considerable gash there. Mari was trying to stop the bleeding with a towel. The buzzing subsided enough for me to hear, "Put pressure on it. I'm going to get the first aid kit."

"She'll be fine," Kyler drawled, leaning against the island now. He waved around that damn lollipop as he stared at me. "Won't you, *Sunshine?*" He popped the candy into his mouth and crossed his arms.

I set my jaw, turned away from him, and closed my eyes. I didn't have to answer him. *Breathe in.* I could ignore him. *Breathe out.* I could block him out. *Breathe in.*

"Careful," Kyler whispered next to my ear, and I could feel his breath. "You might start breathing fire."

Breathe in. The scent of the lollipop flooded my senses. Strawberry. *Breath in.* "If you don't take a step back, I'm going to shove that lollipop down your throat."

The breath of his chuckle set my teeth on edge. *Breathe in.* "I'd like to see you try."

Breathe. Out. My eyes shot open, and I grabbed the first thing I saw with my uninjured hand. I whipped around, aiming for his opposite shoulder. He caught my wrist. But I'd been expecting that. I dropped the weapon into my waiting bloody hand. I aimed for his waist.

He used my momentum against me and spun me with his grip, pulling my back flush against him. He held me there with a tight grip on my uninjured wrist across my collarbone. "Predictable," he whispered in my ear, ripping my weapon of choice from my hand. "You tried to stab me with a spoon?" He gave a low chuckle.

"The spoon was a distraction." While he was talking, I had planted a foot on the cabinet door in front of me. Using it for leverage, I threw my head back and pushed off the cabinet simultaneously. He made a choking sound mixed with a grunt. I used my free hand to grab the wrist that held me, slipping under his arm to drop down and twist out of his hold. I pushed him toward the sink, twisting his arm behind his back to pin it. His abdomen slammed into the countertop. The lollipop flew out of his mouth with the impact. I leaned in to whisper, "Don't. Underestimate me." I released him, leaving a bloody handprint on his wrist, and reached for the lollipop in the sink. I rinsed it off in the still-running water and popped it in my mouth. I may have added a little sway in my hips as I walked away and leaned on the island.

Laughter rang across the kitchen. Mari stood in the doorway, gawking. Her eyes shifted between Kyler and me, holding back a full-mouthed smile. Kyler pushed himself off the edge of the sink, clenching his jaw. He shot daggers at me with his bright green eyes.

I didn't hide my grin. My hand stung. My head was spinning. There was blood soaking the sleeve of my sweatshirt. But I didn't care. That was exhilarating. The satisfaction I had from beating him was worth it all. My instructor once told me my greatest strength was that people would underestimate me. I didn't look like someone who could kick someone's ass or hold my own. They would try to take advantage of that and be sorely disappointed when I handed them their ass.

I slid the lollipop from my mouth, waving it at him before I plopped it back on my tongue. He rubbed his wrist where I'd twisted it. It was covered in blood, and when he noticed, he put it under the still-running water to wash it off.

Mari was in front of me then, tending to my wound. She wasn't holding back her smile anymore. "I've never seen that before."

"What?" I asked, pulling the lollipop from my mouth and studying it. I wasn't sure why I'd grabbed it or put it in my mouth. Something inside me thought it would give an extra "screw you" that I couldn't pass up.

Mari's eyes were sparkling with wonder. "Kyler losing."

"What did Niko lose?" The new, chipper voice came from the same door Kyler entered through.

"Nothing," Kyler grumbled, drying his hands off and reaching behind me for a slice of pizza. He leaned back against the sink and ripped into it with his teeth. Rage radiated off him. This was far from over between us.

"His lollipop." Mari grinned. "Rayleigh bested him." Her grin didn't disappear as she wrapped my hand lightly with gauze.

"Sounds a bit silly, fightin' over a lollipop." He grabbed a plate and started piling it with food from the counter, which already looked like it was dwindling, surprisingly. "And slightly unsanitary." By his voice, I could tell he was the one who communicated with me when I was kidnapped—in my head. He picked up a small cereal box and mumbled, "I can never pass up some Lucky Charms. Mm-mmm." The quirky voice matched his appearance poorly. He was about the same age as the other two, with deep brown eyes shining against his brown skin and black hair cropped close to his head, a beanie covering half of it. He was muscular but small, decently handsome, and the crinkles by his eyes told me he smiled more often than not. When he turned to face me fully, that smile shone brightly. "Welcome to the

Dengalow!"

I made a face. "What the heck is a Dengalow?"

Kyler scoffed while Mari suppressed a giggle.

The other man spread his arms out, "This place! I couldn't decide what to call it since it's not quite a house, not quite a castle. So I made up something fun." He grinned, clearly pleased with the odd name. I could think of a few other names, manor or mansion being the first two. I raised a brow at him, and he cleared his throat. "Anyways," He gestured to me, standing there in a trance. "Lovely to see you up and about, dearie. I assume you're feeling better?"

Despite his quirky nature, his question brought me back to all *my* questions. The momentary distraction of Kyler being a part of this group made me forget that I didn't know who these people were or why I was in their house. "Can someone please explain to me what is going on?"

Mari finished caring for my hand, her smile fading at my tone of voice. She left to return the first aid kit. Kyler was tearing into another slice of pizza, glaring at me. But it was the third person who spoke, "Yes. Of course." He walked over to the table and motioned for me to follow. "I'm sure you have many questions. I'll do my best to answer them."

Shocked that he wasn't taking me to the study as Mari suggested earlier, I only stared at him with an eyebrow raised. I blinked away my confusion, threw the lollipop stick away, and followed him to the table.

He took a bite of something on his plate and looked at me expectantly. My brain latched on to the most obvious question. "Who are you?"

He gave me a close-lipped smile and swallowed before answering. "You can call me Theo." He took another bite of food.

I nodded, waiting for him to continue. When he didn't, I clarified, "And why am I here?" I knew remaining calm and clear-headed was the only way I would get answers. I had to stay focused on the questions and prepare for the most ridiculous answers to avoid being caught off guard.

"This is the safest place for you." He took another bite.

"Why did you rescue me from those men?"

"Because you were in danger." Another bite.

I pinched the bridge of my nose and took a pointed, deep breath, letting it out heavily. "Why did those men kidnap me?"

He swallowed and pushed his now empty plate away. He crossed one leg over the other and placed his clasped hands on his knee. "Because they believe you to be one of the most powerful fae in all the realms."

There it was— the most ridiculous answer. I blinked at him. "Sorry. What?" I couldn't voice all the questions that came to mind. They were coming too fast. Like Mitch's rapid-fire Nerf gun: What is a fae? Most powerful fae? In *all the realms?* How many realms were there? How did they exist? Were they fae, too? How was I fae? Was my family fae? Were they even telling me the truth?

He smiled fully again. "Ah, yes. You don't know anything about your history, do you?"

What is he talking about? I was born in Wisteria Falls. I grew up there. With my family. My friends. I went to Wisteria Heights. I visited the hospital too many times to count. I developed a love for cooking. I remembered every teacher I ever had. Every trip I'd ever been on. Boating trips. Summer camp. Trips to the meadow with Arabella and my dad. Both of which I'd lost within the last two years. Arabella lying on a gurney in a hospital. Dad screaming as his life ended. Mitch. *Mitch.* Hooked up to machines. Comatose.

My heart rate picked up as the questions zoomed through my head.

Not again...

I stared at Theo. He stared back. Mari walked in, freezing in the doorway. Kyler was sitting on the counter but had stopped eating and was watching me with an intense curiosity.

My vision started fading.

Breaths became ragged.

Mari took one look at me and pulled her phone out to start dialing.

Kyler jumped off the counter and ripped the phone from her hand. "Don't." He turned his attention back to me. When his eyes found mine, he said, "Focus." He wasn't moving toward me. He stayed across the room, arms crossed, as he instructed me, "Calm yourself."

The oxygen didn't exist in the room. My lungs were fighting for air. The hammer in my head was obnoxiously loud. "Take in your surroundings. What can you feel?" His voice was firm. Strong. I hated that he knew what was happening to me. Hated that he was doing this. "*Come on, Sunshine.* What do you feel?" He gritted out.

I closed my eyes against my better judgment and did as he said. I felt the chair beneath my legs, soft but supporting. The table under my hands, smooth but textured. The floor at my feet, solid but cold. A hand grabbed mine, warm but callused.

"What do you see?"

His figure stood across the room, his attention entirely on me. Mari knelt in front of me at the table, my hand in hers, her eyebrows knitted together. The pile of food on the island was more like scraps compared to when I arrived.

My chest expanded with air, and my eyes rolled back into my head as I let it out. When I focused again, Kyler was browsing the island for something else to eat as if nothing had happened. He had just walked me through a panic attack like he'd done it a thousand times.

I'd never been talked out of one like that. Kaleb had been there for most of mine, his physical touch and gentle words pulling me from the panic. I wasn't sure what to make of what just happened, but I knew I would eventually have to thank him for what he did.

Mari was still kneeling before me, gripping my hand. I slowly pulled free from her grasp and looked at Theo, who hadn't moved from his relaxed position. Mari stood and slid into the chair next to me. None of this made sense. Fae? Other realms? Magic powers? It wasn't possible...was it?

I addressed Theo, "Tell me what I need to know." Not everything, not right now. I just needed to know the essential things for now. Finding out the impossible existed would take a lot more time and convincing. "*Only* what I need to know."

Theo blinked. "Alrighty." He gave a tiny bow with his head in understanding and began. "You are a valuable asset. We," he gestured to himself and the other two, "have been assigned to protect you. Others are trying to capture you. We do not intend for them to be successful."

I nodded, matching his story with what I overheard while held captive. And everything else that happened lately. A different thought occurred to me. "Were those people involved in my brother's accident?"

Theo nodded.

My heart dropped to my stomach. Mitch was almost killed because of these creatures. Were they after my entire family? Were they involved in Arabella's accident? Dad's? They both *died*. What if—

"Will they—" I swallowed thickly. "Will they try to finish the job?" I knew he knew what I meant.

"They already think he's dead." My head twisted to Kyler. He was back to shooting daggers at me with his eyes.

"*What?* How? Why?" The high-pitched whine of my voice was unpreventable.

Theo answered, "What he means to say is—well. Yes. I suppose he meant what he said. The reason, though," he pressed on, even though Kyler's dagger stare met his momentarily, "there are things you don't know about us. Our kind." Again, gesturing to the three of them, he said, "Things you don't *need* to know right now, as you kindly requested. Just know that Mitchell is safe and healing."

I nodded, appreciating Theo's ability to understand me at that moment. "What happens now?" Because I had a feeling that things wouldn't go back to how they were. They couldn't. It wasn't possible to forget any of this. Any of what happened the last few days.

"The others will not give up their mission. We will have to make a plan. But for now, you will stay here—"

"No!" I slapped both hands over my mouth too late. My hands moved to my temples, and my eyes widened as I looked at Theo, whispering, "Please. Can't I stay with Kaleb?" I didn't want to be stuck in this house, with these people, with Kyler, whose glare was still burning into my skull.

Theo's gaze fell to the ground with a sigh. He didn't have to say the words for me to know his answer, but he did anyway. "I'm sorry." When he looked up, his eyes said enough, "This is the safest place for you."

My fingers tangled in my hair and curled into fists. I couldn't be locked in this house. I would go crazy not being able to see Mitch. The twins. *Kaleb.* Something he said clicked, and my gaze flew to Theo's piercing stare. "What about school?"

"You can still attend your classes. Niko and Mari are enrolled there for that very reason." Theo stood and walked to the door leading to the library. He faced me before stepping through and said, "Until we can figure out a plan to stop the others, you will always be escorted by one of us outside this house." The idea of spending any time alone with Kyler made my blood boil. "Understood?" Theo looked between the three of us, waiting.

Both Kyler and Mari nodded.

All of them looked at me. I could leave, just not alone. I wasn't trapped, just... closely watched. I met Theo's gaze. "Okay."

At my confirmation, he left the room. There were so many thoughts running through my head. I needed to write down the questions I had. I didn't want to forget anything.

Mari started to say something, but I cut her off. "I'd like to be alone."

Her shoulders dropped. "I'll take you to your room."

She led me out of the kitchen, but I felt Kyler's gaze follow me until we disappeared around the corner. No, he wouldn't forget what I did to him in that kitchen. Good.

Mari walked me to my room without a word, keeping her head hung and her hands folded in front of her. I wondered if the warm, gentle person I'd just begun to know would become someone I'd learn to trust. I didn't know if she chose to be here or if this was just a job for her, but she seemed too genuine not to care. Her laugh when I bested Kyler was sincere, as was her being impressed by me. She acted like it was the best part of her day. It was almost as if— "Are you and Kyler siblings?"

Mari's body straightened at the sound of my question. She grinned over her shoulder and said, "No, but we might as well be. We grew up together. We trained together and have been on several missions, too. He's an ass most of the time, but you learn to love it." At the look of disgust on my face, she giggled. "Or continue to hate it."

I tucked away that information, hoping we could bond over Kyler being an ass sometime. I brought the conversation back to where my mind had wandered. "So, at school... Do you go by Amariel?"

"Yes, but I prefer Mari."

"Okay," I paused, thinking of the encounter I just had. "Why does Theo call Kyler Niko?"

"They've known each other a long time. He's always been Niko to Theo." When I gave her a quizzical look, she went on. "Kyler's full name is Nikylo."

"Oh." What an interesting name. "How long have you been going to Wisteria Heights?"

"I started a couple of weeks ago. We weren't supposed to interact with you for fear of bringing too much attention your way. But I suppose that doesn't matter anymore." She gave me a small smile. Before I could voice my next question, she answered it. "Braxton asked me to Prom of his own accord. He and I were fast friends. He wanted to make sure I had someone to go with. He's charming." She looked down at the ground, "He introduced me to your other friend, Leighton. We all have French together." Of course, I already knew this information, but some color made its way into Mari's cheeks. I smiled to myself, pieces coming together in my head, but I stopped myself from going too far. I didn't know Mari that well, and I wasn't sure if I wanted to bring Mari into our group until I knew her better.

"So, I can still go to prom?" That was the last thing I should be worried about right now, but I *was* looking forward to it.

Mari scrunched up her eyebrows, "Yes, of course. Why wouldn't you be able to go?"

"Besides the obvious?" I held up my hands, "I don't know. Just with everything going on, I wasn't sure."

"Don't worry, we'll still have a fun night dancing." She smiled shyly, and I returned it. When we returned to my room, she lingered in the doorway as I walked in. "Do you need anything else for the night?"

Looking around the room, I saw a new silk nightgown lying on the bed, a pitcher of water by the bed with an empty glass again, and my medicine. I saw the toiletries I needed in the bathroom. None of it was mine, but it would suffice. Except for the medicine. Which I only wondered about for a second before remembering that Kaleb was with Kyler earlier that day. That also explained why he complained about Mari's partner on the phone. I imagined they wouldn't get along too well, no matter what he said about it in the courtyard the other day.

"Could you bring me a notebook and pen?" I needed to write down my questions. I didn't want to forget anything when I was finally able to ask. I was still doubting that any of this was even real, but if it was, I was going to need answers.

She nodded and disappeared out the door, letting it close most of the way behind her. After staring at the door momentarily, contemplating an escape, I decided to change into the nightgown. Exhaustion was closing in, and I didn't feel the need to run right now, no matter how much Kyler annoyed me. You'd think after being unconscious for three days, my body would be well rested, but apparently not. I felt like I hadn't slept in a week.

The bedroom door creaked open behind me when I stepped out of the bathroom. A male cleared his voice, and I whipped around to find Kyler standing in the doorway, notebook in hand. I froze. Heat rose up my neck, spreading to my cheeks and ears. He had another stupid lollipop in his mouth, switching it from one side to the other with his tongue. His eyes traveled down to my feet and back up again, not missing one curve that the nightgown revealed. I tried using my hands to cover myself, but it didn't do anything for me. Kyler, however, lifted one side of his mouth at my attempt and threw the notebook on the bed, turning and leaving without a single word.

I stomped over to the door and slammed it shut. I leaned against it in an attempt to calm myself down. A dark chuckle echoed from the hall.

Ugh! It was bad enough that I had to stay in the same house as him. Now he'd seen me in this silly nightgown. I thought of calling and complaining to Ken and Leigh but realized I didn't know where my phone was. That should have been something I asked Mari for when she left, but instead, I'd asked for a stupid notebook.

I walked over to the bed and snatched it up. I sat at the desk with a huff and started writing down the questions from the list in my head. The first attempt at writing a question tore the page with how strongly

I wrote the words:

Why is Kyler an asshole????

I ripped the page out, crumpled it, and chucked it at the wall. It fell between the desk and the wall, so I told myself I'd pick it up later. The second attempt to write a question was calmer, and I managed not to rip the paper this time. It stemmed from one of Theo's two insane statements.

What is a fae?

They were telling me I wasn't even a human, but I looked exactly like a human. If the people in that portrait were what fae looked like, why didn't I have the same features they did? Where were my pointed ears and enhanced beauty? I felt like an average human, not the "most powerful fae in all the realms," which led to my following questions as I added those.

What other realms are there?
Where am I from?
Is my whole family fae?

The last question held me up for a moment because if my whole family was from another realm, why didn't my parents tell us? What could have kept them from telling me I'm not human? As I added those to the list, I wondered if there were any clues or hints that we weren't human. But I guess since I didn't know the difference between a fae and a human, I wouldn't be able to spot it anyway. I added that question, too. Then:

Are you fae????

Theo said I didn't need to know anything about "their kind" but seemed to be referring to only himself, Mari, and Kyler. I wondered if it had anything to do with what Aaidan and the Kool-Aid man said when I was kidnapped. That thought stumbled into a hundred more questions, and I wrote them all down.

When I finished scribbling as many questions as I could remember, I decided that sleep might help me think of more. I set the pen on top of the notebook and slid to the floor to find the paper I'd thrown, thinking it probably fell under the desk. But when I crouched down to look, it wasn't there. Huh. I stood and walked to the side of the desk to see if it got stuck between it and the wall. Nothing. I checked under the desk again before deciding I didn't care that much— no use losing sleep over a stupid piece of paper.

    I took one of the pills from the bottle on my nightstand, crawled under the fluffy white comforter, and fell into a deep sleep.

XVII
Paradise

I jolted awake. The room was dark, but I sat up and looked around for whatever woke me. Nothing seemed strange or out of place.

The pale moonlight illuminated the room. I swung my feet to the floor and padded to the balcony doors. They were locked from the inside. Why hadn't I checked earlier? I unlocked them and stepped out into the cool night air. I wrapped my arms around myself and took in the railed balcony I stood on. The spring breeze brought the smell of wet soil and sweet grass. I inhaled the scent and sighed. It reminded me of the meadow this time of year.

Despite its size, the tiny sliver of moon was bright. It shone on the surrounding forest, making it clear that I was either facing away from the main road or we were in the middle of the forest.

The sound of rushing water hit my ears. The rivers near Wisteria Falls all ran down the gentle slopes of the mountainside it rested on, convening in one spot to create a beautiful waterfall in the middle of the forest somewhere. By the volume of the rushing water, it seemed we were in the middle of *that* forest. I mentally added it to a new list of things to ask in the morning.

I peered over the edge of the balcony and saw I was on the second floor of the house—or whatever Theo called it. The Dengalow? It took up a massive plot of land within the trees. The structure of the house was made up of large stones and glass. It was strange but oddly beautiful. Some of the pieces looked like genuine crystals, but I couldn't tell from where I stood.

The balcony was at one end of the house, and if I leaned over the railing, I could see the other side, but it was a long way away. How big was this place? And how had I never known this place was here? Granted, we were in the middle of the forest near the falls, and I couldn't see any roads, so no one likely knew about this place. But everything inside seemed so—

A shadow passed over the moon. My gaze shot to the glowing crescent, expecting to see clouds, but there were none in sight. It must have been an owl or a bat because I couldn't see anything else in the sky.

Another cool breeze passed through the bars of the railing, causing goosebumps to pop up all over my bare arms and legs. A shiver ran through me, sending me back through the glass doors to seek the warmth of the blankets on my bed. I closed the glass doors behind me and locked them again.

When I turned back to the bed, something on the desk caught my eye. Or rather, the lack thereof. The pen was there, but that was it.

The notebook was gone.

I whipped my head to take in the rest of the room. Thanks to the moonlight, there weren't any dark shadows, and I could see every inch of the empty space. There was no one there, but the notebook disappeared *somehow*.

I hurried over to the door and touched it to ensure it was shut. I grabbed the door handle and hesitated momentarily before opening it to peek outside. The halls were empty and quiet, a single light illuminated from the end of the hallway—no sign of anyone. I opened the door a little farther, and the thought of making a run for it crossed my mind again. If everyone were asleep, perhaps I would make it... but I quickly changed my mind and shut the door, locking it. I wouldn't know which way to go if I tried to run. So what was the point?

Thinking the lock alone might not be enough, I ran over to the nightstand, throwing the things on top of it to the floor. When it was cleared, I pulled it quietly over to the door. It wasn't very heavy, but it would alert me if someone tried to get in. I pushed it flush against the door so I would know even if it opened a crack. Satisfied with my quick thinking, I climbed back into the bed and pulled the covers to my chin.

If the notebook had been stolen, whoever was in my room probably woke me up. The noise of the door closing could have easily been loud enough. But why did they take the notebook in the first place? They brought it to me at my request and gave it willingly, so why take it back? And in the middle of the night? While I was *sleeping*? It seemed strange.

The thoughts consumed me as I drifted off to sleep once more.

The dream that greeted me wasn't like my night terrors. This one brought me to a place surrounded by trees I'd never seen before. I was lying on a forest floor, the ground beneath me unbelievably soft. I pushed myself to a sitting position and took in the shades of green surrounding me. Some of them I swear I'd never seen before. My vision was sharp, more so than usual, and with it, I could see every detail of the leaves and trees that surrounded me, right down to the bright blue bugs crawling on them ten feet away.

I stood with caution, knowing that my dreams tended to turn into nightmares quickly, but this dream didn't feel like one of those. I felt my body still lying on the bed, sleeping, while my mind could fully explore the world around me.

A term I'd heard someone use before popped into my head: lucid dreaming.

That's what this felt like.

The calls of animals came from all around me, as clear as I'd ever heard the sound of a bird's song. I could even hear the flutter of wings and found the hummingbird— no, not a hummingbird. But similar. It was near the leaves where the blue beetles were, searching for— I guess searching for the beetles because it snatched one with its long beak and flew away. *Fascinating.*

I took a step, the forest floor squishing beneath my bare feet like a sponge. The sound of a waterfall drew me toward it. I gently moved leaves out of the way as I traveled to an opening where the noise stemmed from and stopped short.

There was a cliff and the view… It was the most beautiful place I had ever seen. An island filled with unique and beautiful trees, flowers blooming from some in the distance, and multicolored birds soaring over the canopy. A rainbow stretched across the sky, filled with enormous billows of clouds, the sun setting on the horizon.

It was like a painting.

Through the trees below was a small city with buildings and homes, people milling about—a whole community built into the earth itself. I wanted to go down there to visit, to see the goods at the market, and to learn about the culture. It seemed so inviting.

The rush of water that drew me to the cliff's edge was on my right. The water sparkled and danced with colors unlike any I'd ever seen. It was as if the rainbow lived within the water. It fell several hundred feet before disappearing into a hole in the ground.

Following the path from which the water fell, I gawked at a magnificent palace on top of the mountain behind me. The whole structure was built with crystals of every size, shape, and color, creating a rainbow effect as the sunset hit the building. The windows were crystal clear, but the view to the inside was obstructed by something else.

If this were a lucid dream, I could do whatever I wanted. Right?

The first thing that crossed my mind was flying. I always wanted to fly. And right now, I wanted to see where the water from the rainbow river fell. To visit the village below and meet the people who lived in this dream of mine. Standing at the cliff's edge, I closed my eyes and took a big breath.

When I opened them again, I let my body fall forward in a free fall.

The feeling was euphoric. I let out a whoop of excitement, drinking in the air that flew in my face, and watched as the hole in the ground grew closer. The water from the falls sprayed my face as I flew closer to it. The cool water felt so real. As I closed in on the space where the water disappeared, I knew I'd have to slow down soon. Not realizing how I might do that, I tried thinking of something to help.

The void below was closing in fast. And I was falling, not flying. I needed something to help me fly. Wings. Why didn't I think of that before I jumped?

I imagined two great eagle's wings sprouting out of my back, forming the vision clearly in my head.

Nothing happened. A slight panic crept in. I thought that was how lucid dreams worked—you imagined things happening, and they just *happen*. Maybe the wings were too much of a stretch.

A parachute, then. I imagined a backpack stuffed with one and a cord to pull it open.

Still nothing.

The slight panic rose and settled in my chest. I was thirty feet from the pitch-black opening, but there was nothing to stop me. I started pinwheeling my arms in a last-ditch effort to slow down, but it did nothing. The distance closed too fast, and the black hole suddenly swallowed me.

Darkness consumed me.

My eyes shot open as I screamed and shot up in bed. The white comforter covered my body. The sun peeked through the curtains. I must have fallen asleep for longer than I realized.

I put my head in my hands. What idiot tries to fly in their first lucid dream?

Laughter rang from somewhere in the house. Who on earth would be up this early and *laughing*? I did *not* want to find out at this hour, so I pulled the covers over my head and tried to block out the morning.

A loud thunk woke me. I slowly opened my eyes and pulled the covers down from my face. The second I did, something fell seemingly out of the sky and landed hard on my face. "Ow! What the hell?" A headache was settling in, but I couldn't tell if it was from whatever hit my head or the lack of caffeine the last couple of days.

Groaning at the pain and whoever woke me up, I looked around for the culprit. There was no one there. The door still had the nightstand pushed in front of it, untampered with. The balcony doors were locked from the inside. But out of the corner of my eye, I saw the desk was now littered with several books. How in the hell...

I looked at my pillow. A *book* landed on my head? Where the hell did it come from? Again, I scanned the room and saw no sign of someone else being there. *Okay... I must have imagined it falling from the sky...*

I picked up the book and read the cover: *The Origins of Fae.*

My head snapped to the desk, and I threw off the blankets to scoot off the bed—all thoughts of where the books came from vanished, as did my caffeine headache.

Sifting through the books, I read the titles of a few: *Fae Magic, Lineage of the Elementals,* and *The Art of Wielding.* One of the books had what looked like a painting on the front—a floating island above a world of water below. The island had mountains covered in trees and buildings peeking out of the canopies along the edges of the mountains. Several bodies of water were along the island, and cabins lined the water's edge. In the sky were two moons mirroring each other in phases.

My notebook sat next to the books on the desk. I snatched it up, opening to the first page of questions. It wasn't just my handwriting on it anymore. In purple ink, next to each question, was an answer with a citation for a book. Each book listed sat on my desk. If it didn't have a citation, there was either an "in-person" comment or "not yet." Which I assumed meant that it was something I didn't need to know yet. Most of the ones labeled "not yet" were questions about Theo, Mari, and Kyler.

There was a knock at the door. "Come in," I muttered, reading through my list of questions to see if any had real answers.

The sound of the nightstand scraping on the ground caught my attention. I set down the notebook and rushed to the door to move the nightstand. Mari was standing there with her eyebrow raised.

I shrugged, even though I knew my cheeks were tinted pink. "I didn't want anyone to come in without me knowing," I confessed, then gestured to the books, "but I guess the nightstand didn't matter because someone got in here anyway."

Mari let out an exasperated sigh, "Well, actually…" She smiled, "Some of our kind have magic that can move things between realms and planes of space and time." She said that like it was part of an everyday conversation, which to her it probably was.

"Uh huh…" I blinked dramatically, opening my eyes wide, nodding like I understood. I definitely didn't.

"That was probably just Theo sending them to you. He said you might like reading the answers to some of your questions rather than hearing them from someone. Learn things at your own pace." My level of appreciation for Theo skyrocketed. Although I wasn't very appreciative that he'd dropped one on my face, I decided to keep that little bit of humiliation to myself. "Anyway, I was coming to see if you were ready to join us for brunch," she said.

My stomach, again, growled in response, and we both giggled. "I guess I am kind of hungry." I glanced back at the books, wanting to know more about my history, but I knew they would be there when I returned. "What time is it anyway?"

"It's just after eleven." She went to take a step into my room but stopped short, looking at me. I gave her a nod, and she continued over to the wardrobe and opened it. The midnight blue gown still hung there, along with a few newer items.

"How did you know what size clothes to get me?" I asked, unsure if she'd answer me, but I needed to ask anyway.

She didn't turn but sifted through the clothes. "I make clothing back home. It was easy enough to guess your size." She *makes* clothes? I had so much to learn, now including everything there was to know about Mari.

She pulled out a couple of tops, holding them out for me to choose from. I pointed to the lavender one, and she handed it to me. Then, she grabbed some black, legging-style pants to give me.

I laid them over my arm and headed for the bathroom. Her voice stopped me in the doorway. "Do you want me to do your hair?" The question caught me off guard. The last time someone did my hair...

"No. That's okay." Using the hair tie on my wrist, I pulled my hair up into a messy bun. Seeing I could do it myself, Mari nodded and stepped out of the room. She was almost through the door when I said, "I can do these things myself." She turned to look at me. "So long as I know that I have clothes and whatnot. You don't have to draw me a bath, pick out my clothes, or do my hair..." As I trailed off, I noticed a flash of something like hurt in her eyes. "I just don't want to inconvenience you," I said truthfully.

She gave me a sad sort of smile. "Of course. Do you want me to wait for you in the hall, or would you like to walk yourself to brunch?" The honest question felt like a blow to the gut.

But as I thought about the path to the kitchen, I knew I hadn't paid enough attention last night on our way there. "Can you wait for me?"

She nodded, closing the door on her way out. I quickly took care of my needs and changed into the clothes I'd picked out. After splashing water on my face and taming the flyaways in my hair, I headed out the door to find her leaning against the wall. She took in my appearance and glanced a little too long at my bare feet. "Do the slippers not fit?"

Figuring it was rude to tell her I ignored them because I thought I couldn't run away in them, I said, "I don't like to wear shoes unless I have to." Which wasn't a lie, so I didn't feel bad about saying it.

On the way to the kitchen, I searched for the painting of the two people I'd seen the night before. We were almost there when I realized it was missing. In the place where I thought I'd seen it was a painting of a young girl collecting flowers from a meadow in a basket. She was by a lake, the flowers were up to her knees, and her basket overflowed with spring colors. I turned to Mari, who had stopped with me, and asked, "What happened to the picture of the couple from last night?"

Mari lifted one shoulder, "Theo must have found a better place for it. He likes to rearrange the paintings every once in a while." She turned and waved for me to follow. I didn't think she was telling me the truth for some reason.

As we approached the kitchen, the voices within traveled down the hall. Theo was rambling about something, his voice too quick and quiet for me to understand, but the voice that answered was all too familiar.

The warm cadence. The familiar baritone. The hearty chuckle.

Mari gave me a knowing smile over her shoulder, confirming my theory.

I couldn't help myself. With a little hop, I sprinted the remaining length of the hallway.

When I reached the door, I paused for half a second, searching for the human belonging to that warm honey voice. A joyful sob escaped me when I saw him, and I dashed across the room to his open arms.

XVIII
Run

Kaleb's smile was full of joy when he saw me. He took two steps toward me before I leaped into his outstretched arms, wrapping my legs around his waist. He pulled me close, arms wrapped as far around me as they'd go, and his nose pressed into my shoulder. I buried my face in the crook of his neck, laughing through the tears flowing down my face. A mix of joy and relief filled my soul. "What're you doing here?" My voice was muffled against his neck. It didn't matter. He was here. He was okay. I was okay. Everything was okay.

It wasn't Kaleb who responded to my rhetorical question. "It was a two-to-one vote," Kyler grumbled from somewhere behind me. Not caring about whatever that meant, I pulled myself closer to Kaleb, relishing his warmth, breathing in his scent, and committing it to memory—lavender and cedar.

After an obnoxious sigh from Kyler, I unwrapped my legs from Kaleb's waist, and he lowered me to the ground. He pulled away, only enough to see my face, and I smiled at him, tasting the tears on my lips. His smile dropped, and he pushed me back suddenly, scanning me from head to toe before his wide eyes met mine again. "You're not hurt? Are you okay?" The questions seemed the same, but I knew they meant two different things.

"I'm not hurt." I didn't want to mention that I *was* hurt but had already healed, again not wanting to tell him too much too fast. "And I'm okay. Now." I wiped the tears from his face and wrapped my arms around his neck again. He hesitated only for a moment, then squeezed me around my waist, burying his face in my hair and taking his turn to breathe me in.

"Ugh... Enough with the lovey-dovey bullshit." I let go of Kaleb enough to see Kyler standing near the island, arms crossed and brow furrowed. "Can we eat now?" His question was aimed at Theo, who was setting a plate of food on the island now set up buffet style.

Theo clapped his hands once over the food and opened them as if it were an offering. "Help yourselves."

Kyler wasted no time snatching a plate and throwing food on it. I turned back to Kaleb, who was watching me with an intensity I'd never seen before, eyes darting to Kyler every few seconds before concentrating on me again. "Forget him," I said, placing my hand on his forearm—

"Yeah, forget him," Kyler mumbled, "the guy who saved you while this coward," he thrust his finger toward Kaleb without looking up, his voice rising as he continued, "*Let* you get kidnapped by a bu—"

"Uh uh!" Theo cut him off. "This isn't about you, Niko. Zip it." He made the gesture with his fingers across his lips.

Kyler growled at him but didn't say another word. Again, my appreciation for Theo grew exponentially. I caught his eye and mouthed, "Thank you." His only response was a slight, curt nod.

I grabbed Kaleb's arm around the elbow, a familiar gesture, and led him to the island. We grabbed plates and filled them up before heading to the table.

Mari cleared her throat, "Actually, the table outside is set for brunch."

I squinted, looking at all the food and plates inside, but realized we were missing the silverware and beverages. She finished getting her food and led the way through the door.

We stepped onto a vast terrace, a table close to the door. The rest of the deck consisted of a lounge area with a fire pit, a jacuzzi, and a plethora of plants, some of which didn't look like anything I'd ever seen. The edge of the terrace overlooked the forest, and the sounds of the rushing water were more prominent on this side of the house. There wasn't any sign of a road from this view either, which made me wonder just how far from civilization we were.

I was curious enough to walk over and peek over the railing. Sure enough, it was a drop off the edge of a cliff, and below, I could see where the rivers converged to make the falls. From this height, I couldn't see the lookout meant for tourists, so that ruled out anyone knowing the house was there apart from the people living there. But, damn, what a view.

Looking out over the forest, the rocky hills full of trees went for miles. Wisteria Falls was nestled into the side of a mountain range, the town sitting south of the Falls. It was a beautiful place to live. If I had to leave—

"Thinking of jumping?" Kyler's voice yelled from the table.

I whipped around to find a wicked grin on his face. I squinted at him. There was no way he could have known about that dream. But the sparkle in his eye told me something different.

Deciding to ignore the thoughts accompanying that, I went to the table and sat between Kaleb and Mari. Kyler sat on the other end next to Theo.

A pitcher of orange juice sat on the table, along with a carafe of coffee and a small jar of creamer. Each spot at the table was set with a juice cup and a mug.

Kaleb reached for the carafe of coffee and poured some into my cup before filling his own. I went for the creamer, but he beat me to it and poured some into my coffee, stopping when it turned the perfect shade of brown. I raised my eyebrows at him, a small smile playing on my lips as I said, "Did you want to cut my waffle, too?"

A low chuckle came from the other end of the table, but I ignored it as Kaleb's cheeks turned pink. His voice was barely a whisper when he spoke, "Sorry... I just—" Words seemed to have escaped him. His gaze dropped with his hands to his lap.

I rubbed his forearm, "I was joking, Kaleb." He didn't look up, so I shook his arm slightly to make him look at me. His eyes finally lifted to mine. "Thank you. But I'm okay, really. These guys have been really nice and accommodating." *Except Kyler,* I thought to myself.

Kaleb seemed to follow my thought and glared at Kyler across the table. "Yeah, I'm sure it's been lovely." He said through his teeth.

Kyler stared at Kaleb, but something on the table caught my eye. I blinked. Because surely I didn't just see his spoon stirring the coffee itself. When I opened my eyes again, he held the spoon as it circled his mug. I squinted, my eyes finding his again, but they were still on Kaleb.

His piercing green eyes conveyed much more than words ever could. I glanced at Kaleb and saw the same glare on his face. What happened between the two of them? Kyler had been assigned to watch Kaleb at his house, but I never expected the tension between them to come to this, nor that they would be glowering at each other across the table.

They both took a sip of their coffee. Kyler finished first and laid the first blow. "Lover Boy over here wouldn't stop asking about you."

Kaleb choked on his coffee and slammed his cup on the table. "Of course, I asked about her! She's my *best friend!*"

Kyler raised his eyebrows, taking another sip of coffee before responding. "I think there's more than just friendship on your mind," he turned to me, "Right, Sunshine?"

I didn't want to be dragged into whatever this was, so I said, "I think you should leave."

Kyler gave me a devilish grin, tilting his head. "This is my house." A throat cleared, but he pressed on. "He should leave." He gestured with his coffee cup.

"You brought me here!" Kaleb shouted.

"Because I thought it would help *her* get the stick out of her ass!" He used his free hand to gesture at me.

"Says the guy with a pole stuck so far up *his* ass that shit's coming out of his mouth instead!" The words were out of my mouth so fast I didn't even realize *I'd* said them until everyone was staring at me.

Theo and Mari burst out laughing, breaking the tension at the table. Kaleb held out his fist, a smug look on his face, and I high-fived it. I switched my hand to a fist, but he left me hanging. Scrunching my eyebrows together, I figured he was probably distracted by whatever just happened, so I let it go, dropping my hand.

Theo picked up the conversation as the rest of us continued to eat. He said something about switching shifts with those who needed a break from their current positions with Jordin, Mitch, and the twins.

I was only half listening, running back through the conversation in my head while pushing half-eaten food around my plate. Somehow, Kyler got Kaleb to admit something, and that tension caused this feud they now seemed to be in. But that meant there were definitely feelings on Kaleb's side, and I didn't know how to address that. But I guess it was time to hit the problem head-on instead of letting things go unsaid.

"Can we be excused?" I asked. Theo looked up mid-conversation and nodded, continuing his instructions to Mari and Kyler. I stood, nudging Kaleb to get up, too. "Come on. We need to talk." I downed the rest of my coffee and waited for him to stand.

He took a bit longer but eventually got up and followed me inside. I walked through the kitchen and into the hallway, trying to retrace my steps back toward my room. Halfway there, I changed my mind and turned to the next open door. It was the piano room.

I sat on the piano bench and ran my fingers along the ivory keys, remembering the only song I ever taught myself. Kaleb stepped into the room and sat heavily in the armchair, elbows on his knees and head in his hands.

"Kaleb." Not knowing how to start the conversation slowly, I said, "Is what Kyler said true?"

He didn't answer, holding his head and slightly rubbing his temples. I waited, knowing he'd heard me and was searching for the right words. "I don't know." Well, that wasn't the answer I was expecting, but hearing him say it made me think maybe we were on the same page. "I can't tell if they're feelings for you or if they're lingering feelings for Bell." As he said that, his head was still in his hands, but he lifted his head to look at me when he spoke again, "I care about you. I do. I would do anything for you. And Kyler was right... I shouldn't have left you alone in the grocery store."

"Kaleb, you couldn't have known—"

"But I still shouldn't have. Especially after you said you felt like someone was stalking you. It was stupid." He crossed the room, took my hand, and knelt before me. "You matter to me, Rayleigh. I don't know what I would have done if you… if you hadn't come back from that. Knowing I could have been the reason why…" He looked down to where he held my hand. "You know what I mean. Losing someone you care so much about is devastating. I've seen how it's torn you apart. Twice. And then seeing the effect almost losing Mitch had?" He shook his head, his eyes finding mine again.

"I don't know what these feelings are, Ray. I wish I knew. It would be so simple, so easy for us." He gave a small, nervous smile, "You make me laugh, you're incredibly smart, and you're strong. So strong, Ray." He swallowed hard, the sound of it reaching my ears before he continued, "When I— when I saw you today—saw that you were safe and unharmed," his eyes gleamed silver, "something inside me cracked open, and I wanted to wrap you up in my arms and never let go. The joy I felt having you in my arms is something I've never experienced before." He gave another smile. "I'm not going to push you to try this because I'm still not certain myself. But I'm willing to try if you are." His eyes shone, a little glimmer of hope in them.

The entire confession took me by surprise. I didn't know where to start. His feelings were similar to mine, making me wonder if we were both just getting in our own way. His past interest in Bell was the main reason why I didn't want to try anything. The weird feelings I'd been getting lately weren't always constant, but they were getting stronger. He'd been there for me through so much. Bell, Dad, and everything that's happened with Mitch. He's always been there to make me laugh or hold me on my weakest days, knowing exactly what I might need to help cheer me up. He was one of the nicest guys I'd ever met. And he was right. It would be *so* easy for us.

But did I want that? Did I want easy? Obviously, we had our issues, but it didn't make the decision any simpler. Was there something wrong with me for not being able to love him like that?

"If I'm being honest, I don't know either, Kaleb." I pulled on his hands and scooted over on the piano bench for him to join me. "You and I have been friends forever, but everything you said is true, too." I hooked my arm in his and pulled him closer, laying my head on his shoulder as we sat hip to hip. "It's weird because of Bell, mostly, but I don't know what these weird and confusing things I'm feeling are. I definitely love you." I lifted my head to find his wide eyes on me. I wasn't prepared to say that, but there it was. I didn't regret the words. I never would. "But I don't know if it's romantic love. I love our friendship and how you know too many things about me. I love the stupid innuendos you make and the excitement you get when they make me cringe. I love how much you support me and care for me. I love how much you *love* Kaleb. You care so much. I see it every time you look at me. You're always there whenever I break down or have a problem with someone. You listen, talk me through it, or let me ramble, knowing I don't want your advice but need you to listen." He laughed a little at that. "There is so much going on right now. I don't know if it's a good time to start something—" He tried to turn away, but I cupped his cheek and turned his face back to mine. "You could have gotten hurt at the store, too."

Too late, I realized I may have made a mistake putting my hand on his face like that. His eyes traveled to my mouth and back up to my eyes. So close. We were so close. I didn't get to finish what I was saying— He lifted his hand to my face, caressing my cheekbone with his thumb. I didn't know we would end up here. But neither of us was pulling away from the other. He leaned in slightly, closing the distance between us at an agonizing pace, his eyes moving between mine and my mouth. When my breaths shortened and I didn't back away or give him any sign to stop, he closed the remaining distance.

His mouth met mine with a tender touch, barely a whisper. Something inside me stirred, a whisper of wind and rain. Embracing that feeling, I leaned into him more, our lips fully meeting. His mouth moved to accommodate mine, and his hand started to travel back into my hair when he pulled back to look at me, breathing uneven and eyes shining with—

Someone cleared their throat from the doorway. Kaleb jumped up so fast that he slammed his knee on the piano, spewing a string of curse words while the strings hummed a tune to his sailor's song. I sat on the bench, mouth gaping at how scared Kyler made Kaleb. Maybe he was embarrassed because we got caught. It sent my mind reeling. Red traveled up my neck as I glared at Kyler.

He was standing in the doorway, lollipop and all. Why did he always have one in his mouth? "Sorry to interrupt what I'm sure was a pleasant chat." Somehow, I felt like he knew it wasn't pleasant at all. "But I have to take you home now," he said, looking pointedly at Kaleb, who was still slightly limping from his fight with the piano.

"What!" He looked between Kyler and me, "I've only been here an hour. Give me at least one more."

Kyler removed the lollipop from his mouth and looked me up and down before settling his piercing green eyes on my own. "Sorry. Not gonna happen." His gaze flicked to Kaleb. "Come on, Romeo. Time to go." He found my glare again and rolled the lollipop on his tongue before slowly closing his mouth around it.

Ick. I shook the image from my head, turning to watch as Kaleb walked toward me. I stood to hug him, but he walked past me, head down, and didn't attempt to look at me again. "Kaleb…" I tried. He kept going.

Kyler decided to open his foul mouth, "What's wrong, stud? Don't wanna say goodbye to your girlfriend?"

Kaleb was so close to Kyler that when his fist flew toward Kyler's jaw, I didn't have time to stop him. With one hand, he stopped Kaleb's fist. He used his momentum against him, just like he had with me. Stepping back to straddle the entrance, he twisted Kaleb's arm behind him and slammed him against the doorframe opposite him. Kaleb let out a hefty grunt at the impact. Kyler had barely moved. He had taken just one step to get the force he needed to slam Kaleb into that frame. He stepped up behind Kaleb, removing the lollipop with his free hand and leaning into his ear as a lover might. "Don't ever. Try that. Again."

I gawked at them, frozen in place. What else could I do?

Then Kaleb squeaked, breaking my stupor. I ran to remove Kyler's hand from Kaleb and shoved Kyler back against his side of the doorframe.

He let me, smirking as he popped the lollipop back in his mouth and stepped into the hallway. "We leave in three minutes, kid," he said over his shoulder.

I made a vulgar gesture to Kyler's back and could have sworn I heard him chuckle. Kaleb was still leaning against the doorframe but glared after Kyler. "I see what you mean, now. He's an asshole."

I laughed, "It took him slamming your face into the doorframe to realize?"

He didn't laugh like I expected him to. Instead, he pursed his lips and stepped out into the hall. "I'll see you tomorrow." He stalked down the hall, turning the same corner Kyler had, and disappeared just like that.

I couldn't move my feet to follow him because I didn't know what I would say if I did. Instead, I stood in the doorway of the piano room, wondering what the heck just happened.

XIX
Extraordinary Magic

When I returned to my room, all I could think about was Kaleb. The books on my desk would have to wait. So much was running through my head already, and I had to process that before adding new information. I closed my door and slid down against it, letting the thoughts flow.

His confession didn't entirely catch me off guard, but when he opened that door saying he was willing to try, it lit a fire inside me.

I'd never had feelings like this before. A crush? Yes, but those are superficial. My feelings for Kaleb were complicated and platonic—I thought.

I threw my head back against the door and stared at the ceiling. Was I ignoring romantic feelings for him because of his interest in Bell? Was I not entertaining the idea simply because of her? *Did* I want to go there with Kaleb? If he hadn't interrupted me, I would have said that it didn't seem like the right time… but maybe that was why it *was* the right time.

But then he just left and acted like he didn't just kiss me after all that tension between us. Or at least, what I thought was tension. Was what I felt romantic feelings building up this whole time? Our friendship was intimate and wonderful, but did I want more?

I let the thoughts flow through my mind and grasped onto the one I felt when he kissed me.

I slowly traced my lips at the memory of how his fit so perfectly against mine. He was so gentle and sweet. He hadn't been greedy, giving just as much as he took. My only other experience with kissing was on a dare in third grade. It was wet and sloppy, and it wasn't something I wanted.

But *Kaleb*... I chose that. Kind of. I didn't plan to kiss him, nor did I ask for it, but was it unwanted? No. Something in me begged for it. Needed it. Because I wanted to see if I felt anything...

And? My inner voice broke through the silence.

Something stirred inside me. The wind and rain felt strange, but it also felt... familiar. A sense of ease and comfort. But is that what romantic love felt like? Comfortable? Or was there something more to it? I always imagined loving someone would feel wild and free, a euphoric sense of happiness that radiated through my blood—

Like when I saw him today, I ran into his arms and felt like nothing could separate us. At that moment, a spark of something came alive inside me, and it stirred again when he kissed me...

Not knowing how Kaleb felt was killing me. I needed to talk to him. But clearly, we weren't allowed to be alone without Kyler barging in. With an exaggerated sigh, I pushed myself off the floor, making a mental note to ask for my phone the next time I saw one of my hosts.

Across the room, the books still sat on the desk with the notebook beside them. I stared at them from where I sat, wondering where to start.

Deciding there was no better way than to jump into it, I hauled myself up and plopped down at the desk. How Theo knew textbooks were my favorite way to learn beats me, but I made a mental note to thank him later. Grabbing my notebook, I found the citation to my first question:

What is a fae? Origins of Fae pg 26

I pulled that book from the pile and opened it. It was thick but well-read, staying open on the desk when I laid it open.

> A faerie, sometimes referred to as a fae, is a spirit of the earth. What started as a small species hidden among the elements became human-like in size and appearance, able to wield the elements they associate with.

That explains why I fit into the world I knew so well, seeing as we were made to be human-like. But wielding elements? It sounded like the shows I watched as a kid were based on these faerie creatures.

> After centuries of feeling small and weak compared to other species, the faeries discovered how to harness the powers they were hidden amongst and collectively strengthen their species. Faeries can control or wield one element, such as air, earth, water, or fire. Rarely has there been a faerie that can wield more than one.

Already, more questions popped into my head. I read the rest of the pages cited for that first question and learned they changed their appearance centuries ago. Not only did they change in size, but they also started *using* the elements they used to hide among as a power source. Creating magic with water and air, fire and earth... That seemed impossible. But if I understood correctly, which I'm pretty sure I did, I could control one of the elements... but which one?

I wrote my new questions down and then picked up two books cited for the next question:

What powers do fae have? *Fae Magic pg 122, Art of Wielding pg 45*

I prepared my notebook for more notes and opened the books to the correct pages, laying them out next to each other. Between the two books, I learned how the four types of fae controlled their powers. Air elementals were called Annysians, fire elementals were Ignalians, Omonians were water, and Udarians, earth. The book also talked about the Evanians, who could control more than one element but had been extinct for centuries.

I set down my pen and released a loud breath through my lips, rubbing my temples as I processed. Mentally, I was preparing myself to go through more questions and texts, but I didn't even know if I wanted to open the other books yet. My brain already hurt.

This was all so impossible to believe, and my instinct was to leave this house and never return. But something deep within me told me to think about it. Why would this make sense in my life? The connections I started making made it almost impossible to write off.

For instance, fae grow more rapidly—physically and internally—causing the young to have trouble adapting to their quickly changing bodies. Thus, they are clumsier for the first fifteen years or so. So before a faerie gets their full powers—which would happen soon for me since they usually come in between the ages of seventeen and twenty-one—they are far more clumsy.

Another trait that made me feel like I *was* fae was their quick healing abilities. The last few days alone could prove that. Even before whatever Mari gave me, the bruises and cuts from my dreams were barely visible by the end of the day.

The one that didn't fit was the beauty of the fae. If the people in that portrait were what the beauty standard was in this other world, I definitely didn't fit the bill. Maybe that was something that came in with my powers...

It all seemed too fictional to be true. Arabella would have jumped at the opportunity to ask question after question, aching to learn all she could about magic and where she came from. It made me wonder how different this would be—learning all of this together. She'd probably tell me I was overreacting and overthinking, telling me to accept our fate and own the magic we were born with. She wouldn't hesitate or panic like I had. We were opposites when we wanted to know details and information. She would listen and absorb like a sponge, whereas I had to take it in chunks to make it make sense, hitting the books and breaking down how things worked. We balanced each other out, able to fill in the blanks for each other when one of us didn't understand or missed something to solve the problem.

But she wasn't here to help. It was just me.

I briefly wondered what her life might have been like if she had survived. Sometimes, I wish it had happened that way—that *she* had lived. Not that she deserved it more, but because she saw so much more in this world than I ever could, she wanted to live her life full of adventures.

A knock sounded at my door.

I took in my surroundings and realized I had taken the liberty of studying on the floor.

The books were spread out around me. Some lay open, and some stayed closed. I hadn't even touched the book of paintings. I filled my notebook with twice as many new questions as old ones. I thought I might be brave enough to ask Theo or Mari in person, but only time would tell. I removed the books from my lap and answered the door.

It was Mari. "I thought you might be getting hungry." Hungry? *How long have I been up here?* She peered around me at the books scattered on the floor, and her lips quirked up in a smile. "Have you been studying this whole time?"

I felt my cheeks warm slightly, "There's a lot to learn, and I—I wanted to get a head start." I sighed, my brain feeling like it was about to explode. "But my head is so full of new information I don't think I can look at any more textbooks."

She giggled. "It must be overwhelming, learning about an entirely new world. Not to mention the magic." I nodded. She looked past me at the books again, and her eyes lit up as they found mine again, "Would you like to see something?" She put her hands up in defense at my wary glance, "I promise it's not more information, but it might help you grasp what you learned a little better."

Besides the fact that I *was* hungry, the way she lit up about whatever she wanted to show me made me nod. "Then can we eat?" I asked, finally feeling the pang of hunger.

She nodded excitedly and reached her hand out to me. I stared at her extended hand for a split second, unsure how to interpret the gesture. But as I glanced from her hand to her face, the excitement there waived any doubt I had, and I laid my hand in hers.

Almost immediately, she pulled me from my room, dragging me down the hall as fast as she could. We weren't running, but her exhilaration was intoxicating, and it started rubbing off on me. A smile spread across my face, and a weight lifted off my chest. I hadn't felt this light in a very long time. Wherever she was taking me, there had to be something extraordinary there.

We passed several closed doors, the piano room, and just before we got to the library, she pulled me into a room I'd never seen open before. The floor was mostly bare, aside from an intricate rug and a single chair near the tall window that overlooked the forest outside. Mari stopped in the middle of the room, letting go of my hand, and spread her arms wide to gesture toward the walls as she turned in a circle. "These all represent parts of Niccodra." Her joy made her whole face light up. It was incredibly contagious.

With the smile still on my face and slightly breathless, I turned my attention to what she referred to, and my smile melted into awe.

Paintings covered the walls—but not ordinary paintings. They were full of magical creatures and places, painted with colors I didn't even know existed.

The one closest to me had intricate details of houses built on the branches of enormous trees. Waterways ran through the branches and spilled onto the ones below. A small waterfall fell over the edge to the depths of the forest unseen. Some of the branches made pathways to other ones, interconnecting them like the streets of a city. Some buildings looked like businesses on a central tree apart from the houses. It looked like a marketplace within a town, all woven and constructed neatly into the wood of the trees.

The painting next to it was a cliffside. Its walls had windows and doors built into them, layered on top of each other to be what looked like homes. Sections were jutting out of the cliffs made of rocks and tree branches to look like balconies, all high above the body of water below. Sitting on top of the water, but still connected to the cliff, was a little cluster of shops with some labeled as a bakery or grocery store. It, too, looked like a small city.

The next painting drew me in immediately. It was a cavern with light spilling through a single hole in the ceiling. A small rainbow waterfall drizzled through. The water within the cave that wasn't hit by the light seemed to have a luminescent glow. Some other small waterfalls trickled down the walls of the cavern. The painting seemed to move as I studied it, coming to life as I watched how the water flowed and moved in the collection at the bottom. The area was lined with flowers that glowed against the dark walls they crawled over. I wanted to visit this cavern if I ever ended up in Niccodra. It called to me through the painting.

"Come here," Mari beckoned from a picture near the window. "I want to show you something." Her face was bright and smiling. The euphoric feeling I felt on the walk to this room was still there, and I knew it was because I was starting to feel more comfortable around her.

I made my way over to her, taking in each of the beautiful creatures and people, who almost seemed normal, on the path to her. I had yet to study those paintings. When I stopped beside her, I glanced at the picture she was waiting to show me. It was a man with pointed ears and striking features on his dark brown skin. The high cheekbones, the sharp jaw, the full lips. His eyes shone a bright green and—

"Are his eyes *sparkling?*" I stepped closer to inspect myself, but Mari caught my shoulder, holding me back.

"Watch," she whispered with a hint of knowing. She lifted her finger to the corner of the painting and pressed against the colors collected there.

I stared at the part of the painting where her finger was and almost asked what was so special about that particular spot. But then a gasp escaped me as a ripple of something I could only describe as magic left her finger, and the painting started to *move*.

My jaw went slack as I watched the man on the canvas come to life. He started moving his muscular arms in intricate loops and practiced moves to the rhythm of unheard music. It wasn't as smooth as a video might be because I could still see the paint strokes, but I could tell exactly what was happening. As the man moved, so did the earth around him. When he finished his rhythmic movements, he stepped back into his starting position and prepared to repeat the routine, the earth falling effortlessly back into its original place.

Mari lifted her finger from the painting, again freezing the Udarian in his starting position. "Pretty cool, huh?" I heard the smile in her voice but was still staring open-mouthed at the painting that had just *moved* before my eyes. How was something like that even possible? *Moving pictures?* It would make more sense if it were a video, but I reached out and felt the strokes of the paint on the canvas. The tips of my fingers tingled as I ran them down the textured surface, but that was the only indication that anything was different about this painting.

"How?" I breathed. It was all I could manage to say.

Mari let out a small giggle, "We all have different powers, but this magic is within the painting." I didn't miss the way she worded the sentence. There was a difference between what she was, what I was, and whatever created this painting. But I tried to put those questions aside as she said, "To make it move, you only have to possess magic, and the power within the painting responds to your touch." The tingling in my fingers... She stepped around me to another painting of a fae, this one a female with skin so pale it almost looked like an icy blue. "Do you want to try?"

My eyes widened. *I can make paintings move?* The thought was ridiculous, and I wasn't sure I was ready to accept that that power ran through me—not yet. I shook my head, but when her shoulders sagged, I said, "But can you show me again?" I pointed at the pale female standing in a pile of snow with her arms spread out as if feeling the wind around her.

Mari obliged my request and touched the painting, bringing the wind to life as it blew the fae's white blonde hair around her face. The fae threw her head back and inhaled deeply, and I knew from the books I read that she was grounding her power with the breaths she took. She was an Annysian.

"Incredible," I whispered as Mari lifted her finger from the painting, freezing the air wielder in place once more. I turned to look at the other paintings in the room and watched as Mari showed me the other two types of fae. The Ignalian's controlled fire crawled slowly up the trunk of a tree but didn't burn the bark. The Omonian moved the water to slowly take the shape of a giant wave that crashed back into the river.

"Do all the paintings of your world move?" I asked, taking in the walls around me and wondering how they might come to life.

"No. Only those done by the *kallit* can come to life." She laughed as she took in my confused expression of yet another new word. "*Kallit* are like the artists of our world, but they carry so much more power within them. Each stroke encaptures the movement of that specific swatch as it moves throughout the entire painting." I looked up at the painting of the Annysian again and took in as much of the details as I could, not understanding in the slightest what Mari meant but still enamored by it. The intricacies of this artwork made me want to see the process one day because it seemed like so much more than just a canvas, paints, and a paintbrush—like Jordin used.

I turned to ask Mari another question, but it froze on the tip of my tongue when I saw the expression on her face. She wasn't looking at me. Her attention was on the wall near the door. She had her finger on a painting I hadn't noticed, the world coming alive before her. I walked over to join her in front of the magnificent painting that covered most of the wall.

The colors flew off the huge canvas as I took in what I immediately knew to be the entire realm of Niccodra. Lush green landscapes covered eight islands of varying sizes. Waterfalls cascaded down the mountainsides of each and continued to flow off the edge of the isles into the enormous body of water below. I knew that was the center of the planet, and I briefly wondered how the islands could float above it before remembering that the realm was filled with magic.

As I took a step closer to the painting, I noticed the small structures of the homes among the trees and along the water's edge, carved into the mountains and rising from the ground itself. Whoever painted this one didn't include the realm's life force but captured the beauty without it.

When I looked at Mari again, I noticed her eyes shining with tears as she took in the beautiful canvas. Knowing exactly what that look meant, I asked, "Why does this one make you sad?"

Mari sniffled lightly and turned her shining eyes to me. "I just forgot how beautiful Niccodra was."

I squinted at her. "What do you mean, 'was?'"

She took a deep breath through her nose and sighed. "Niccodra hasn't looked like this for over a century." Her voice hitched, and the second it took her to catch her breath was all it took for me to realize she said a *century*—as in one hundred years. And *she* forgot what it looked like. *How old is she?* She didn't look a day over seventeen.

Questions littered my brain that I tried to remind myself to write down in my notebook as Mari's eyes came back into focus and settled more on me as she went on, "Rayleigh, Niccodra is—"

A knock sounded behind me, making me jump slightly as I turned toward the intruder.

Theo. "Ah, there you are, dearie." He gave me a smile that made his eyes crinkle and deep dimples in his cheeks appear. "I was coming to find you in your room but heard your lovely voices here." His eyes turned to Mari momentarily and seemed to communicate something in that glance because she straightened, pursed her lips, and gave him a slight nod. Like she'd been reprimanded silently or something. I wondered if his interrupting us when he did was by accident or if he knew Mari was about to say something she shouldn't. The thought left my mind as he turned back to me. "Have you eaten?"

I shook my head, "Mari came to get me for dinner but wanted to show me these first." I gestured to the paintings around us, glancing around again to take them in. I mentally added the room to my list of places to return if allowed. I felt I didn't get to look at them all closely enough. Perhaps when I returned, I'd be ready to accept that I had magic within me and be brave enough to try bringing one of the paintings to life myself.

"Yes, yes. The *kallit* are extremely talented magic wielders, aren't they? Puts my simple pastime art to shame." I raised an eyebrow as he chuckled to himself. He, too, took a moment to stare at the painting of Niccodra behind me. An emotion passed over his eyes that was too brief for me to catch before he turned them back to me. "Did you get a chance to look at the books delivered to your room?"

I nodded, then remembered *how* they were delivered. I squinted at him. "Next time, can you make sure not to drop one on my face?"

The smile on his face faltered slightly, his eyes flicking to Mari briefly before recovering. "I apologize for my mistake. I must have… misread where your head was on the pillow." Mari coughed slightly, to which Theo eyed her without saying a word, and again, I felt like he silently communicated something.

I narrowed my eyes even more and asked, "Why were you trying to drop one on my pillow?"

His smile slowly disappeared, and he answered too slowly for me to believe what came out of his mouth was the truth. "Well— you'd been sleeping for a while, and I wanted to make sure you were awake in time for brunch."

Out of the corner of my eye, I saw Mari's hand cover her mouth, but not before I saw the smile she tried to hide. My eyes flicked back to Theo. I wanted to believe him, but he wasn't making it easy. "You could have just knocked on my door…"

His smile returned. "Of course. Yes. Next time, I will be sure to knock on your door to wake you up." He said through slightly gritted teeth, making it clear there was something he wasn't saying. He fixed a smile on his face again and took in my appearance, bare feet and all. "If you'd like to get some shoes on, we will be leaving shortly. After you eat, of course."

I made a face. "Leaving? Where?" I was beginning to think I would be stuck in the house unless I was going to school. But they said I could leave, just so long as one of them was with me.

Theo gave me a knowing look and almost whispered, "The hospital, of course. To see Mitchell."

All thoughts of whatever Mari was about to say before Theo arrived vanished. I gasped, my heart rate picking up. I'd forgotten about Mitch. How did that happen? A mix of happy and sad tears filled my eyes as Theo's crinkle-eyed smile reappeared. I took a single step toward the door but paused. I'm unsure what made me do it, but I spun on my heel and walked up to Mari. She stiffened at my sudden approach and gave a wary smile as I stopped right in front of her.

"Thank you. For this." I gestured to the room. "And…" The words caught in my throat, but I cleared it and pressed on. "And for the company." Before I lost my nerve, I wrapped my arms around her in a quick hug. She had been nothing but kind to me since I met her. I didn't show my appreciation earlier when she was there for me, and I wasn't entirely sure I knew how, but a hug was easy. It was how I showed my friends I appreciated them, and I thought, given time, Mari and I could become that.

Her body was stiff for a moment before it relaxed, and she returned the hug, saying, "Anytime, Rayleigh." I pulled away to see her cheeks slightly flushed and a smile once again lighting up her face.

Without saying another word, I hurried out of the room to grab shoes.

꿋 ꔀ ꗚ ꕜ

When I got to the kitchen, Theo waited patiently with his hands behind his back. He gestured to the food on the counter, "Help yourself."

When I realized he was the only one in the kitchen, I asked, "Where's Mari?"

Theo smiled, "She went on an errand for me. She will be back late tonight."

"Oh." My shoulders sagged slightly. Mari's presence had become a welcomed one and gave me a sense of calm I hadn't felt since I woke up in their house. Now, my anxiety seemed to be settling in, and I missed that lightweight, floating feeling I had when she was around. It was much preferred over feeling like a horse was sitting on my chest.

"Eat, dearie." Theo pulled me from my thoughts again. "We don't force our guests to do anything they don't want to, but I'm afraid you'll starve if we don't keep reminding you to eat." His smile was genuine, but my grimace wasn't. It did seem like every time I'd eaten in this house I hadn't felt hungry until someone asked me if I was. I'd have to be more mindful because I knew my anxiety could make me forget to eat.

The spread of options for food was smaller than usual, but I didn't think I could handle much at the moment anyway. My anxious stomach always took less to appease whenever it decided it *was* hungry.

After stuffing my face with a sandwich and some grapes, I turned to Theo, who was in the same position I'd found him in when I entered the kitchen. "Ready?" I nodded, and he gestured with one hand to the door off the kitchen.

It opened to a garage where a white Jeep awaited us. Climbing into the passenger seat, I shoved my hands under my thighs to hide their shaking. Apparently, that didn't fool Theo because he looked from where my hands were tucked to my face and eyed me warily before opening the garage and starting the Jeep to back it out.

"Is everything all right, Rayleigh?" he asked, pulling out onto a drive concealed by the trees around us.

Not knowing what I would say, I shook my head. I'd been so distracted by everything happening to me that I forgot entirely about Mitch and hated how selfish that made me. He was hurt. *I* hurt him. And I hadn't thought about him for days. I watched out the window, holding back the tears I felt coming, not wanting Theo to see them if they did fall. Excitement ran through me at the thought of seeing Mitch, but it was accompanied by disappointment in myself for not asking to see him sooner. Even if I had, would they have even allowed me to go before now?

"Did you learn anything interesting from the books you were reading?" Theo interrupted my thoughts.

A laugh escaped me. The tears building behind my eyes dissolved at the change of subject. "Interesting is not a strong enough word for what I learned."

"How would you describe learning the intricacies of the magic, the fae, and Niccodra, then?" I could hear the smile in his voice, even though I still stared out the window.

We were still on the driveway leading away from the house, but the density of the trees started to thin, and I could see a road ahead with cars rushing past. "I would say the word that crossed my mind the most while reading was unbelievable." Many of the things I read were still unrealistic, but that was because I was still fully immersed in human life. I felt like a human, looked human, and fully believed I was human until twenty-four hours ago when the possibility of being something more gave me a little thrill.

"I'm sure it's all a bit overwhelming, learning you aren't actually from here. That you have powers. That you're a different being altogether." Overwhelming was a good word choice. It was the one Mari had used, too. We reached the end of the driveway and turned onto the road. I looked back to where we exited and noticed it didn't look like a driveway, just a slightly bigger opening with the grass covering the entrance to blend in. Anyone driving past that point would never know there was a house deep within the dense trees.

I turned slowly back to Theo. "Yeah. It's a lot to process. I'm still not sure I believe it all." We were approaching an intersection I recognized, and the familiar rock with 'Wisteria Falls' carved into it came into view, confirming my theories of how hidden the house was above the falls. No one would ever know it was there. Fascinating. "Can I ask you some questions?" I said, thinking about the ones in my notebook labeled 'in person.'

"Absolutely, dear." He said that as if he'd been waiting for me to ask. "What would you like to know?"

I took a breath and let it out slowly. The questions I wanted answered pertained to where we were going. "Why did the people who kidnapped me try to kill Mitch? And how is it that they think he's dead?" After all, Mitch was in a public hospital. It wouldn't be that difficult to find out if he were there, right? Not to mention that everyone at school knew he was in a coma.

"Ah, starting with the easy questions, I see." He winked. "We think the people who kidnapped you are trying to rid you of any connections you might have here in Wisteria Falls." My eyes widened at the blunt answer. I guess I shouldn't be surprised. His answers were short and to the point last night, too, even if some of them seemed obvious. "They believe he's dead because our kind, that is, Niko, Mari, and I, have powers different than yours." That confirmed what Mari hadn't flat-out said but insinuated earlier. "Some of us have the power to manipulate the mind."

My head swung to him, and my jaw dropped. It took me a second to process whether I had heard him correctly, and then I blurted, "Manipulate the mind!? What does that even mean?" Had they used it on me? Was everything that happened just them messing with my head?

He chuckled nervously, "Don't worry, we've never used it on you." His words made me wonder if they could read minds, too. "It means that we can make one think one thing happened when really something else happened." That power... That was something I didn't think anyone should have. It could be misused so easily. "When

Mitchell was hit by the car, for instance, part of our team was nearby and on the scene before the local authority. They made it look like Mitchell had died on the scene and was being brought to the hospital for hopeful revival. He was pronounced dead upon arrival, leading the two men responsible away from the area and leaving Mitchell safely in the hands of our team. We have a member of the team posing as a doctor at the hospital to handle such incidents discreetly."

My eyes widened as my head turned slowly to Theo, a realization dawning on me. "Doctor Smiles." His name came out in a whisper.

Theo pursed his lips. "Didn't you ever wonder why you always had the same doctor growing up? Even in the ER?"

Yes. Yes, I had. But not until recently. Why didn't I question that earlier? Although I'm sure if I mentioned it to Jordin or even Dad, they would have thought I was crazy, telling me it was just luck that we always saw Dr. Smiles. Or maybe they already knew… "Is my whole family fae?"

We were getting to the outskirts of the city now, still several minutes from the hospital. Theo cleared his throat and made a face, seemingly debating how to answer the question. Finally, he said, "The family you call your own is not your true family."

XX
Hurts Like Hell

My heart dropped to my stomach. "What?" The people I knew, the people I loved and cared for, the people who raised me, played with me, and grew up with me, weren't my *true* family? What did that even mean?

Theo seemed to realize it might have been too much information because his mouth opened and closed like a fish out of water. When he finally found words, he stumbled over what to say next. "Of course — I mean, you must understand— Oh my… You and Arabella were born elsewhere and brought to Jordin and Greg for safekeeping." My eyes widened at this even more shocking information, but he rushed on, trying to salvage the conversation. "They already had Mitchell on the way, and your birth parents trusted them with your lives. They thought leaving you two with them would keep you the safest."

My head started spinning. I thought the information about my powers was intense. Learning that I wasn't even properly related to the people I called my family was worse.

The lie of not knowing *what* I was didn't even compare to the lie of not knowing *who* I was.

I tried to take deep breaths, not wanting to panic, but I wasn't sure it was working. The oxygen in the car seemed to disappear. My heart rate kicked up a notch, and my vision blurred. I closed my eyes and tried to focus on breathing like Kaleb always had me do.

Breathe in.

Breathe out.

Slowly.

But the world was slipping away from me.

It wasn't working.

Static filled my ears, blocking all sounds out.

A voice in my head spoke. *What do you feel?*

The words were familiar, but the panic was blocking my ability to think of why. Instead, I focused all my energy on the answer to that question.

The seat I was sitting on, comfortable and soft. My hands under my thighs, touching the textured fabric. The seatbelt across my chest, restricting but safe. A hand on my shoulder, a light touch of comfort.

I opened my eyes, knowing the next part was to focus on what I could see. The inside of the Jeep, black and pristine, came into focus. Theo's hand on my shoulder, his eyes wide but caring. The familiar cityscape outside the window.

Theo's soft voice broke through the static that filled my ears. "That was too much. I apologize." He removed his hand from my shoulder as I acknowledged his apology.

My heart rate was still slowing, my breathing was shallow but fulfilling, and I asked, "How long was I... panicking?" It didn't look like we'd gone very far from the moment I closed my eyes to now.

Theo cocked his head. "Just a few seconds, it seemed like. Much like when we were in the kitchen last night."

"Hmph," I grunted. Coming out of panic attacks was not easy for me. Not simple. Never quick. But these last two... I didn't like the idea, but I'd have to thank Kyler for teaching me to handle my panic attacks by myself. The thought of the arrogance that would roll off him when I did made me immediately regret that decision. He wouldn't be subtle about it, that was for sure.

Seeing that we were almost at the hospital, I turned to Theo. "Can we put a pin in this family history conversation?" I felt there wasn't enough time to cover everything before we arrived. As far as I knew, Mitch was my brother. I didn't want to think of him as anything else when I walked into that room to see him.

Theo released a breath. "Absolutely, dear. Whenever you're ready." He was focused on the road, and I watched him, forehead slightly scrunched, as his facial expressions subtly changed every few seconds. I wondered what conversation he was having in his head. He seemed to be scolding himself, and I gave a quiet laugh before turning my focus ahead.

We turned into the hospital parking lot a few minutes later, and I was out of the car the moment it was in park. I was halfway to the door before Theo even turned it off.

He informed me that Mitch had been moved to a different room because he wasn't an ER patient anymore and led me to a room on the second floor. There, I found Mitch lying perfectly still in his bed. Jordin and Chief were sitting at a table in the corner of the room.

Jordin jumped up as soon as she saw me, quickly covering the distance between us. Before she could wrap her arms around me, I held a hand up to stop her. Her arms retracted to hug her stomach. Her eyes flicked from me to Theo and back nervously.

"I'm here for Mitch," I said. She held my gaze for a moment before dropping it and giving a curt nod, stepping aside for me to pass. There were so many thoughts and emotions running through my head that I needed to talk to Jordin about, but not right now.

I stepped up to Mitch's bed. His different casts, the machines he was hooked up to, and the healed scratches on his face. I reached for his hand but pulled back at the last second and lay my hands across my waist. The last time I held his hand—

I didn't want that to happen again. No risks. The thought of hurting him more than I already had— I couldn't do it.

I stared at him. He looked so much better than the last time I saw him. Color had returned to his face. Someone had given him a bath to wash away the blood and dirt. He looked relatively healthy, all things considered. Did that mean he would wake up soon? I didn't want him to feel like I wasn't there for him. But I also didn't want to hurt him again accidentally.

A warming sensation ran along my arm, where it rested against my waist. An overwhelming feeling coursed through me. One that reassured me and made me think, *I can do this. I can trust myself.* There was no chance of me falling asleep and having a nightmare. There were too many people watching. They wouldn't let that happen again.

Slowly, I reached my hand out again and touched Mitch's. The warmth surprised me. I slowly sat beside him and raised his hand to hold with both of my own. I knew the others in the room were watching. They saw my hesitation, but I didn't care. Right now, it was just me and Mitch. Tears welled in my eyes as I watched him sleep. He looked so peaceful. He didn't look like the weird, wild kid I grew up with. The one that woke me up with Nerf bullets last week. The kid I went on adventures with.

A favorite memory of mine popped up, and deciding that he might be able to hear me if I talked, I told the story out loud.

"You probably don't remember, but I know you've heard this story before," I started, smiling through the silent tear that fell. "I was four years old. You were two. We were playing in the living room, and Ma had gone next door with Arabella to get something. Knowing she would only be gone for a minute, she left the front door slightly ajar. I had the brilliant idea to go on an adventure, grabbed your hand, and walked out the door, not caring that you only wore a diaper. I led you to your favorite red wagon sitting outside and helped you climb in. Once you were settled, I started pulling you down the sidewalk towards the corner store half a mile away." I laughed a little, shaking my head at my courage those days. "When Ma got back to the house and saw we weren't where she left us, she freaked out. She looked *everywhere*. The house. The backyard. The basement. Our rooms. Even our secret hideouts. She didn't think we'd take off like that. When she stepped out the front door to check the yard, a neighbor waved her down and told her she saw us walking down the sidewalk. Alone. She threw Arabella in the car and drove in the direction they pointed. She spotted us halfway to the store and pulled over, yelling my name. When I stopped, she parked next to me and yelled, 'Where in the world are you going?' As she got out of the car to get us, I looked at her seriously, 'I was just takin' my Mitchy to the store!' In a very matter-of-fact tone." The memory had me so caught up in the past that it was hard to return to reality. "I got in so much trouble that day, but being the adventurous child that I was, I—" My eyes finally focused on Mitch again, who was looking right back at me with a small smile on his face.

"That's my favorite story." He said.

A happy sob burst out of me. "Mitch!" My voice was a broken whisper, but I jumped to hug him. At his grunt of pain, I pulled back. "Oh, I'm sorry, I'm sorry. I just— you're awake!" And I jumped on him again, squeezing the life out of him.

"Ray!" Pain laced his strained voice, and I pulled back again to stand next to his bed, keeping hold of his hand but tensing every muscle to keep myself from leaping onto him again for another embrace.

"I'm sorry— you're awake! Do you feel okay? You're smiling!" Each word was louder than the one before. He was laughing a bit but clutched his side with his free hand. "You're okay!" The term was relative. I could clearly see he wasn't pain-free. But he was talking and awake and okay! I smiled at him, wiping tears from my eyes, and wondered how it was possible—

It dawned on me, and I turned to Jordin. She was standing between Theo and Chief at the foot of his bed, tears stained her face as she smiled. "When did he wake up?" I asked, knowing that coming out of a coma wasn't easy. It wasn't like the movies where they wake up and ask where they are. They wake up slowly, each day a little more aware. But as I looked back at Mitch, he seemed fully awake and functioning. If I had paid attention, I might have noticed that he no longer had a breathing tube. That his hand was squeezing mine back with surprising strength. His casts weren't hard but soft, as if he was getting ready to move. The only thing he was hooked up to was an IV. I tilted my head, scrunching my forehead a bit, then tilted it the other way to look straight at Theo. "And how is he functioning this well?"

Jordin's smile had disappeared, and she opened her mouth to answer, but when she saw me looking to Theo for answers, she pursed her lips and dropped her gaze to Mitch instead.

"Doctor Smiles is a part of our team, as you know," Theo started, but then the doctor stepped into the room and closed the door behind him.

"Hello, Rayleigh. Lovely to see you again," he beamed at me and walked to the other side of Mitch's bed. "I hear you've been learning some things about yourself lately?" He grabbed Mitch's chart from the bottom of the bed and checked his vitals on the machine against it.

All I could do was nod. The casual way he mentioned things meant the other people in the room must already know everything. Jordin and Theo knew. Doctor Smiles. But Chief? I squinted at him. "You too?"

He nodded. "Been assigned to this town since you were brought here."

My mind was going to explode. "Is there anyone else I should know about that's a part of your *team*?" I asked, directing my question to Theo again.

Theo shrugged. *Actually* shrugged. Like it was no big deal that I just found out nobody in my life was who they said they were.

I looked back to Mitch. His mouth had turned slightly down, and his eyes were wide and shining. When I met his gaze, he gave me a small smile that didn't quite reach his eyes. "I only just found out," he said as if it wasn't the most insane information he'd heard in his entire life. Maybe he didn't know what we were talking about.

"Found out what?" I asked, slowly taking my hand from his to lay my arms across my waist again.

He raised an eyebrow at me, "That you're a loser." A huge smile broke out on his face as the others in the room suppressed a laugh. I tried to hold back my laughter but failed miserably, giggling through the pain in my chest. I plopped down on the edge of Mitch's bed, and he reached for my hand again, a smile still plastered on his face as the laughter died down. I let him take my hand and held his gaze as his smile faded, and he said, "I don't care what you are, Ray. You'll always be my sister. No matter where you are in the universe or what blood runs through your veins," He gave a wild grin, "you're still my annoying big sister who sucks at Nerf gun wars," I gasped and tried to pull my hand away in mock frustration, but he held on tight, his smile tightening, "That I love so much." His voice broke a little, and I noticed tears in his eyes. Mine spilled over at his last words. "And that will never change."

I shook my head, "Why does this sound like a goodbye?" I said, the words barely a whisper as I took in the pained expression on his face. "You just woke up. You can come home soon. *I* can come home."

He shook his head. Why was he shaking his head? "I can't go home, Ray." His voice was quiet but firm. "They think I'm dead."

Hot tears spilled down my face as the words slammed into me. If he wasn't going home— "No… No! You have to stay!" I turned to Theo and Jordin. "He has to stay!" I was on my feet again but didn't let go of Mitch's hand. "Can't you just—just protect him or something? Like you have been here?"

Theo answered quietly, "They know we're hiding something. They don't know what, but if they find out…" He trailed off because he knew I knew how that sentence ended.

I turned back to Mitch. He was blurry through the tears in my eyes. "I don't want you to go. I just got you back." My voice was cracking. I was breaking. Mitch was the only family I had left. And even if he wasn't my actual family, he was still my brother. Just like he said. In my heart, he was my brother. He always would be. I looked at his face. The tears spilled down his face, leaving tracks on his cheeks. But there was acceptance beneath his sadness. He knew this had to happen, and there was no stopping it. "I can't lose you, too." My voice was a squeak, barely audible. But I knew he heard me.

With a lot of effort, he sat up on the bed and faced me. "You'll never lose me, Ray. I'll always be with you." He placed his hand on his heart. "Right here." This time, he pulled me into a hug, ignoring the pain he must have felt. I squeezed him as tight as I dared, my tears falling on his shoulder as his fell onto mine. We stayed like that for a few minutes, just holding each other, before someone cleared their throat. I almost ignored it, not caring if something else had to be said. But Mitch released me and pulled back slowly, taking my hand again as he sat up fully and faced the four people now standing at the foot of his bed.

Doctor Smiles spoke first, directly to me, "Theo has informed me that you don't know everything about our kind." I was wiping the tears from my face, trying to compose myself as he continued. "Mitchell's condition when he arrived was very dire, but with my... abilities, I was able to speed up his recovery enough to get him functioning on his own again."

"So, what, you have like— healing powers?" I said a bit sarcastically.

He nodded, "In a sense, yes." I gaped at him. "But I'm sure you'll learn more from Theo and his team later. For now, know that Mitchell is fully healed from his internal injuries, with the more external ones mending on their own. We didn't want it to seem too suspicious." He stepped back, apparently done explaining himself to me, and wrote more notes on his clipboard.

I turned to Theo, my mouth still gaping. I knew he was the one in charge here. I closed my mouth, pressing my lips together before asking, "Where are you taking him?"

Theo looked at me with sad eyes. "I can't tell you that."

"How long will he be gone?"

"I can't tell you that either, dearie." My gaze fell. I should have expected that answer. "Just know that he will be safe. And he won't be alone."

There it was—the reason for me to acknowledge Jordin. I looked up at her through my eyebrows. "You're going with him?" My voice was hollow and harsh.

She nodded. Tears still lined her eyes, but she held them back. "He's my son," she whispered.

I clicked my tongue. "Of course. *Of course.* He's your *son.*" I tried to remind myself that Jordin wasn't really my mother, but it didn't matter. "I'm your daughter!" My voice was louder than I intended, anger lacing each word. "Or at least I thought I was. Did you even care about me like that?" Mitch squeezed my hand, pulling a little to grab my attention, but I ignored him. "When Arabella died, you couldn't even look at me! I needed you!" My voice cracked as tears threatened to unleash. "I was crumbling into *nothing,* and you treated me like it was *my fault.* How was it my fault, Jordin?" The words were spilling out of me now—a waterfall of words I never said. I couldn't stop them. "The man who hit us was drunk! *He's* the reason Arabella died, not me!" I reeled in my anger a little. "I don't even know why you cared so much. She wasn't even your daughter."

Jordin couldn't take it anymore. "She was too! And you—" Her voice cracked through the pain. "I treated you like my own children! I loved you! I still do—"

"You have a funny way of showing it!" She recoiled at my harsh tone, but I went on, "Where were you when Dad died? Huh?" When she didn't respond, I answered for her. "You were gone. You were never home. You *left us*! We had to grieve him without you," My voice broke. "Do you know how hard that was? Do you even know what happened that day? We had to listen to Dad screaming as he died. And you were a shell. A ghost in that house." The feelings I had never processed into words finally came to the surface. "It felt like I was grieving you too." The words barely made it out in a whisper.

Jordin's face fell, fresh tears spilling down her face. After a moment of silence, she made a bold choice and walked toward me. I didn't feel like backing away, so I let her approach. But my eyes were on the ground. She placed both hands on either side of my face and lifted it to look at her. Her eyes flicked between mine, back and forth a few times before she spoke. "I had no idea—" She started, swallowed, and tried again. "You didn't deserve to go through that, sweetheart. Any of that." She wiped away some of my tears and said, "I'm so sorry I wasn't there for you."

She meant it. I could tell. Hell, I might have forgiven her for it right then. But there was more to pile on now. I gently removed her hands from my face, and hurt flashed across her face as I said, "You've kept too much from me." I knew that she probably didn't have a choice, that it had to be kept secret, but that didn't mean I wasn't hurt. "I need time." I took a step back, and she mirrored me.

"I understand," she whispered. Then she walked back to the corner table and sat with hands in her lap, shoulders slumped, and head hanging.

Theo walked toward me and stopped beside me, his shoulder touching mine. His voice was low enough for only me to hear, "You'll need to talk to her before you leave." He wasn't looking at me but staring at the wall ahead.

"I know," I said because I had a lot of questions for her. "I just— need a few minutes." Mitch still gripped my hand, but his other was in Doctor Smiles'. The doctor had his eyes closed, both hands wrapped around Mitch's. Was he using his power? How did it work? Was he listening to the inner workings of his body as he held his hand? I made a mental note to add it to my list of questions in my notebook. Turning back to Theo, who was still shoulder to shoulder with me, I said, "When will he be leaving?"

Theo dropped his gaze to the floor. "He will be brought to a temporary safe house when you leave. Then we will move him to a more permanent location on Saturday."

"Why Saturday?" I watched Doctor Smiles release Mitch's hand and step back to make notes on his clipboard.

"Prom is that evening." He said it like it was the most obvious answer. When he saw that I was still confused, he explained. "Aaidan and Koladon will be distracted trying to get to you."

What felt like cold water trickled down my spine. They were going to use me as a distraction to move Mitch, like bait on a hook. And if what they were saying about me being the most powerful fae was true, it would work. Aaidan didn't seem like the type to pass up on an easy opportunity to get what he wanted. A shiver ran through me at the possibility of seeing my beautiful torturer again.

My gaze fell to Mitch. He was now answering Smiles's questions, who charted the answers as he went. If being a distraction would keep Mitch safe, I wouldn't hesitate. Theo and his team must have known that, which would explain why they planned it without telling me. But I didn't like not being told things. Yes, too much information overwhelmed me, but being uninformed wasn't any easier. Too many secrets had been kept from me. My entire life had been a lie, and I still didn't know the half of it.

Without looking at Theo, I said, "I don't want to be kept in the dark anymore." Knowing everything was exciting and paralyzing, but I could handle it. I'd treat it like another class in school, learning new things that seemed impossible but would help me to live my life to the fullest. I'd have little study sessions, maybe a PowerPoint or two, to ensure I understood the new world I was being introduced to. Perhaps

I'd even make Theo quiz me. I just hoped none of it was as dull and confusing as Trig. "When we get back to the house—"

"Dengalow," he corrected with a smirk.

I had to bite my lip to hide my own. "When we get back to the *Dengalow*," I mocked, but my smile faded, "I want to know everything. Maybe in small chunks, but I need to know. I'm tired of secrets."

Theo breathed a sigh of relief, "Absolutely." He stepped back to look at my face, then over his shoulder at Jordin, still studying her hands in the corner. When his eyes met mine again, I could see the request in his eyes. "You should start with her. She has important things to tell you." I dropped his gaze, but Theo caught my chin and made me look at him. His deep voice rumbled through me. "She cares about you. Even if she didn't know how to show it properly." He released my chin and clasped his hands behind his back. "She was only trying to protect you."

My gaze flicked to Jordin, and I took a deep breath. I squeezed Mitch's hand to let him know I would be back and walked over to where Jordin sat. I stopped and waited for her eyes to find mine. I motioned with my head for her to follow and turned to the door without checking to see if she did.

XXI
Eyes Open

We found a private family waiting room down the hall, and I sat heavily in one of the chairs, leaning my head back against the wall. Jordin followed me meekly, shutting the door behind her and sitting on the edge of the chair across from me. She set her hands in her lap again and started twiddling her thumbs.

When it became clear she wasn't going to speak first, I sat forward, put my elbows on my knees, and let my hands hang loose between them. I stared at the top of her head. "I don't know what to ask, Jordin. So you're going to have to start talking."

She shrugged, not looking up. "I don't know where to start." Her voice was quiet, laced with sadness. Perhaps even something more profound.

"How about the beginning?" I offered.

Her head finally lifted, and her eyes reminded me of a lost puppy, but she took a breath and said, "Your mother's name was Analisa." The sound of her name made something come alive inside me. "She's a fae just like you, but she was born in a time of war. It wasn't safe for her in your realm. She was brought to our doorstep with a note asking my parents to care for her like their own. It said that one day, her family would come back for her when it was safe again.

"Your Grams didn't hesitate. She raised Analisa as my sister, not knowing anything about her or where she came from. We looked similar enough to pass as sisters, so no one questioned our relationship."

Jordin took a deep breath. This was the most I'd heard her say in years. "When we were in high school, Analisa started to develop her magic. At first, it was easy to write off as random luck, like her car starting only because she asked it to or things happening at just the right moments. But then weird things started happening. She would run her hands along the grass, and flowers would grow in the wake of her path. Or she would swim in the lake, and the water would bubble. We didn't know what was happening.

"Then, one day, a man showed up. He said someone was coming to help her learn her magic and how to control it. Once she could control it, she could return to her realm with her family. The only problem was she didn't know anything about her family in the other realm. As far as she knew, we were her family, and she didn't want to leave. But when told she had magic, she was beside herself with questions. They sent a young woman, or at least she looked young, to help Analisa learn about where she came from and how to control her magic. Her name was Libella. She looked like an Amazon goddess. A warrior. She was tall and beautiful, and her laugh filled the room with joy. She answered all of Analisa's questions with grace and patience, practicing her magic with her as often as she could without being discovered. We went to the meadow by the lake. That was her favorite place." Jordin's eyes softened as she looked up at me. My mother... She practiced magic in *my* meadow? "And it was secluded enough that no one would see her using her magic. Her magic entranced me, and Libella was kind enough to let me tag along to see what she could do. Sometimes, Analisa and I would sneak away from home in the middle of the night to practice her magic. Her favorite thing to do was make creatures out of water. She would have them dance around us, floating in the air and leaving wet kisses on our faces." Jordin smiled at the memory.

"The next time someone came for her, it was the man who would turn out to be your father, Rafael. He was part of the Omada assigned to protect her on her travels back to their realm. He would help her if she failed to use magic to protect herself." Jordin sat back in the chair, taking a deep breath. "Saying goodbye was the hardest thing I'd ever done. She was my sister, and it felt like I would never see her again. But she left with a promise to come back whenever she could, but I knew it was unlikely.

"I cried for days after she left, having spent so much of my life with her, I didn't know what it would be like without her." That was how I felt after losing Arabella. Maybe that was why Ma disappeared after her death. She was reliving history, in a way. "Eventually, I returned to my life and got used to her being gone. Greg certainly helped me get through it the most." A sad smile crossed her face at his name.

"Analisa showed up on my front porch a few years later. I was so surprised to see her that I didn't even realize she wasn't alone when I leaped into her arms. Rafael was standing behind her with you and Arabella in his arms." She closed her eyes as her smile disappeared. "You weren't even one yet. When I noticed you two and saw the expression on Analisa's face… I'd never seen such worry. I knew immediately something was very wrong. All the joy I'd felt when I first saw her melted away. Ushering you all inside the house, I shut the door and told Greg to close all the blinds. Rafael handed Arabella off to Analisa, but you…" Her eyes found mine, silver lining them. "You took one look at Greg and reached out your little tiny hand for him. He was so taken aback but didn't hesitate. He lifted you from Rafael's arms and pulled you close. You laid your head on his shoulder and fell right to sleep.

"Rafael and Analisa smiled sadly at each other, and he nodded to her. Then she turned to us and told us that the war was still going on in their realm, and it wasn't safe for you two to be there. She begged us to take you in, knowing you'd be safe here, but promised to send others to help protect you. One look at Greg, and I knew he was ready to help. To take you in. He was already holding you like you were the most precious piece of treasure he'd ever owned. Of course, we hadn't known that day that Mitchell was on the way, but I don't think Greg would have changed his mind either way.

"Analisa told me she wouldn't be able to visit for fear of leading the wrong people here who might try to kill you and Arabella. She also said that she wouldn't be able to return to her home and would have to go somewhere else until things... settled." Jordin found her hands in her lap again, thumbs twiddling away. "I wasn't allowed to know all the details. I don't know where your parents went or if they're still alive. I don't know what war was happening or if it's even over. I don't even know the full extent of your mother's powers." She looked up at me. "What I do know is that they loved you," she choked out, "and they didn't want to leave you here, but they didn't have a choice. They were being hunted and had barely made it here without being caught. They told Greg and me that Doctor Smiles was a part of their team and that you were only to see him whenever you were hurt due to the difference in your blood and anatomy. It's slight but enough for regular doctors to catch and find suspicious. They also said the new local police chief would be there if we ever felt like anything was wrong.

"The third guard was Theo, but he kept to the shadows when watching over you. He never made himself known, kept close watch on you, and was always aware of where you were. You and Arabella were so active and clumsy throughout your life, always seeking adventure in the forests and the lake. Your powers remained hidden for the most part, but when you two hit high school, the same signs your mother gave started to show. I told your Omada what I noticed, and they began to keep a closer eye on your two, knowing that the first sign of your powers could give away your location. They did their best to shield you and cover your tracks, but it didn't always work. We knew someone discovered your existence the day you turned sixteen. Theo and Chief told us they felt someone from their realm enter ours. They didn't stay more than half a mile from you two after that, knowing that something could happen at any moment.

"The only night they were all too far away was—" She stopped and cleared her throat, hesitated a moment, and then her eyes lined with silver again. "The night Arabella died."

My hand flew to my mouth. Arabella's death wasn't an accident?

But the man who hit us was a drunk… he was convicted. He said he wasn't drinking but had blacked out and couldn't remember anything from that night. It occurred to me then it must not have been a drunken blackout but something different…

Jordin sniffed and went on. "By the time Theo arrived at the crash, Arabella was already gone. But you… You were still alive but only just. Hanging on by a thread," she sniffled. "He said that you would have been gone if he hadn't arrived when he did. He did what he could to make sure you'd arrive at the hospital alive and then went to the man in the truck who had barely been injured. He interrogated him to determine if someone else was pulling the strings, but his memory had been wiped completely clean. Theo took responsibility for the accident and doubled his efforts to keep you safe after that, knowing he had to call in more support soon after. Whoever was hunting you was sure that you both died in that accident. We were told they left our realm thinking the job was done. But they returned a few months later because they could still sense your magic.

"During those months following Arabella's death, I didn't know how to handle the grief of losing her. Even though she wasn't my flesh and blood, I had raised her as such. All I could think about was how I needed to find a way to contact your parents. To tell them I failed to protect their daughters. I couldn't even look at you without seeing your mother and asking myself how I would tell her." She buried her face in her hands, giving in to the grief. When she recovered, I had tears streaming down my face, too. "But you were right. I saw you falling apart, and all I could do was think about how much I wanted to tell you that it wasn't your fault… but I couldn't. I wanted to tell you everything whenever your grief overwhelmed you, but I knew it wasn't the right time. I knew that telling you wouldn't make it easier. Or better. So I distanced myself from you, knowing you had Greg to comfort you."

She tried to wipe away her tears, but more replaced them so quickly. "The day Greg died…" Her voice cracked, and something broke inside me, too. "I was told they could smell you in his car. Your blood from the accident that morning was dried on the seat but fresh. He heard from Theo before he left the house again that they were on the hunt that morning. He had known it was possible they would come for you, so he made sure Theo and Chief were near the house before he left. None of us thought the tracker would send them after Greg…" She took a shaky breath, letting it out slowly before continuing again. "Theo told me he was on the scene when you arrived after the crash. He didn't let you see him, but he was the one who stopped you from running up to the flaming car."

Tears flowed freely down my face, but I made no move to wipe them away. Dad died because of me… because I was clumsy and cut myself open and bled in his car. If I hadn't fallen that morning, he might still be alive…

Jordin's soft but stern voice interrupted my thoughts, "Rayleigh, you cannot blame yourself for Greg's death. I know that's what you're doing, but it's not true."

"But I'm the reason he's dead!" I sobbed.

Her knees hit the ground before me, and she made me look at her. "You did *not* kill him, Rayleigh. Those—those *monsters* did. You may have been the one they were after, but it is *not* your fault he's dead." She reached for my hands, and I let her take them. "Greg wouldn't have changed anything about that morning if it meant you were safe." The sorrow in her voice mirrored what I was feeling inside. "He loved you more than anything. You meant the world to him, and I know you felt the same way about him." Jordin went silent for a moment, her words echoing in my head. When she spoke again, her voice was barely a whisper. "I'm so sorry you had to grieve him on your own. I couldn't comfort you in the way that I should have. I handled my grief by throwing myself into work and taking over Greg's position at his company. I didn't think—" She paused, her tear-filled eyes finding mine. "I didn't think you would need me like you needed him." The truth of that sentence hit hard. She didn't think I loved her like I did Dad… how could she? Besides Kaleb, he was the only one who could ever get through to me. Jordin was never able to comfort me like that. I didn't realize how much that might affect her until this moment.

Making a decision, I squeezed her hands to get her to look at me. "Jordin, just because we didn't always see eye to eye doesn't mean I didn't— don't need you. That I don't *love you*." The words cracked something open in both of us. A happy sob tore from her as she pulled me into a strong embrace, one I hadn't felt or returned in over a year. After a moment's hesitation, I squeezed her back, releasing all the pent-up anger and grief I'd been holding onto.

We stayed like that for a while, allowing me to process everything she said, her mother's embrace never ceasing.

It was all so much. Knowing I'd been hunted my entire life. That Arabella had died alone when it was meant to be both of us. Dad died because of a bloodstain I'd left in his car. I still didn't know enough of the details of my life, but I did know that no one around me was safe. I pulled away from Jordin to look at her again. "Why did they go after Mitch?" I asked because that was what didn't make sense to me. He was walking home from school alone. I wasn't with him. There was no reason for them to target him.

Jordin moved back to the seat across from me, wiping her tears, and she shook her head. "I don't know. Theo thinks they changed tactics because they had learned something else about you, but they won't give me any more information." She took in my expression and sighed. "We should probably get back to Mitch. It's getting late, and I don't want to take up any more of the time you have left with him."

She stood, pulling me up with her, and made to move toward the door, but I pulled her back. She stopped and met my eyes. "I'm sorry you lost your husband." I wasn't sure I'd ever said those words to her, thinking she didn't care. "And I'm sorry you almost lost your son. You didn't deserve any of this."

Her eyes filled with tears again, but she didn't let them fall, blinking them back again before saying, "I lost a daughter, too." She laid a hand on my shoulder. "But we can't lose you. Promise me you'll do everything you can to learn your magic. It's your strongest weapon. I've seen what it can do." She smiled. "Learn it. Own it. Control it. Show those monsters what you're made of."

I gave a sobbing laugh, not even sure what my magic could do yet, but I knew she was right. "I promise. So long as you promise to keep Mitch safe." A nod, but I added. "And make sure to bring the Nerf guns with you. He'll beat you, but I'm sure you'll learn quickly."

She laughed. "I'll make sure to grab them from the house on our way to the safe house." When she turned to walk out this time, I let her pull me behind her.

॰ ॰ ॰ ॰

When we got back to the room, Smiles was gone. Theo and Chief talked in the corner, and Mitch sat in bed watching the little TV. Jordin stopped in the doorway and motioned for Chief and Theo to meet her in the hall. She told me on the walk back that she would give Mitch and me a few minutes to ourselves before they left.

As soon as the door closed, I said the one thing I'd kept to myself but *needed* to tell someone. "Kaleb kissed me."

Mitch's jaw dropped, but he quickly recovered. He threw his hands up and exclaimed, "Finally!"

"Excuse me, what?" The words came out through a laugh.

"You heard me." He chuckled a bit, patting the bed beside him. "Tell me everything."

Rolling my eyes, I sat down next to him, leaning on his shoulder, and relayed the story of the piano room. He had a devilish smirk the whole time, but when I got to the part about Kyler, his eyebrows tried to disappear under his hair. "Kyler did what now? I don't even know this guy, but he sounds like a total twat!"

"Right?!" At least someone agreed with me on that. I realized Mitch hadn't been around to hear about anything else since Kaleb asked me to the dance, so I went back and told him the whole story from the last time I saw him up until the kiss. I left out the details of how unfortunately attractive Kyler was and how it confused my brain, though, thinking they were unimportant details.

"This Kyler guy is supposed to protect you? Sounds like he would rather eat hot coals." He and I both laughed a little at that. Then his face turned more serious. "What are you going to do about Kaleb?"

I let out a sigh, "I don't know Mitch. He's been my best friend for so long. I don't want to lose that if things don't work out."

"Yeah, but what if things *do* work out? What if that happiness you felt when you saw him today was just the start of something new?"

I cocked my head at him and gave a knowing smile. "When did you become so smart?"

He shrugged, a smile playing on his lips. "Just promise me you're not going to try to kiss Kyler."

My jaw dropped, and Mitch laughed as he saw the pink filling my cheeks. I shook my head as a laugh started to bubble out of me, too. I knew he said it to get a rise out of me—typical Little Monster move. I was glad I hadn't mentioned how confusing things with Kyler were. He thought it was hilarious that Kendall and Leighton thought Kyler was treating me the way he was because he liked me.

I soaked in those moments with Mitch, not knowing when or if I'd ever see him again. The laughter faded between us, and he noticed me staring at him. "No. Don't start with the tears. You and I both know we won't be able to stop." He was right. We both cried way more than any average person should. But even when I took a shaky breath to try and will the tears away, they still spilled down my face.

"I'm gonna miss you, Mitch." I threw my arms around his neck, and he returned the embrace, either ignoring the pain or it had lessened since I had left him with Doctor Smiles.

"I'm gonna miss you too, Ray." He held on for as long as he could until someone knocked on the door to his room.

Jordin peeked her head in as we pulled apart. "It's time, sweetheart." Mitch and I both nodded. A nurse came in behind Jordin, and we all helped Mitch transfer to the wheelchair she was pushing. Theo and Chief were in the hall waiting for us when we emerged. Outside, Chief led us to his cruiser and opened the back door for us.

The roar of an engine made my head turn. I closed my eyes and let out a frustrated sigh at the sight of the familiar black Audi as it pulled up behind the cruiser.

Immediately, I turned to Theo. "Why can't you just take me home?" I asked, knowing that's precisely why Kyler was there. After saying goodbye to Mitch and Jordin, he was the last person I wanted to be in a car with.

Theo looked at me plainly. "I have to escort Jordin and Mitchell to the safe house. I most likely won't be back at the house until tomorrow."

Kyler stepped out of the car and rounded the front of it to meet us at the back of Chief's cruiser.

Still addressing Theo, I said, "And where's Mari?"

Mitchell was watching the conversation like a tennis match. Then Kyler came into view, and his eyes widened. "*That's* Kyler?" My head snapped to him in an effort to get him to *shut up*, and he bit his lip to keep the growing smile from appearing. He failed.

I scowled at him and turned to Kyler, who was leaning against the back of the cruiser, his leather jacket and tight black jeans fitting him perfectly. He was so infuriatingly attractive, and I couldn't stand it.

Kyler smirked. "Talking to your little brother about me, Sunshine?" His deep voice rattled my bones.

I clenched my teeth and twisted back to Theo. "Why can't Mari pick me up?"

"She's busy," Kyler answered.

I whipped back to Kyler. "I wasn't talking to you."

He sneered, "Obviously."

Theo cleared his throat. "Niko," he warned, then addressed me, "Rayleigh, I'm sorry, but Mari is busy tonight with something else. Niko will be taking you home." He came to stand between Kyler and me, with whom I was still having a staring contest. "Right now, you need to say goodbye to Mitchell and Jordin. The longer we are outside, the bigger the risk we take."

His words settled the hate that had been boiling to the surface. I turned away from Kyler to face Jordin and Mitch, who were both gaping slightly at the interaction they just witnessed. My cheeks suddenly felt hot. They'd just seen how much Kyler rattled me. Great.

I took a deep breath and stepped up to Jordin. "Remember what you promised me?" She nodded and gave me a reassuring smile. "Good." I reached for her and wrapped my arms around her middle tightly. "I love you, Ma."

She let out a short sob, burying her face into my shoulder as she squeezed me tighter. "I love you too, sweetheart." Her voice was muffled in my shoulder, but I knew calling her Ma was what caused her to break open a little more. While she told me the story earlier, I realized nothing she did was wrong. Sure, she could have handled some of it better, but she was still my mom, even if the same blood didn't flow through our veins. She pulled away and wiped the tears from her face before kissing my forehead and stepping behind Mitch.

Mitch already had tears in his eyes, but I could tell he was holding them back for me. I crouched in front of his wheelchair and put my hands on his knees. "Don't cause Ma any more trouble, Little Monster. She's been through too much, okay?" He nodded.

"Write to me if you can. Tell me all about your magic and what you learn." I nodded at his request and stood to hug him. He whispered, "I love you—more than the sun."

I choked back a sob. "I love you, too, Mitch. More than the sun." Sniffling loudly, I stepped out of his embrace and helped Chief get him into the back seat. Once he was settled, I gave him one last hug before shutting the door. I hugged Ma before she climbed in next to him and waved as they drove out of the lot, Theo following in the Jeep.

When they disappeared around the corner, I took a deep breath, wiped the tears from my eyes, and turned to face the last person I wanted to be in a car with. He was leaning against the front of his car with a lollipop sticking out of his mouth. Asshole.

I stomped to the car's passenger side and tried to yank open the door, but it was locked. The sadness I had felt saying goodbye to my family turned into fuming rage as I turned to Kyler and watched a smile slowly spread across his face. I yanked on the door handle several times, clenching my teeth as the arrogance dripped off him.

He pushed off the front of the car and turned to face me. "Patience, Sunshine." He sauntered over, making me back up against the car door to keep space between us. But he didn't stop his advances. He closed the distance, and my breath caught at his sudden closeness. My rage boiled to the surface, but something else in me warmed at his nearness. I hated it. I shoved whatever that feeling was deep inside me as his scent overwhelmed my senses. Smoke and something else I couldn't place, but the strongest was the strawberry lollipop he had in his mouth. It filled my nose against my will, weaseling its way into my memory.

He reached behind me, his hand grazing my hip as he found the door handle. The car beeped, signaling that the doors had been unlocked. I was pressed against the door, but he roughly pulled the handle. The movement forced me into him, and my hands flew up to stop me from getting too close. They landed flat on his chest. Air caught in my lungs. I could feel his steady heartbeat beneath my palm. The warmth of his body seeped through his shirt. His chest rising and falling to the beat of his strawberry-scented breaths on my cheek—

I came to my senses and *pushed* as hard as possible to get him back off. My push was either much weaker than I intended, or he was as solid as he felt through his thin shirt because he barely moved. But it was enough. I turned around and opened the car door the rest of the way, climbing into the front seat. I went to slam the door, but he grabbed it. "Don't."

Scowling, I let go of the door and buckled my seatbelt instead. He closed the door gently, and the minute he stepped away, I reached to open the door so that I could slam it again to piss him off. But the door locked. "Ugh! Screw you, jackass!" I gave him a vulgar gesture through the window.

He unlocked the car again to get in the driver's seat and chuckled darkly. The car started with a roar, making me roll my eyes so far back into my head that I almost gave myself a headache.

It was difficult not to admire the inside of the car. It was gorgeous, but I never wanted him to know that. Instead of looking around the car as my heart wished, I stared straight out the windshield as he pulled onto the main road. Instead of turning away from the city toward the Dengalow, he headed into the city.

"Where are you taking me?" I growled.

"Somewhere for you to blow off this steam."

XXII
New Blood

I shouldn't have been surprised that Kyler knew where my gym was, but that didn't stop me from whipping my head toward him when he pulled into the parking lot. "How the hell did you know I train here?" It was the one secret that only two other people knew about, and I'd been adamant about keeping it that way.

His answering look told me enough: they'd been following me much closer than I assumed. But he answered anyway, "We know the owner." Of course, they *knew the owner*. He was probably involved in the group protecting me. Something occurred to me.

"Did someone follow me here the day I was kidnapped?" The memory of the person stalking up to my car flashed in my head.

Kyler looked at me sideways for a moment before answering. "Yes."

"Why do you have to be so creepy with the hoodies??" I was glad to finally know the people behind the hood were just there to protect me, but they could have been more subtle and less creepy.

He made a face, "What? I drove off before you got to the lot."

My face dropped. "Then who was the man in the hoodie?"

"Probably a stalker," he mocked, getting out of the car. "Remember, someone *kidnapped* you?" He closed his door before the slew of curse words flew out of my mouth.

I sat back in my seat, crossing my arms. There was no way I was going in there with him to do *any* training. When he noticed I hadn't gotten out of the car, he rounded the front and came to open my door. Petty as ever, I reached up and locked the door from the inside just before he reached the handle. I knew his windows were tinted, so he couldn't see the smug look on my face when the door didn't open when he yanked on the handle. Two can play at this game. I chuckled at my small victory, but then the car beeped, and I swore, rolling my eyes at my stupidity. The now unlocked door swung open, revealing a scowl on Kyler's face. "Out."

"No." I didn't look at him, but I could feel the irritation radiating off of him.

He put a forearm on the car and leaned far enough that I could feel his hot breath on my cheek as I refused to look at him. "Out, Sunshine."

"I'm not going in there with you." Out of everyone I knew, I did not expect Kyler to be the first to discover that this sacred place of mine existed—or at least the first to reveal that he knew about it.

"And we're not leaving until you've blown off some of this steam." His breath still smelled like strawberries even though he'd finished the lollipop on the drive here.

"Why? It's not like you even have to deal with me at the house. I'll stay in my room."

He laughed, the sudden burst blowing my unbound hair into my face. "That won't matter." Before I could ask what *that* meant, he said, "Plus, you haven't been here in five days. It shows."

My head snapped to look at him. "What do you mean, it shows?" I started. I didn't realize how close he was until my nose almost touched his. "I pinned you to the countertop just fine yesterday." The words came out a little breathier than I wanted, the distraction of the short distance between us suddenly overwhelming.

As he noticed my sudden change in tone, a wicked smile grew on his face. His voice became more of a growl, "We both know I let you pin me to that counter."

His insinuation didn't make it easy to hide the heat rising to my cheeks. But I wasn't going to back down. "Bullshit. I bested you. And I'll do it again."

He chuckled and stood up straight. "I'll be happy to prove you wrong, Sunshine. Inside." He stepped away from the car, holding the door open so I could exit, but I just sat there with my arms crossed. Mostly because I still hated the way he called me Sunshine. But I also saw right through him. He'd goaded me into beating him again. To get me to go inside. I couldn't let him think that he 'let me' pin him.

I looked at the studio. The lights weren't on, and neither was the sign. "It's not even open."

Kyler held his hand up, and a tiny key dangled from a keyring hooked on his pinkie finger. Seeing no way out of this, I groaned loudly and unbuckled my seatbelt.

As much as I hated to admit it, he was right. I hadn't been at the studio in a few days and felt my body craving the training—the movements, the release, the structure. I hated the idea of showing Kyler what I could do, but I needed this. He knew it, too, which made it worse.

Of my three guardians, why did he have to be the one who knew the most about me? I couldn't stand him, and it seemed to me that the feelings were mutual. Yet he still noticed enough to help with the panic attacks and that my training was something I needed, mentally and physically. Whether he knew that or not, I surely wouldn't be surprised if he did.

He grabbed a pack from the trunk as I slammed the door, which earned me a scowl, but I grinned back. *Serves him right.* He unlocked the gym and held the door for me to walk into one of my favorite places.

Kyler flipped on the lights to reveal an empty mat before us. I peered down at my current clothes and realized I didn't have the proper clothing for a training session. Before I could relay that tidbit to Kyler, he held out a bag and pointed to the bathrooms. Clenching my jaw, I snatched the bag from him and went to change.

When alone, I opened the bag and saw what he'd given me. It was all brand new, tags and all. I grunted, not caring how he knew my sizes but still curious nonetheless. Perhaps Mari had gotten them for me. I'd have to thank her later.

As I changed into the new outfit, I realized this could be a good thing. I'd take my anger out on him. I may not be able to hit him, but I could undoubtedly throw him over my shoulder and onto the mat a few times. Kyler was bigger than my coach, both in mass and height, but I was mad enough at this point that I felt as though I could flip an elephant over my shoulder.

I emerged from the bathroom to find that Kyler had changed as well. Sporting gym shorts and a cut-off shirt, he was stretching his arms while standing in the middle of the mat. "How do you even know how to do this?" I demanded, walking to the edge of the mat, stopping to cross my arms while he waited for me in the middle.

Kyler shrugged. "Training back home includes similar moves to jiu jitsu."

"Training for what?" I was stalling. I didn't want to get in a grappling match with Kyler. Mainly because the last time he grabbed my bare torso, he left a mark. The cool air in the gym bit into my exposed skin. The clothes he'd given me to wear were a bright green sports bra and matching leggings. Neither of which covered the mark on my ribcage. But I didn't care. I wanted him to see it. To see if he'd react at all. It had faded on the outer edges a bit, but at this point, I was starting to think it was a permanent mark. That could very well be true, but that didn't mean I had to like it.

"Quit stalling and get out here." He didn't break eye contact, which meant he was either great at self-control or didn't find what I was wearing attractive, which would be a mistake on his part. Because I saw myself in the mirror before I came out here. I knew I looked good. But his eyes didn't wander, which meant he wouldn't see the mark. *Dammit.*

I pulled the rubber band from my bun, which had become too messy, and switched it to a tight ponytail. Kyler watched my every move, calculating. I stepped onto the mat. "Are we sparring, or are you going to attempt to teach me something?"

He cocked a brow at me. "Both."

"If I win, you have to stop calling me Sunshine."

He chuckled, "And if I win, I get to call you Sunshine anytime I want."

I narrowed my eyes. "Deal." Because I knew he wasn't going to win.

Just as I finished tightening my ponytail, Kyler moved to grab me from behind, pinning both arms to my sides. "Show me how you got out of this hold Aaidan had you in." His breath was warm on the shell of my ear, and suddenly, my entire body was hot despite the chill I felt moments ago. Every inch of bare skin that Kyler touched felt like it was on fire, but not like the burn on my ribs.

No. This was different.

This was my body betraying me.

I hated it.

His breath whispered in my ear, meaning he hadn't moved his face away yet. I almost let myself think of why that could be. But then I remembered why we were here and did what he asked.

I took a deep breath, dropped my weight to bend my knees, and stepped out sideways. I briefly shifted my hips in the other direction before bringing that leg behind both of his. Straightening the leg that was now behind him, I hugged both of his knees and dropped our weight back. I landed on top of him with my shoulder blades against his chest.

But that's where the similarities ended. Because Kyler knew the counter move. He was still holding on to me and used the momentum I gave to pin him to the ground to his advantage. He kept us rolling and managed to pull himself out from under me. He swung his leg over my waist, pinning me down with his weight, straddling my hips.

The position he ended up in, with hands on either side of my face to cage me, was called "the mount."

Kyler gave me an evil grin like he'd won, but he was far from it.

I wrapped both arms around his right elbow, pulling it toward where his stomach met mine. Holding onto his elbow with one hand, my other grasped his hand, and I pinned it to my chest. I trapped his right foot against my backside with my opposite foot and bucked my hips while rolling to the left simultaneously. It took more effort than it usually did against my coach, with five days off and Kyler being heavier, but it worked.

Kyler's legs were still wrapped around my waist, but I had moved both hands to pin his arms to the mat next to him.

He broke my hold and grabbed my left arm into a Kimura, then bucked his hips to throw me off him and straddled me again. He pinned my hand above my head and held me down by my collarbone with his other forearm. This left his face very close to mine, and our heavy breathing mingled closely as his eyes sparkled with the almost victory.

I flared my nostrils and went to make my next move, but Kyler jumped off me and pulled me to my feet with the hand he still held onto. It took minimal effort for him to haul me to my feet. I didn't appreciate that I was out of breath, and he was ready to go again immediately.

I stared at him, my jaw slack. "You forfeited the match."

Kyler grinned, "Nah. I won, Sunshine."

"No. You didn't. I didn't tap out." My breathing wasn't quite normal, but I was ready to go again.

He raised a brow, the grin slowly disappearing. "You want to go until you tap out?"

"That's how it works, dumbass." I crossed my arms as he took me in, knowing I wouldn't be the one to tap out, and that would be the last time he called me Sunshine.

Finally, he shrugged and started towards me. Jaw set, eyes focused on me. I bent my knees, arms loose and ready as I began to move my feet to circle him. He followed suit, his clothes clinging to him from the sweat we worked up in the first match. It gleamed on his skin. It didn't seem like we sparred long enough to produce that much sweat, but if he felt the instant heat I did when he touched me, it would explain the amount of sweat we were dripping.

His eyes were on mine, but mine were on his arms, watching. Tracking.

When he made his first move to grab me, I shoved my hand in his face and grabbed his left knee with my hand, pulling his leg up between mine. I wrapped both hands around his thigh, shoving my shoulder into his exposed side. I let go of his leg with my arm closest to his body and grabbed his waist, moving the leg I had a grip on over my left leg. I straightened my other leg and sat down, taking him with me. His weight pulled us on our sides, and I pushed his shoulder down with my own to get his back flat on the ground. I got both arms on either side of him before he made his counter move.

He slid out from under my cage, avoiding my leg mid-swing to straddle him. Instead, he grabbed both my legs and shoved me onto my side. I couldn't move my legs because he had a grip like a bearhug on them as he pinned me down with his body weight.

But I knew my way out.

I placed my hand on his head and pushed while I shimmied my legs back and forth, slipping them from his bear hug. He was fighting to keep hold of my legs as I held his head, but he couldn't keep them in his grip. When my first leg was free, I pushed to a half-stand. I used my leg strength to get my other leg out while leaning onto his back, wrapping my arm around his neck and under his armpit, and locking them together against his chest.

He had been so focused on gripping my legs that he didn't expect the headlock. But that didn't deter him. He put his hands between my arm and his chest and pulled down, making my chest go flush against his upper back. And he pulled out of my hold. He sat back on his knees with a grip still on my forearm.

With a sharp pull, he jerked me forward. He moved so fast that I couldn't follow as he grabbed my back leg in my momentary lack of control. Using his shoulder, he shoved me onto my back, but his grip on my leg loosened. I swung my free leg under him and up around his waist. I pulled the leg he used to flip me out of his grip and wrapped it around his waist on the other side, getting him in a closed guard.

He did what I expected and put his hands on my waist to break out, but I reached up and pulled his head down to my stomach, the move causing my face to heat, but I ignored it. I pushed his hand into his chest and loosened my legs. I placed my feet on his hips and pushed while holding him in place. I adjusted my hips and pressed one hand against his chest. I moved one leg around that arm and onto his shoulder, the other quickly following on the opposite side to meet it. I shoved my hand between my legs to grab one of his— I couldn't tell which— behind the knee.

My legs were locked around him in a triangle hold, and I held him there, waiting for him to tap out. There was no way he was getting out. He may be big, but my legs were strong. My coach was never able to get out of my leg holds. Yeah, he was smaller, but it didn't seem to matter. I had Kyler trapped, and he and I both knew it.

That didn't stop him from trying to get out, though. He struggled in my grip, trying everything he could. He finally got his leg out of my hold, but his head and arm were still deadlocked in my triangle. I could see his face turning red.

"Tap out, dumbass," I said through gritted teeth. I could hold him, but he was strong and making it difficult. I didn't want to hold him any longer than I had to.

Kyler's answering noise was too close to a feral growl to understand. I assumed he said, "No."

"Tap out!" I squeezed my knees tighter to show him I wasn't even using my full strength. "Don't be *stupid*, tap out! Now!"

Finally, I felt it— the tap on my leg.

I released my grip and moved to get up, heaving breaths because it took a lot to hold him for that long while he struggled against it.

Kyler was still bent over on his hands and knees, sputtering and coughing after the momentary lack of oxygen. His face was red, and I couldn't tell if it was from being headlocked or because I'd won.

He wasn't looking at me, but it was probably because he was still trying to recover.

"Coach says you shouldn't wait to tap out," I said between breaths, hands on my hips.

"I'm fine," he growled.

"You could have passed out."

"I said. I'm fine." He pushed himself up and turned toward me, still breathing heavily. "Again."

My eyebrows shot up as I laughed. "I just kicked your ass! You want me to do it again?"

He just squared up and waited, his breathing becoming steadier. His face was full of determination. I thought about refusing to go again, but I had to admit it felt good sparring with someone different. Coach was fun, but sparring with Kyler felt real. Like I was fighting against someone. Not only was he bigger and stronger than my coach, but I had pent-up anger to use against him. Somewhere to place that anger and use the hidden strength I knew I had. Maybe it was something to do with my Fae powers coming in, but I could feel my body changing. Adapting to something new. Growing into something else. My stability was better, and my muscles were becoming more defined. My whole life, I thought it was just bad luck that I was so clumsy, but now I knew that wasn't it at all. I knew training helped develop all those things faster, but knowing my body was different from normal humans made sense that I had caught onto jiu-jitsu so quickly.

"Square up," Kyler said, becoming impatient with me.

I stepped up across from him on the mat, bending my knees, and said, "Just remember you asked for this."

We went until Kyler made me tap out.

Not because he won. No.

Because I was exhausted from holding him in the locks and chokes until he tapped out. He was fuming by the end. He thought he would teach me something, but all I learned was how stubborn he was. He never tapped out right away. No matter how many times I confidently told him to. He always struggled to get out of my hold for several seconds before finally tapping out.

All the moves he knew were basic and first-level for me. It was easy to break his hold and avoid his attempts at locks. He almost had me a couple of times, but if I made a little squeaking noise like I was in pain, his grip faltered. I may or may not have taken advantage of that.

Turns out he had a weakness for someone in pain.

I had no such mercy. He would grunt and yell because he was frustrated, but it didn't affect me. I thought he was letting me win after the second round, but he came out of that hold with rage seeping off him. It was slightly terrifying.

For the last one, I ended up having him in a straight ankle lock, and he tried for a whole minute to escape while I just calmly kept repeating through my strained voice, "Just tap out."

When he didn't, I twisted his foot a little to make it more painful and impossible for him to move in that position without injuring himself. He growled and tapped the mat so hard I thought he punched a hole in it.

He'd been pacing the mat for several minutes now after I told him I was done. I was leaning against the wall at the edge of the mat. I didn't understand why he was so upset. It was just sparring. *What a sore loser.*

He should have been exhausted, too. We'd been at it for almost two hours, but he never seemed to run out of breath. He always jumped right up, grabbed a drink of water, and was ready to go again.

He stopped pacing and looked at me with his brow scrunched. "Where did you learn to fight like that?"

The answer seemed obvious, so I stared at him and opened my arms to gesture at the gym around us.

He shook his head and stalked toward me, stopping inches from me. He searched my eyes as he said, "I know your coach, remember? Rifner can only teach you so much."

I cocked my brow at him. "I don't know who Rifner is, but he's not my coach."

Kyler's brows scrunched together again. "He owns this place."

"Okay? And? There's more than one coach here." Maybe where he's from—*we're* from—there's only one instructor.

He squinted at me. "What's your coach's name?" The little space between us shrank even more as he leaned in to hear my answer. I had to look up at him now. I debated not telling him, but there was no point.

"Tom." The twins' adoptive dad had mentioned in passing one day that he taught jiu-jitsu. After my dad died, I asked him if he could teach me, knowing that the twins could find out at any moment, but Tom promised not to tell them. He said he was teaching them privately at home, and if I ever wanted to expose my secret, he would be happy to have me join training at their house.

Something like recognition flashed in Kyler's eyes at his name.

"Tom is your coach?"

I started to shake my head. "Don't tell me he's part of this group of people here to protect me." Kyler's lack of answer was enough. If that were true, "Do Kendall and Leighton have something to do with this too, then?" I squeaked.

Kyler turned away from me and growled, "It's late."

But I grabbed his elbow before he got too far, his skin still hot from our time on the mat. When he stopped, I let go, but he didn't face me. "Don't lie to me." My voice was stern but soft, if only because the thought of the twins being a part of it— if they knew this whole time

"They don't know anything," Kyler said.

When he didn't go on, I said, "But?"

"Yes. Kendall and Leighton are similar to you."

My stomach flipped. Was anyone who I thought they were? The twins— I grew up with them. We'd been best friends since kindergarten. They were in the dark like me, but… To ensure there weren't any other surprises, I asked, "And Kaleb?"

From where I stood, I could see Kyler's jaw flex and his shoulders tense. "No." His nostrils flared, and he growled, "He's not involved."

His tone brought my temper to the surface. "What's your problem with him?" I demanded.

He whipped around so fast that I stumbled back half a step into the wall behind me. "He's an asshole!"

"You're one to talk!" I snapped.

"You can't even see it!"

"See what?!"

"He treats you like a child!" He snarled. "Like you can't do things for yourself. He's basically trained you to need him every time you have a panic attack! Do you understand how selfish that is?" His voice had risen to a yell, his green eyes shining with hatred and his nostrils flaring. His breath was hot as it hit my face.

"Why does it matter?" I tried to yell back, but my throat tightened around the words. "At least he cares!" Something about what Kyler said was true, though. I still needed to thank him for teaching me to control my panic attacks alone. But Kaleb's way still worked, which shouldn't give Kyler a reason to hate him. He was trying to help, too. In the only way he knew how.

Kyler's mouth opened to say something, but he closed it again, changing his mind. He searched my eyes for a moment and then stood up straight. I hadn't realized he was leaning over me until that moment. He'd been inches from my face. No wonder his smoky, strawberry scent was filling my nose. He took a deep breath and repeated, "It's late." His voice was low, but the fight had gone out of him. Maybe the exhaustion finally hit. With one last look at me, he stepped away and turned toward the door again. "Let's go."

I stood there for a minute in shock. Kyler had to be the most confusing person I'd ever met. His actions and words spoke different things. One minute, I knew he hated me with every fiber of his being. The next, I was trying to decide if he cared for me or was jealous. It was starting to get annoying.

But my exhaustion was starting to overwhelm my body. I didn't want to fight about this anymore. I shouldn't care what Kyler thought anyway. I barely knew him. He was there to protect me, and that was it. Kaleb had been there for me most of my life. I cared about him, and he obviously cared about me. So what if his methods of helping me were different? It still *helped*. And it made me feel safe.

As I walked to the door Kyler held open, I asked, "Can I get my phone back?" I hadn't talked to Kaleb since our kiss. It had taken a back burner to the other events of the day. It felt like several days had passed since I'd seen him. Held him. But I knew we needed to talk sooner rather than later.

Kyler blinked at me. "I— we don't have your phone."

Odd. I assumed they were holding my phone so I couldn't contact anyone and accidentally send my location to the enemy. But if they didn't have it— "It wasn't on me when you—" I hated that I had to say, "—rescued me?"

He locked the gym door and headed to the car, shaking his head. "You didn't have anything on you. We assumed you'd dropped everything at the store when they took you."

Well, that's strange. The last person who could have it was Kaleb. But if he didn't have it... where was it?

XXIII
Sorry Not Sorry

When we arrived back at the house, I barely made it to my bed before passing out. The exhaustion must have been enough to keep the dreams away because I forgot to take my medicine beforehand. But the night terrors stayed away. I woke up refreshed after what felt like the best night of sleep I'd ever had. I thought maybe I hadn't moved during the night because I slept so hard, but the blankets on the bed said otherwise. They were crumpled and crowded around me when I woke to the sun shining through the window.

It had been past midnight when we left the studio, but Kyler stopped for food on the way home. We'd both exhausted all our energy at the gym and were starving. He almost ordered the entire menu at Taco Bell, and then he turned to me and asked what I wanted. I gaped at him. Only for a moment, though, before my stomach demanded I order twice as much as usual. We silently devoured every last bite before returning to the house. We hardly said anything to each other on the drive, but I still felt something radiating off him as he drove silently, munching on his food. It made me wonder if part of my magical abilities could sense other people's energies or if Kyler just wore his emotions on his sleeve.

He didn't even make sure I knew the way to my room before disappearing to wherever his was. I made a mental note to explore more of the house during the week, but at least I knew how to navigate to my room.

As I walked into the kitchen that morning, Theo was at the stove watching a spatula flipping a pancake. I blinked. Theo smiled at me, holding the spatula with the pancake on it. "Top of the mornin' to ya, dear! Can I—"

I put my finger up to stop him. "Not yet," I grumbled, refusing to believe I'd just seen the kitchenware making breakfast on its own. I needed coffee. Theo made a gesture as if locking up his mouth with a key and tossed the invisible key to me as if to say, 'Whenever you're ready.' I followed my nose to the coffee pot and poured myself a big mug, adding the creamer already sitting out. As I savored the first sip, I turned around and leaned against the counter, watching to make sure Theo was indeed flipping the pancakes he had tried to offer me. "I'm a beast before my coffee," I mumbled, knowing it was no excuse, but sometimes I couldn't handle people in the morning.

I stretched my sore muscles this way and that between each sip of coffee until I finally felt the brain fog melt away. I turned to Theo and said, "Good morning, Theo."

He looked at me and held out his hand. At first, I just stared at him like he was crazy. Then he pointed to his lips before holding out his hand again. I bit back a smile, reached into my pretend pocket, pulled out the invisible key, and handed it to him. He mimed unlocking his lips, then smiled at me, "Good morning, dearie."

"That's his favorite joke." I jumped a little at Mari's groggy voice. I must have missed her entrance into the kitchen. She walked up to Theo and hugged him with a peck on the cheek. The gesture felt comfortable but not romantic. I wondered if I could pluck up enough courage to ask about them later. "He uses it whenever he's told to be quiet." She grabbed a hot pancake from the spatula Theo extended to her and bit into it before grabbing a plate and piling a few more on top. She pulled a fruit bowl from the fridge and brought it to the table to sit.

I looked from Mari to Theo, who was still flipping pancakes, and asked, "What time are we leaving for school?" I didn't want to assume they waited until the last second like I did. We had plenty of time this morning, but it didn't seem like Kyler was up yet, and I wanted to shower since I hadn't before crashing last night. The nightgown under my robe felt like it was sticking to my skin. It was disgusting.

"You probably have forty minutes before Kyler is ready," Mari offered, "fifty max. And when he's ready, he leaves. Whether I'm ready or not." She gave me a pointed look, and I shook my head knowingly. We both chuckled a little.

I moved to the counter and grabbed a couple of pancakes. Theo saw my plate, glanced up at me, then at the plate again. He grabbed two more pancakes, put them on top of the three I already had, and nodded, satisfied with his work. I raised my eyebrow at him, to which he said, "I heard you trained for quite a while last night. You must have worked up a big appetite."

"Trained?" Mari said as a blush rose to my cheeks. So Kyler hadn't gone straight to bed last night. I wondered if he told Theo how many times I'd pinned him. I grinned at the thought as I dug into my pancakes.

Theo looked at Mari, "She and Niko went to Rifner's studio last night after hours. Niko wanted to see what she was capable of." He gave me a knowing look, then said, "Apparently, Rifner hasn't been training her. Tom has."

Mari choked on her food. "What!"

"Why does it matter who trains me?" I asked defensively, wondering if they understood the question through the pancake I'd stuffed in my mouth. I was more confused by their reaction than why Kyler wanted to see what I could do. I swallowed, "Besides, wouldn't you have known that if you talked to Rifner?" I stuffed another bite of pancake in my mouth.

"Tom wasn't supposed to interact with you just yet," Theo said, flipping another pancake. How many did they need?

"Why not?" I asked, washing down the pancake in my mouth with some coffee before continuing. "Kendall and Leighton are my best friends. I knew Tom before he started training me."

"Knowing Tom and training with him are two different things, Rayleigh." Mari sounded irked. "He wasn't supposed to get involved in your training."

"And he seems to have taken it upon himself to do it secretly," Theo mused.

"To be fair," I held up one finger to stop them from going on as I swallowed another bite. "Tom only mentioned that he taught jiu-jitsu. I asked him to train me."

Theo squinted his eyes at me and then trained them on Mari, "Do you think he ran it by Rifner and had him cover for him?"

"*Again*, why does it matter who trained me?" A hint of desperation crept into that question as they still hadn't answered it.

"Because," Kyler walked into the kitchen and headed straight for the coffee pot behind me. He looked like he just stepped out of the shower. His dark curls were still damp, and some stuck to his face. It made his blue eyes pop. *Wait, blue??* I blinked. They were green. My mind was playing tricks on me. "He is a councilor to the fae. One of the most powerful," Kyler continued, and the scent of his cologne invaded my nose. "He's been teaching you far more advanced techniques than he's supposed to."

"Okay... and?" None of what they said made any sense. First, what was a councilor, and why was he teaching *me* jiu-jitsu? Secondly, it was jiu-jitsu. They're bound to teach more advanced moves when you get the easy stuff down, so why would that be an issue? I decided to save the first question for later, thinking it would need more time than we had to explain, but I asked the second.

Theo flipped one more pancake onto his pile and handed the entire plate to Kyler, who was still between us getting his coffee. I gaped at the stack of pancakes, but after what he ate last night, that looked like a snack.

"Your magic has been bleeding into your training," Theo directed at me. "Tom has been teaching you to use magic with your fighting."

My jaw dropped, as did the pancake I was holding. Luckily, it landed on my plate. *I've been using magic this entire time? Without knowing?* "But how?" I asked out loud, needing to know the answer.

"Through your breath work," Kyler said, leaning against the island counter while he ate his pancakes with his hands.

But how could I do that without knowing? I mean, yeah, Tom made me concentrate on my breathing when doing certain moves, making sure to breathe out on the ones that took the most effort. But that was normal for any workout, wasn't it? When I was taught how to squat correctly in gym class, we were told to breathe in on the way down and out on the way up. It seemed easy enough to connect that to my moves in jiu-jitsu, which is why Tom started teaching me more advanced moves. Or so I thought.

"You're telling me that I've been using magic… without knowing I'm using magic?" That made no sense. Primarily because I hadn't even known magic existed when I started training. I didn't feel any different. There was no power in my veins or spark in my fingers. I wasn't sure what magic felt like, but I was pretty sure I would be able to feel something. But if I couldn't feel the magic… I thought about the books I was given to study, how the fae used to be a part of the elements, and now the elements were a part of them. I wondered if it just flowed through them— *us,* I reminded myself. Perhaps it was possible the magic wasn't noticeable.

All three of them were watching me process. Theo spoke first. "While fae *are* generally faster and stronger in jiu-jitsu, you have only been training for a few months. Niko has been sparring for years. And from how he described your knowledge and strength in sparring with him last night, it's clear some magic is involved."

Oh.

Oh.

A cocky grin spread across my face as I slowly turned my head to Kyler. "Because I couldn't possibly beat you without magic."

Kyler smirked, "Not a chance."

"Did you tell them how many times you had to tap out?" I mocked.

"How many!" Mari shouted from the table.

"Without magic, it would have been zero," Kyler gritted out.

I gave him a mock smile. "I don't need magic to beat you."

Kyler grinned. "Wanna go again, Sunshine?"

"Sure." My voice went low. A challenge. "Let's make it thirteen."

"Thirteen??" Mari spat her food across the table, followed by a hearty belly laugh. Theo must have joined her at the table, his laughter echoing hers.

Kyler's cheeks started to color. He faced the laughter and repeated through clenched teeth, "If it weren't for her magic, it would have been zero."

"Keep telling yourself that, sweetheart," I purred, pulling his attention back to me. I lowered my voice to a whisper as I leaned across the space between us. "I think you like being stuck between my legs."

As soon as the words left my mouth, I knew they'd been a mistake. The color in Kyler's cheeks faded, and a slow smirk spread across his face as he leaned in a little further. His breath graced my ear as he whispered, "I think you like it more."

My cheeks warmed, and I pursed my lips. Hating that he turned the insult meant for him back on me, I stalked out of the kitchen. "I'm going to take a shower."

I only heard Kyler's answering laughter and the other two asking what he said to make me storm off. When I got to the bathroom, I turned the shower all the way to cold.

१ मे स र

Thirty minutes later, I was waiting in the kitchen alone when Theo walked in and announced that Tom and the twins were coming over that night.

"Wait, they're coming here?" I said, not believing I'd have someone close to me to share this crazy experience.

Theo smiled. "Yes. They will likely stay with us, so our team will be less spread out."

"How long are they going to be staying?" I asked.

"The plan is to figure that out. Tom filled the girls in over the weekend, telling them as much as they could handle. We will be filling you *all* in on more details tonight."

"I hope you have a PowerPoint or something cool," I mumbled. I was glad I took a few minutes after my shower to write down all my new questions from the last two days. I'd have to remember to bring my notebook to the meeting.

Kyler stalked into the kitchen, saying, "We're going to be late." He beelined straight for the garage door, not bothering to check if I followed him.

Theo bid me goodbye, and I headed to the garage just as Mari hurried into the kitchen with her backpack and my own. "You left this in your room. I went to see if you were ready, but you were faster than I thought!" She smiled as I thanked her, and we both hurried out to the garage.

Kyler had pulled the jeep out of the garage and sat idling, waiting for us. Mari shook her head, "See, this is what I mean. I'm honestly surprised he's still here."

I laughed, "He can't have actually left you behind before?" It seemed absurd to leave Mari if she wasn't ready the second he was. What if she was in the bathroom or something?

"Oh, he's tried!" She paused, looking at me for a moment before going on. "Let's just say he can't get very far without me." She winked and opened the door to the backseat for herself.

I wasn't sure if she was trying to be nice by letting me sit in the front or what, but it wasn't something I was used to either way. Sitting in the front seat next to Kyler was not my first option, but the backseat often made me car sick. That was why I always drove, whether it was to school or into the city for groceries or shopping. I was hardly ever the passenger. Honestly, it probably had more to do with fearing loss of control than my mild nausea. Maybe it *was* a control issue, but it had only been a few days, and I was already sick of being driven around. I was not a passenger princess. I missed driving. I missed my car. Would Chitty even start at this point?

That wasn't even the worst of it. I couldn't go anywhere or do anything whenever I wanted, and I was on someone else's schedule—not my own.

Somehow, my freedom had slipped out of my hands, and Kyler was one of the people in control.

I grumbled in frustration, opened the front passenger door, and got in, ignoring Kyler's noise of annoyance. The door hadn't even closed before he started down the driveway. "You couldn't have waited two seconds?" I snapped, slamming the door.

"We're late," he retorted.

"Two more seconds wouldn't have killed you!" I said, clicking my seatbelt in place.

He ignored me, turning up the radio instead, and I had to bite my tongue so I didn't yell at him over the music for being immature.

I rolled down the window, which got me a look from Kyler, but I didn't care. I liked feeling the spring air on my face. As he pulled onto the highway and the breeze picked up, I put my hand on the window frame and lay my chin on it, letting the wind whip my hair all around. It would be a rat's nest when we got to school, but whatever. I stuck my arm out the window and made waves against the wind, pretending to dodge the air pockets. Arabella and I used to do that constantly, pretending we were flying instead of our hands. It was such a silly little motion, but it felt freeing. Like I could do anything.

Kyler turned the music down at one point so it wasn't blaring through the speakers, and I was surprised to find that he didn't listen to metal or screamo music. It was more contemporary rock and indie music. I mentally tried to keep track of some titles to add to my playlist whenever I got my phone back. It slightly annoyed me that we had similar taste in music, though.

We arrived at school five minutes before the first warning bell, so I didn't understand why Kyler had been so adamant that we were late. But I didn't say anything as I got out of the Jeep and headed to Chem.

Mari and Kyler slowed to have a quiet conversation behind me, but I didn't stick around to hear what either of them said. It probably wasn't any of my business anyway.

When I walked in the doors, both Ken and Leigh squealed and hurried over to tackle me with hugs. The excited hugs became more emotional as I realized I hadn't seen them since I was kidnapped, and I pulled them closer. Emotions ran over me as we stood there, wrapped in each other's arms. No words were exchanged, but the embrace spoke volumes.

I couldn't believe how much had happened since last week. Our lives had taken the most unexpected turn, and who knew what else life had in store for us? Of course, Prom was on Saturday, but Theo said it would be a distraction as they moved Ma and Mitch to a more secure location. But who knew what was going to happen after that? Would we all go back to the other realm together? Would we stay here? Would I even be able to return to where we came from if I was being hunted?

I almost whispered something to the girls about it, but another arm wrapped around my shoulder. I looked up to find Kaleb had joined us in the group hug. I decided the comment to the girls could wait and moved to pull Kaleb closer to me. That was where I felt the most safe —with my people.

A few minutes remained before the bell rang, so I told the girls I would talk to them later and pulled Kaleb aside.

My cheeks suddenly felt flush as I looked at Kaleb. He seemed oddly shy when I asked if I could talk to him, but I knew why. "Hi," I whispered, only because I felt it was all I could get out. My nerves had gotten the best of me, too, I guess. The last time we'd seen each other, less than twenty-four hours ago, he'd kissed me. And I kissed him back.

"Hey," he said, avoiding my eyes.

Now wasn't the time to address the kiss or any of the feelings that came with it, so I jumped to why I'd pulled him aside. "You don't happen to have my phone, do you?"

He scrunched his eyebrows together. Clearly, that was not the conversation he thought we were having. "No. Why would I have it?"

I shrugged, "I haven't seen it since—" I lowered my voice as much as possible, "the grocery store." I wasn't sure what the other kids at school knew of my absence last week, but I didn't particularly feel like explaining that I'd been kidnapped and knocked out for a few days.

Kaleb was thinking, then pinched the bridge of his nose. He didn't look at me when he released it but held his hand out as if he were giving me the answer. "Why don't you ask Kyler?" The way he said Kyler's name told me what I already knew: he was jealous.

I raised my eyebrows at him. "Kaleb," I paused, lifting his chin with a finger before continuing, "First off, you have nothing to be jealous of." Not a total truth because Kyler was stupid hot. *But* there was no way in hell I'd give him the time of day. He'd have to have a total personality transplant. "Second, I did ask him, and he said he didn't see anything when they rescued me."

Kaleb looked like he didn't believe either statement, but after searching my eyes, his shoulder sagged, and he dropped his gaze to the ground. "Sorry."

"Hey," I said, lifting his face to look at me again. "I still don't know what this is," I gestured between us. "But I will say this: You have a significantly higher chance than he ever will, okay?" I smiled, which he tried to return as the bell rang for class.

Before he could walk to his seat, I wrapped my arms around his waist for a hug. It was just as much for him as it was for me. He didn't hesitate and wrapped me tight in his arms. I could have stayed there all day, wrapped up in his warmth, without a care. He turned his head slightly and put his mouth to my hair in a gentle kiss. It made butterflies jump to life in my stomach, making the things I had to say to him later more evident.

Mr. Blake cleared his throat from the front of the classroom, and I pulled away from Kaleb to head to my seat, my ears hot.

I sat down next to Kyler, who didn't bother acting like he knew anything more about me than the next guy. The last time I'd been in this classroom was when I failed to remember any test knowledge and lost thirty minutes in the bathroom. Then, I was gone for two days. After all of that, there was a slight moment of panic over what my grade would be like. Before I let that set in, I decided to talk to Mr. Blake when he dismissed us to start our lab for the day.

After he finished explaining something called a Lichtenberg figure, I left Kyler to gather the supplies while I went to talk to Mr. Blake.

If he was surprised to see me back in school, he didn't show it. "How can I help you, Ms. Foster?" He turned back to his pile of papers to grade.

"I was just wondering if I could get the assignments from the last two days of class," I paused, looking away when my embarrassment got the best of me, "And perhaps a redo on the test from last week?"

Confused, he asked me, "Why would you want to redo a test you aced?"

My jaw went slack, but I recovered quickly and asked, "I... aced the test?" There was absolutely no way. I didn't turn it in. I hadn't even written my name on it. It was blank.

Mr. Blake shuffled through the papers on his desk and pulled out a test, handing it over to me. The name at the top was mine. That and the answers written were in my handwriting. A red pen marked A+. I looked from the paper to Mr. Blake and back, unsure if I should tell him I never finished the test. Thinking about my current predicament, I decided it wouldn't matter in the long run. "Oh. I thought I'd done much worse."

"As for the assignments and lab work, there weren't any. Only a lecture, which you can find on the class website." He went back to grading papers, a clear dismissal from his desk.

I stood there, staring at the paper I held in my hands. When I eventually returned to the desk, Kyler had begun the lab without me. Kaleb watched me as I returned to my seat, his brows raised in question. I held the test up, showing him the grade. He just shrugged, unaware that anything was strange about me acing the test.

I glanced at Ken, who noticed the exchange. When she saw the test, her face went white. Her reaction was more what I was looking for. I widened my eyes, pursed my lips, and nodded. She and I would definitely be talking about this later.

I sat down heavily, placing my test face down on the table before bringing my attention to the lab Kyler was doing. He didn't acknowledge me, but I wasn't about to let him cut me out of another lab. He was setting up the acrylic and the nail, so I grabbed the balloon to blow it up. I hated the feeling of being shocked, so I decided to disturb Kyler's perfectly messy hairstyle. As soon as he finished setting up the materials properly, I pounced before he could stop me.

The balloon made contact with his head, and I rubbed it back and forth quickly to create the static electricity needed for the experiment. His head turned in slow motion toward me, the snarl on his face as he realized what I'd done was priceless. With a mocking smile, I pulled the balloon away from his head, and his hair stood straight up. I laughed.

"That was a mistake," he said through gritted teeth, not moving toward me nor touching the nail to finish the experiment.

My eyebrow lifted, a cocky grin appearing. "No, it was a perfect opportunity to make you look like a twat."

"No," he lowered his voice so only I could hear it, "you don't understand. I can't touch that nail."

"But you're the one holding the static charge," I said sweetly.

He closed his eyes and pinched the bridge of his nose. "You'll have to touch the nail and me. The charge will travel through you to the nail." He opened his eyes, and his piercing stare pinned me in place. "It'll work."

"No!" I wasn't sure how he had known I would question the chances of that working. "I did that so I didn't have to get shocked. You touch—"

"I. Can't." He bit out, trying to communicate something with his eyes. Suddenly, this didn't seem like a joke anymore. Something about how he said that made me feel unsafe. I wasn't sure if it was because of what would happen if he touched the nail or what would happen if it traveled through me. After reading his expression, though, I decided it would be worse if he touched the nail.

I nodded nervously, swallowing the lump in my throat and turning to the setup. I placed my left pointer finger on the top of the nail and then pointed my other index finger at Kyler. His brow was scrunched together. This wasn't a joke anymore. He was bracing for something. He took a deep breath before slowly moving his finger toward mine. He glanced up right before his finger touched mine, and his eyes shone with something I couldn't place.

Then he closed the distance between our fingers.

A jolt of energy exploded through my body. Way more intense than it should have been for a simple static charge from a balloon. Our eyes were locked, and Kyler's eyes had a lightning pattern flow through the irises, the color breaking into different pieces of blue and green. It was a beautiful mosaic of colors.

I was sure the moment only lasted half a second, but it felt much longer. Our gazes were still locked, and our fingers were stuck in a barely-there touch.

Something felt off. The room had gone silent. I tore my gaze from Kyler's and looked around the room.

I gasped.

Everyone was frozen in place.

XXIV
I Don't Wanna Be Friends

My gaze shot around the room. I still hadn't let the gasp I'd sucked in out. Not until I took in every single face. Every single person. They were all stopped mid-experiment. Some were still setting up the pieces, others had their balloons blown up, and a couple had static-filled hair, but no one was moving.

Kaleb was frozen, looking directly at me, a glower clear on his face. I sighed. From the look on his face, I knew he had watched the exchange between Kyler and me and saw the playful, evil gremlin side of me that could have been mistaken for flirtation. My stomach dropped. After I had just told him Kyler was nothing to worry about. I sighed.

The reality that he was stuck in that expression reminded me we were in a crisis, and I should be focusing on that. I turned to Ken and Leigh. They were leaning into each other, likely whispering things between themselves, frozen.

I whipped my head back to Kyler. I couldn't be the only one not frozen in place. He hadn't moved his finger away from mine, but I could see his chest rising and falling. His eyes. The crackling between the colors was still going, but slower. They weren't locked on mine anymore, either. They were darting back and forth between my eyes, our barely touching fingers, and the table.

"Kyler," I said, my voice barely a whisper. "What's going on?"

His eyes were on the table when he said, "You made me do this."

My eyebrows shot up. "How did *I* make you do this?!" I gestured animatedly with my free hand all around us. "What even is *this?*"

The energy that traveled through me had dissipated, and Kyler pulled his finger away from mine. "Because of my—" he searched for a word, "—abilities, I am already full of energy. Adding a static charge to it can create catastrophic events." He used both hands to gesture to the small piece of acrylic the nail had touched.

Or what *used* to be acrylic.

In its place was a frozen explosion of the material with the nail hovering above it. The experiment was meant to create a lightning strike within the surface that would only be visible once we blew some ink toner onto it. It looked like the acrylic had been blown to pieces, even with me as the bridge to tame the static charge.

I glanced back up at Kyler, then around the room again to all the frozen students. "That doesn't explain everyone being *frozen in time!*"

Kyler closed his eyes, his face falling into an expression I'd never seen from him before. "I had to use my other abilities to stop time so the pieces wouldn't fly everywhere and hurt the other kids."

Two things went through my mind at that moment. One, he said kids like he wasn't our age. I gave myself half a second to wonder if that could be true, but that was a conversation for another time.

And second, but most importantly, *did he say stop time??*

It felt like my eyes were bugging out of my skull. He went on like it was a casual conversation: "We have to start this experiment over, just the two of us, to make it look like it was right before the charge went through you to the nail."

"What?" I deadpanned. I was still slightly freaking out about the fact that he *casually stopped time.*

He pinched the bridge of his nose and gestured to the counter where he had initially gotten the materials. "Go grab another piece of acrylic and put it where the exploded one was."

I gaped at him. He *froze time.* To stop people from seeing the explosion or getting hurt by a piece of acrylic flying because of his powers. *What is he?* I asked myself, knowing that nowhere in my fae books did it mention anything about an electric charge within them.

Kyler snapped his fingers in my face. "Come on, Sunshine. I can't hold this for long." I met his gaze and realized the veins in his forehead were starting to pop, and his neck muscles were tense. Whatever he was doing, it wasn't easy.

I sprang into action, running over to the counter, and decided he could explain more about himself and his powers at a different time. This was an act now, ask questions later moment. I retrieved the new piece of acrylic and another balloon because I didn't see the other one I used, and hurried back to our table.

Kyler swept up the pieces of the exploded resin and shoved them into his pocket, careful not to disturb the nail as it hovered in place. I slid the new piece in place, blew up the balloon, and swiped it against my head this time. Kyler stepped back from the table, and I went to place my finger on the nail.

"Stop!" Kyler threw his hands up, careful not to grab me and lose the static charge.

I whipped my head to him. "What! You said to do it again!"

"You weren't touching it with that finger. Switch and put your other finger to mine, but don't touch me before you touch the nail."

I saw what he was trying to do. He was recreating the scene precisely as it was before the static charge fully hit the acrylic. He raised his hand with a finger pointed at me and stood exactly where he was when I realized the room was frozen. I adjusted my stance to where I had been and looked to him for approval. He nodded, jaw set. I hovered my other finger over the nail and locked eyes with Kyler. Recreating the connection of our fingers without touching him, I dropped my finger on the nail.

The room exploded with noise again, everyone talking over everyone else. Kyler nodded almost imperceptibly and brought his hand down. A small bead of sweat appeared on his temple, and he swiped it away before it tracked down his face. I wondered how much power he had to make a room full of people freeze like that. There were so many things I needed to ask him, but it was never the right time for questions when they popped up.

Deciding to put a pin in that conversation, I turned away from Kyler and found Kaleb again. He had stopped glowering at me but still wore a scowl as he worked on his experiment. I sighed and turned back to my table to sit down while Kyler applied toner to the acrylic to reveal the frozen lightning pattern inside. He didn't pay any attention to me, so I ignored him, too, getting lost in my thoughts.

Kaleb had every right to be angry with me. I would have been, too. I was careless and playing with his emotions, even if it wasn't intentional. Kyler got under my skin so easily that I acted before thinking about the consequences, and karma was coming back around. I didn't think I would lose Kaleb if I said I just wanted to be friends, but I had basically flirted with Kyler in front of him right after I said that Kaleb had a better chance than him. The close proximity to Kyler was making things complicated, both in class and at his house. Not to mention, I had no idea what kind of conversation went down when Kyler brought Kaleb home after our kiss. It couldn't have been good if Kaleb was acting as mopey as he was when I got here this morning.

With a thought forming in my mind, I pulled out my notebook and ripped off a small piece of paper. I knew it wasn't a great idea, but I was feeling reckless. Scribbling a note as quickly as I could, I folded it in half twice and stood up from my table. I turned to walk towards the back of the classroom and dropped the folded note on Kaleb's table when I passed.

I didn't stop at his table but made my way to the girls' table and leaned onto it. They were applying their toner to the acrylic, so they didn't notice my approach. "Hi," I said, my voice cracked a little. I hadn't realized my emotions were so close to the surface.

When the girls shot their heads up to me, they skirted the table to hug me again. "We were so worried about you, Ray!" Ken whispered in one ear.

"Yeah, so much has happened!" Leighton said in the other.

"I know," I replied, my throat constricting my words. "But it's going to be okay." My false confidence was so convincing that I almost believed it. "There's so much I have to tell you guys. I can't wait for you to come over tonight." The original list of things I had to tell them had grown since I'd seen them last. Each new thing was more insane than the last, with the latest classroom incident taking the cake.

Leigh pulled away first. "It'll be a sleepover just like old times," she said, the smile she gave me not quite reaching her eyes. I wondered if something else was happening with her aside from finding out she was fae or if it was just all the information dumped on her over the weekend.

Ken finally pulled away, too, a sad look in her eyes when she smiled. "I don't even know how I feel about any of this yet," she whispered, her honesty hitting so close to home.

"We've got each other, though," I said, grabbing each of their hands and lowering my voice so only they could hear. "Together, we'll be the greatest fae warriors. Nerf wars prepared us for this." They both started giggling, thinking of our summer's past on the battlefields of the grove behind my house. The teams were always the same: Ken, Kaleb, and me versus Leigh, Mitch, and Bell. It was always intense and taken seriously, and if it wasn't, you were the first one out.

Ken tried speaking through her giggles, "Remember when Bell tried to do a roll between the trees, and she didn't realize you camouflaged yourself into the grove floor?" Both Leigh and I burst into fresh bouts of giggles.

"She rolled right into me! I shot her straight in the gut!" I laughed. There were so many memories of us battling in the grove between Kaleb's and my houses, whether it was Nerf guns in our later years or stick swords in the earlier years. We always made the best of our summers, pretending we were in medieval times and all fighting a dragon or in dystopian lands fighting for survival or another world altogether, going on an adventure across the magical forests. Who would have guessed that four of us were actually from another world? The smile on my face faded to a softer one as I took in my best friends. "This is just another adventure we get to go on together. Only this time, we have real magic, and there are actual bad guys to fight."

The girls' smiles faded. "Were they there that day?" Leigh said quietly. "At the mall?"

I had forgotten all about the mall. She didn't even remember disappearing, and when we told her, it seemed like she didn't believe us. But her face told me that she believed us now. "I don't know," I said honestly because Kyler hadn't actually answered that question last night. "We'll have to ask Theo tonight. He's really good at answering all of my questions." I thought about my notebook at the Dengalow and wondered if my new questions had been answered.

Mr. Blake cleared his throat right next to me. I jumped at the noise, as did the girls. He didn't smile, but his eyes sparkled with a knowing look. "Ladies. I'm sure your conversation is very important, but are you finished with your lab?"

I pursed my lips and looked back to the table I shared with Kyler. He was sitting with our redone experiment in front of him, elbows propped on the table and his chin resting on his clasped hands. I couldn't see his face because his hair hid it, but I figured he was probably glaring at the wall. He was good at that.

The girls moved around the table to showcase their experiment to Mr. Blake, so I returned to my seat.

When I passed Kaleb's table, he reached out his arm to stop me. I looked into his sparkling brown eyes as he silently asked for permission. When I nodded, he pulled me to him in one fluid movement, both arms snaking around me and pulling me close. I relaxed into his hug, and he whispered, "I trust you." My back tensed, as it always did when someone breathed near my ears. "I'm sorry I let him get under my skin. He deserves the glares, not you."

I relaxed my arms and shifted to look at him. "Meet me in the courtyard after lunch?" I smiled, knowing he had to have read the rest of the note if he was apologizing.

He returned the smile and nodded, kissing my forehead gently before letting me go. The place where his lips touched tingled as I stepped out of his embrace, making me bite back a smile.

I finished the walk to my table and plopped down on my stool, thinking of what exactly I would say when I got to the courtyard. Kaleb didn't deserve to be left in the dark, but I also knew there was only so much I could tell him.

Kyler's deep voice startled me out of my thoughts as he said, "You can't tell him anything."

I snapped my head to him, "I know, dumbass. But what I *do* say is none of your business."

"It's my business if it's about me." He smirked.

"It's not." Lie. My ears got hot. Technically, it was about him, but not in the way he was insinuating. I needed to make sure that whatever conversation they had in the car didn't affect Kaleb's decisions or choices when it came to me. Things were still unknown between us, and my life was already going off the rails, but I didn't want to drag him along on the crazy train without telling him at least a little bit of information. I cared about him and wanted him in my life. And he needed to know that.

"By the color your ears just turned, I don't believe that for a second," he mocked.

"If I didn't know any better, I'd say you were jealous."

"And if I didn't know any better, I'd say you were lying to him."

"About what, exactly?" My quiet voice turned to a whispered shout. "Because you're not wrong! I can't tell him anything about who I am because it'll either put him in danger or make him think I'm crazy."

Kyler clicked his tongue. "You have to lie to him about that. But you could at least tell him the truth about us."

"There is no us, *Kyler,*" I snapped.

"Ooo… do that again."

"What?"

"Say my name again."

I sneered at him. "I hate you."

"Sure you do, Sunshine." He winked. Actually *winked*.

I crossed my arms, "You aren't supposed to call me that anymore." He'd said it a few times already today, and I'd let it slide in the moment, but we made a deal last night.

"Pfft, I won. Which means I get to call you *Sunshine* all I want."

"You forfeited! I automatically won!"

"Forfeit actually means the deal is null and void. But I definitely came out on top that first match." The insinuation in his tone made my insides curdle.

"Oh my god! Your ego could rival Tony Stark's."

"Most girls like him."

"Well, I'm not most girls!" I retorted. Glancing at the clock, I realized it was almost time to leave. I stood up to clear the table.

"No, you most certainly are not," Kyler murmured before standing up to help. "Let me guess, you're a Steve Rogers kind of girl?"

Something occurred to me then. "How do you even know those characters?"

He cocked a brow at me, "Everyone knows the Avengers."

I lowered my voice, "But you're not from here. So, again, how do you know who they are?"

He chuckled, "I did my research." He walked away to put the reusable supplies back, and I rolled my eyes. Of course, he'd had to do research. Otherwise, he would have been way out of the loop.

I took the acrylic with the frozen lightning pattern now etched into it and placed it on the shelf for display. When I looked closer at the design carved into our piece, I saw that the resin had slightly cracked along the lines of lightning. That wasn't supposed to happen, was it? I checked the other ones already on display, confirming none had cracks. Could Kyler's lingering energy have made it a little overzealous? Or was it *my* magic? Either way, it was hardly noticeable unless one looked closely. I put ours toward the back just in case and walked back to the table as the bell rang.

Kyler had already disappeared, but the twins and Kaleb were waiting for me as I packed my bag. I shoved the test I didn't take into my bag and remembered I needed to talk to Kendall.

I zipped up the bag and met my friends in the doorway, where we all walked to our next classes together, Ken and I splitting off to Spanish while Kaleb and Leighton went to their math class.

Ken nudged me when we were alone. "Talk." Her eyebrows were raised at me, but I wasn't exactly sure what she was referring to.

Before we reached the classroom, I pulled her into the bathroom. After checking the stalls to ensure they were empty, I leaned against the bathroom door to ensure someone else couldn't come in without me knowing. "How did I ace that test? I didn't even write my name on it!"

Ken shrugged, "I dunno, Ray. My guess is as good as yours."

Whatever it was, it didn't make sense. With my handwriting and everything, there was no denying how strange it was.

Ken cleared her throat and caught my eye. "Care to explain what happened in class?"

I was unsure if she was referring to my chat with Kaleb or time-stopping because she would be the only one who might notice, so I asked, "What do you mean?"

She gave me a deadpan expression. "Flirting with Kyler?"

Well, I wasn't expecting that accusation. "I wasn't flirting!" I said a little too quickly. "It's payback for all the shit he's put me through."

Ken angled her head, "It looked a lot like flirting from where I was sitting." She didn't have to mention that Kaleb saw it, too. She didn't know what happened yesterday unless Kaleb told her, but I could tell she knew something happened between Kaleb and me by the look she was giving me. She was the most honest friend I had. Sometimes a little too honest, but at least she called me out on my shit.

"Whatever. I wasn't flirting." Before she could object, I said, "We don't have time to argue about this." I braced for my next question as she gave me a pointed look. "Did you feel anything weird in class?"

She cocked her head. "No. Why?"

The warning bell went off for class, but we were right next to Spanish, so I talked faster. "Something weird happened. And you were with me the last time something like this happened."

I didn't have to be specific for her to follow. Her eyes widened. "No one around you could see you?"

"Not exactly," I said, pausing to figure out how to word it. "Everyone around us was frozen in place."

"Us?"

I grimaced, "Kyler and I."

Her eyebrows shot up before furrowing again, "Wait. You and Kyler were *both* moving? And you could talk to him?"

I nodded. When she said nothing else, I dropped the last bomb: "Kyler was controlling time."

The blood drained from her face. She looked like she was going to pass out. When she finally spoke, it sounded like she'd seen a ghost. "He can... control time?"

"I guess? I'm still not sure exactly how, but he admitted to doing it.

I don't have any idea what he is, and I was going to ask you if Tom told you anything this weekend, but you look as clueless as I am."

She was shaking her head, her mouth slightly open. "I've no idea. What kind of creature can control time?"

I took a steadying breath and let it out slowly. I probably wouldn't get the answer from anyone but the source. Knowing that he could be that powerful, able to control time and freeze everyone in the room, was terrifying. What other kinds of powers could they have?

Ken tilted her head, "Wait. Why *did* he stop time?"

"Well, that—" The class bell rang. We'd been in the bathroom longer than I realized. "I'll tell you later." And we both rushed for class across the hall.

When lunch rolled around, I passed the girls' table with my food and told them I'd be outside with Kaleb. I was surprised to see Kyler sit at their table on my way out the door. He tracked me across the lunchroom, his piercing stare going straight to my soul. I squared my shoulders and continued to the courtyard, doing my best to ignore him.

Kaleb wasn't out there yet, so I sat down to eat my sandwich. My nerves were getting the best of me, making my stomach churn with anxiety. I could only nibble on the sandwich.

After everything that had happened the last few days, I knew Kaleb was the only person I wanted to share everything with. He was there for me through every other life-altering circumstance, and I knew he would want to be there for me in this situation, too, given the chance. But I also knew I couldn't tell him everything right now. Not until I made sure it was okay for him to know. He would have to trust me completely, knowing he might not find out what all of this was until I was allowed to tell him. I was unsure if there were any rules about humans learning about fae, so I could only promise to tell him so much. Jordin and Mitch knew, and Grams, but only because they had to. I didn't even know if things between Kaleb and me could last, mostly because I wasn't even sure where I'd be a year from now.

But I had made my decision.

I was starting to wonder if Kaleb had forgotten about me when I felt warm hands cover my eyes.

"Guess who?" Kaleb's exaggerated girl voice sent me into a fit of giggles.

I tapped a finger playfully on my chin, "Hmmm, Kendall?"

"Nope!" The high voice answered.

I touched his hands as if feeling for the answer. "Leighton?"

His hot breath caressed my ear, "Guess again, girlie." It was his normal voice again.

I couldn't stop another giggle from escaping and placed a hand on his forearm. "If you don't stop calling me girlie, this will never work," I teased.

He gasped in mock surprise, making me laugh. He pulled away from me and let me turn to face him. "Ya know, I don't think Leigh will be too happy you guessed her name after feeling my man hands." He wiggled his fingers at me, smiling. I couldn't ignore the fact it wasn't his full, winning smile.

"Your hands are so warm and soft, though!" I grinned.

He chuckled a little, and as it faded, his eyes searched mine. I knew he was trying to gauge what this conversation would be about. He shook off the nerves and extended his hand to me. "Shall we?"

"We shall." I grabbed his hand and stood up, linking our arms.

"What brings us to our courtyard stroll today?" He asked, a bit softer than his usual cheery tone.

"Two things," I started. "First, I wanted to make sure that whatever Kyler said to you yesterday on the ride home didn't affect you and me," I said bluntly.

Kaleb let out a frustrated sigh. "No. Nothing he said affects us." He looked at me sideways as if that was all he was going to say. But I waited for him to go on. He sighed again, "He mocked me the whole way home and said I don't deserve you."

My face softened. "Kaleb... Did you at least fight back?" I wasn't surprised that Kyler bullied Kaleb after what he interrupted yesterday, and I didn't expect Kaleb to physically try to fight him after what happened. But it would make me feel better if he stood up for himself.

His face turned a bit pink. "I tried. I threw a few insults his way and told him you can decide on who deserves you on your own." He quickly whipped his head to me, "Which you are not property! I just meant, like, deserves your love or whatever…" He trailed off, his cheeks turning a darker shade of pink, making me giggle.

"Kaleb, you are more than deserving of anyone's love. And you already have mine, remember?"

He smiled, "You're deserving too, ya know." He nudged me.

"I know. Which brings me to my next point." I took a moment to calm my beating heart and said, "Remember our last courtyard stroll?" He nodded but didn't say anything, so I continued, "You said you didn't want to ruin anything between us by confessing your feelings for me." That day, I was certain I didn't feel anything towards him. But that was then…

"I remember." He took a deep breath before continuing. "I never wanted to make you uncomfortable, but my feelings were starting to change, and I didn't know how to process them at the time, especially because we'd already talked about us before."

Hearing him say it out loud had me biting my lip. My stomach was in knots as I thought about what to say, but I pushed through and made a bold step outside the friend zone. "My feelings have started to change recently, too, Kaleb." If he was surprised, he didn't show it. I suppose the fact that I let him kiss me yesterday was revealing enough. A smile did start playing on his lips, though. "But there is a lot to consider before I say what I want to say."

"Consider? Like what?" His tone was even but playful.

"Like the fact that I was just kidnapped and tortured and then brought to someone else's house for safety."

He narrowed his eyes, "Yeah. Why are you being kept at *his* house? Wouldn't the police have a better idea of protecting you?" The way he bit out 'his' made me bite my lip to keep from laughing.

I released a breath through my lips, making a funny noise, and said, "There's a lot I can't tell you. But consider his house a safe house—like witness protection." Kaleb could always tell when I was lying, so giving him a version of the truth was the better option. "Theo, Mari, and Kyler are part of a special operation to protect me."

"Kyler and Mari are in high school."

"I know, I know. It seems a little strange, but you have to *trust* me." This was the first step before I could take things any further. Because if he didn't trust me with this, there was no way we could make this work, no matter how we felt about each other. "Kyler is a jerk, yes, but Mari and Theo are the exact opposite. You met them. They've been nothing but kind to me and have been taking good care of me." The next part of my story would make or break whatever was between us. Kaleb's concentration was on the path ahead, but the look on his face told me he was having difficulty processing everything. I stopped walking and made him do the same, turning him to face me. Once I caught his gaze, I said, "I don't know what my future holds. The people who kidnapped me are still out there, and they aren't giving up. Theo says it's going to be unpredictable, and things could change on a dime, but—" I stared straight into Kaleb's honey-brown eyes. His focus was entirely on me, hanging on every word. I gave him a small smile as I said, "I want you to be there."

Kaleb's eyes were shining, full of hope. "As your friend?"

My smile grew, "If that's what you want." I moved closer to him, which had me tilting my head back to keep my eyes on his. "But I kind of want to see where this goes." I placed a hand on his chest. His heart was beating wildly under my palm. I searched his eyes as what I said started to sink in, and a smile broke out on his face. I put a finger up, "But just know, this could all get a little messy, and I might have to keep some things from you right now because I don't fully know what's going on or what I'm allowed to tell you."

His smile had grown, but he was nodding. "I trust you'll tell me what you can when you can." His smile faltered a little. "And even though I don't trust Kyler or his motives, I trust *you*." He reached up to tuck a piece of stray hair behind my ear, and his hand trailed my jaw until he reached my chin, tilting it up slightly. My breath caught as he said, "You mean so much to me, Rayleigh. I don't want to lose you. And if that means I have to deal with Captain Asshole," I smiled at the nickname, "then I'll deal with it. For you. Because you're worth it."

The butterflies in my stomach released themselves, and I couldn't hold back my smile anymore. He still had his hand under my chin and held it there as he started to lean in. My heart was racing, and I closed my eyes, anticipating the feeling of his lips on mine again. Yesterday's kiss was so unexpected, but this time. This time, I knew it was coming, and the butterflies in my stomach traveled to every part of my body, enough of a sign to me that I had been suppressing these feelings for far longer than I thought. I felt his breath on my lips as I waited for him to close the space between us.

"Well, isn't this heartwarming?" The new voice startled me into opening my eyes. Kaleb was still standing before me, his hand under my chin, and his eyes closed for the kiss that never reached my lips.

He was frozen.

I twisted around to the voice behind me and saw familiar stark blue eyes and blonde hair.

Aaidan.

XXV
Vengeance

I stepped in front of Kaleb to face Aaidan. My hands started to shake, but I clenched them into fists, ignoring the feelings creeping up. I couldn't have a panic attack right now. Kaleb was in danger. I needed to protect him. I wouldn't let anything happen to him.

Aaidan was leaning against a tree, examining his fingernails like he had better things to do than whatever he was doing here.

"What do you want?" I spat, the raging beast inside me paced.

"Tsk, tsk, tsk..." He looked up at me through his eyebrows. "You should be nicer to the people who hold your loved ones hostage." He gestured toward Kaleb over my shoulder, but I didn't dare look. If I looked away, it would give Aaidan an open target.

"Being nice to someone who kidnapped and tortured me isn't something I feel like doing today."

He let out a low chuckle. "Of course, how could I forget."

"Let him go." I gritted out.

"From what I just heard, you probably don't want me to do that." He gave me a tight-lipped smile. "Unless, of course, you want him to find out who you are. If that's the case, I'll just—" He raised his hand as if to wave off some spell from Kaleb.

"No!" I didn't know how his magic worked, but I definitely didn't want him to do that.

Aaidan lowered his hand and smirked. "I thought so." He pushed off the tree and closed the distance between us with three sauntering steps, keeping about a foot between us when he stopped. If he had come closer, I would have made him regret it. "You are a difficult girl to track down alone, you know?"

That was an excellent point. How did he find me without Kyler or Mari seeing him? Could they see us from inside the cafeteria? "How did you find me?" I asked, adjusting my stance to cover that I was trying to move into the view of the cafeteria doors.

"I wouldn't do that if I were you," Aaidan warned, tracking my every move. His eyes shot to Kaleb again. I followed his gaze. A crystal dagger appeared, hovering near Kaleb's stomach, poised to strike.

I gasped. "Don't!" I didn't move my feet another inch in either direction.

"That's it," he muttered. "Now, be a good girl and get back into place." He gestured to where I was before he showed up.

Clenching my jaw, I stepped back in front of Kaleb. Aaidan lifted his hand and made a twirling motion with one finger. I flipped him off and spun to face Kaleb. The knife still hovered near his stomach, but it moved to aim at his side when I stood in front of him. He looked so happy—peaceful even—in the moments before he was going to kiss me. Tears burned behind my eyes at the thought of anything happening to him. He and the twins were all I had left, and I wasn't about to lose them, not if I could help it. I gritted my teeth to hold back the tears and made a deal with myself: No one else would die because of me.

"Now. You asked how I found you." Aaidan stepped from behind me and into my view, holding up a phone. *My* phone. *Shit.* I knew I had it on me when they took me. "Your sweet boyfriend here—" That was a term I wasn't sure I could use yet "—must not know or forgot that you don't have this." He wiggled the phone at me. "He texts you all the time, you know." He unlocked my phone with my passcode, although I have no idea how he'd figured it out, and started scrolling through my phone. He stopped to read some of them aloud in a mocking tone. "'My guard says you still haven't woken up yet, and I can't come see you til you do. I'm so worried about you.'" He stopped and scrolled some more. "Oh, this one was good. 'I don't even know what to say after that kiss… if I'm honest—'"

"Stop," I snapped, not wanting to hear him read my private texts. The fact that he'd probably already read them made my blood boil. "Just get to the point, whatever it is."

Aaidan stopped in his tracks and angled his head at me. He looked me up and down before returning to the phone and scrolling again. "He texted you about ten minutes ago saying he got caught in class and would be late to your meeting in the courtyard." He clicked the phone off and pocketed it before stepping up next to Kaleb and me. "It was the perfect setup. You see, I couldn't have your Omada knowing I was here. It would have ruined my perfect plan." He snatched my hand. I tried to yank it away, but he easily kept hold of it. He plucked the dagger from where it hung in the air, placed it in my palm, and closed my fingers around the hilt.

The panic I had shoved down earlier raced to the surface. Aaidan released my hand, and I felt my arm move of its own accord. The evil grin on Aaidan's face told me he was controlling it. The blood drained from my face. "No. *Please*," I begged. "I'll do anything." My arm paused. The dagger's tip was mere inches from touching his shirt. One wrong move, and I knew it would cause severe damage, if not kill him. I tried with everything I had to move my hand away or angle the knife from a dangerous blow, but nothing worked. I couldn't move any part of my body from where it was. How was he doing this? Was this another power that Kyler had, too? Controlling people?

Aaidan stepped behind Kaleb and stared into my eyes, his pupils dilating as he said, "You're going to do everything I say. And if you don't, that dagger will go straight through his heart."

The burning in my eyes started afresh, but I blinked back the tears. I focused on Kaleb's frozen face, and my head nodded of its own accord. I had to stay strong for him.

"Good," Aaidan whispered, then moved to circle us again. My eyes stayed on Kaleb. "Now, Saturday seems to be a big day for you and your fan club, am I correct?" I nodded, knowing he was referring to Prom. The whole plan hadn't been laid out yet, but I knew enough. If he asked me specific questions… "What, exactly, are they planning?"

Thinking quickly, I decided to tell the partial truth in case he could somehow tell I was lying. I wouldn't be surprised if that were one of his special powers. "They plan to use me as bait to lure you out."

"Mmhmm. And why are they trying to lure us out?" He mused. "Because we aren't that thick. We know what a trap looks like." He paused in front of me again, something glittering in his eyes. "But I think there's another reason. Perhaps to distract us from something else? Something they've been hiding?"

Shit. "No," I said quickly, trying to think of something he would believe they could be doing. He resumed circling before I could think of anything, though.

"Tell me." He leaned in to whisper, his breath hot on my cheek. "Why did you never bury your baby brother?"

My blood ran cold. He knew Mitch was still alive. How? Theo said they were able to keep it a secret, that they knew we were hiding something but didn't know what it was. If these people were stalking me as closely as it seemed, they would have seen me go to the hospital, not the cemetery.

"He's brain-dead in a coma," I said, letting the hot tears run down my face to sell the lie, unable to hold them back any longer. "Thanks to you," I spat through the anger.

Aaidan's breathy laugh against my ear made me cringe. "Why don't I believe you?"

"Sounds like you've got trust issues," I muttered.

The hand holding the dagger jerked, and I gasped at the sudden movement. But it hadn't touched Kaleb. It was just a slight movement to prove a point.

"That's just a warning, princess." Aaidan's hot breath was on my cheek again as he leaned in further from behind me, his chest touching my back. "Insult me again, and I'll make you draw blood."

I let out the breath I had sucked in and gave a stiff nod. It seemed I was alone in this fight. If that were the case, I'd have to figure out how to make him release me so I could fight him properly. "You must have control issues, too, because it seems you're scared to face me unless you're holding the ropes like a puppet master."

White hot pain sliced across my back.

I let out a scream worthy of a horror film.

It felt like a blade of fire—maybe it was—like he sliced me open and cauterized the wound simultaneously.

My scream echoed through the courtyard. Someone had to have heard it. They would come to save me.

"No one's coming to help you," he said through clenched teeth. "No one can hear you scream. We're invisible to the world." I let out another scream as he scraped the blade across my back again just below the first wound.

A dark chuckle at my scream and the sharp pain stopped, leaving the radiating pain to burn. I let out a whimper of pain involuntarily.

Another voice spoke then, but it wasn't in my ear.

Rayleigh?

Kyler.

A sob tore through me.

What happened?

How he knew, I didn't care. My labored breathing helped to disguise the sob as a result of the pain and not from hearing Kyler's voice.

Aaidan stepped out from behind me and into my point of view again. There were no weapons in his hand. No sign of anything that could have carved into my back, and I shuddered, not knowing what it could have been. Perhaps he'd pocketed it, but the two things that happened took over any thoughts of trying to figure that out. I had to concentrate.

"Someone will find me," I said aloud. Then to Kyler, *Aaidan is here. In the courtyard. He's holding us hostage.* "You can't keep me here forever."

I can't see you, Kyler growled. *Dammit. He must be using his shield. You'll have to let me in.*

"Oh, but I don't plan to. I just need you to agree to help me," Aaidan purred.

While he started in on a monologue, I said to Kyler, *What shield? Let you in? How?*

You have to let me see where you are. Through your eyes. The statement almost made me react physically. Thankfully, Aaidan still held me in place. This was absurd. How could Kyler talk in my mind *and* see through my eyes? I felt a gentle caress on my temple, or was it inside my mind? It was hard to tell. *That was me. Requesting to be let in.* I wasn't sure if knowing he could make me feel something like that inside my head was something I wanted to know. His voice was softer when he spoke again. *Open your mind, Sunshine. Let me in.*

Aaidan was still going on about me leaving willingly with him from the dance. Instead of listening to that nonsense, I concentrated on Kyler's instructions. *How do I let you in?*

You… It felt like he took a deep breath before starting again. *You have to trust me. Open the door to your mind.* That was it? I could see why that might be an issue, though. I didn't trust Kyler.

But I would have to trust Kyler to save Kaleb. How ironic.

Aaidan had turned his back on me, so I closed my eyes and searched my mind—a door. I needed to find a door. At first, nothing popped up. It was a black, empty space, like a void. I kept searching, thinking of a way in. Not anything specific, just something to open.

Something appeared. A massive oak door, with intricate designs carved into it and swirls made of iron. It was beautiful. I didn't look at it too long, knowing I had to concentrate on Kyler. Trust. I had to trust him. Not always, but right now. Reaching out a mental hand to the door, I turned the handle. Bright blue eyes came into view through the crack as it opened. They seemed to be floating in the middle of the blackness around them. They were blue, but I knew they were his. I'd seen his eyes that color before… hadn't I?

Good. Kyler's voice was a low growl as those blue eyes bore into me. *This may feel a bit invasive,* he sounded apologetic. *Open your eyes.*

When I did, Aaidan was studying me. "What are you doing?" He demanded.

I felt a heavy weight penetrate my mind. That must have been what Kyler meant when he said invasive. I tried not to let the feeling of his presence in my mind show on my face. My voice sounded bored as I addressed Aaidan. "I was trying to block you out. You may like the sound of your voice, but I find it annoying."

He roared and leaped forward, putting both hands on either side of my neck, knocking me away from Kaleb and making me drop the dagger.

Get down! Kyler bellowed in my head.

I dropped my body weight, going limp to the ground, and slipped out of Aaidan's grasp. Pain shot through me as my back hit the ground, but I didn't let it affect me. I rolled out of Aaidan's reach just in time.

An invisible force knocked Aaidan twenty feet across the courtyard. He landed hard on the concrete with a sickening crunch. But he rolled and stood back up instantly, looking around for the culprit that neither of us could see.

Kyler's presence in my mind disappeared. He must not have been using my eyes to see anymore. He was here. I pushed myself up, ignoring the stiff pain in my back, and ran over to where Kaleb was still frozen in place. His hand had moved slightly from its original position. I must have bumped it when Aaidan knocked me down. His feet were still planted in the same place. The dagger I had been holding was lying on the ground, its crystal blade gleaming in the sun. I checked Kaleb's side, where I had held it against him, and saw no evidence of it being there. Relief washed through me. He wasn't hurt.

The fight behind me dragged my attention away from him.

Kyler must have used his power to knock Aaidan away from me because I hadn't seen him show up. But they were in a fistfight now— kind of. Neither was making contact because they were both quick and well-trained. I watched in awe at how easily they dodged their opponent's strikes, hardly letting the other make contact. Kyler hit Aaidan's jaw once, and Aaidan made contact with Kyler's gut, but that was all I could determine with how quickly they were moving.

Finally, Aaidan threw a punch that Kyler swiped out of the air and spun him around to pull him flush against his chest, just like he'd done with me in his kitchen a few days ago. But this time, Kyler was doing it to cause damage, so he had a tight chokehold to cut off Aaidan's airway.

"If I pass out, it'll release him." Aaidan choked out, his eyes looking toward Kaleb.

"Stop!" I yelled to Kyler, not wanting that to happen.

"This isn't the time for sentiments, Sunshine," Kyler grunted, holding tight to Aaidan but didn't squeeze any harder. "If I don't take him out now, he'll keep coming back."

The inner battle in my head was crazy. Both ways sucked, but I didn't want Kaleb to find out this way. It would be too much at once. I also didn't want Kyler to *kill* Aaidan. But if Kyler let him go, he would try to capture me again, or worse. Someone else could get hurt. Someone else could die.

But I also had to make a new plan. A better one. He knew Mitch wasn't dead, so we had to change the plan anyway.

"Let him go," I said. Then, to Kyler, *They know Mitch is alive.* His eyes flashed. *We have to come up with another plan.*

Aaidan was straining against Kyler's hold, a slow smile spreading across his face. Blood shone on his teeth from where Kyler's fist connected with his jaw. He knew he was about to get away with this.

Kyler tilted his head until his mouth was touching Aaidan's ear. "When I let you go, you're going to leave. If you come back, I will not hesitate to kill you. Unlike her, I don't care if Kaleb finds out. I can deal with that later." I didn't know how his voice could go any lower, but it did as he growled, "And if you touch her again, it'll be the last thing you ever do." Those words made my insides turn to putty, but I didn't acknowledge it. I couldn't. Not now. Not ever.

Aaidan gave a tight laugh. "Looks like someo—"

Before he could finish that sentence, Kyler threw his fist into Aaidan's side so hard I swear I heard a rib crack. Aaidan grunted at the impact, and Kyler released his neck, shoving him to the ground. "Leave," Kyler demanded.

Aaidan spat a mouthful of blood onto the ground and pushed himself to stand, wobbling on his feet. Good. "You won't win this," he directed at Kyler. He gripped his ribs where Kyler's fist had landed and gave me one last look before limping down the path.

XXVI
Enemies

Kyler watched Aaidan until he disappeared, then turned to me and covered the distance between us in three strides. His anger had dissipated into an expression I'd never seen on Kyler's face. He stopped inches from me, making me take a hesitant step back. His eyes flashed an emotion I couldn't place. "Where did he hurt you?"

I had forgotten all about the white-hot pain Aaidan caused before Kyler appeared. "How do you know he hurt me?" That was my first question, but before he could answer, I asked another. "And how did you know I was in trouble?"

His nose flared, but he didn't answer me. Instead, he reached out and turned me around to look at my back. I tried to stop him because I was sure Aaidan had cut through my shirt to leave my bare back on display, but Kyler was too strong. A sharp hiss through his teeth told me it was worse than I thought. "This needs to be healed. Immediately."

"Why won't you answer my questions?" I said, tired of not knowing everything and trying to piece it together myself.

"This isn't the time or place," Kyler said, sounding tense. "Mari will be out in a minute. She'll take care of your back, then we'll deal with

Kaleb."

Kaleb. His innocent face was still frozen, awaiting our kiss. How were we going to unfreeze him without him knowing something else happened in the last ten minutes?

Wait, did he say Mari was going to heal me? I had so many questions. I made a mental note to start bringing my notebook everywhere I went. These questions were getting out of hand.

I walked through what I knew as we waited on Mari.

Both Mari and Smiles could heal people. Aaidan and Kyler could stop time. Kyler and Theo could talk to people in their minds. Aaidan could control people. Kyler could sense when something was wrong with me. *I might have to make a chart.* I thought to myself. I also noted that none of those related to the elemental magic I read about. *What are these people??*

"I already told Theo this, but I don't want any more secrets. I want to know it all. Tonight." My brain was still processing a lot from this morning, but at this point, the crazy was just going to get crazier. There was no point in waiting to find it all out. I wanted to know. I'd process it with the twins. All at once. Or I'd at least try.

Kyler scoffed, "Don't worry. Theo's got a whole presentation ready."

Ha. Good. He listened.

Mari came around the corner, running straight for me. "Rayleigh, are you alright? Kyler said you were hurt."

I nodded but kept my eyes on Kaleb. How could we act like none of this happened? There was evidence everywhere.

Mari joined Kyler to look at my back, and she inhaled sharply. "Oh my god...did he use—"

"Yes," Kyler growled.

"What?" I said, becoming a little uneasy at how concerned they seemed. "What did he use? Is it really that bad?"

"Nothing I can't take care of," Mari said confidently, ignoring my first question. "This isn't going to be pleasant, Rayleigh. Quick healings never are."

"How exactly are you going to heal me?" I asked.

"Do you need to use me?" Kyler's question was directed at Mari.

Why would she use him to heal me? I had no idea what she was about to do, so I couldn't object if she said yes.

They were silent a moment before Mari finally said, "If Rayleigh is okay with it."

The statement took me aback. "What do you mean? How would you use him?"

Again, silence for a moment before she spoke. "His... abilities may make it hurt less. But the cuts start at your shoulder blade and go diagonally across your back, down to your waist. So it would be a bit of an... *intimate* touch."

I wasn't sure what that meant, but deciding to get it over as quickly and painlessly as possible, I said, "Just do it. Whatever it is. Less pain, please."

"Alright," Mari said. "I'm going to have Kyler place his hands directly on the wound, and my hands will go over his. You won't feel much pain, but you may initially when he touches the open cut, okay?"

"Okay." I breathed, closing my eyes for whatever was about to come. Even with her description, I still didn't know what to expect. All I could think of was Kaleb and how everything that happened might change things for us, even though I didn't want it to. He deserved the truth. He deserved to know he was in danger. I knew that. But if I told him—

Searing pain cut through my thoughts as Kyler's hand pressed under my shoulder, causing me to hiss, but it subsided quickly, replaced with a warm sensation of comfort that spread through my body from where his hand was placed. His other hand lay under my other shoulder blade on my ribcage, his fingers slightly wrapping around my waist. The same searing pain came and went, turning into that same sensation as it spread through my body again. Kyler made a noise that was similar to the one I made simultaneously. I didn't want to acknowledge that it sounded like the noise I made whenever I slid into a hot bath, but I couldn't ignore it either.

The bliss that ran through me at his touch was not something I wanted to be feeling at the moment. Is this what Mari meant by intimate? If it wasn't, my brain needed to have a serious talk with my body because it was currently betraying me. Again.

The warm, soothing feeling grew stronger, the heat radiating through my body and causing all sorts of things to come to the surface that I tried to shove way down. It was proving difficult the longer his hands were on my bare skin.

But my body, of its own accord, leaned into those feelings. Into Kyler's touch as he supported me with his strong, capable hands. *I shouldn't be doing this.* The voice in my head said. But it felt so—

He was healing me. And Mari was helping. I was leaning into both of them. I focused on letting the healing sensation flow through me, and I barely noticed when his hands started to travel—

My eyes shot open as his hands trailed along my waist. I stepped out of his embrace, his hands dropping contact.

Mari was standing off to the side, her cheeks slightly pink from whatever secondhand embarrassment she experienced. I couldn't even look at Kyler. I didn't want to see whatever smug look he probably had on his face.

I closed my eyes briefly and let out a long breath. "Is it done?"

"Yes," Mari whispered. "I'm going back inside." And she disappeared before I could open my eyes.

Kyler was still behind me. His labored breathing from whatever powers he used to help heal me slowly steadied. "We need to close up your shirt," he muttered.

Not sure if I wanted him to be that close again, I dropped my head back to stare at the sky and let out another long breath. If Kaleb realized my shirt was torn apart, he'd know something happened. It had to be fixed. I brought my chin back down and said over my shoulder, "You can do that?"

His jaw was slack, eyelids heavy with exhaustion, but he nodded. He took a step toward me hesitantly, and I turned my back to him. He closed the rest of the distance and reached for the shredded parts of my shirt. He gently fingered the fabric, careful not to touch my bare back again.

The sensation of his fingers so close to the small of my back made the muscles there tense, and a giddy feeling traveled through my body. I scolded myself but then remembered that that happened when anyone was about to touch my back. Kyler was no different.

His fingers worked their magic, and I could tell when he finished because I couldn't feel the tiny pulls on my shirt anymore. He didn't make any attempt to back away, though. I couldn't make my feet move either. We stood there in silence for a moment. His strained breaths hit the back of my neck, causing the hairs to stand on edge, and goosebumps appeared on my arms. My breathing hitched.

I swallowed thickly, took a deep breath, and turned my gaze back to Kaleb. I reminded myself of the circumstances and mentally told myself to snap out of it.

"Can we please help Kaleb?" My voice was breathy, so I cleared my throat. He had been trapped in that stance for so long. Wait, how was he still frozen with Aaidan gone? I looked at Kyler over my shoulder. His eyes were glassy. He still hadn't stepped back. "Are you controlling him now?"

Kyler nodded. "I had my control ready the minute Aaidan let up. Even if he tried to release him before I made him leave, I would have immediately taken over."

"Then why did you let him go?" I wondered since that was the only reason I made Kyler release him. Other than the fact that I didn't want him to kill him.

"Because," Kyler let out a long breath, "Aaidan could have taken back control or something worse." He walked toward Kaleb, and I followed. "Get back into position, just like class earlier. Exactly where you were before he was frozen."

Heat traveled up my neck, definitely turning my ears red. "Are you going to be standing there when he wakes up?" I asked, eyeing him right next to Kaleb. I didn't know if 'wakes up' was the correct term, but I didn't care. I wasn't about to let Kyler stand this close as I prepared to kiss Kaleb, especially after what had just happened with the healing thing and my shirt. Not to mention how he interrupted our last kiss.

Kyler squinted at me. "What were you guys doing?" He glanced at Kaleb, saw his face, and where his hand was. I saw the realization as it crossed his face. He clenched his jaw, nose flaring and hissing through his teeth before looking at me again. "He was about to kiss you." Not a question, but I nodded anyway.

My mocking comment from earlier floated into my mind. Maybe he *was* jealous. The thought was absurd. Why would he be jealous? He hadn't shown the slightest bit of interest other than being an ass to me. Sure, we'd had some banter back and forth, but I was not interested. No matter how much my body tried to convince me otherwise.

"Can we just do this?" I asked, getting impatient and slightly embarrassed with where my brain was going. I didn't want to think about Kyler and his jealousy when I should be thinking about Kaleb. I just told him I wanted to see where things went between us, which meant forgetting about other possibilities, even though I didn't consider Kyler one of those.

Kyler bit back whatever he wanted to say, huffed loudly, and said, "Yep. I'm going to walk way over there," he pointed toward the cafeteria doors, "shout when you're in position." And he turned on his heel.

"Thank you," I blurted. Kyler stopped, but he didn't turn back. "For saving me. Us."

Kyler glanced over his shoulder. His brooding stare softened slightly, but he just nodded and sauntered off to the cafeteria doors.

Ignoring the sudden need to hug Kyler, I faced Kaleb again. My pulse quickened as I walked to stand in front of him. The hand holding my chin had dropped a bit, so I moved it back to my chin and used my other hand to caress his cheek with a soft touch.

A moment. That's all I stole, staring at him. Admiring him. He was so handsome and kind. Caring and gentle. A little selfish at times, but I was okay with that. I was a little selfish myself, bringing him into danger. Letting him be a part of my insane life. There was no way I could have predicted any of this happening. The truth would come with time, and I wanted to share it with him. To tell him everything about me. But I wanted to do it the right way and tell him myself, on my own and with no surprises. When it was just the two of us.

I dropped my hand back to my side and tried to step into the place of happiness and joy I was feeling before Aaidan showed up. "Ready," I said, figuring Kyler would hear.

The moment Kaleb could move again, his grip on my chin

tightened, and he pulled me closer until my lips met his in a gentle touch. I didn't realize how much my emotions had built up over the last ten minutes. They were so intense I felt like crying. Instead, I leaned into him, deepening the kiss, wrapping both arms around his neck. His hands landed on my waist and trailed to my back, where he pulled me to him, closing whatever gap was between us.

The kiss turned steadily into a greedy one, and I ran my fingers into his hair, closing his curls into my fist. He moved his mouth against mine with an enthusiasm I matched. Wanting— No. *Needing* more. His hand traveled up my back, and I let out a soft whimper, a mix of pain and pleasure, as he ran over the freshly healed wound through my shirt.

He stopped the movement of his hands and pulled back slightly, concern written on his face. "Are you okay?" He said, a bit breathless. "Is it too much?"

"I'm fine," I said, though tears had started falling down my face, and the place where his hand had touched was still tingling. "I'm just —" I smiled. "I'm overjoyed." It wasn't a lie. I was happy to be wrapped in his arms and finally let myself feel the feelings I'd ignored for months. But there was so much more I had to tell him. I didn't even know if he would stick around after he found out. But as we stared into each other's eyes, I knew.

Kaleb made me happy. I wanted to open up to him. To let him see every part of me. Secrets and flaws and all.

He smiled back at me, kissing me again and leaving us both breathless when the bell rang. He pulled away, finding my eyes, "Me too, Ray. I've never been happier." He moved to wrap one arm around my shoulders while mine found his waist. I looked up at him from under his arm, and he snagged one more kiss before we made our way through the cafeteria doors.

We both were smiling when we walked inside, but there was that little piece of me that had me on my toes. Watching. Waiting for something else bad to happen. I tried not to let it consume me.

XXVII
Don't Blame Me

The mixed feelings throughout the remainder of the day were intense. One minute, I couldn't stop thinking about Kaleb and the feelings I now accepted that altered my brain chemistry in a good way. The next, I knew Aaidan was still out there and, despite Kyler's threat, he could come back at any time and do worse things. I would know. I'd been the victim of some of them.

I tried not to show my newfound fear when I was with Kaleb. It wasn't as hard as the other thing that kept bothering me. Every time I leaned back in my chair, the tender flesh on my back would react, and I was reminded every freaking time of Kyler's hands there. I knew without his help, the wound would be much worse. His tender touch and the bliss that accompanied it in the moment—

Whatever my body was feeling, my heart wasn't in it, and my head knew it wouldn't happen, so I pushed those feelings aside every time.

Each time those thoughts popped into my head, I reminded myself that it was because of the healing magic, and I got that wound from trying to protect Kaleb (and being mouthy while doing so). This would bring me to everything that happened with Kaleb in the moments after, making me smile. How had I ignored my feelings for so long?

Kaleb managed to be waiting outside both of my classes after lunch, and the grin he gave me both times made me forget every bad thing that ever happened as he kissed me. He would pull away to look at my face, only to steal one more, grab my hand, and walk me to my next class.

When I couldn't see him, anxiety about what could happen next took over. No matter how many butterflies I got when he kissed me or held my hand, that little voice in my head told me he should know what happened. He should know about me and the danger he was getting himself into. How he'd almost been hurt.

He was only human. And they would use my feelings for him against me if they got the chance again. There's no way he wouldn't be caught in the crossfire. We had to protect him. Mari assured me Kaleb was being guarded as closely as I was, but that wasn't good enough for me anymore. Not after what just happened in the courtyard.

I found Kyler right where he said he'd be after class, leaning against the Jeep. I walked straight up to him and said, "I want Kaleb to come stay at the house."

Kyler barked a laugh, "No way, Sunshine."

"Yes! He needs protection, too. He's only human." This was one thing I was not negotiating. Kyler didn't seem like he was going to budge, either. So I crossed my arms and leaned back on my heels, raising my eyebrows and shrugging, "If he's not coming to the house, then I'm going to his."

Kyler pushed himself off the Jeep, closing the distance I'd left between us. When I didn't back down, a scowl appeared on his face, "He can't come to the house."

"He's been there before," I countered, holding my ground even though he towered over me. I lifted a hand to poke him in the chest. "*You* brought him there. You can do it again."

He looked down to where my finger dug into his chest and back up to my eyes, a smirk playing on his lips. "Not. Gonna. Happen." He pinched the finger digging into his chest and dropped it a short distance away from him. "You can't tell him anything anyway."

"So I won't!" I threw my arms up for emphasis. "He can stay in my room while you tell me everything you've been keeping from me!"

His eyes darkened, and he set his jaw. His voice rumbled, "He's not staying in your room."

"But he's coming to the house."

"No." Kyler bit out, his eyes sparkling with defiance.

"Yes."

He took another step toward me, leaving hardly any space between us. "The answer is no, Sunshine." His smoky breath hit my face.

I had to tilt my head back to keep eye contact, making it clear he wouldn't win this. "Then I'm not going home with you." I twisted on the heel of my foot, flicking my ponytail upward so it smacked him in the face as I walked away.

I didn't get very far.

Kyler whipped me back around by the shoulder, and before I saw what he was planning to do, he grabbed me by the hips, lifted me off the ground like a child, and threw me over his shoulder. He gripped my thighs to hold me in place and walked back toward the Jeep.

I threw my fists against his back and yelled, "Put me down, asshole! You can't force me to go with you!" He wasn't listening, though. Instead, he tightened his grip on my thighs, making it harder to kick my legs. "Dammit, put me *down*!" But it didn't matter how much I struggled or how hard I punched him. It wasn't going to work. He opened the back door of the Jeep and threw me in. The gentleness I'd felt earlier in the courtyard was gone entirely. I sat up quickly to try and bolt out the still-open door, but he slammed it shut and leaned against it.

Idiot.

I went to the other door and tried to open it.

I let out a long sigh.

He had child-locked the doors.

I clenched my jaw and climbed into the front seat, reaching for that handle. It didn't budge. "UGH! Screw you, jackass!" I hit the window with my fist for emphasis.

He had a smug smile tugging at the corner of his mouth. I gave him a vulgar gesture through the window before sitting in the driver's seat and crossing my arms tightly to my body. I couldn't believe he was kidnapping me, locking me in the car like a child. All because I wanted to protect my— boyfriend? Is that what he was now? I wasn't sure, but Kyler didn't seem to care anyway.

What did he have against Kaleb? Why couldn't he come to the house to stay safe? The only thing that came to mind was some hardcore jealousy. Which still didn't make sense if it were true. If he wanted to show interest, there were better ways to do that than being a straight-up ass.

I thought about the moment in the courtyard when his hands started traveling. I'd stopped him, but what made him do that? Thinking about how he made me feel with a simple touch— I *hated* it. Hated that he could do that to me. Hated that my body reacted. But... if he was feeling the same way. If his hands traveled because he felt it too. Maybe—

Channeling the acting skills I learned during my sophomore year in theater class, I turned to the window and knocked. When Kyler glanced at me over his shoulder, I tilted my chin down, looked up at him through my lashes, and slightly stuck out my bottom lip. He still had his back leaning against the back passenger door of the Jeep, and the windows were closed, but I knew he could hear me. "Please let me out."

He shook his head once.

"I promise I won't leave." I turned down the corners of my mouth slightly.

He narrowed his eyes. "I don't believe you."

I turned my little frown into a slight smile, "Come on," I smiled sweetly, "I trusted you earlier."

There. A flash across his eyes. I had him. He raised his chin and looked down at me, a smile playing on his lips. "If you run again, I'm throwing you right back in there."

I nodded, widening my eyes to prove my innocence.

He reached for the handle and opened the door for me.

I pounced, pinning him to the car with my new toy against his neck.

He wouldn't have known this, but I went to the courtyard before meeting him by the car to see if it was still there. Something about it was calling to me—calling my name. So when I returned to find it still lying on the ground, I pocketed it.

Now, I held that crystal dagger up to his throat with a sneer on my face. He looked at me with utter surprise. "Don't *ever* lock me up like that again," I ground out. "Got it?"

Kyler's eyes flashed blue for half a second, and a wicked grin played on his lips. "You never cease to surprise me, Sunshine." I snarled, pressing the blade deeper, but not enough to draw blood. To my surprise, he leaned into the blade, causing that drop of blood to appear at the point. His hoarse whisper gave me chills as he said, "I won't lock you up again."

"Promise me," I demanded.

Kyler slowly raised his hand and wrapped it around the hand holding the dagger. I tried to keep it in place, but something about the gentleness with which he covered my hand made me give in. He lifted the hand with the dagger away from his throat and brought it down between us. He lowered his chin, bringing his face close to mine, holding my gaze the whole time. "I promise *never* to lock you up. *Ever* again."

A shiver ran down my spine at the words. The promise I felt run through my blood. He was so close. His nose inches from mine. His hot breath danced on my lips. Smoky. Strawberry. He held my gaze. My mouth slightly parted as I breathed in his promise. His gaze dropped—

"Eh-em."

I jumped away from Kyler and swung my head toward the person who, thankfully, interrupted us.

Mari.

I sighed in relief, but it only lasted a moment as I took her in. Her stance said so much: arms crossed, hip popped, head tilted, glaring through her brows. She was *pissed*.

But she wasn't directing it at me.

Oh no. That look was pointed at Kyler.

He rolled his eyes at her expression, pushing off the car and turning to get into the driver's seat.

Her gaze fell on me. Her face softened, but her eyes lifted in surprise. "What was that?" She asked with a hint of accusation in her tone.

I shrugged, trying to ignore that my cheeks had been the color of a beet from the moment she showed up. "He told me Kaleb couldn't come to the house." I casually held up the dagger between two fingers before pocketing it again. "So I threatened him with my new dagger."

She nodded slowly and bit her lip to avoid saying anything other than, "Uh huh…" She dropped her shoulders and gave me a knowing look before she said, "You want Kaleb there to protect him, right?"

I grabbed my elbow and gave a one-shoulder shrug. "I can't think of any better way to do that."

She put an arm around my shoulders, leading me to the backseat of the Jeep. "Neither can I."

I looked at her sideways as she opened the door for me, waving to someone over my shoulder.

When I turned to see who it was, a huge grin spread across my face as I saw Kaleb trotting our way with a mirroring grin. I whipped back to Mari. "He's coming?!"

She smiled in return. "You wouldn't have come with us. Kyler knew that."

I blinked. The smile was still plastered on my face. I must not have heard her correctly. I blinked a few more times before I said, "I'm sorry. What?"

Mari shrugged and gestured toward Kyler. "He told me to get him after class." I glared at the back of Kyler's head in the front seat. He knew this whole time Kaleb was coming to the house. *He* suggested it. So why did he start that argument with me? What was the point? To get me riled up? Get under my skin? Make me hate him? Because it was working. I *hated* him.

But now I had to consider it was his idea to bring Kaleb to the house.

Stop being so confusing! I screamed in my head. Kyler's head turned slightly, but I spun away from him, not wanting to think about what was happening inside his head.

Mari disappeared, and, thank goodness, because Kaleb walked right up to me and wrapped his arms around my waist, capturing my mouth with his. I placed my hands on his chest and felt his heartbeat against the palm of my hand. I pushed him away before he got carried away and looked up at him with a stupid grin on my face. "Are you always going to greet me like that?" A disgruntled noise came from the driver's seat, but Kaleb answered me with another kiss. I blushed and gave him a little push so I could climb into the car. He followed me into the backseat, our backpacks landing on the floor in front of us, and grabbed my hand as soon as he shut the door.

When I glanced at the front seats, Mari and Kyler were facing forward, not paying us any attention. I pulled my lips into my mouth and looked at Kaleb. He stole one more quick kiss before putting his arm around my shoulders and pulling me over to lean on him.

Mari cleared her throat, "We're going to stop at Kaleb's house so he can grab some things. Then we'll stop by your place so you can get your prom dress since we likely won't be stopping at your house again this week."

The fact that we were still going to Prom surprised me. It's my first and last dance. It might be the last human thing I'd ever do, depending on how the night goes. Aaidan's threat today would likely change the plan for Prom, though, so who knows if I'd actually get to go. I hoped I would, though. I wanted to, even though I was bait for the enemy. I wanted to dance with Kaleb in my lavender dress, wear a corsage, take fun pictures, and be a teenager. Usually, that kind of thing didn't interest me, but with Kaleb…

When I looked up at him, his eyes were already on me. "Did you get a tie?" I asked.

"I did," he whispered. "I also got shoes similar to yours."

I lifted a brow, "You got sparkly silver high tops?" I suppressed a giggle.

"No." He poked me, smiling. "They're lavender."

"Hmm." Who would have thought we'd end up here? Cuddling in the back seat of a Jeep, talking about Prom after deciding to try dating and getting attacked by a maniac? Not me. Definitely not me. On all accounts. The first three were pleasant surprises, but the last one made my smile fade. I tried to turn away before Kaleb saw the worry lines appear on my face.

He didn't miss a beat. "What's wrong?"

What could I say? I couldn't tell him the truth—not yet. Not until I knew everything for myself. I decided a bit of truth wouldn't hurt. "I still get anxiety about being kidnapped," I whispered. "I'm worried they'll come back. Prom is the perfect excuse."

His face dropped. "Ray. You know I'll protect you." Kyler scoffed, and I shot a look to the rearview mirror, where I could see his face. Kaleb grabbed my chin and pulled my attention back to him, trying not to grit his teeth as he said, "We will *all* protect you. You'll be safe." He kissed my scrunched-up nose. "I promise."

We pulled up to Kaleb's house, and he ran inside. A few minutes later, he returned with his duffle and a garment bag. He placed both in the trunk and then hopped back in, pulling me to him again for the short ride to my house.

Kyler and Mari were silent in the front seat, but every once in a while, Mari would turn to give Kyler a look, and his head would turn slightly toward her, raising his brows or smirking. They had to be speaking mind to mind. But it was so subtle that I wouldn't have seen it if I didn't know about that ability. Kaleb, I'm sure, was oblivious. He was probably too busy concentrating on me, given that he kept pressing his mouth to my head and running his fingers up and down my arm.

The sensation his finger trails left was new to me. It differed from what I felt when Kyler healed me, which I didn't want to think about. This was comfortable and safe and felt like internal goosebumps.

When we pulled up to my house, I hopped out of the car to skip inside. I heard another door open and slam shut behind me. I turned to see Kyler stalking after me, glowering every step of the way. I stopped in my tracks to face him. "I can go in alone."

"No. You can't." He didn't stop where I did but shouldered past me.

"You let Kaleb go in alone!" I shouted after him, stomping my way up the path.

Kyler whipped around so fast that I almost ran into him. "He doesn't have two psychotic monsters after him!" His smoky scent washed over me. "You are our top priority. I couldn't care less what happens to him." He thrust his hand at the Jeep for emphasis.

"Then why did *you* arrange to have him at the house?!" I yelled in his face. "Some part of you obviously cares!"

"Not about him!" He growled. His breathing became ragged, and his smoky scent became stronger.

"Then *why?*" I shouted, and then, because I couldn't help myself, "And why do you smell like smoke?"

He took a quick step back, his face taking on a blank stare, and turned toward the house again. He quickly covered the distance to the front door, leaving me to hurry up the rest of the path. Somehow, between where he left me standing and the front porch, he produced a lollipop and placed it in his mouth.

"You didn't answer me." I stomped after him, right up to his chest, and poked him. "Why did you invite Kaleb and then act like my request to invite him was absurd?"

Kyler just stared at me. Arms crossed, leaning against the wall by the front door, switching the lollipop from one side of his mouth to the other with his tongue. When it was apparent he wasn't going to tell me, I cursed colorfully and turned to the front door. I dug my key out of my backpack and unlocked the door, storming inside straight to the garage. After going to the mall last week, I never had the chance to bring my dress in from the car.

If I hadn't been so focused on my anger at Kyler, I might have seen the back door wide open.

I might have noticed the muddy footprints from the back door into the house.

I might have even realized the lights were on in the hall upstairs.

But I didn't notice.

Not until I came back into the house with my dress and shoes in hand and found Kyler with his back to me, standing in the hallway and blocking my way back to the front door. He flexed his hand beside him, signaling me to stop. *Stay where you are, Sunshine.* I heard him say in my head.

I couldn't see around him, but I heard a dark chuckle that wasn't Kyler's. That's when I saw the muddy footprints leading from the back door, and I knew that whoever was standing on the other side of

Kyler had already been in the house when we arrived. Maybe they were searching for me. Or perhaps they were searching for Mitch. I don't know. But whoever it was wasn't there on friendly terms.

"I wondered when our paths would finally cross, Nikylo." The other man spoke slowly, deliberately. "Adarachi says you've been giving him a fair bit of grief."

"Adarachi has a lot to learn." Kyler's low voice rattled my bones.

"He also informed me of your plans for Saturday."

How did he know our plans for— right. I told him. But I didn't tell him the whole plan!

You need to sneak out the back door and get back to the car, Kyler said. *He can't see yo—*

"I may not be able to see Rayliana, but I know she's here," the other man said as if he'd heard everything Kyler spoke into my mind. Was he talking about me? How did he get my name wrong?

Shit. Kyler's voice echoed in my head.

"She holds quite the grudge against you, tavi," his dark chuckle sounded again. Who was this guy? "Even if I hadn't heard her yelling outside, I would have *smelled* her hate. It's potent." He clicked his tongue. "A shame, consid—"

"Oh, *shut up!*" I said, stepping around Kyler. "I'm tired of listening to shitty monologues." The man standing in the hall raised his brows as he took me in. He did not look as menacing as he sounded. He was shorter than Kyler, though not by much. For whatever reason, he was wearing a crisp black suit. His chin-length blond hair was pin-straight. He had a five o'clock shadow, and his eyes were a soft hazel.

"You've got quite a mouth on you, don't you?" He mused.

Kyler looked at me with a warning. *Don't.*

"Might as well speak out loud, tavi," the stranger said, sounding bored and annoyed. "Your inner dialogue is impossible *not* to hear."

"So is yours," Kyler growled. "Tell Adarachi to come on out and play." Wait, Aaidan was here? Where?

The man dipped his chin in surprise, "You've grown stronger. Tell me, how did you get past Adarachi's shield?"

"Like I said," Kyler gave him a wicked grin, "he's got a lot to learn."

"Can we just skip to the point of why you're here?" I bit out, starting to worry about the fact that Kaleb and Mari were still in the car and Aaidan was supposedly here somewhere. Is that where he was? Did Mari know what was going on? How did they even know we were at my house? Maybe they didn't think we'd show up here. It was, after all, the most obvious place for me to go. So why come here at all?

"Adarachi believes your brother is still alive and well." He steepled his fingers in front of him. "We came here after his incident at the school to see if it were true." He held out his hands and looked around the empty house.

Aaidan slithered down the stairs, glaring at me, but spoke to the other man. "Upstairs is clear, Koladon." *Ohh, so* that's *the Kool-Aid man.* "Looks like no one's been here in a week."

"Because I haven't been, dipshit," I spat. "And, like I told you earlier, my brother is in a coma."

"And I still don't believe you," he countered, taking a step toward me, which made Kyler step in front of me again. Aaidan stopped and looked at Kyler. He tilted his head slightly to the side, and a crooked grin spread slowly across his face. "Always on guard duty, huh, Nikylo?" Aaidan struck so fast that I didn't even know what happened until I felt the blood spilling out of my cheek. My hand flew to the stinging wound he'd left with the stiletto dagger he now held up to his nose and inhaled deeply.

Kyler snatched Aaidan's wrist with a snarl. "I warned you what would happen if you touched her again." His low voice was laced with warning. If he had spoken to me like that, I probably would have pissed myself.

Not Aaidan, though. No. Aaidan ripped his hand from Kyler's and stepped right up into his face, whispering, "I don't think you have it in you."

Kyler took a step back. "Oh, you have no idea what I'm capable of." As he spoke, he reached for my hand behind his back. "But it's not me you should be worried about right now." His hand wrapped around mine, and a strange sensation moved through my body. It felt as though gravity itself released me from its hold.

All I saw before the sensation consumed me and my vision cut out was a flash of fire as the house I grew up in exploded around me.

XXVIII
Immortals

My body slammed into something warm and familiar, but my vision still hadn't recovered. The sound of an explosion and a roar came from somewhere nearby. I heard tires squeal and realized that noise was coming from the car I was now inside. We were speeding off down the road and away from the action behind us. *How did I get in the car?*

"Rayleigh." A rough voice spoke near my ear, "Are you okay?"

My heart was racing. What I saw before I blacked out—what I heard seconds ago—could only mean one thing.

My house was gone.

Along with every memory that had been held within it. It was gone. Up in flames. I could hear the remnants of the gas line exploding. My heart sank into my stomach, and a sob broke out of me.

"Rayleigh," the rough voice whispered my name again, this time more intensely.

"I'm not hurt," I sobbed, knowing that was what he wanted to hear, "but I'm not okay." My whole life had literally and figuratively gone up in flames. From being told I wasn't human to finding out my family wasn't really my own, and now my childhood home was exploding behind me.

Strong arms wrapped around me as my body started to shake. I didn't think twice as I curled up into the embrace. My emotions overwhelmed me, and I tried not to let panic be the one that took over. I focused on the things around me, ultimately counting the strokes of comfort up and down my spine as I thought of all I'd lost.

The snow globe Dad got me that I meant to get repaired.

The books Arabella left behind that I told myself I'd read.

Home videos of Mitch, Bell, and me at Christmases and birthdays.

Pictures of the family I would never see again.

All of it was gone. I'd never step foot in that house again. There wouldn't be any mementos to keep—nothing to remember them by but the memories in my head.

The soft caresses down my back were becoming slower, and the arms around me had loosened their hold. My vision finally recovered, but my tears blurred the view. I tried to blink them away. It took a few tries, but eventually, the back of the Jeep became clear.

Kaleb was passed out, leaning against the door on the opposite side of the backseat. There was no way I couldn't tell him anything now.

The warm, familiar seat I thought I had slammed into wasn't a seat at all.

It was Kyler.

I was in his lap.

I used his chest to push myself up, and he groaned—a sound of pain.

My head snapped to him, and all thoughts of my house left my mind.

His head was lolled back against the headrest, and he looked on the verge of passing out. His eyes were half closed, his breathing labored, and his skin had paled at least four shades lighter.

I removed my hand from his chest to find it covered in blood. *I* was covered in blood.

Oh my god.

There was a gaping wound across Kyler's stomach. He was losing blood. Fast. It flowed freely out of the wound.

"Kyler?" My voice cracked. "What the hell happened back there?"

Did I lose time? Did I pass out? When he didn't answer me, I rearranged myself to straddle his lap, putting my knees on the bench on either side of his legs. I reached up to cup his face with both hands and lifted his head from the headrest. "Kyler. Open your eyes," I begged. His eyes were moving under his eyelids, but they weren't opening. "Kyler!"

"How bad is it, Rayleigh?" Mari's voice came from the front seat. We were still speeding down the highway.

"It's bad! Really bad," I choked out, still trying to get Kyler to open his eyes. "What happened?"

"Aaidan caught him in the stomach," Mari answered, continuing in a calm, instructive voice, "Tell me what you see, Ray. Describe the wound."

I blinked back the tears that had reformed and moved my bloody hands from his face to focus on his stomach. "He's losing a lot of blood!" I said, peeling back the shredded pieces of his shirt to better assess the damage. "Th-there's a gash in his stomach," I took a deep breath before continuing, "about the length of my forearm. It goes from his sternum to his hip and is about as wide as two of my fingers." I sniffled. "I can't tell how deep it is, but judging by the amount of blood, I'd say it's deep." I didn't want to inspect it further in case his organs started to peek out. I never thought I'd be thankful for all the times I'd been injured and dealt with blood. Or else I would have blamed all this blood on the queasy feeling I was getting.

But the queasy feeling came from the fact that Kyler looked like he was dying.

"Okay, Rayleigh?" Mari said calmly. How was she so calm? "I need you to help me with this. Just like Kyler helped you." Was she about to talk me through magically healing a deadly injury like it was a regular Tuesday? "Rayleigh?" Her voice was more stern this time.

"Okay!" She was indeed going to do just that, it seemed. "Okay, I'm ready. What do I need to do?" I asked. Kyler's head had fallen back onto the headrest again, and his breathing had become shallow.

"Place both hands on the injury, covering as much of it as possible," Mari said.

I did as she instructed. The skin surrounding the open wound felt cold and clammy. The blood started to seep between my fingers as I added slight pressure. "Okay. Done. What now?" My voice began to shake, so I took another deep breath, knowing that crying or freaking out or having a panic attack right now was out of the question.

"I'm going to reach back and touch you. All I need you to do is focus all your thoughts on closing the wound, okay?" I nodded and then voiced my agreement, realizing she couldn't see me. "You're going to feel a lot of energy pass through you, and it might be painful, but keep your focus on mentally stitching that wound up." This was ridiculous! "Ready?"

If it was going to feel anything like what happened to me earlier, I definitely wasn't ready for that feeling again. But at least I knew what was coming. Unless being on the healer side of it felt completely different from being healed, then I had no idea what to expect aside from Mari's warning.

Regardless, I knew after the initial pain this would work. "Ready."

Her hand found my hip, and I thought she oversold the energy bit.

Then it hit me.

It felt like being shocked all over again by the balloon electricity through Kyler's touch, but this was even more magnified. My entire body went tense, and my head flew back at the intensity of the energy flow.

"Concentrate, Rayleigh!" Mari's voice sounded far away.

I fought the force that held my head back and tipped it down to see my hands on Kyler's stomach. Blood continued to seep through my glowing fingers—

GLOWING FINGERS?! Holy shit! My eyes bugged out of their sockets. I had glowing fingers! How did I have glowing fingers?? *Concentrate!* I scolded myself.

I looked past my *glowing fingers* and imagined the wound beneath my hand stitching itself together.

The first sign that it was working was when the blood flow slowed to a stop. Then, I felt the skin start pulling itself together under my hands. "Should I release pressure as it closes?" I said through gritted teeth, the energy straining my muscles and making talking difficult.

"Yes! Let it breathe." Her voice was a bit strained, too, but it seemed like it could be from reaching behind her and not because she was using magic powers to heal someone. "The blood flow should have stopped."

"It did," I said, then did what she said and eased the pressure as the wound started healing under my glowing hands. "Why are my hands glowing?" I spat, not able to stop myself from asking.

"It's the power flowing through you. It's normal."

"Nothing about this is normal!" I barked, looking up at Kyler's face to see if there were any changes. His face was still pale, a sweat had broken out on his forehead, and his brow was furrowed.

"My power's almost out, Ray," Mari said. It was good to know their powers had limits, even if now was the worst time for them to run out. "We'll have to finish when we get to the house."

I looked down at Kyler's stomach as Mari's hand slipped from my hip. I sucked in a sharp breath as the glowing stopped and revealed the half-healed gash. "The wound isn't closed!"

"We're almost there," she croaked. "Theo is right behind us. He's already contacted Smiles."

I lifted my hands from the wound on his stomach, but the minute I did, blood started oozing from the wound again. "He's bleeding again," I choked out, replacing my hands over the gash to hopefully slow the bleeding until Smiles could get there.

"Take off your shirt and use it to put pressure on it," Mari instructed. She turned onto the hidden driveway and sped through the trees.

Ignoring my embarrassment at being left in a sports bra, I pulled off my shirt, balled it up, and pressed it on his stomach to stop the bleeding.

I looked at his face again. It had gone slack. Using one hand to hold my shirt in place, I reached up to Kyler's neck with the other, searching with two fingers for his pulse.

There wasn't one.

"*No!*" I shouted, switching positions so my knee could hold down the shirt and put both hands on Kyler's chest. I started pushing down as best as I could over his heart, but with the angle he was at, I didn't know if I was doing it correctly.

"What happened?" Mari's voice was laced with concern.

"No. Pulse." I said between compressions. Hot tears began streaming down my face. I'd never had to give someone CPR before, and I was glad they required us to learn it in gym class last year, but this is not the situation I would have thought I'd use it in.

Mari screeched us to a halt, threw it in park, and flew out of the car. I dared to look up for a second to confirm we'd made it to the house. She ran into the garage, disappeared around the corner, and reappeared seconds later carrying a satchel. She wrenched open the back door and dug one hand into the bag while placing the other on my arm. "Put your hands back on the wound, Rayleigh."

"You're out of power!"

"Just do it!!" She snapped. Her eyes bore into mine.

They were glowing purple.

What the hell?!

Turning back to Kyler, trying to ignore the glowing purple eyes, I did as she said, throwing my now bloodied shirt out the door and placing my hands on his wound again.

The energy blasted through me, but I was prepared this time. I fought the force that tried to throw my head back and kept my gaze on my hands as they started to glow, mentally picturing the wound closing again. This time, the intensity of the energy caused me to yell as it flowed through me into the wound.

The bleeding finally stopped.

The flesh of his stomach had stitched itself together.

As soon as the last piece of skin was sealed, a warm sensation flooded my body, and I stopped yelling, instead breathing as deep as I could.

Mari slipped her hand away. The glowing stopped. The warm feeling continued but started to fade. Quickly. I reached two fingers for his neck again.

He still didn't have a pulse.

I replaced both hands over his heart and pushed onto my knees on either side of his legs, leaning forward to yell in his face, "You don't get to die today, dumbass!"

The first compression felt like fire against my hands.

The second flooded my body with that familiar warm sensation.

The third sent that blissful feeling I'd felt in the courtyard all the way to my toes. It consumed me and made me want to arch my back into the feeling, but I kept my focus on Kyler. On his heartbeat. On his face for any sign of life.

As the sensation surged through my body anew, I prepared for the fourth compression, but a sputtering cough made me pause.

Kyler's face regained color, and the cough was to clear his airway.

"Oh, thank God," I whispered, sitting back on my heels again. My forehead fell to lay against my hands on his chest.

The coughing stopped, and a gravelly whisper made me lift my head, "Hey, Sunshine." A hint of a smile played on Kyler's lips, though it looked like it pained him to do even that.

"Hey, dumbass," I whispered, my voice hoarse.

"You saved me." There was a hint of a question in those three words.

I raised my eyebrow at him, a smile playing on my own lips. "Yeah, well. Now we're even."

Kyler stared at me, his eyes shining with something I couldn't quite figure out.

I broke our stare, unable to take it any longer, and took in the space around us. One glance down at myself reminded me I was no longer wearing a shirt and still straddling Kyler, blood all over both of us and the backseat. Not only that but Kaleb was still passed out on the other side of the car.

I maneuvered my way off Kyler's lap and out the car door Mari had swung open. She disappeared around the other side of the car and out of sight. Kyler took his time sitting up, taking in the new scar he now wore on his abdomen. He peered at me, and I reached out my hand to help him out of the car. If his wound healed anything like mine did, it would still be tender to the touch for several hours, but it wouldn't hurt internally. He accepted my help, swinging his legs out of the car one at a time and onto the driveway. I pulled lightly to help him stand, watching his feet to ensure he could do so independently. *Man, whatever powers these guys have, they sure do recover fast from dire situations.*

Once he was steady on his feet, I went to slip my hand out of his grasp, but he gripped my fingers tighter before I could.

I looked up. His face was several inches from mine, but the minute our eyes met, there was no space at all.

"Thank you," he whispered, reaching up with his free hand to tuck a piece of stray hair behind my ear, his thumb lingering to wipe the blood from the scar on my face that Aaidan had given me. My eyes fell, but the breath went out of me when he tilted my head up to find my gaze again. "He will pay for this."

I couldn't find words, so I just nodded as my eyes started to burn.

Kyler almost died. I'd been *worried* about him.

And I saved him.

This guy I thought I felt so much hate for was slowly becoming someone I cared about.

But that was all this could be. Because there was someone else I cared about more.

I forced myself to take a step back. His hand fell away from my face. I reluctantly pulled my hand from his grasp, and he let me this time. As soon as I was a good two feet away, I allowed myself to take a deep breath.

Before I could say anything, though, a huge gust of wind pushed me forward from behind. Half a second later, a similar gust *pulled* me backward. I twisted to see what could cause such a force, but the ground shook before I could turn around. My balance wasn't quite steady from the traumatic events I'd just gone through, and I had to bend my knees to prevent myself from falling.

Once the ground settled beneath my feet, I finished the turn. What I saw had me backing up several steps right into Kyler before I could stop myself. He placed his hands on my shoulders to keep me steady as I took in the massive creature that had landed on their lawn.

"No. Fucking. Way," I breathed.

This was not possible.

I was dreaming.

No. This was a *nightmare*.

This creature in front of me was the monster I dreamt of.

But it was also from some of my favorite movies.

It was magnificent, yet terrifying.

Beautiful, but impossible.

Not real.

"That's Theo," Kyler whispered behind me.

"HA!" Was my immediate response, only because that couldn't *possibly* be true. "That is *not* Theo." I laughed, hysteria building up in me as I found the word in my brain for what it actually was. "That," I pointed at the creature before me, my hand giving away my fear as it shook, "Is a *dragon*."

And that was the moment the earth tilted. I heard Kyler say my name as my body fell of its own accord. His arms wrapped around me, stopping my fall before everything went black.

१ म स र

"Rayleigh," the voice was so soothing. "Come on, Sunshine. Wake up." Why? It had been *such a peaceful rest.*

A huff of hot, smoky air rushed over my face. My bleary eyes opened slowly, and after a few blinks, I saw Kyler struggling to lean over me. Why was he so unsteady?

Then I saw his shredded shirt and the blood coating his torso, and it all came back to me. He was still weak from being torn open. I'd saved his life. Then a dragon—

I shot up so fast that I almost collided with Kyler's face. I stared at him, my eyes widening as I whispered, "Is there really a dragon behind me?"

He chuckled, offering me his hand as he stood. "See for yourself."

"*No.* Are you joking?" I stared at his impassive face, ignoring his hand to help me up. I didn't think I'd be able to stand right now. "You *have* to be joking. Dragons aren't *real!*"

He shrugged, looking behind me, "Looks pretty real to me."

That same huff of hot air hit me again, and I scrambled to my feet, completely ignoring Kyler's hand. I whipped around to find the golden dragon settled on the lawn, watching me.

"Breathe," Kyler whispered from too close behind me, probably hovering in case I fainted again—because, *Holy shit! A dragon?!*

"Breathe, Sunshine," Kyler repeated, laying his hands on my shoulders as I backed into him again.

I finally took a deep breath and let myself take in the sight of the creature before me, even if I still didn't believe what my eyes were telling me.

The dragon, because I refused to believe *that* was Theo, was the size of a small school bus. Its tail was wrapped around its legs, the end flicking like a cat's tail, and the wings were tucked in tightly to its body. The golden scales covering its entire body shimmered even though the sun was hidden behind the clouds. The golden eyes matched the color of the scales but were glowing like the light of a fire.

On top of its diamond-shaped head were two horns with a slight s-curve ending in a sharp point. They looked like they could do some serious damage if rammed into something, point first. Along its neck and tail were small, sharp spines laying flat against them, but they stopped at the base of its neck.

The wings were folded, but from what I could tell, they resembled bat wings, protruding from the shoulder and connecting all the way back to the thighs. Who knew what his wingspan was, but if I had to guess, I'd say it was at least double the length of his body—that is if you didn't count the tail.

My eyes found their way back to the dragon's face. His golden eyes pierced me with a stare. Another smoky breath sent smoke from its nostrils into the air between us. It was a good twenty feet away from me, but I felt the heat of that smoke as it surrounded me.

"He's going to shift," Kyler said behind me. I'd forgotten he was even there, so I jumped at his voice, and he chuckled. "He's requested that you either close your eyes or turn away."

"Wait, he's going to do what?" I spun out of his hold, whipping around to face him.

"Shift. Back to his human form," Kyler stated as if that wasn't the craziest thing in the entire world.

Mari walked over at that point, looking much better than when Kyler was in distress. "Aw, man. I wanted to do the grand reveal," she pouted, a smile on her lips.

"I know." Kyler rasped. "Theo always gets the attention."

I gaped at them. My eyes flicked from Mari to Kyler and back a few times before I finally said, "You can *all* transform into dragons?" My voice came out much softer than I intended, the accusatory tone losing its effect.

Mari nodded, but Kyler said, "Technically, it's called shifting."

They watched me closely. Waiting. Letting it sink in. Kyler had a smug look on his face as he leaned against the Jeep, still weak.

I knew they were waiting for me to freak out. To say something. To have a panic attack. To pass out again. Something. But as I stood there staring at them, I didn't feel any of those things coming up to the surface.

All I said was, "Huh." Not a question. Barely an acknowledgment. I think I depleted my energy to the point where I couldn't give them any more reaction than that. Exhaustion hit me, and my shoulders sagged. So much had happened today, and it was only 4 p.m. The most recent events played through my mind, and I flicked my gaze to Kyler. "My house?"

He shook his head.

My stomach dropped. I already suspected, but the confirmation was still a blow. "What happened?" I asked, terrified of the answer I would get.

"Let's go inside," Theo's voice came from right behind me. I screamed and jumped a solid three feet away at his sudden appearance, which made him chuckle before finishing his thought, "We're safer there."

Just because I was curious. To make sure. To confirm I wasn't crazy. I slowly turned around to where the dragon had been a moment ago.

Nothing.

I glanced sidelong at Theo again and took in the robe he now wore. It was a silky black robe that fell to the floor, with gold-threaded designs spread over the material. I could tell he wasn't wearing any shoes, and his usually brown eyes were shining gold like the dragon's that had pierced my soul moments ago. Realizing something, I shifted my gaze to Kyler once more. "Do your eyes change color?"

Kyler raised one eyebrow, "Only when I tell them to."

I narrowed my eyes on him. "I've seen them turn blue. Or at least flash blue." I was sure it wasn't in my head anymore.

This time, both of Kyler's brows shot up. He looked at Theo without saying anything. Out loud, at least.

Theo's eyes flicked between Kyler and me. "Hmm... Interesting."

"Why is that interesting?" I asked.

Theo didn't answer, though. Instead, he laid his arm around me and turned to lead me inside. "We will do our best to answer all your questions, including that one. But we must do so inside. It is not safe out here in the open."

I started to go with him, then remembered, "Kaleb!" I spun to get him, but Mari, who was directly behind me, held up her hand to stop me.

"He's already in the house," she said. When my eyes bugged out of my head and fear crossed my face, she said, "I brought him in while you were meeting Theo's dragon."

I sucked in a breath. If he'd woken up— "Did he see—"

She held up her hand again. "No. He was still unconscious."

My jaw dropped. "No way." When she didn't say anything, I voiced my question. "You carried him into the house *by yourself?*"

Mari wrinkled her nose and nodded.

"Ha!" Whatever she did to recharge her energy, she got it back fast. Kaleb was at least one-eighty and over six feet tall. I could have carried him from the car to the garage if I did it like a fireman, and that was only fifteen feet. She carried him all the way into the house and, hopefully, put him in my room. I gave Mari a slow once over and noticed she was much more toned than I realized. "I want to train with you," I stated very seriously.

A big smile crossed her face, "Okay!"

Remembering my other stuff in the car, I stepped around Mari and grabbed my backpack and dress. As soon as the dress unfolded, my body sagged.

It was covered in Kyler's blood.

I closed my eyes, letting out a long sigh. "Guess I'll have to find a new dress for Prom," I stated. Exhaustion hit me then, and I wondered out loud. "Is it even worth going if I'm just going to be bait?"

"You're not just bait, Rayleigh," Theo offered and was next to me again, ushering me inside. "We have a plan."

XXIX
Demons

Theo led me to the kitchen, where a vast assortment of food, once again, covered the island. Where did they keep this much food? At least I knew why they had such big appetites now.

"Eat, dearie," he instructed. "It'll help with the exhaustion." Then he disappeared down the hallway.

Kyler and Mari helped themselves, piling food on their plates. I stared at them, wondering how on earth these two people, and the one who disappeared down the hall, could turn into *dragons*. They looked like normal humans. Then again, so did I. And apparently I wasn't. But *still!* The idea was ridiculous.

I *had* just seen a dragon on their lawn. A magnificent, beautiful dragon. Granted, I passed out, but I was starting to think I could blame that partially on the exhaustion. I wasn't sure I would ever get used to the idea of dragons, though.

"Eat, Sunshine," Kyler said, pulling my attention away from my thoughts. "You used a lot of energy today." I took him in, his shirt still shredded in the middle, and dried blood caked his shirt, abdomen, chest, and even his face where I'd grabbed it. I looked down and saw my clothes covered in blood, too—his blood. My hands were covered in it, too. I went to the sink to scrub them off before turning to the island of food.

Giving into the demand of my stomach's growl, I grabbed a plate and started serving myself a healthy assortment of goodies. I watched the other two mindlessly eat their food while stacking more on their plate. I figured now was as good a time as any to get some answers.

"How did you get hurt at my house?" I asked Kyler.

He sighed through his nose as he chewed his food, leaning next to Mari on the counter. "Aaidan shifted in the middle of us moving to the car," he said through a mouthful. "His claw caught my stomach before I could complete the jump."

"Uh huh…" I said, not understanding the last bit at all. "And how *did* we get to the car?"

He swallowed his food and tilted his chin slightly, staring at me for a moment before lifting his chin and saying, "One of my powers is manipulating time and space," he offered.

"And what does that mean exactly?" I said, disbelieving.

Kyler grinned, setting his plate down.

Mari choked on her food, "Kyler, no!"

I made to ask her, "What?" but then Kyler disappeared from where he was next to her.

My jaw went slack. *Where did he—*

I screeched, throwing my plate full of food in terror as he appeared a foot in front of me. He threw his head back, laughing as he caught my now empty plate with one hand and my waist with the other before I could stumble backward. The food was still midair when I watched it disappear. I clapped my hands over my mouth to stop the screaming. The pieces of food I'd carefully picked for myself fell from somewhere right above me back onto the plate Kyler held out.

Removing my hands from my mouth and forcing myself to take deep breaths, I slowly tracked my eyes back up to Kyler's, which were glittering with amusement. "What the fuck was that!" I wanted to slam my hand into his chest, but remembering his injury, I controlled my anger and only lightly pushed myself out of his grasp.

"I believe humans call it teleporting," he chuckled, handing me my full plate back.

Teleporting? The idea seemed impossible. But then again, *so did a dragon.* And I just witnessed both things within the last twenty minutes.

"I'm surprised you only screamed," Mari chuckled. "I would have decked him."

My eyes traveled to hers, and amusement shone there, too. "I thought better of it, ya know, since he almost *died.*"

She smiled, shaking her head, then turned to Kyler, "I'm surprised you had that energy in you."

"Pfft, it was only a scratch." He rubbed the new scar on his chest as he returned to the counter and resumed his position next to Mari. Leaving me speechless across the room.

This was a side of them I hadn't seen. Kyler had become more… Alive? Playful? Comical? Whatever it was, he seemed less of an asshole and more of a human. And Mari seemed to have a strong and spicy side, making me like her even more.

I stared at them, knowing there was more to learn about them and suddenly feeling like they would make it more fun than overwhelming.

Maybe I should lean into the lighter side of it, treat it more like a lesson, and learn as much as I can—as if it were an ordinary subject in school. The energy to freak out right now wasn't there anyway. The answers I was going to get were going to be way out of pocket, but I reminded myself that this was real, and I was learning. *Where's my notebook when I need it?*

"Okay, moving on," I said, scooping some mac and cheese on my plate while thinking of my next question. "How did Kaleb happen to pass out?"

"That was me," Mari claimed, raising her half-eaten wildberry pop tart.

"One of your powers?" I asked casually, to which she nodded. "Do you have more than one?"

She nodded but looked bewildered and said, "Rayleigh, are you okay?"

"Yeah!" I lied, a fake smile on my face. They both looked at me with an eyebrow raised. I knew they were used to me having panic attacks or running away from information, but I wanted to know everything. And that meant absorbing the information they gave me, no matter how crazy it all seemed. Before either of them could speak, I released a breath and went on, "I'm just processing the best way I know how. Ya know, trying not to panic or freak out after everything that happened today."

They eyed me warily, but I didn't feel like explaining my processing system. I followed Mari when she moved to the table, leaving Kyler leaning against the island alone. He still wore that amused expression, and his eyes were trained on me. He didn't even look away to see what he was putting in his mouth. Even from this distance, I could feel something like pride coming from him, but I turned to Mari and tried not to acknowledge how that made me feel.

"I have healing abilities and can sense and change emotions," Mari stated.

I nodded, shoving a bite of mac and cheese in my mouth. The first taste of food sent me into a frenzy, shoving bite after bite into my mouth until I had to take a minute to breathe. Whatever energy I lost today gave me the appetite of a blue whale. Focusing on what Mari said, I knew the first part, but the second one made me think. I swallowed the food and said, "How did that make Kaleb pass out?"

She pursed her lips. "I flooded his body with the chemical responsible for making you tired. I may have been a little overzealous because I didn't know how long things would be… crazy."

I took a deep breath but nodded, letting it out through my lips. Simply because I needed to know, I asked, "Have you ever used that power on me?"

She shook her head, "Only once. When we rescued you."

That made sense. Exhaustion hit me so hard that night. If her powers knocked me out for three days— "Will Kaleb be asleep for as long as I was?"

"No, he will likely wake up later tonight. You had some serious injuries after your kidnapping, so I wanted to ensure I could heal you properly without freaking you out too much. Hence, the three days." She watched as I ate more of the food on my plate, silently contemplating everything she said.

Unable to think of any more questions for her, I turned to Kyler. "Besides the teleporting thing, do you have other powers?"

He nodded. "You've seen a lot of what I can do."

"Really?" I cocked my head. The times I'd seen his magic ran through my head, and I guessed, "Freezing people in place?"

A nod. "Physical manipulation or what humans call telekinesis."

I squinted at him, thinking. There had to be more to the teleporting power, but the way Kyler kept staring at me told me there was something else I was missing. I tilted my head at him, trying to remember—

Don't think too hard, Sunshine. Kyler grinned at me from the counter.

"Ah," I gave an exaggerated nod. "Mind communication. Right."

"Well, that's not all," he said, pushing off the counter to get a glass from the cupboard. He turned to fill it with water in the sink before continuing, "I can also read minds." He said, taking a sip of water as he leaned against the sink this time.

Heat flooded my cheeks. If he could read minds— *Nope.* I scolded myself, not wanting to remember everything I'd thought or felt about him. He could have been reading my mind right there.

"Don't worry," he smirked. "I don't usually use that unless I need to interrogate someone. Like Aaidan."

I narrowed my eyes on him. "Is that why you let him go in the courtyard?"

He gave a curt nod. "I can also plant ideas or images in their minds." He took another sip of water, and I watched as he swallowed. I suddenly felt parched.

My eyes snapped to his. "Stop it."

He smiled—an actual, full smile.

And he had dimples.

Dammit. I swore to myself. Of course, he had dimples—just one more thing for me to find attractive about him.

I shook myself out of it. "Why did you let Aaidan go?"

"We need him to lead us back to whoever sent him." Theo's voice carried across the kitchen as he entered from the hallway. He was no longer wearing the silk robe but corduroy brown pants, a tan button-up, and what seemed to be his favorite beanie. I hadn't seen him without it until this afternoon.

"Who sent him?" I asked, but Theo held up a hand to stop me and then used that hand to gesture to the hallway he had come from.

Kendall appeared, followed by Leighton and then Tom. I let out a little squeal and jumped from the table, running over and barreling into the twins. They stumbled back as I wrapped them both in a hug, and they laughed at my enthusiasm.

After a moment, I let go and turned to Tom. He gave me a small smile, which I returned before moving in for a quick hug.

"Rayleigh," Theo's voice was commanding but gentle. I pulled away from Tom, and Ken and Leigh each took one of my hands in theirs while I faced Theo. "Please, finish eating so you can get cleaned up. Then we will go to the study for my presentation."

My eyes shot to Kyler, "You were serious?" He gave a slight eye roll but nodded. I couldn't help the giggle that escaped as I looked back at Theo. "You put together an entire presentation?"

Theo looked from Kyler to me, then shrugged. "I thought it would be easiest to tell you everything as if you were in a classroom. You seem to enjoy learning that way. And from what I've heard, you're a spectacular student."

I narrowed my eyes at him, glancing at Kyler for a moment. But there was no way he knew that was how I tried processing all the information. At least, there was no way he could have told Theo about it with enough warning to make a presentation, which meant the idea came before this afternoon. Theo wasn't wrong, though. I was a good student. But I couldn't shake the feeling that he might not have devised the idea alone.

Mari walked up to where I stood with the twins and hugged Kendall. "Glad you guys made it!" Wait, when did Ken meet Mari? I eyed the encounter but didn't say anything.

"Us too," Ken said, hugging her back. She glanced at Leigh over Mari's shoulder and waggled her eyebrows. I narrowed my eyes, wondering what I missed.

When Mari let Ken go, she turned to Leigh and said, "Hi!"

A smile spread across Leigh's face. "Hi," she said softly as Mari pulled her into a hug. Leigh returned the hug, color rising to her cheeks when she saw my shocked face.

My eyes shifted from Ken, who was biting her lip as she watched me put the puzzle pieces together, to Leigh and Mari, whose hug lingered a second too long to be casual before Leigh stepped back. Oh. *Oh*. Gosh, had it been that obvious the whole time? Damn. I thought I was observant, but how did I miss that? I grinned stupidly at Leigh as Mari strolled back over to the table, a lighter gait to her step.

Yes. I thought to myself. *Definitely yes.*

ᚠ ᚼ ᛋ ᛐ

"When were you going to tell me?" I asked on the way to my room, poking Leigh in the side. Ken had nicely pointed out all the dried blood on me and said I needed a shower.

"I only recently figured it out myself. I mean, I still find guys attractive, but *girls?*" I had never seen her act so giddy in my life. "They're just so pretty!" When she saw me smiling, she shrunk into her shoulders a little. She was still grinning as she scrunched her nose and said, "I also didn't know how you'd react."

I stopped short in the hallway, grabbing Leigh's arm so she did the same. Ken pulled up short ahead of us when she noticed. "Leighton," my voice had dropped into a more serious tone. "You can love *whoever* you want to. It won't change how I see you or feel about you. I love you! That's not gonna change. Okay?"

She gave me a shy smile as tears formed in her eyes and nodded.

"Good." I grinned at her and poked her side again. "I still expect you to tell me everything, though. I don't care if it's a guy or a girl. If they make you this giddy and excited, I want to hear all about it. Okay?" A giggle bubbled out of her, and the tears spilled over her crinkled eyes. "And if she hurts you," I pointed back toward the kitchen where Mari was, "I'm still going to beat her up." I remembered how Mari had carried Kaleb in alone and added, "Or at least I'm going to try. She did carry the tank that is Kaleb into the house by herself earlier..." We all laughed then.

I took her hand and continued down the hall again.

"Where is Kaleb?" Ken asked.

Guilt rose in me, knowing he was still passed out somewhere. I hoped he wasn't in my room because that's where we were headed. "He's here. Somewhere. But he's… napping?" I said, not knowing what else to call it. Mari said she had made him sleep, but I knew he wouldn't be happy when he woke up—wherever he found himself.

Ken gave me a look. "They let you bring him here?"

I shrugged, "I didn't really give them a choice." I wondered if telling them this next part was wise, considering I didn't even know what would happen next, but I did anyway. "We're kind of dating now."

Both of the girls gave me dramatic sidelong glances. "Since when?" Ken asked, although something told me she didn't seem too thrilled by the news.

"Lunch?" I scrunched my nose at her, but her face didn't change. "Why do you seem upset by that?"

She forced a smile and said, "I guess I'm just surprised, that's all."

"Yeah, I for sure thought you and Kyler had chemistry," Leigh piped in.

Oh no. Was it that obvious? "No way! I—" I was going to say that I hated him, but that wouldn't be true. Not anymore. Not after today. "I told you guys, I'm not interested in him like that." Which was not a lie. Even if my treacherous body tried to convince me otherwise. No matter what my friends saw, I was not changing my stance on this one.

The girls exchanged a glance. "Whatever you say, Ray." They said in unison.

"Why can't you guys just be happy for me?" I huffed.

Leigh sighed, "If you're happy, we're happy for you." She put her hand on my shoulder and leaned in, "And you still have to tell us everything, too." Laying my frustration aside, I suppressed a giggle, and she joined me. Ken still looked wary, but she gave me a genuine smile.

We finally reached my room, and they both gasped when I opened the door. No sign of Kaleb. Thank goodness. My books were still scattered across the floor, my notebook among them, and it looked like new books had appeared on my desk, too. I'd have to thank Theo later.

"Make yourselves comfortable," I said, turning to the twins. They had stopped in the doorway, jaws dropped.

"This is your room?" Leigh gaped.

I laughed. "Yep!" I'd gotten used to its size and beauty, but it made sense for the girls to be impressed. I was, too, when I first arrived.

Kendall didn't waste any more time. She ran and jumped onto the bed, sinking into it with a joyous expression. When I shut the door, Leigh was walking over to the balcony doors to admire the view.

After scrubbing the dried blood off my arms and torso, I emerged from the bathroom in an extremely comfortable, oversized sweatshirt —that smelled amazing—and loose black leggings. The girls were sitting among the books on the floor. I plopped down with them, thinking we had a few minutes to spare.

"So what did Tom tell you guys?" I asked, curious if they already knew more than I did.

Ken shrugged, flipping through *Fae Magic*. "He didn't really tell us anything. Just that we come from a different realm."

"And that we have elemental magic," Leigh added, shuffling through the books on the floor. "He didn't have time to tell us much else, though. He had to cover for Kyler at Kaleb's last night."

I was glad to hear they never left Kaleb unguarded, but I squinted. "Wait, who was with you two, then?"

Ken pursed her lips, and Leigh blushed, saying, "Mari came over."

My jaw dropped. "No wonder you two were so friendly with her in the kitchen!" I pointed at Leigh. "You made sense," I said, switching my point to Ken. "You didn't."

They both laughed. "She's adorable!" Ken said. "And so sweet."

"Oh, I know! I've been staying with her the last couple of nights." I chuckled. "She's probably the only reason I still have my sanity after being stuck in this house with an asshole and a guy who calls me 'dearie' and can never tell how much information is too much information."

They both laughed, and Leigh said, "Mari does have a very calming personality, doesn't she?"

"She does," I said. Leigh's face lit up, and I couldn't help but smile. It was so nice to see her genuinely happy about something. I had started to worry.

"Wait," Ken said, "if Tom was with Kaleb, and Mari was with us, and I assume Theo was with you...where did Kyler go?"

"Ugh," I dropped my head back to stare at the ceiling and said, "He was picking me up from the freaking hospital."

I dropped my chin back down to find Leigh grinning at me over the book of paintings she had picked up. "Why'd you say it like that?"

"Because he's the last person I wanted to see! And then," I hesitated but knew they'd find out soon enough, so I sighed heavily and went on, "he took me sparring."

Ken lit up, "Wait, like jiu-jitsu?"

"Yeah," I said quietly.

"We practice jiu-jitsu!" Ken gestured between herself and Leigh.

I pursed my lips but didn't say anything. Leigh squinted at me, "You knew that already, didn't you?" She gave me a knowing expression, licked her lips, and smiled. "How long has Tom been teaching you?"

I gaped at her, and Ken shrieked, "What! Tom is teaching you, too?"

But I didn't answer her. I was still staring open-mouthed at Leigh. She waved me away, "Oh, come on, Ray. I can put pieces together. Mr. Piper lets me out of class early, too." She winked.

I was too shocked to answer. Of course, she would be the one to put it all together, but damn, she was good. She laughed to herself and went back to her book.

"Wait, so how long has Tom been training you?" Ken asked, closing her book and focusing on me.

"Like six months?"

"And you didn't tell us?" Ken nudged me, "Is that why you were always 'busy' after school?" I nodded, and she glanced off into the distance, thinking. "*That's* why Tom was never home when we got out of school." Leigh nodded as if that was one of her clues, too. "He was too busy teaching *you*!"

Leigh squinted at me, "Why jiu-jitsu?"

Shrugging, I pulled my knees to my chest. "When my dad died, I —" I took a shaky breath, realizing this was the first time I'd spoken this out loud, "I needed to find a way back to myself again. To get stronger, both physically and mentally." I huffed a laugh through my nose, "And I was tired of falling down the damn stairs."

Both girls chuckled, having seen me do just that a few times. Ken laid her hand on my knee. "I get it. We both do." She reached for Leigh's hand. "Tom was never great with empathy, but somehow, he knew teaching us jiu-jitsu might help. He always said it was a great way to release emotions." She smiled, "In a way, it's connecting us back to our parents, too."

I always wondered how they'd gotten past their grief after losing both parents. Knowing it was similar to how I'd dealt with it made me feel that much closer to them. They'd gone through some of the same shit, and I was just now realizing it. Sure, they hadn't been kidnapped and weren't being hunted, but they lost loved ones and just found out they weren't who they thought they were. I looked at my best friends, tears shining, and whispered, "I'm really glad I don't have to go through all this alone." I smiled through the tears that had slipped down my face.

The girls returned the smile, both now squeezing my hands. Ken said, "Us too. It's a lot to take in!"

"Did you guys believe Tom when he told you?" I wondered, remembering my hesitancy and anxiety. "Because I'm pretty sure I had like three panic attacks!" I laughed. "Oh! And I fainted right before you got here."

They giggled, and Leigh said, "Well, we definitely had questions! But Tom had to leave, so he did the only thing he could: he showed us his magic."

My jaw dropped, "He showed you?" They both nodded, smiles spread wide. "I've only seen Kyler and Mari's magic. And I found out what they are." I nudged Ken, who knew I'd been trying to puzzle it out.

"Wait, you *did?*" I nodded. When I didn't fess up, she tapped my knee repeatedly and demanded, "Tell us!"

I just shook my head, "They'll want to show you."

The girls just stared at me. Leigh finally whispered, "Is that why you fainted earlier?"

"How do you do that!" I smacked her thigh, still shocked at how well she put things together.

Her laugh echoed mine, and when she finally caught her breath, she sat back against the bed. "This is all so crazy," she breathed. "We have magic. Your friends are—" she looked to me for an answer, but I just pursed my lips, shaking my head, "—some crazy magical creatures?" I nodded, and she shook her head in awe. Then, she seemed to remember the book in her lap. "*And!* There's a whole other realm!" She turned the book around for us to see.

Ken snatched it, pulling it closer to study. "This is where we're from?" She exclaimed.

"Yeah," I said, leaning over to peer at the pictures. "There's a room full of magical paintings just like these that Mari showed me yesterday." Gosh, was that only yesterday? No wonder my body was exhausted. It'd been through so much the last two days.

"Magical paintings?" Leigh said, mouth dropping open. "As in 'pretty' magical or as in 'magic' magical?"

"As in, they move when you touch them."

Both of the girls' jaws dropped.

"I wanna see!" Ken said, throwing the books off her lap and jumping up to open my bedroom door. "Aww, man!" she whined, making me turn to see what stopped her. Mari was on the other side of the open door with her hand raised to knock. "I wanted to see the magic paintings!"

Mari lowered her hand, chuckling. "I promise we'll go on a tour later." She glanced at Leigh and me, "Ready?"

I turned to Leigh and winked, which made her cheeks glow a bright pink as she tried to hide a smile. She stood, offered me her hand, and pulled me up beside her. I leaned in close and whispered, "I've never seen you so smitten."

She bit her lip and hooked her arm in mine, following Mari down the hall. I could hear the smile in her voice when she whispered, "She's just really pretty."

XXX
You

We followed Mari into the library, where a bookshelf had been pushed in like a door, revealing a room beyond it. It held more books, a desk, and several places to sit around the room: a couch, where Kyler was lounging, two comfy chairs, one of which held Tom, and Doctor Smiles had taken the swivel chair behind the desk.

Ken immediately plopped herself into the empty chair near Tom, looking over her shoulder at Leigh and me as she did with a smirk because she knew that left Leigh, Mari, and me to join Kyler on the couch. Great. I stuck my tongue out at Ken, who just winked before turning to chat with Tom.

Leigh and Mari sat down on the opposite end of the couch from Kyler. I sighed, knowing they'd done that on purpose. But, instead of sitting down right away, I walked over to Smiles, who stood up to greet me when we came in.

"I hear you helped save Kyler from a nasty cut," he said by way of greeting. "And with human techniques, nonetheless."

I gave a tight-lipped smile, "Mari healed him, and I used my knowledge of CPR, that's all."

His eyebrows stretched toward his hairline. "That's all?" He looked at me as if waiting for me to go on, but I just shrugged. "Rayleigh, you saved his life. Don't let anyone tell you otherwise. Including yourself."

Embarrassed by the praise I was receiving, I thanked him and turned back to the couch.

I sat down next to Kyler, who I had felt tracking me around the room from the minute I stepped through the door. I left as much space between us as possible, but it didn't feel like enough. His body radiated heat through the inches separating us. I wondered if that was part of being a dragon. Although Mari never seemed to radiate heat...

Kyler took in my comfy sweatshirt with an eyebrow raised.

"What?" I asked through gritted teeth.

"Nice sweatshirt," he commented, the corner of his lip twitching.

I rolled my eyes and leaned back onto the couch. "How's your stomach?" I asked, trying to switch the conversation away from my wardrobe choices.

Kyler huffed a laugh, the smoky scent of his breath washing over me. He shifted a little before answering. "Good as new, thanks to you." The smell of strawberries filled my nose, and I glanced over to see he'd popped another lollipop in his mouth.

I rolled my eyes and whispered, "At least now I know why you always smell like smoke." He cocked a brow at me, the lollipop stick interrupting the smirk that played on his lips. "Why lollipops?" I asked before I could stop myself.

He pulled the candy from his mouth and leaned over the space between us to whisper, "Because," his mouth was so close to my ear that my neck stiffened, and my shoulder jerked up to my ear, sending a ticklish sensation down my back, "Sunshine and lollipops go together."

My cheeks heated at his answer. I tried to cover it up with a scoff, but that didn't stop the feeling that went through my body. I leaned away from him to look at his face. "Stop doing that," I angry-whispered.

"Doing what?" He broke the devilish smile by popping the lollipop back into his mouth.

"Making me *feel* things! It's so violating."

"I didn't do anything." He used the time it took for the heat to travel up my neck at my confession to let his eyes wander down my body and back up again. When his eyes finally found mine again, they were a fierce green. His voice was deeper, if that was even possible, when he said, "That's all you, Sunshine."

My stomach dropped. *Shit*, I mentally scolded myself. I'd basically admitted he made me feel things. I almost changed the subject again by asking him about the color-changing eyes, but someone cleared their throat, and Kyler leaned back in his lounging position. My head snapped in the direction he faced.

Theo stood beside his desk, hands behind his back. "Is everyone ready?" A collective agreement echoed in the room. "Good." He looked between Ken, Leigh, and me. "I need you three close to each other, so Mari," he pointed between her and Ken several times, saying, "you switch with Kendall here."

Mari sighed but stood so Ken could sit between Leigh and me.

"Good," Theo said. "Kendall, if you would please grab both Rayleigh and Leighton's hands."

"Uhh, why?" She asked, sounding as skeptical as I felt.

Theo sighed, like he knew she would ask, and said, "Please just do as I ask."

Ken raised her eyebrows, but Tom spoke next, using his fatherly figure voice, "Kendall."

That was it. That's all he had to say, and she reached for both our hands, but she may have rolled her eyes a bit. Tom and Theo nodded at Ken as Leigh and I threaded our fingers through hers. It wasn't like we hadn't held hands before. It was just strange for someone else to request that we do.

Theo turned to Kyler and gave him a nod. When I followed his gaze, Kyler was reaching for my hand. I snatched it away before he could touch me.

Kyler tried to hold back his grin, but it didn't work. "What's wrong, Sunshine?" He whispered so only I could hear, "Afraid you'll like it?"

I snarled at him but swallowed my retort when Theo cleared his throat. "Rayleigh, please." His eyes shone with sincerity, making it hard to keep the scowl on my face. "Trust me."

I sighed and looked back at Kyler. "Don't burn me." And I put my hand back on the couch instead of placing it in his outstretched hand. Theo didn't say I had to make it easy for him.

He smirked around the lollipop stick, flipped his hand over, and laid it on top of mine. A tiny spark between us made me jump slightly, and he let out a dark chuckle that made me shiver. He didn't curl his fingers around my hand, though. He just lightly rested his on top of mine. His hand was warm, rough from calluses, but…comforting.

I gritted my teeth. Even after the day's events, it still frustrated me that I found his touch comf—

All thoughts left my mind as a tingling sensation started at my hand, spreading up my arm and through my whole body before crawling down my other arm to where Ken gripped my hand. The room around me disappeared. Ken screamed a moment before Leigh did as I assumed the tingling sensation and darkness overtook them. Theo's voice came through the void surrounding us. "Ladies, please. Relax. We're going to show you a few things, and this is the easiest way to do so." As he spoke, the black void changed.

We weren't in the library anymore. I mean, we were. I could feel the couch beneath me, Ken's hand squeezing mine as if her life depended on it, and Kyler's still lightly lying on top of mine. But the scene before us developed into an open field of tall grass next to a river with a tree line straight ahead. Four figures stood in the grass. I recognized them all from the paintings Mari had shown me.

But this wasn't a painting. When Theo said presentation, I thought he meant powerpoints and videos, not *this*. It was like we were standing—sitting—in the field right in front of the figures.

"Before you, there should be four Fae," I heard Theo but couldn't see him. "Each one is a pure-blooded form of each line. Annysian, Ignalian, Omonian, and Udarian. They—"

"How are we seeing this?" Ken interrupted, panic lacing her voice. It was strange to hear the usually calm and collected one sounding so panicked.

I felt more than heard Kyler chuckle, but Theo answered. "It's a mind link called *myados*. We will get more into our powers later," The Fae before us all stepped back except one. Her bright blue eyes shone against her pale skin. "The Annysian is going to demonstrate her powers."

Ken's hand relaxed in mine as the blonde-haired female turned away from us and started moving her arms. It was similar to how I'd seen it in the painting, but now I *felt* it. It was as though I stood in front of the air wielder as she pulled the gusts of wind around us. My hair blew around my face as I watched her take a deep breath, her movements pulling the air towards her. Then she let her breath out as she pushed her hands straight towards the ground. The tall grass before her split down the middle from the breeze blowing it apart in a trail to the tree line. She took another deep breath and pulled her hands back, moving them in a delicate pattern before slicing her arms across her body while pushing the breath out. A muffled crack filled the air. At first, it seemed like nothing had happened. Then, several yards away, the tree trunk split down the middle, with each half of the tree falling opposite ways.

My jaw hit the floor. If what Kyler and Theo told me earlier was true—

"That's what I am?" I breathed.

Tom's voice came from somewhere, "As far as I can tell, yes." Ken and Leigh gasped, but Tom said, "I sensed it in you the moment we started training." The Annysian stepped back to where the other Fae waited, and the fiery, red-headed male stepped up. Tom was still talking as the male stepped into position. "Your powers haven't made an appearance yet, but I've been preparing your breathwork for when they *do* surface. Your stress the last few months could be suppressing them, but you could also be a late magic bloomer."

As what he said sank in, a smug grin grew on my face. I couldn't help myself. I slowly turned toward where I knew Kyler was and gave the space there the cockiest grin. "That means I beat you fair and square."

Kyler growled, "I know." Even though I couldn't see him, I knew he was pissed. But me? I was *ecstatic*. He may have been six-four and packing muscle, but I was stubborn and always knew my way out; the breathwork was just a tool I'd been taught. Ha!

A sharp inhale made me turn back to the fae demonstrations. The

Ignalian had somehow called fire to one of his hands. With his other one, he rubbed his thumb and middle finger together and quickly opened his hand — a fireball appeared. Because of the texts I'd studied in my room, I knew the fire wielder had created the spark for his fireball with the friction between his fingers. Theo reiterated that to the girls as I watched the fire dance up the Ignalian's arm with wide eyes. The fire adhered to his arm, but it wasn't hurting him. Incredible.

"The fire-wielders are the rarest in our realm," Theo said as the wielder shot his fiery hands toward the tree the Annysian had brought down, lighting it aflame in one blow. We were several yards away, but I could feel the heat from across the field. One of the girls gasped as Theo said, "They are the most powerful Fae while simultaneously being the most dangerous." Yeah, I could see that. My jaw was again on the floor as the male linked his fingers in a bowl shape before lifting them up and outward. The flames grew higher on the tree, licking the leaves of the trees still standing. "As you can see, they cause destruction very easily, and if it isn't controlled properly, it can be deadly to anyone in the immediate vicinity."

I immediately decided I was thankful I couldn't control fire. I didn't want that kind of power.

The Omonian stepped up as the Ignalian stepped back from his raging fire, his eyes dancing with flames. The water wielder's tan, dewy skin seemed to have a layer of water settled on it as they turned their body toward the river nearby. Keeping their eyes on the raging fire, they wound their forearms around each other in a circular motion, and the water in the river started to rise, taking the shape of a ball, growing bigger with each circle their arms made. When it was the size of a small car, they lifted their hands straight up. The ball rose into the sky and followed the movements of the Omonian's arms as they stretched and arched over the field, stopping and pointing straight over the fire, which started to catch on the trees still standing. The water wielder yanked their hands apart, and the water spread into a thick sheet above the fire just before the Omonian brought their hands down to the ground, the water falling with them. The fire sizzled out under the wave of water that crashed into it. The mist from the fall of water touched my face with a cool whisper.

At this point, I don't think my jaw was ever going to leave the ground. The way these Fae were wielding elements like it was nothing more than breathing was incredible. That much control must take years to hone.

Last was the earth wielder, which, in my opinion, was the coolest. The Udarian was barefoot as he walked to the still-smoking tree on the ground. He bent down to touch the blackened bark in what seemed like mourning as he bowed his head. He stayed like that for a moment, and the tree moved with him when he stood back up. He used a slicing movement with his arms to break apart the tree into several pieces without touching it. Hovering in the air, they started to spin as his hands directed them. When the wood slowed, it was shaped like logs. He stacked them into three walls, making what seemed like an open-walled house with them. Once they were stacked neatly, he put his hands on the ground again and pulled the dirt up with him as he straightened. He molded and shaped the earth within the walls of logs until it resembled a home, complete with dirt packed into shelves, a table, and small mounds around it as places to sit. The paintings I'd seen of Niccodra made so much more sense now. The Udarians must have built most of the homes within the realm out of earthly elements within the trees, the ground, and the rocky cliffs.

I could smell the freshly dug-up dirt and sweet grass the Udarian now stepped back from. Whatever this mind link thing was, it was powerful if it could do all that.

Kyler lifted his hand from mine, and I immediately missed the warmth there.

Theo came back into focus as the scene of the four Fae disappeared. "Now that you've seen some of what the Fae can do, are there any questions?" Theo had the presence of a teacher, and it made me wonder if he did this back in the other realm.

Leigh raised her hand, to which Theo lowered his head as permission to speak. "So if Rayleigh is—what was it? Archesian?"

"Annysian," Theo corrected as Ken chuckled.

"Omniscient," She said, taking a breath to go on.

"An-ny-si-an," Theo broke it into syllables, and I giggled with Ken. We both knew Leigh had trouble repeating new words, and she'd be laughing with us if she weren't so concentrated on getting her question out. Most teachers learned the hard way that having Leigh repeat things back to them wouldn't work. It was something she dealt with throughout her school years, and she really struggled in the first few years. But she'd been able to adapt and accept her differences as we grew older, laughing at her mispronunciations or saying it so confidently even we questioned if it was wrong.

She held her hand up, "Whatever." She smiled, then finished her question, "If she's *that*, what are Ken and I?"

"Excellent question," Theo said but gestured to their foster father. "Tom, if you would be so kind."

He gave a curt nod, trying and failing to wipe the smile from his face, and turned in his chair to face us on the couch. "Your parents were both Omonian, so it only makes sense that you both are as well. They were strong water wielders, and from what I can tell, you two will fall right into their footsteps."

The girls looked at each other and smiled. "Cool," they said together.

"If there are no more questions about the fae," Theo started, but I shot my hand in the air. "Yes, dearie?"

Lowering my hand, I pulled my knees to my chest. "I read about another line of fae in the books you gave me."

Theo blinked. He looked at Kyler and Tom before his gaze settled on me again. "The Evanians." I nodded, and he continued, "They were a rare type of Fae in our world. They possessed the ability to wield more than one element."

"Can you show us?" I heard Ken ask, reaching for my hand in anticipation.

"I'm afraid not," Theo's voice was deeply regretful. "Evanians have been extinct for longer than we have been alive."

Leigh cleared her throat. "How did the Avanons have more than one element?"

I pursed my lips to keep from giggling as Theo sighed in frustration. "Evanian," he enunciated with a hint of frustration. His eyes snapped to Kyler briefly before his face softened, and he turned back to Leigh. "Sorry for my outburst." That was an outburst? He barely even raised his voice... "Our knowledge of the Evanian lineage is buried deep within our *Kyllindro*. Even I don't have access to that. But we do know that it was not because of intermixing elemental lines. Each elemental power is passed down as a human's genetics are passed down. So if your mother is a water wielder but your father is a fire wielder, you get one or the other, not both. The others lay dormant in the lines," Theo sighed. "I assume only one parent needed to be Evanian for them to bear a child with such abilities, but I cannot be sure without access to the knowledge." Theo's gaze slid to Kyler's again, and I tried to ignore the fact that they were having a silent conversation.

I hugged my knees closer, knowing none of the information about the Evanians really mattered, but I had been interested nonetheless. Perhaps there was more to learn in the books Theo gave me.

He cleared his throat, "Now that the questions are out of the way, we will move on to the other half of the presentation." He nodded toward Kyler again.

Letting my arms fall to either side of me, I braced myself for Kyler's hand on mine as Ken threaded her fingers through mine on the other side. This time, as Kyler's warmth seeped into the back of my hand, I could have sworn he curled his fingers slightly around mine before the tingling sensation flowed through me to Ken, and the room went black again. Another strange feeling went through me as his hand touched mine, like a magnetic charge that would keep our hands attached even after he was told to let go. I tried to ignore it and focus on what appeared around us.

The scene that formed was similar to the one we'd just seen with the Fae, but no river flowed nearby, nor did any trees line the field—just a grassy meadow with mountains far in the distance.

"Try not to scream," Theo said, his voice deep with amusement. I grinned, knowing what was coming. The gusts of wind that accompanied the beat of a dragon's wings came from behind us. It was amazing just how silent those wingbeats were, and it made me wonder if it was part of their training to be stealthy with their flying.

The twins gasped with fear and awe as the golden dragon I'd seen outside landed heavily in the field several yards away. Ken's grip on my hand tightened, but I couldn't tell if it was excitement or fear in that squeeze.

"This is my other form," Theo said. "We are what you call Drakalasson. Or dragon-shifters."

"You're joking," I heard Ken's deadpan whisper.

"Dead serious, actually," Theo chided. "I had it all planned out to show you the transformation, but it will have to wait until later."

The tall grass in the field swayed on the winds created by five more dragons as they approached; various sizes and colors landed in a semicircle facing us. Is this how children of their world learn these things about themselves, through a mind link? Or do they go to these types of presentations in person? How do they learn about the other species that inhabit their realm? It occurred to me that there had to be more than just fae and dragon shifters, starting with whatever magical creature made the paintings Mari showed me.

"While a dragon's color doesn't depend on their lineage, the powers they possess do," Theo's voice interrupted my thoughts. I focused back on the dragons before us, but the scene faded slightly, so I could see Theo standing in front of the dragons on the field. "Unlike fae, dragons can possess more than one type of magic. Some ancient magic in the blood allows us to hold up to three types of magic, depending on our heritage. My sire line is directly linked to the Parevim line, giving me the ability to move or control inanimate objects or people." As Theo explained the dragon's powers, I saw it demonstrate with a boulder that sat in the middle of the semicircle. Or I assumed that was what was making the boulder move, seeing as nothing was touching it.

My eyebrows raised as I looked from Theo to Kyler, who just winked at me, moving his lollipop from one side of his mouth to the other. I made a face at him, but the events in the courtyard popped into my mind. "Aaidan too, right?"

Kyler raised his brows in surprise and nodded, but Theo answered, "Aaidan has two powers. That is his lesser power."

"Which is why I was able to take control of Kaleb so easily without him realizing," Kyler whispered so only I could hear.

"His stronger power," Theo went on, "comes from his mother's bloodline, the Fyxenal. They can become invisible or put up a shield that hides anything behind or within it." The boulder in the scene behind Theo disappeared suddenly and reappeared. As Theo explained their powers, I wasn't sure which dragon was doing what, so I just focused on the boulder disappearing again.

"That's how Aaidan hid you from me," Kyler's voice was low, laced with something like regret. I turned to see his solemn face staring at the boulder he'd projected with his mind. "Why I couldn't see you were in trouble," he clenched his jaw.

My jaw went slack as I tried to think of what to say and how to reassure him that what happened wasn't his fault, but Theo went on before I could. "Mari and Doctor Smiles both come from the Dynkoi line. Healers, for all intents and purposes, but also able to sense and control emotions. That's harder for us to show you in a demonstration like this, but perhaps later." He nodded to Mari, who returned the gesture before Theo faced us again. "Then there's Kyler's other two lines, Ravault and Lunnox."

I heard Leigh whisper, "I hope there won't be a test on all this." Both Ken and I snickered.

"The former can control time, either freezing it or speeding it up—but never rewinding it." The way he said that seemed ominous. Like someone tried, and something terrible happened instead. "That power is also where the teleporting comes from. Opening pockets of space to somewhere near their current position." One of the dragons disappeared from the end of the line and reappeared on the opposite end. I blinked dramatically at the ease of such a movement, remembering Kyler scaring the shit out of me in the kitchen. He seemed to remember, too, because his fingers twitched on my hand, and I turned to see him wink at me again. I made a face at him and turned back to Theo. "They cannot, however, create portals to other realms or faraway places." I sagged in relief, knowing it was impossible to create a random portal to take me back to Niccodra. I'd have to be taken somewhere specific. Before I could ponder where the portal might be, Theo continued, "The latter allows him to show you the demonstrations with the fae and the dragons here. He can read minds and manipulate you into thinking or seeing something that isn't there, making it look and feel very real. The stronger the dragon, the bigger the illusion they can create."

"Sounds dangerous," I muttered.

"It is," Kyler mumbled, his finger fidgeting on the back of my hand.

I frowned at him. "You sound like you hate your magic."

His gaze found mine and held it momentarily before turning back to Theo. "It is a power some should never have." The knowing tone in his voice made my stomach drop. What happened to make him feel that way about his magic? Did he do something he regrets? Or did someone do something to him?

"The final line of dragons," Theo interrupted my thoughts, "is called the Solina line. Like the Evanians, the Solina line is thought to be extinct due to being hunted down by a past dragon lord. The Solina line was already dwindling when the dragon lord went on a hunting spree to kill them all, but he made sure there was no way the blood could be passed on. Their powers, while mysterious, are pretty straightforward," he paused, catching my eye before going on. "They are seers."

My eyes widened as the girls gasped with me. "As in, they can see the future?"

A nod. "And the past, in most cases. There were limitations, I'm sure. But the dragon lord who slaughtered them thought they were too powerful for the world, and no one should have the power to know the future." Theo took a deep breath and sighed. "It is unfortunate that we do not have such powers anymore because they used to be fantastic at gathering historical information for our *Kyllindro*." Theo clapped his hands, making the girls and I jump. "Anyway, that is all the types of powers that you should know right now. Any questions?"

When his question was met with silence, the girls started mumbling something about food, and the weight of Kyler's hand disappeared from mine, the scene of dragons with it. I glanced over to see him pull the now-empty lollipop stick from his mouth. He was chewing the gum from the center, and a smirk played on his full pink lips, and I—I was staring at them.

I yanked my eyes from his smug smile and stood abruptly. "Can we take a break?" I practically shouted.

Not only was that a lot of information, but I needed to pee, and my stomach begged for more food. We'd been in there a few hours, breaking everything down, and I needed a minute before we dove into the next portion.

"Of course," Theo said, gesturing toward the door that led to the hallway.

Kendall and Leighton asked to be taken to the kitchen for food. Mari obliged, and I followed them out. Tom, Smiles, and Theo stayed behind in the study to discuss something before joining us. I went toward the bathroom down the hall, leaving Kyler sprawled on the couch with his stupid lollipop gum and a stupid grin on his stupid face.

The sun had fully set, which meant it was past nine. Through all the information swimming around in my head, I wondered if I could tell Kaleb any of it without giving too much away. Theo told me I could tell him whatever I felt necessary but to leave actual titles of our kind out of it. He said to say something like, "I'm not from here. I have magic powers, and so do the people protecting me. But I can't tell you exact details about what they are." Which, in all honesty, was all the information he needed. That and the fact that I was in danger meant, by default, he was too.

As I mulled over how to say any of that, I wondered when exactly he would wake up. He'd been asleep all afternoon. Surely Mari's power wouldn't keep him asleep all night?

I emerged from the bathroom and turned right into a solid body. "Oof!" I said the same time he did. When I looked up, I let out an exasperated sigh, "Jeez, couldn't you have stood off to the side a little, *dumbass?*"

Kyler grinned, "Can't you watch where you're going, *Sunshine?*"

I rolled my eyes and went to go around him, but he placed an arm in front of me, hand on the wall. I slowly cocked my head to see a dark look on his face. "Let me by," I ground out.

"Answer me a question first," he said, those green eyes dancing. I crossed my arms and faced him with an unmistakable scowl. He took that as a sign to go on. "Why are you wearing my sweatshirt?" His gaze traveled to said sweatshirt, and I unfolded my arms to look at it myself.

That's why I recognized what I thought was the soap scent when I put it on earlier. It was his smoky strawberry scent with that hint of something else I still couldn't place. "It was in my wardrobe," I stated, wondering why his sweatshirt ended up there myself, but not caring at the same time. "And it looked comfortable."

He was still looking at the sweatshirt when I glanced back at him. His eyes slowly tracked their way back up to mine. His pupils had dilated, darkening his gaze. "Give it back," he growled.

"Make me," I snapped, turning to escape the other way. His other hand slammed into the wall on that side, caging me in. His face was so close to mine. I knew I could drop down and escape that way, but something about the situation made me face him again. "If you want it so bad, take it," I snarled.

His lips curled into a wicked grin. "I bet you'd like that, wouldn't you?"

My breath hitched, but I decided to use his trick against him this time. To play along. I placed my hand on his chest and gave him a slight nudge. He let me push him back against the opposite wall, his grin slipping away, and his eyes flickered blue. I leaned in. "Not as much as you would," I whispered in the space I left between us.

A pounding on a door down the hall made me take a step back. Kyler made a guttural noise and pushed off the wall. "Your boyfriend's awake," he mumbled, stalking off in the opposite direction of Kaleb's shouts.

XXXI
Odds Are

I'd been staring at Kaleb's door for five minutes. The only reason he stopped pounding on it was because Mari came running when she heard the noise. She flew around the corner, saw me frozen there, and slowed to a halt in front of me with a weak smile.

"You okay, Ray?" She asked, careful not to speak too loudly.

I shook my head. "I'm trying to think of what to say," I confessed. She gave me a knowing look and nodded. She knocked on the door and, once he stopped pounding, told him I would be there in a minute.

His hoarse voice answered, "Okay."

She turned back to me. "Do you need help?" She offered, taking in my slumped shoulders and arms crossed loosely at my stomach. "Or company?" She added softly.

I took a deep breath and let it out slowly before I gave her a thankful smile, "No. I should probably do this alone," I whispered.

"Okay. Shout if you need anything." She slipped something into my hand and turned to leave but then seemed to remember something and spun on her heels to face me again. "If he wants to stay, you can take him to the kitchen for some food."

If he wants to stay. That wasn't something I'd considered. The fact that he might not want to. I just assumed I'd tell him what I could, and while it might take a minute to understand, he would accept it.

I nodded to Mari, and she continued down the hall, leaving me alone again.

That was three minutes ago. I was still staring at the door, contemplating my best choice. No matter what I decided, it wasn't going to be easy.

Finally, I took a deep breath and knocked on the door.

"Yeah?" Kaleb's voice came through the door.

I used the key Mari had given me and opened the door enough to slip inside before shutting it behind me.

"Rayleigh," he sighed the moment he saw me and immediately closed the distance between us, reaching his arms around me and pulling me close. The relief in his voice made my heart twinge. He probably thought something happened to me. Or that he'd been kidnapped until Mari told him I was there.

I wrapped my arms around his waist and squeezed him as tight as I dared, laying my head against his chest. His heartbeat was erratic, but it was starting to slow. "I'm sorry I made you wait."

"What happened?" He spoke into my hair, holding me like he'd never let go. I might have let him. This was the safest I'd felt all day.

"So much," I confessed, tears burning behind my eyes. I decided to start with the easiest thing to tell him but the hardest emotionally. "My house is gone."

That made him pull back to look at me. "What? How?"

I spent some of the time in the hall trying to think of how to word things so it wasn't too much, too fast. "The bad guys rigged it with bombs. Kyler—" Another thing I'd had to think about how to word, "—is well trained and was able to detect the bombs and get us out of there before I got hurt."

Kaleb's brow was wrinkled, and his jaw clenched. "The last thing I remember is watching you disappear into the house. Why can't I remember anything else?"

I pursed my lips, knowing he wouldn't like the answer. "You got knocked out."

He searched my eyes in panic before they softened, and his head dropped, "And I couldn't be there for you."

"Hey," I raised my hand to cup his cheek and lift his gaze back to mine. "You couldn't have done anything. There were *bombs*, Kaleb. If anything, I'm glad you were *safe*."

"Yes, but you weren't!"

"I was, though. Kyler kept me safe."

"But I want to be the one that keeps you safe!" He countered, his voice rising slightly.

My face softened, and I realized this could be jealousy as much as anything else. "Kaleb," he let me pull his face to mine, and I gently kissed his lips, then laid my forehead against his. "There's so much you don't know," I whispered.

"Then tell me!" He pulled his forehead away from mine, capturing my face gently in his hands. "Tell me how I can protect you. Tell me what I can do to keep you safe. Please." The last word was a whisper. His molten brown eyes searched mine, waiting for a reply.

I took a deep breath. There were two ways this could go. I could say that I'm not allowed to tell him anything, and he would leave or decide to stay anyway because he cared that much about me.

Or...

"I'm not from here," I confessed.

He blinked. "Here... as in Wisteria Falls?"

"Here as in... Earth." I made a face as I said it, knowing it sounded ridiculous.

Kaleb let the words sink in, and I saw the moment his brain accepted them as genuine. His brows slowly rose as his jaw dropped. "You're an alien?"

"Ha!" The noise escaped me before I could help myself. Then I laughed through my nose as I thought about what that word meant and shrugged, "By definition, I guess you could say that I am."

A look of horror crossed his face, "Oh god." He took a step back, and I let him. This information was a lot to take in, I would know. I couldn't expect him to take it all in without being a little freaked out. I sure didn't.

"You process this however you need to," I said, raising my hands to show him I wouldn't force this on him. "I can't tell you everything, but I can tell you some. If you ha—"

"You're from *space*?" He interrupted, looking at me with crazy eyes, his mouth slightly open.

I shook my head, trying not to laugh. "No. But I'm from a different, uh, realm?" This was becoming a lot harder than I thought. I hoped I wasn't scaring him off, but it wasn't looking promising from how he backed away, shoving his fingers through his hair in distress.

"Are we talking like— like Narnia or— or Asgard?" He asked, his hands moving frantically in front of him like that would help him gather the information he needed to understand.

When I went to answer his question, I paused. "You know, I'm not really sure. But if I had to guess, I think Asgard?" The paintings I'd seen of floating islands and waterfalls felt similar enough to it.

"Do you have like— like superpowers or something, too?" His breathing was quickening, and he was stumbling over his words.

"Kaleb, breathe," I said, knowing he might hyperventilate if he didn't take a deep breath soon. I would know. I reached out my hand and left it palm up toward him, offering the comfort he always provided me.

He looked down at my outstretched hand. I waited. He looked up to my face, eyes still wide, then back to my hand. Slowly, his face relaxed, and he lifted his hand to set it in mine, taking a deep breath as he did so. I closed my hand around his, but he didn't look up from where our hands met. It looked like he was waiting for my skin to change to scales or something else alien-like.

"I'm still the person you've known since kindergarten," I said. "There are just things I didn't know about myself until recently." His hand was trembling in my own. "I don't have to tell you anything else. We can stop with this. You can go home." I paused but continued when he showed no signs of wanting to take me up on that offer. "But I told you because I wanted you to know." His gaze had not moved from our hands, so I leaned down to put my face in his field of vision. "I wanted you to know because I care about you, and you shouldn't be left in the dark."

He lifted his head, and I straightened myself as he did. "I care about you, too," he whispered. "I'm glad you told me, it's just... It's *weird*!" He made a face. "I'm dating an *alien*."

I laughed, "No! You're dating me. Rayleigh. Your best friend and favorite person in the whole world," I teased, giving him a big grin, which he had a hard time not returning. I gave a slight tug on his arm, and he let me pull him closer, the smile on my face fading. "But being a part of my life, being close to me, means you're in danger too." He wrapped his arms around my waist, and I did the same to him, meeting his eyes with honesty. "Things have... happened lately where you could have been hurt." His eyes widened, but I hurried on. "Thankfully, Kyler and Mari were there to protect us. But I needed you to know that. You should know that you've already been in danger and that you still are if you want to continue to be with me."

His eyes softened as he looked up at me. "Rayleigh, I can't imagine giving you up just because being with you puts me in harm's way. There's danger everywhere, and I would throw myself in front of all of it for you if I could." He leaned down to put his forehead on mine but paused and scrunched his eyebrows, "You're not going to grow antennae and try to cut me open and put something inside me, are you?"

"No!" I laughed again, "I'm not *that* type of alien. I'm technically not an alien at all. I'm just not from Earth, goobis." I used the old nickname we used to call each other and squeezed his back where my hand lay. I guess it was a ticklish spot because he started squirming a little. I tickled him some more to get him laughing.

"Okay! I get it!" Through the laughter that bubbled up, he said, "You're not going to turn into a creepy alien!" I laughed with him, loving how easy this conversation seemed to be going suddenly. His smile faded as he caught my eyes again. "I can live with the fact that you're not human," he reached up to put a piece of stray hair behind my ear, "but are you going to have to go back to this other realm?"

That was a question I hadn't thought to ask Theo. I searched Kaleb's eyes and saw something like hope there. "I don't know," I said honestly. The sparkle in his eyes started to fade. I put my hand on his cheek. "But I promise you'll be the first to know when I find out, okay?"

He gave a slight nod and leaned into my hand. "What happens if you do leave, though?"

"Let's cross that bridge when we come to it, okay?" I whispered, replacing my hands around his waist and tugging him closer. While I didn't want to leave, I knew it was possible, and I had a feeling Kaleb would not be allowed to come along. "For now," I glanced down at his mouth, then tracked my way back up to his eyes slowly, only to find he'd done the same thing, "I want to be a little selfish." I gave him a sheepish smile.

His hand brushed my cheek, "Me too." His fingers found their way into my hair around my ears. He used that hand to tilt my head and lowered his lips to mine. The gentle brush of his lips made me want to melt into him.

My heart started racing, and I felt like he stole the breath out of my lungs as he hungrily claimed my mouth more fully with his. I moved to wrap my arms around his neck and threaded my fingers through the curls on the back of his head, pulling him closer. A deep moan escaped his mouth, and he placed his hands on my hips, walking me backward to the wall by the door until I was pressed against it, his soft lips never leaving mine. His hands trailed up from my hips, fingers brushing under my sweatshirt and touching my bare waist.

I made a little noise against his mouth, and that must have unleashed something inside him because he pressed himself fully against me, pushing my body flush with the wall, and he kissed me more fiercely.

But something sharp dug into my back. "Ow!"

He pulled his mouth from mine, his eyes wide with horror as they met mine. "Are you okay? Was it too much?" He breathed heavily.

"No, I'm fine." I was trying to catch my breath. "It wasn't you. It's just, it felt like something was poking me in the back," I said. He furrowed his brow and stepped back, pulling me away from the wall so we could both examine it.

There was nothing there.

Kaleb turned me around to look at my back, but I knew he wouldn't find anything. "Nothing," he said.

We were both still breathing heavily, but I could tell the heat of the moment was over. Instead of addressing it, I grabbed his hands and gave him a small smile. "You hungry?"

His stomach gurgled in answer.

I giggled and kissed him quickly before pulling him toward the door. "I'll take that as a yes."

On our way to the kitchen, I told him who he could expect to see in the house. While he was surprised to hear it, he didn't seem to care that he'd "be the only human," as he put it. I still didn't think of myself as anything but human, but now that he called me an alien, I would just let him have that one.

As I watched a smile spread across his face, I couldn't help but notice that he'd been taking this all *way* better than I expected. I had an inkling that could be for a very different reason.

When we entered the kitchen, the twins hurried over to greet Kaleb, who embraced them both tightly before asking in a hushed tone, "So you guys are aliens, too?"

The girls looked at me with a question in their eyes, and I just gave them a look that told them to play along, so they nodded back at Kaleb.

While he was distracted by them, I walked toward Mari. As I stepped away, I heard him say to the twins, "You guys promise you won't try to probe me with your weird mind powers?" Little did he know, he was asking the wrong people to make those promises.

Mari smiled sweetly as I approached, "Everything go okay?"

I nodded, squinting at her. "A little too okay, if you ask me."

She gave me an innocent look, so I raised my brows. She gave in, "I didn't want him to freak out on you. It seemed like you were already stressed enough trying to figure out what to say, so I gave him a little nudge of understanding," she shrugged. "Kyler helped, too."

My eyebrows shot up higher. The fact that these two were spying on my conversation with Kaleb was unnerving, even if they did it for my benefit. "How did Kyler help?"

"The alien idea," she smirked. "But when that started to freak him out, I had to step in again." She searched my eyes briefly, then said, "We weren't listening to the whole conversation, just so you know."

"How did you know I was thinking that?"

She gave a small chuckle. "I don't need to be able to read minds to know what you're thinking, Rayleigh. Your facial expressions speak volumes. It's like when someone wears their emotions on their sleeves, but your thoughts can be read through your facial expressions." She wasn't wrong there. I relaxed my face to a neutral one, and she laughed. I smirked.

The idea that Kaleb's reaction wasn't entirely his own made me feel a little guilty. But he knew the truth, even if it wasn't all of it. He knew the most important thing: that he would be in danger if he wanted to continue to be a part of my life. And he still stayed—that decision he made on his own. I looked at him, laughing at something he said to the twins, then leaned in as Ken whispered something in his ear. "Thank you," I said to Mari. Kaleb looked up at me then and smiled. I mirrored it and walked over to take his outstretched hand while he continued chatting with the girls, trying to figure out what he could compare them to that he knew.

He pressed a kiss to my head between his replies, and I leaned into him, interlacing my fingers with the hand draped over my shoulder. The girls both watched the exchange warily.

"So this is real?" Ken interrupted their train of thought, looking more at Kaleb than me.

I felt him nod. He started to say something else, but I didn't hear it because Kyler walked into the kitchen.

His broad shoulders were rolled back, his stride confident, and his eyes avoided me completely. I didn't want to think about him right now, but he did help me with something crucial, and I needed to thank him. I knew that if I walked across the room right now, though, Kaleb and everyone else would wonder what was going on.

Instead, I decided to try using the line of communication between us.

Kyler? I reached out with my mind.

He stopped dead in his tracks and turned his gaze toward me. It pierced right through my soul.

Thank you.

He didn't say anything. He just held my gaze for a moment, gave a slight nod, only for me, and then continued to the food.

I wanted to know why he kept helping me with Kaleb when it was clear that he couldn't stand him. It seemed obvious that he cared, but he told me earlier it wasn't about Kaleb. Which only left one option: Me. I wondered if it was because he was assigned to protect me or if he only started to care about me after he met me. Although, I didn't know how that could be true because I wasn't actually nice to him. He should hate me. I should hate him. I shouldn't think about how he makes my heart race whenever he's close to me or how it felt to watch him almost die. Or the magnetic pull I felt every time he was close to me. Or how his scent of strawberries and smoke made me—

Better stop staring, Sunshine, Kyler's voice interrupted my thoughts. *Someone's gonna get jealous.*

I could hear the smirk in his voice and realized that I was doing exactly what he said. Staring. At him. *I was spacing out,* I retorted.

He chuckled in my head, a low, dark noise that made my insides queasy. There was no evidence of his laugh on his face, though. He was leaning against the counter and siping the coffee I'd just watched him prepare while I was 'spacing out.' *He just asked you a question.*

Dammit, I was still staring. I lifted my head from Kaleb's shoulder to look up at him. He was waiting for me to answer. "Sorry, I'm exhausted. What did you say?"

His eyes were hard to read, but he repeated himself. "Were you able to get your dress from your house before—"

"Before it blew up?" I finished for him. "Yeah, but—" I hadn't told him that Kyler bled out in the car. How was I going to tell him that my dress got destroyed because I was saving Kyler's life after being attacked by another dragon?

"It got singed on the way out," Kyler offered, occupying the spot next to me. He wasn't looking at me but at Kaleb. "We'll get her a new one. For now," his gaze dropped to mine, "Theo would like to continue your lesson."

"Lesson?" Kaleb said, looking down at me, too. "What lesson?"

I didn't know what to say other than the truth, so I said, "About where I'm from." I could see the question in his eyes, but I shut it down before he could voice it. "You can't sit in. I'm sorry."

His shoulders dropped in defeat. "I knew you'd say that." He looked at Kyler. "How long will I be locked in my room?"

Kyler cocked a brow at him. "You haven't eaten yet, have you?" When Kaleb shook his head, Kyler continued, "Eat. Mari will keep you company." He turned to me then, "Ready?"

I looked between Kaleb and Kyler; something odd about how pleasant they were being toward each other. But I wasn't about to question it. I turned to Kaleb and kissed him on the cheek. "I'll come find you when I'm done," I promised, releasing his hand. Turning to the girls, I hooked an arm in each of their elbows, marching us down the hall leading to the library.

XXXII
Up In the Clouds

Smiles and Theo were waiting when we walked into the study. "Welcome back, ladies," Theo said. "If you'll resume your seats, I will pick up where we left off."

"And where's that?" I asked, plopping into my spot on the couch. "You said we finished with all the types of magic."

"Indeed we did," Theo nodded, clasping his hands behind his back again. "We are going to move on to the politics and other properties of our magic."

"Oh. Okay." I forgot I had written those questions down. Kyler followed us in but didn't resume his seat next to me on the couch, instead opting for the chair next to Tom. I shoved the disappointment I suddenly felt way down. I shouldn't care if Kyler sat next to me or not. In fact, I should have been grateful that he couldn't distract me anymore. Although, that meant we probably didn't get any more cool visuals either.

Theo clapped his hands once, and Smiles shut the door. Theo reached for something on his desk and said, "We only have a little time to cover the rest of this, so please hold all questions until the end." He walked straight up to me and held out my notebook.

I looked up at him in surprise, reaching out to take it and the pen he offered me. "Thank you."

"I wanted to make sure I answered as many of them as I could here, but for those that I can't," He gestured to my notebook.

"Thanks," I said again, hugging the notebook and smiling. He winked and returned to his desk, taking up his post front and center.

I opened the notebook and saw that the new questions I had written were answered—again, with the purple pen. More citations from books I assumed were all in my room or something like "in-person" or "not now." His earlier presentation mostly answered the "in-person" questions, and I'm sure more of them were about to be included in this next portion. Only three questions weren't answered, not even an "in-person" remark. I decided to address those when Theo was done with his next lesson if he didn't answer them during it.

Theo cleared his throat. "Each species has separate rulers," he began. "While our species coexist on Niccodra, we still have our own hierarchies of power. Drakalasson are ruled by their King and Queen, and power is passed down through their bloodline. Fae, however, have councilors, one from each elemental type. They are elected based on who is more capable of leading, not necessarily the most skilled or the strongest of their kind."

"Why are ther—?" I started, but Theo held his hand up. Right. Holding questions 'til the end. "Sorry," I whispered, sinking into my seat.

Theo clasped his hands behind him again and continued, "No human communities exist in Niccodra due to their inability to survive there for long without the correct oxygen levels." I gulped. I sure hoped they were right about me not being human if they planned to take me to Niccodra. "Long ago, the Fae councilors and Drakalasson royalty decided collectively that humans could not be brought to the realm against their will. This abolished slavery, which some dragons had been taking advantage of, mainly because the human lifespan only lasted about a year once they arrived. However, because of where the realms connected, some humans ended up in Niccodra by accident. And if they didn't die within the first few hours, they were sent back to Earth with their memory wiped of anything they might have seen."

Theo pulled a map of Earth up to show us where the portal was.

I sat straight up when I recognized the spot on the map. "Wait a second… That's my meadow!" Theo nodded. "There's a portal to Niccodra there?" My brain started processing things faster than my mouth could say them. "Did my dad know? Did my mom? Is that why she—"

Theo, again, held up a hand for me to stop. "Rayleigh, dear. Please. Save your questions for the end." He pointed to my notebook, where I already had a ton of notes, and I let out a breath, writing down the questions that flooded my mind as fast as possible.

He went on to talk about the planet of Niccodra and its power. It had eight islands: Delgia, Gitapodi, Nykeraki, Diplopela, Krevatisto, Fotypas, Pipistrella, and Eliorra. The planet was one of two that circled a blue star called Andromeda. In the center of each island was a water cave that acted as a farm to grow crystals called Xoutallos, or Xouta. Andromeda fed power into the water of the caves each time its light shone through the single entrance on the ceilings.

"The crystals are harvested regularly and used to recharge our dragons' powers." Theo held up a bag, and I recognized it as the one Mari had shoved her hand into when I needed to save Kyler. He pulled out a piece of crystal within and held it up. It didn't look like a single color, but many shades of red, orange, and yellow, not blended but wholly separate, like a fire.

"There are several different color themes, one for each type of power," Theo explained, replacing the fire-looking crystal with one with teals and purples. "If a dragon has multiple powers, it needs to recharge with each type of crystal that corresponds to its powers. Or it can choose to enhance one specific ability by using multiple of the same crystal."

Theo replaced the purple and teal crystal in the bag and set it down. "That's the end of my presentation for now." I raised my hand, but he held his up, and I lowered mine in defeat, letting him continue. "It's late. I will take in all your new questions and answer them tomorrow, okay?" I nodded. The girls had gotten up to leave with Tom, finding Mari at the door to show them to their rooms. Kyler sat with one leg over the arm of his chair, but as Theo approached me, he sat upright, put his elbows on his knees, and rested his chin on his clasped hands. He stared at nothing in particular.

Theo stopped in front of me, and I handed him my notebook, which contained almost a whole new page of questions. Once he tucked it under his arm, he said in a low voice, "There were some questions in your notebook that I cannot answer." He glanced at Kyler, who was still staring at the wall, before looking at me again. "Niko has to be the one to give you those answers."

My stomach dropped. I had a feeling Theo would say that, but that didn't mean I had to like it. I glanced at Kyler, who was avoiding my gaze. I stepped toward him, but he stood abruptly and practically sprinted out the door before I could say anything.

I thrust a hand in the direction he went as I turned to Theo, "I don't think he wants to talk about it."

"Follow him," Theo said. "You need to know."

My heartbeat started thrumming in my head. His tone told me this was important. Too important not to chase after Kyler. The questions felt silly, but perhaps they weren't that at all.

With a dramatic sigh, I hurried after Kyler. I stepped into the library in time to see him disappear down the hall toward my room. I picked up my pace to catch up to him and entered the hallway to see him vanish into a room I'd never seen open before.

When I finally made it to the doorway, I froze mid-step.

It was Kyler's room.

My jaw dropped. I thought *my* room was huge. His was at least double the size, and the ceilings were twenty feet high. Half the room was similar to mine: a bed, wardrobe, nightstand, desk, and a bathroom on the far end.

The other half was filled with what looked like a giant cushion covered in rocks. If the rocks were what I thought they were, that was where he recharged in his dragon form, the rocks being the crystals that Theo just showed us. My jaw had dropped at the sheer size of the dragon's makeshift bed. If he filled that entire space when he shifted, then his dragon was *twice* the size of Theo's.

I couldn't comprehend the man sitting at the desk with his head in his hands turning into a golden dragon that size. Although... would he be gold? Or would he be a different color? Would I get to see him transform into one of those magnificent creatures?

I shook the thought from my head, unsure if I even wanted to see that, and asked from the doorway, "Why did you run away?" I asked.

"I didn't," he said without looking up.

"Looked like it to me." I crossed my arms and leaned one shoulder on the doorframe, unable to make myself step into his room but trying to be casual.

"It's not a conversation for everyone to hear," he muttered.

My stomach started tying itself in knots. "Why not?" My voice was soft, but something else crossed my mind, and I tilted my head at him. "How do you even know what the questions are?"

He lifted his head out of his hands and plucked something from his desk, only to toss it at my feet.

When I bent to pick it up, I let out a tiny gasp.

A purple pen.

My head snapped to where Kyler was watching me with an intensity I'd never seen from him. "*You* answered my questions?" I started connecting the dots. "And sent me those books?" He nodded. "Why did Theo say it was him?"

He scoffed, "Theo wouldn't know the first place to look for any of that information. The book collection in the library is mine." My eyes widened, but no words or thoughts came out. Kyler studied me for a moment, then answered my question before I could ask it again. "You weren't exactly a fan of mine when you first came here. I decided it would be best if he covered for me."

He was right. I don't know what I would have thought if I knew Kyler was the one answering my questions. A realization had me clenching my jaw as I whispered, "You evil bastard…" I clicked my tongue at him. "You dropped that book on my face on purpose, didn't you?" That got a sly grin out of him, which earned him a vulgar gesture.

He chuckled, the sound easing the weird tension in the room. "Since we're telling all Theo's secrets, he can't communicate mind to mind either." Kyler sighed, "The night we rescued you, he used our bond." He gestured between us. "We didn't want to hinder the rescue."

Squinting, I clarified, "So he can't talk to other people in their minds? Only you can?" He nodded. *Interesting.*

I let the silence linger and took in more of his room. Bookshelves lined two of the four walls. They were overcrowded with books that ranged from ancient-looking to brand-new. Loose papers were stacked on his desk in a few different piles, along with more books. In fact, there were books *everywhere.* On his nightstand, in his bed, along the cushion on the floor. I wouldn't be surprised if there were several in his bathroom. I wondered if any were fiction or if he only had books like the ones he'd been sending me.

The smell of the room wafted under my nose. *Oh my God...* The last component of Kyler's scent, the one I hadn't been able to place, was books. It was a mix of stale vanilla and tall, sweet grass. It reminded me of the meadow.

When my gaze fell back to Kyler's, his eyes were locked on me. Studying me. Watching. But it didn't take long for him to stand and cross the room, stopping a few feet from me with his hand on the door. "Do you mind coming in so I can close the door?" He asked softly.

The blood drained from my face. He wanted to be alone with me? *In his room?* I uncrossed and then recrossed my arms, "Why?" I squeaked.

"Because this conversation isn't one I want someone to overhear." He gestured with his head across the hall. I followed his gaze to a door I recognized. It was the one I'd stared at for five minutes earlier—Kaleb's room.

"Oh," was all I said before taking a deep breath and a single step into Kyler's room.

It was enough for him to shut the door behind me. He pointed to a window seat that had been concealed by the door and said, "Please, sit."

He was unusually polite, so I gave him a pointed look before crossing the distance to the window seat and sitting precariously on the edge of it. I wasn't sure where this was going, but it seemed like a bomb was about to go off, and Kyler held the detonator.

The window seat was big enough for both of us, but he elected to stand and lean a single shoulder on the wall next to it. He hadn't taken his eyes off of me.

He took a steadying breath before answering the questions that had been burning in my mind for a week. "The mark on your torso was an accident," he started. Another deep breath. "But it wasn't controllable." He scrunched his eyebrows together. "It's a rare phenomenon that it happened before your powers developed, but in our realm, a dragon can choose a Fae they believe complements their power as their rider. It's called a Kavaltis bond."

"What?" I deadpanned. Surely, I hadn't heard him correctly.

He smirked, "Do you actually need me to repeat it?"

"*You* chose me as your *rider*?"

"No," he said quickly, his smirk disappearing, "my *dragon* chose you."

"Aren't you one and the same?" My voice went up a whole octave.

"Yes, but no."

"That doesn't make sense!" I shouted.

"I can't control who my dragon chooses!" He shouted back. He pushed off the wall and turned away, shoving his fingers through his hair. "I never understood the magic, but my dragon can make two choices without my knowledge, and this is one of them. When I caught you that day at school, he made the connection without warning, catching me off guard." I remembered the hissing sound he made when he dropped me.

Something he said reminded me of another one of my questions. "Is that how you knew I was in trouble in the courtyard?"

He nodded. "When your emotions of distress or panic heighten, I can sense it through our bond. It's also how I could enter your mind and see through your eyes," he said cautiously.

"I thought that had to do with your other powers."

He shook his head, starting to pace in front of me. "When a rider bond is made, it creates a connection so that during battle, if the rider falls off or is in trouble, their dragon can find them faster and hopefully rescue them."

I nodded because that actually made sense. "Are there any other things this bond does?" I asked, thinking it could be why I felt certain things when I was around him.

"Well, my ability to talk to people in their minds can only be done at a short distance. With you," he paused, marveling at something, "with you, there could be miles between us, and I could still find you. Talk to you. Feel you." He shook his head in disbelief, then brought his gaze to meet mine. "And aside from others like me, I've never had anyone reach out to me in my mind like you did in the kitchen tonight," he whispered. "That connection, that bond—you found it on your own. It took me by surprise. I didn't even know you could feel it."

I tried to ignore my now racing heart and took a deep breath, coming to my last question on the subject. Then I could get the hell out of here and control my now intrusive thoughts. "So, what, the mark of this Kavaltis is just a permanent handprint on my torso?"

He cocked a brow, "It hasn't changed?"

I tilted my head at him, "Changed?" I hadn't studied the mark closely since I first noticed it. I just saw the slow fading around the edges and tried to ignore it for the most part.

"May I—" he cleared his throat as if the words had gotten caught there, "May I see it?" It was the softest tone I ever heard slip from his lips. He gestured to where he knew the mark lay.

My lips parted as all oxygen left the room, considering the question. The thought of lifting my shirt to show Kyler made bubbles start in my stomach, but I wasn't sure what made me so nervous. It's not like he hadn't seen it before— at the training gym and this afternoon when I used my shirt to keep him from bleeding out.

Kyler hadn't moved toward me. He just stared at me, eyes wide and pleading. He was giving me a choice. I didn't have to show him. I could tell him no. He'd given me all the answers I needed to know. So I should leave.

But a small part of me whispered *yes*. Because I was curious—about what he said. About it changing. I wanted to know if he was right. If it was different.

Slowly, I stood up. He stepped forward to stand what felt like inches from me but was probably two feet. I could sense his trepidation from where he stood. The blood rushed to his ears that were peeking out through his black curls. Was he *nervous?*

Breathing became difficult, and I wasn't sure if it was because I was about to be shirtless in front of him or something else entirely.

I reached for the hem of my sweatshirt— *his* sweatshirt— and lifted it over my head. It was a last-second decision to remove it entirely because I knew a bunched-up, oversized sweatshirt would get in the way if I wanted to see it, too. Kyler grabbed it from my hands and set it on the window seat where I had been sitting a moment before. His breathing seemed steady, but I couldn't help but notice it was a bit ragged. He *was* nervous.

I knew studying my torso from several inches above my head would be an odd angle, but I hadn't expected him to lower himself to his knees in front of me. It brought him level with where the mark was, but the sight of him kneeling before me caused my breathing to hitch. I swear a smile tugged at the corner of his mouth before he looked up at me through his lashes.

He lifted his hand. "May I?" He breathed.

The words sent chills down my spine, but I nodded. Trying to compose myself, he returned his gaze to where the mark was and reached out his hand to run his fingers across it. Goosebumps appeared all over my body. Kyler gave me a questioning look, a smile playing on his lips again. "It's cold," I lied because it felt anything but.

He smirked, and from this angle, that simple gesture made my body turn to putty. His gaze returned to the mark, and oxygen filled my lungs as I mentally chastised myself.

"Look," he said because I hadn't been paying attention to why we were in this position.

Slowly, I dropped my gaze to where his fingers had grazed my skin. What I saw was not the handprint I initially saw burned into my skin. There was still some semblance of a hand, but there were clear patterns with shapes, lines, and dots. A slight glow slowly faded from the lines, and they appeared midnight blue against my skin, which had faded back to its normal color.

Kyler reached toward me again, and his finger lightly grazed the mark, the sensation leaving a tingling feeling in its wake. "These symbols represent me. My magic." His voice told me he was as amazed as I was. "This one here," his fingers traced the innermost pattern, following the lines toward the center of the mark. Every inch of skin he touched seemed to come alive. "It represents my Lunnox line," he breathed, moving his finger to trace another symbol. This one curved around the bottom of the mark and reached just below my sports bra. I inhaled sharply when his finger dragged along that line, but he went on as if he hadn't heard it, even though his cheeks turned a darker shade of red. "This is the Parevim line. And this," he followed the lines to the outer part of the mark that ran along the most sensitive parts of my ribs, coming far too close to a ticklish spot on my waist. I tried not to pull away as he said, "Is Ravault." His eyes traveled up to mine. They were shining with wonder, and all the tension that had just built up between us was magnified with that one look.

"What?" The word barely made it out of my mouth because the oxygen in the room still hadn't returned from the moment he touched me. The mark had already been sensitive, but his fingers left a burning trail over each symbol, making it hypersensitive. A familiar magnetic pull filled the space between where his fingers traced and where he still knelt before me, studying me. Were all of those feelings because of the bond?

"I've just never seen one before," he said, slowly pulling himself up from the floor to stand in front of me again. Now, there *were* only inches between us. That pull was apparent on every part of my body this close to him. "Do you want to see mine? I haven't checked it since the connection, either," he confessed.

"You have one, too?" I asked, wondering when I could have left a mark on him. But when he held his hand up between us, I realized it was the hand he had caught me with that day—the one he'd flexed as he walked away from me. But there was nothing there. I narrowed my eyes at him in confusion, "Where is it?"

He grinned, "You have to run your fingers across it. Like I did yours."

Another shiver ran down my spine. This was starting to border on dangerous territory, but I reminded myself it was the bond. Nothing more. I lifted my hand to run my fingers from the heel of his hand to his fingertips, a sensation I knew all too well.

He inhaled sharply, holding his breath while we watched the intricate lines and patterns form on his hand. They differed from mine, and there seemed to be less of them.

But Kyler swore under his breath.

"What?"

His eyes were swimming with curiosity at whatever he was reading on his hand.

But he never got to answer me.

The lights in his room went out, leaving us in utter darkness.

XXXIII
Flares

My heart started racing. "Kyler?" My panicked voice echoed in his dark room. I couldn't even make out the furniture.

Kyler let out a loud sigh, "Come on." I felt the sweatshirt being tugged back over my head, and I pushed my arms through. "I told them not to do this," he mumbled, more to himself than me. He latched on to my wrist and dragged me along behind him.

What was he talking about? Do what? Scare me half to death? Why wasn't Kyler panicking? How could he see where he was going? The lights were *completely* out. There was not even a flicker to see by. Even the moon—

Wait a second.

There was no source of light *anywhere*. Which meant the lights hadn't turned off—

My vision was being tampered with. Again.

"What's going on?" I voiced, panic lacing the question as he tugged me around the corners of the house.

"We're almost there."

"Almost where?!"

He stopped, causing me to run into him, and dropped my hand.

As soon as he did, my vision was restored, and my ears were filled with multiple people shouting, "SURPRISE!"

Leigh and Ken were holding a cake. They were surrounded by Kaleb, Mari, Theo, Tom, and now Kyler, who had a tight-lipped smile, arms crossed as he leaned against the counter.

Kaleb closed the distance between us and placed a paper crown on my head, followed by a kiss. "Happy Birthday, Rayleigh."

My birthday.

How could I forget?

A glance at the clock told me it was barely midnight. I gave Kaleb a tight smile. "You planned this?"

He shrugged and stepped beside me, placing an arm around my shoulders and leading me to the cake the twins held. The number eighteen displayed on top in candle form.

"Happy Birthday, Ray!" They said together.

"Make a wish!" Mari said, clapping her hands with excitement.

I stared at the cake. The candles melting. The flames flickering.

Eighteen. I'd made it to eighteen.

But Arabella hadn't.

She should be here.

Our birthday last year was the most challenging day of my life. Losing her was terrible, but knowing she hadn't made it another year with me broke something inside me. She wasn't there to build our annual birthday fort in the living room. Or to carry on the tradition of baking a cake together. Or help me blow out the candles. There was no Nerf battle. No uno tournament.

She was gone.

It wasn't the same without her.

I thought if I just forgot about my birthday this year, it wouldn't hurt as much. That I wouldn't feel that pain again. Everything that happened last week was a lucky distraction. And it worked. I had forgotten about my birthday.

Yet there I was. Staring at the burning candles, Theo finished his rendition of 'Happy Birthday,' which he had started to fill the silence.

Knowing everyone was waiting on me, I closed my eyes briefly in the pretense of making a wish and opened them again to blow out the candles.

Everyone cheered.

Everyone except Kyler.

He locked eyes with me and dipped his chin, a level of understanding in his eyes. Something in that nod told me he knew exactly what I felt, but he said he never read my mind. I wasn't sure I wanted to know where that pain in his eyes came from.

Kaleb pulled me into a tight side hug and kissed me on the head. I plastered a smile on my face and tried to be in the moment. To celebrate. Even though I didn't feel like celebrating at all.

Theo cut the cake, and Mari handed me the first slice. I took it with a smile and headed to the island to set it down, taking a small bite. It tasted like ash. I tried not to let it show.

Ken said something about presents, which drew my attention to the pile on the table. It seemed like a lot had been planned before tonight, especially considering what the day had erupted into.

Exhaustion was hitting me hard. It had been a long day, and I wasn't sure opening presents was something I wanted to do.

Leighton noticed my solemn mood and slid up next to me. "You okay, Ray?" Her voice was low so no one else would hear, and she plastered a smile on her face while she watched everyone else listen to Kendall, who had started telling her favorite story about me.

"I've just got a lot on my plate," I confessed, reaching for her hand to comfort myself. She obliged, stepping closer to me so I could lay my head on her shoulder.

"A lot happened today," she sighed. I was going to voice my agreement, but I decided she already knew. Instead, I chose to take in her company and warmth as I processed my twin's missing presence.

The girls and I talked a lot about what it felt like for Arabella to be gone over the last year and a half. I told them that if I ever got quiet and distant in situations like this, to give me the time I needed to grieve her absence, and then we could continue whatever we were doing before I went silent. They never missed a beat. Never pushed me or questioned my mood changes. One of them would always approach me and make themselves available to lean on or as a hand to hold, while the other would distract anyone else in the room until I was ready to join the conversation again. I felt like they understood more than anyone. They both confessed that they often had intrusive thoughts of losing each other and how it would make them feel. We had all lost so much over the last two years. It was hard to believe it had all been a part of some evil scheme to get to me and my powers.

And thanks to this surprise party, I didn't get to find out what those powers were. Kyler's reaction told me there was something more to them than he initially thought.

I found him across the room, engaged in conversation with Tom, but he felt my gaze on him and met it. *Don't think I've forgotten about the mark on your hand,* I told him through the bond. *I need to know what it means.*

He returned to his conversation as if nothing had been said. But I saw the imperceptible nod. He could have been nodding at something Tom was saying, but I knew it was for me.

Ken grabbed a small bag from the table and set it on the counter. "Whenever you're ready," she whispered.

I saw the writing on the bag and released Leighton's hand immediately, snatching the gift. It was from Ma. I reached into the bag and pulled out a card.

> *Happy Birthday, Rayleigh! I've been putting these together for years, knowing you'd have to leave us one day. I wanted you to have something to remember your time here. I hope you know how much we love you and that you will always be a part of our family. I hope to see you again soon, sweetheart. Be safe. Love, Ma*

A tear slid down my cheek, and I ripped the tissue paper out of the bag to pull out a photo album. It was filled with pictures from birthdays and Christmases, days in the meadow with Dad and Arabella, and pictures of my friends and me in the heat of a Nerf battle in the backyard. Memories that I could take with me and never forget. Memories that I would cherish for the rest of my life.

I wiped away the tears and smiled. She knew this day would come and had prepared for it. I wished I hadn't been so resentful of her over the last year. So many things could have been different.

Mari set down a decent-sized cardboard box in front of me. "We couldn't save all of it, but…" she slid it closer.

I put the photo album on the counter and opened the box. The top was covered with books. Arabella's books. They had saved them from the fire or perhaps grabbed them before. It didn't really matter to me then. I had them. I smiled at Mari and pulled out some of the books, stacking them on the counter.

Under them were some of Dad's old CDs alongside his old walkman, old video tapes with the camcorder, and a small box that I knew was filled with notes I'd received from Dad whenever he was away for work. I hadn't touched that box since he died. I left that untouched and looked up to Mari and Theo. "Thank you. This—" The words got stuck in my throat. I swallowed thickly, "You have no idea how much this means to me."

Mari smiled at me, and Theo dipped his head.

Kaleb stepped up next. He held a tiny box in his hands. They were shaking a little. "I wasn't sure what to get you because I know how you feel about your birthday." He hadn't been a part of the pact I made with the twins, but that didn't mean he was any less aware of my emotions surrounding this day. "I had it custom-made."

Curiosity got the best of me, and I took the box from him. It opened on a hinge, and when I saw what lay inside, my gaze snapped to his, tears shining in my eyes. "Kaleb…" I breathed, trying to hold back the tears so they wouldn't blur my vision when I took in the contents of the cushioned box.

It was a shining silver bracelet with two small pendants. One was a silver sun with a circular periwinkle gem set into the center, and the other was a crescent moon with several lavender gems set into its curve. Kaleb gently flipped each pendant over, revealing an engraving on the back of each one. The one on the sun said, "More than the sun," while the one on the moon said, "To the moon and back."

Unable to hold back the tears, I lifted the bracelet from its cushion and held it out to Kaleb, setting the empty box on the counter. "Will you put it on for me?" I choked out, holding my wrist out to him.

"Of course." He gave a tearful smile, carefully took the bracelet from my hand, and wrapped it around my wrist, clasping it in place. It rested next to my scarred moon tattoo.

I rolled my wrist over to admire it before lifting my gaze back to his. His honey-brown eyes were still shining with tears of his own. "Thank you," I could barely whisper the words. I gently grabbed both sides of his face and dragged him down to kiss him tenderly. He wrapped his arms around me and pulled me closer, breaking the kiss and wrapping me in his arms. I twined my arms around his neck, burying my face in his shoulder.

He gave me something I didn't know I needed. Something that I never thought could bring me such joy. A reminder of the family I had and the love I shared with them. Arabella and the moon. Mitch and the sun.

Kaleb had known, though. He knew I would need it. How much my siblings meant to me and that, no matter what, our love for each other would always be there.

I pulled away, thanking him again for being the most observant friend.

There were still more presents on the table: two big bags and one small box. The girls grabbed a bag each off the table and handed them to me, stepping back so I could open them. I had a feeling I knew what was inside. Most of the sorrow I'd felt had passed, and I knew both Leigh and Ken had sensed that, too. Otherwise, they would have held off on these gifts until morning.

I took a deep breath, and instead of reaching in and pulling them out, I grabbed the bottoms of both bags and tipped the contents onto the counter.

Four fully loaded Nerf guns slid out, and I grinned, knowing full well that the twins would carry on the tradition of a birthday battle no matter where we were. The twins revealed their weapons from behind their backs, which meant there were two extras after Kaleb and I grabbed ours. We'd both snatched one up the minute they hit the counter with a laugh.

The girls already had their guns aimed at me. I turned to Mari and Kyler, who were standing nearby with curiosity. As if they knew they weren't a part of this tradition. Smiling, I said, "Do you want to join?"

Mari's face lit up, and she hurried to the counter to grab the remaining two guns, holding one out to Kyler. But he didn't make a move to grab it.

Instead, his eyes locked with mine, no hint of a smile or teasing as he said, "You said Nerf wars were only for family and friends."

"I did." I lifted my chin as I repeated, "Do you want to join?"

His hard gaze softened as he took in those simple words. Something shifted within him. Those words meant more than just joining in the battle—to both of us. He may still be an asshole and drive me crazy, but that didn't mean things couldn't change. After all, if we were bonded, that meant there was something more between us than him just being my guardian.

His eyes didn't leave mine as he gave me a mischievous smile and reached for the Nerf gun Mari extended to him.

XXXIV
All You Need to Know

The battle didn't last long, as it was already past midnight, and we had school in the morning. Kyler had taken Mitch's spot while Mari filled Arabella's, both on Leighton's team. I may have regretted that decision when I realized how good their aim was. And how fast they were. I shouldn't have been surprised, though. In the end, Ken, Kaleb, and I got cornered in the kitchen and pelted with bullets until their guns were out of ammo. We laughed ourselves silly, landing on the ground in a heap by the end of it.

After the day we'd had, it was a nice short break from the chaos and what was sure to come in the next few days. Theo said the plan for the dance could wait until tomorrow and told us all to get some rest.

I walked with Kaleb to his room at the end of the night, giggling about him getting shot straight in the mouth by Mari. He had bet her that she couldn't make the shot. He not only almost choked on the bullet but had to pay her twenty bucks in the end. He also had to fork it over to Kyler and me because we bet on her, too.

"How was I supposed to know she's basically the next James Bond?" He squeaked. I swear he was worse at shooting than I was.

My laughter echoed down the hall as we stopped outside his room.

"Weren't you paying any attention during the game? She hit every mark!"

"Come on! No one is that good." His smile was spread from ear to ear as he watched my laughter ease. He reached up to tuck my hair behind my ear, and I took in the happiness on his face.

"Thank you," I said, barely a whisper. "I needed a little fun today. It was—" I couldn't tell him exactly what made the day chaotic because it would bring up too many questions that I couldn't answer, "—a hard day full of information and exhausting situations."

He pulled me closer, and I wrapped my arms around his waist as he cupped my face in both hands. "You deserve to celebrate your birthday no matter how hard the day before is." His eyes switched focus between mine as he held me there. "I know how hard this day is for you, but we wanted to make sure you knew just how much we care about you, no matter where you are." He kissed the tip of my nose and laid his forehead against mine.

Tears welled in my eyes as I relaxed into him with a deep breath. He was so thoughtful and kind, and looking at him now, I asked myself how I hadn't seen it before. Or maybe I had written it off as being my best friend rather than anything romantic.

Butterflies started gathering in my stomach as my eyes fell to his lips, and I moved to close the distance between us.

The tears disappeared as he returned the kiss, and his fingers tangled their way into my hair. Knowing whose room was across the hallway from his and not wanting to get caught again, I reached behind him and turned the knob on his door to let us in, never breaking the kiss but backing him into the room. He spun us around once we were inside and shut the door with his foot.

His kisses became more frantic as he removed his hands from my hair to trail them down my back instead. The feeling sent a frenzy of internal goosebumps down my entire body, and I never wanted him to stop.

His tongue touched my lips, and my chest heated as I parted my lips for him. The moment his tongue touched mine, that heat in my chest turned to a raging fire, making me move my hands to his chest to push him up against the door.

All these feelings were new to me. The kisses. The fire. The emotions. Kaleb's hands were still trailing down my spine, sending waves of electricity throughout my body. No one had ever kissed me like this before, let alone touched me in a way that made my body sing. I could see why it was addictive. The need for more of him. The way I wanted to crawl all over him and explore every part of his body with my own.

He must have followed my train of thought because his hands found the bottom of my sweatshirt, and his fingers touched my bare skin, trailing along the spot above the waistband of my leggings. His touch made me shiver with excitement.

He broke our kiss. "We can stop," he panted. His forehead leaned against my brow, eyes locked on mine. His hands stopped trailing, fingertips resting on my bare skin. He waited for permission. I could see the want in his eyes—the question. I was sure it reflected my own.

Instead of answering him with words, my eyes fell to my hands on his chest, and I watched them trail down and around his back before looking back up to him. His eyes had also followed my hands, but they locked with mine again as my fingers grabbed the hem of his shirt in the back, and I slipped my hands underneath to lay precisely where his hands were on my back. His warm skin sent waves of heat into me as our gazes locked. But I didn't stop my hands there. I ran them slowly up the curve of his back and around his sides against the soft muscular skin and found my way up his chest until he lifted his arms so I could remove his shirt, revealing eyes full of desire.

I'd seen Kaleb shirtless at pool parties or during a hot summer day in the heat of a backyard war. Hell, I saw him shirtless last week at his house. This time, though—this time it was different. I wanted to study every inch of him, touch every curve and dent along his body. I dropped his shirt on the floor, and my hands found their way back to his bare chest, which was now on display. I ran my fingers along his naked torso. The feel of his skin was so soft and warm against my fingertips, his skin a shade darker than my own. His muscles were defined enough to let me know he'd been working hard in the gym this year.

He let my fingers explore for a moment before he got impatient, and his hands found their way back to the hem of my sweatshirt. He ran them up my back, lifting the sweatshirt away from my body just as I'd done to him.

It felt reminiscent of earlier when I had removed it myself.

For a very different reason.

My breath caught in my throat.

The bond mark.

My eyes snapped to him. "Stop!" The word came out harsher than I meant, but his hands stopped immediately, and confusion replaced the desire on his face.

I couldn't tell him. I couldn't show him. Yes, Kyler had to run his fingers across the mark to make it visible, but did I have to do something to make it disappear? Would Kaleb be able to see it? I didn't want to find out and explain it to him right now.

"Is everything okay?" He was furrowing his brow, looking at my hands pressed on his bare chest as I pushed myself away, pressing him back into the wall again. "Ow!" He hissed. I must have pushed harder than I thought.

I dropped my hand from his chest and used it to fix my sweatshirt back into place while taking a few steps back. "Sorry! I just—"

He stepped away from the wall and turned around to examine it, finding nothing there. But when I saw his bare back, my hand flew to my mouth. A long, jagged scar ran across it that I had never seen before. My jaw went slack as I took in the raised scar tissue there.

"Kaleb," I whispered, reaching out to trace my fingers along the scar. It looked old, but when my fingers brushed it, Kaleb whipped around with another hiss of pain.

He sneered at me, which made me recoil, pulling my hands with me. When he saw how I reacted, his expression dropped to one of resentment. "Sorry, that's just—" his eyes flashed with pain before he focused on me again, and they softened. "It's tender."

"What happened?" My voice was barely there. I knew I had scars he didn't know about, but they were more recent, and I wasn't sure how to tell him how I got them. As far as I knew, he didn't keep things from me, and I thought I knew about all his scars. When we were younger, there was a day in the tree house where we were all comparing scars, telling stories about how we'd gotten them, and seeing who had the most. I won, being the most adventurous and clumsy of all of us, but Kaleb didn't have many to share that day. And he never mentioned a scar on his back, nor had I seen it when he'd been shirtless around me. Or maybe I hadn't been paying close enough attention.

His head dropped, and he stared at the ground for a while before speaking. "I don't know that I'm ready to talk about it," he whispered.

Acid boiled in my stomach. That meant it wasn't an accidental injury like most of mine were. This was serious. The fact that Kaleb hid this from me made my heart hurt. I thought we told each other everything. I realized then that it could be much more traumatic to talk about than I was thinking, and I reached to tilt his chin up.

"Kaleb, you don't have to tell me what happened, but I want you to know I'm here for you." My voice cracked, thinking of what could have happened to him. He was avoiding my gaze, but I pushed on. "Your secrets are safe with me. *You* are safe with me. Always." When he still didn't meet my gaze, a thought popped into my head, and I clenched my jaw. "Did someone do that to you?" My voice was rough. The idea of anyone putting their hands on Kaleb made me want to throat-punch them. Who would want to hurt him? What could leave a scar like that? Kaleb was silent, which gave me my answer. "Was it your dad?" I seethed.

He whispered, "I said I don't want to talk about it." His eyes met mine, tears pooling and then spilling down his face. "Please don't make me." He choked out.

I dropped the tension in my shoulders and cupped his face in my hands. "Okay." I rubbed my thumb along his cheekbone. "Okay. I'm sorry. I won't bring it up again." The tears spilled down his cheeks at whatever horrors he was keeping from me. He didn't need me to focus on that, though. And I didn't need to know right now. He needed me with him in the moment. To meet him right where he was. "I'm with you," I recited his words. "Right here." I placed one of my hands over his heart on his chest. "You're safe." I slowly wrapped my arms around his torso and pulled him close, holding him tight and laying my head on his shoulder while he laid his cheek on my head.

I thought I knew everything there was to know about him. We'd spent so much time together that it was almost impossible not to know. And it hurt that he didn't feel like he could share his trauma with me as I could with him, but I knew it was a different kind. One that happened behind closed doors. Everyone knew about my dad and sister dying, but only those closest to me knew how it affected me, and only Kaleb truly knew how bad my panic attacks were. Kaleb's past was different, but it was also his to share. I couldn't force him to do that. He would never do that to me.

His body began to shake, and I felt the sobs working through it. I squeezed him tighter, carefully keeping my hands away from the tender scar I now knew was there. I pressed kisses along his shoulder and neck occasionally, trying my best to comfort him.

We stayed like that for a while before his body finally relaxed into mine. I kissed his shoulder again and pulled away to look at his face. His eyes were puffy and red, his cheeks still wet from the tears, but the sniffling had stopped. I'd never seen such sadness on his face before. This guy only showed happiness most of the time. It just goes to show that even some of the happiest people in your life could be going through something awful, and you would never know.

I helped wipe away his tears and led him over to his bed. "You should sleep," I told him, pulling back the covers for him.

He crawled over to the far side of the bed, and I pulled the covers up over his legs, but he stopped my hand and met my eyes. "Stay with me." If the look in his eyes didn't do it, the crack in his voice did.

My shoulders dropped, "Of course." He lifted the blanket for me, and I crawled in next to him.

He wrapped his arm around my hips and pulled me flush against him in one swift movement, making me his little spoon. He settled his chin between my shoulder and neck, his other arm worming under my body and around my waist. One of his legs nudged the back of my knees, and I obliged with a small laugh, letting his leg slip between mine. He took a deep breath, and his body relaxed into me as he released it into my ear. "Goodnight, girlie."

I shook my head and suppressed a smile, but I heard a smile in his voice. I wanted to keep that smile, so I said, "I thought I told you that this won't work if you keep calling me that."

He turned his head to kiss my cheek. "Yet here we are."

I turned to meet his mouth with mine and kissed him quickly. "I'm starting to regret my decision," I teased.

He let out a laugh through his nose. "Don't lie. It's growing on you."

I turned my head back to lay on the pillow and adjusted myself in his arms to be as close as I could. "Goodnight, goobis."

He chuckled in my ear, then buried his face in my neck, kissing me there once before laying his head back on the pillow behind mine. I lay there listening to his breathing slow and felt his arms loosen around me before I allowed myself to close my eyes. I hoped that his dreams were free of nightmares and that the horrors of his past wouldn't appear in them.

XXXV
Little Girl Gone

I woke the following day to a loud banging on the door. Kaleb's arm was still draped across me, but he jolted at the sound and rolled out of bed as the pounding continued. I groaned loudly to ensure whoever was at the door knew they were unwanted. Swinging my feet to the floor, I sat on the edge of the bed when the door creaked open, and Kaleb let out a long breath.

"Is she in there with you?" Kyler demanded. I rolled my eyes and started rubbing my temples. It was too early in the morning for his attitude.

Kaleb stepped aside so Kyler could see me and gestured with his arm. "Right where I left her," he said with a sleepy smile. "In my bed." He glanced back at Kyler with that smile still on his face, but it turned into more of a grin.

My cheeks flushed. It was *way* too early for this drama. Kyler's nostrils flared as he took me in. "Breakfast meeting. Five minutes." Those words seemed to take a lot of restraint from him. Like he had meant to say more but could only manage those four. He disappeared from the doorway, leaving Kaleb dumbstruck at the encounter.

"Well, that was awkward," Kaleb mumbled, closing the door and making his way back to the bed.

"You didn't make it any better," I grumbled, feeling the heat fade from my cheeks as the sleepy brain fog cleared and a caffeine headache settled in.

"What do you mean?" He strode straight for me on the edge of the bed, arms outstretched. I stood before he got there, stepping out of his reach with my arms crossed. He paused before me, furrowing his brow.

"You made it seem like we slept together," I said.

"We did *sleep together*," he shrugged, but at the look on my face, he dropped his shoulders and covered the distance between us, placing his hands gently on my arms. "I'm sorry," his tired, whiny voice came out. "He's just— he gets under my skin and makes me nervous when it comes to you. I mean, look at the guy. He looks like he stepped out of a men's fitness magazine!"

I pursed my lips at his assessment of Kyler. "Well, I can't argue with that because then I'd be lying. But his personality came from a dumpster fire." I didn't want to mention that he'd been growing on me. Last night was enough of a confirmation. Kaleb hadn't mentioned it, but I could tell it bothered him that I was being more friendly with Kyler. "Besides," my arms loosened their hold on each other, and I moved them around Kaleb's waist, pulling him closer to me, "I'm dating you, goobis. And I think you're *way* better looking." I winked and captured a kiss from him.

He smiled beneath my kiss before returning it and pulling away. "What is this breakfast meeting anyway? Am I allowed to attend?"

I shrugged, "He didn't say you couldn't." Slipping out of his grasp, I walked to the door. Kaleb may not have mentioned it, but I needed to brush my teeth. "I'll be right back."

The hallway was empty when I entered it. Kyler's door was shut, and he was nowhere to be seen. Didn't matter, though. He shouldn't have been so triggered by me sleeping with Kaleb, even if that was all we did. I didn't know what a bonded dragon and rider relationship was like, but my dating life definitely shouldn't affect it. I'd have to make sure that was clear when I got the chance.

When I got to my room, I headed straight for the bathroom. The clock said it was barely past six when I was done. I glanced at the clothes I slept in and opted to change after the meeting.

As I crossed to the door, something on the desk caught my eye. It was the present I hadn't opened last night. It must have slipped my mind after the Nerf battle. I paused in the doorway momentarily before deciding I could open it after the meeting.

Kaleb was waiting for me at his door. I hooked my arm through his, and we joined everyone in the kitchen. They were all seated around the island, sleep in their eyes, exhaustion seeping from each of them. We all sat around the island while Kyler and Theo faced us from where they leaned against the sink. Kyler still seemed to be seething from the encounter at Kaleb's door because he avoided looking at either of us.

Theo clapped his hands, causing my headache to spike at the loud noise. "The events at the dance this weekend will be crucial to our success—"

"Ugh…" Leighton yawned from her seat. "Why are we discussing this so early on a Tuesday?" I looked over to see her rubbing her eyes.

"Yeah," I yawned. "Can we at least get some coffee?" I said, my voice strained as I spread my arms wide and stretched. Lord knew I would need coffee if they wanted me to remember the details of this meeting.

Kyler turned around and produced four cups of coffee, placing them in front of us. He put the cream and sugar directly in front of me but still didn't look at me. I rolled my eyes and made up my coffee, passing the creamer to Leighton's tired but outstretched hand when I was finished. I took my first sip, closed my eyes, and sighed audibly.

"Everybody satisfied with their morning joe?" Theo smiled, his eyes bright. I still thought it should be illegal for someone to have that much energy this early. But we all nodded, and he went on. "As I was saying, the dance is crucial to our success with transferring Jordin and Mitch. We must make it seem like you are solely there to enjoy yourselves. They will indeed suspect that there is something else going on, but you going," he looked pointedly at me, "will hopefully draw them out—"

"WHAT?!" Kaleb sputtered his coffee. "You're using her as *bait?!*"

Shit. I hadn't given him a heads-up. I laid my hand on his forearm, "Kaleb, I already kne—"

"That's supposed to make it better?" He shouted back. "You were kidnapped and tortured by these people. While these guys were supposedly protecting you!" He gestured toward Kyler, Mari, and Theo. "What makes you think it'll be different this time around?"

"Kaleb," I started, but Kyler interrupted me.

"Because you know about it," he stated, capturing Kaleb's attention immediately. "And you won't let anything happen to her, right?" He raised his eyebrows at Kaleb. "You want to protect her? Here's your chance." Kaleb eyed Kyler, the tension from this morning still lingering. But he didn't want to deny anything Kyler was saying. I could tell he was fighting an inner battle. "We will all be on watch, but she's yours to protect, got it?"

Kaleb shifted his gaze between Kyler, me, and Theo, presumably searching for a way to argue, but eventually, he gave Kyler a curt nod. "On one condition."

Kyler raised a brow, waiting for him to continue.

Kaleb lifted his chin and set his jaw. "Teach me to fight."

A smile played at Kyler's lips, but he dipped his head. "Consider it done."

Oh no. That didn't seem like a good idea *at all*. Kyler teaching Kaleb to fight? Who knew what kind of tension they'd take out on each other? Perhaps Mari could be Kaleb's teacher, and I could spar with Kyler. Though, that didn't seem much better on my end. Maybe Theo.

Theo continued to lay out the plan for the dance, which was pretty straightforward: show up and have a good time, but be on guard and keep communication open.

Kaleb gave me a weird look at that last suggestion, and I couldn't decide if I wanted to tell him that I could speak to Kyler in my mind. On one hand, it would be better to tell him the truth and not keep secrets. But on the other hand, he already thought of me as an alien, so who knows what this new confession would lead to. I decided I would tell him later if it came up again. For now, I just shrugged and continued listening to Theo's instructions.

He gestured to Kyler, though, meaning I missed something, but Kyler took over speaking. "The next four days are going to consist of training. We want you four to be as prepared as possible for whatever might happen. Three of you already train in jiu-jitsu," Kaleb looked at me in surprise, and I just smirked at him, "so we will continue your training there, but also some—" he glanced at Kaleb, likely choosing his next words with care so he didn't give something away, "—other techniques that could help." Who knew what he meant by that? It made me a little nervous knowing what he was. "School hours will remain the same, but we will be in our training facility downstairs each evening after school. Tom and I will be your instructors, while Mari and Theo will be in and out as sparring partners. Any questions?"

Ken raised her hand, and Theo nodded at her. She lowered her hand slowly and hesitated before saying, "Roshan can still be my date to Prom, right?" How had I forgotten about Roshan? I wondered how Kendall would handle her relationship with him going forward. Maybe we could talk later and figure out our crazy dating lives together.

Theo answered, "Yes. As I stated, you will attend the dance as if nothing has changed." He turned to Leighton. "It's my understanding that you no longer have a date for the prom. Is that correct?"

I turned to Leigh in surprise, whose cheeks stained pink at the attention, but she nodded. I wondered when she had talked to Charlie — before or after she learned she was fae. Or maybe she told him for another reason...

"Would you mind being escorted by Kyler that night?"

The pink in her cheeks got brighter, and she started stuttering her words. "I mean—I cou—I don't see—If it's okay—" Her eyes found mine, but I widened mine in caution, imploring her not to finish that sentence. Instead, I gave her a look of encouragement, and she stopped stuttering, looking back to Theo. "I mean... Yeah, I guess."

I glanced at Kyler, who wasn't looking at anyone, but his jaw was set, his chin held high. He must have been told he was doing that because he didn't seem like the type of guy to volunteer to go to a dance, let alone with someone he hardly knew. When I looked back to Leigh, she was peering through her lashes to where Mari stood with a small smile. I knew if I looked in that direction, it would be too obvious, so I just assumed that Mari was smiling back, and I grinned at the thought.

"Any other questions?" Theo pressed. When no one answered, he clapped his hands together. "Alrighty then, off to get ready for school."

The school day passed relatively smoothly, with no sign of Aaidan or the Kool-Aid man (or whatever his name was). I'd thought my house blowing up would have been the talk of the school, but somehow, it had flown under the radar. I was convinced the explosion would have hurt or slowed the enemy down, but that didn't seem to be what Kyler or Theo thought. Everyone was on-site at the school today except Chief, who was still with Ma and Mitch at their temporary safe house, and Smiles, who had to keep up appearances at the hospital.

Since the girls were all getting ready at the house, Ken and Mari told their dates that a car would pick them up on Saturday and bring them to us.

After school, we were led downstairs to a training facility. I didn't know what to expect when we were taken down there, but it was not what I saw when I walked in.

There were several sparring mats, punching bags, and weights like a gym. Then, in another section were some life-size dummies, targets, and other contraptions hanging from the ceiling I'd never seen before. Lining the back wall was a hoard of weapons, ranging from swords and daggers to bo staffs and a bow and arrow. I thought I even saw a mace.

Well, that explained why Kyler was so fit— because there was no way he got to look like he did without a routine. I rounded on him, "You expect us to learn how to use all this before Saturday?"

Kyler chuckled, "Absolutely not. Those are just for display. Mostly." He walked over to a rack on the side full of wooden staffs and what looked like wooden swords. "These are what we will be instructing you with."

"It's like I stepped into one of those medieval times training facilities from my books," Kaleb whispered beside me, his jaw open in awe. I had no idea what books he was talking about, but I smiled as I watched him take in the room around him in wonder.

Some of us giggled at Kaleb's comment, but he didn't care. I nudged Kaleb, "Looks like we get to live out some of those fighting scenes from our childhood days, huh?"

He was gawking at the weapons on the wall but nodded slowly. "Are these all yours?" He directed the question at Kyler, who nodded.

It was my turn to drop my jaw. "Where did you get them all?"

"Won them," Kyler stated as if it were no big deal. Before we could ask him to elaborate, he tossed a staff to each of us and lined us up on the mat. "These are just for practice, mostly for defense against weapons. Saturday, you will all be given these." He pulled a small cylinder the size of a chapstick from his pocket.

"*That's* supposed to prote—" Kaleb's mouth snapped shut as Kyler clicked a button on the small weapon.

It popped into a full-length staff within half a second, extending from both ends of the cylinder. "This is made of rafstos, whi—"

"Bless you," I whispered, making the twins and Kaleb burst out laughing. I tried to hide my smile without much success.

But Kyler didn't find my joke funny, or maybe he didn't understand. Because he tilted his head at me with no hint of a smile and asked, "What did you just say?" He easily twirled the staff around himself, waiting for my answer—a glint of something in his eyes.

"Nothing," I said innocently, earning a few more giggles from my friends. When he didn't continue right away, I gestured for him to do so dramatically, a smile playing on my lips as the other three continued suppressing their laughter.

Kyler squinted at me, "This is serious, Sunshine."

That got my friends to stop laughing. All of them gave me a look. The grin disappeared from my face, and I tried to clear my throat, but that did nothing to hide the red creeping up my neck. "Get on with it then," I said, folding into myself to hide my embarrassment.

Kyler had never used that nickname in front of them so casually before, and they all knew it was what my dad used to call me. The twins hadn't heard someone call me that since he died. He'd called me that in front of Kaleb the other day, but he was so embarrassed by what was said before that I don't think it registered. I'm sure the comfort with which Kyler used the nickname told them all they needed to know about how often he used it. Sure, the girls thought there could be something between us, but that didn't mean the nickname wouldn't be jarring to them. I knew Kaleb would take it the wrong way, though, especially after our conversation this morning. I was sure I'd have to put out a fire later.

I reached for Kaleb's hand, but he pulled it away, clasping it behind his back with the other. When I looked up at his face, he was glaring at Kyler.

My stomach dropped. I knew I should have told Kaleb more about the situation between Kyler and me— How no matter how many times I asked, Kyler wouldn't stop calling me Sunshine. But *I'd* gotten used to it. I'd grown comfortable with it, even. Of course, Kaleb would read more into it than what it was, which to me was just friendly banter. But I'm sure Kaleb only saw a threat like he did this morning in his bedroom. I couldn't help but think that maybe he was right.

Especially when I turned back to Kyler and saw a smug grin on his face.

He'd done it on purpose.

I clenched my jaw. Yes. I would be putting out a fire later.

But I would also be starting one.

Once he saw the look on my face, Kyler's smug one disappeared. He cleared his throat and held the extendable staff out in front of him. "These are made out of rafstos," he glared at me, daring me to speak again, but when I didn't, he went on, "It is the strongest metal in either realm. Difficult to bend and even harder to break. It may look thin and fragile, but it will protect you from most weapons better than a wooden staff."

Kyler collapsed the rafstos staff and grabbed a wooden one, then proceeded to show us the basics of handling. He started us off with the simple spinning techniques before moving into blocking. Since most of our training this week would be learning how to defend ourselves, he wanted to start with defense. The girls and I exchanged knowing looks but didn't interrupt.

Once we had all shown him the proper forms of blocking, he pulled each of us onto the mat to have us practice the blocks against his movements. Leighton went first. I hadn't ever trained with them, but they were also training with Tom, so I knew they'd be good. When Leigh got into position, she looked like a real warrior. It made me smile with pride.

Kyler faced her in his own warrior stance, but I ignored him. I had a feeling it would only make things worse with Kaleb if I watched the sleek movements that I knew Kyler had in his repertoire.

He made the first move, and Leighton blocked it easily. He drove to swing from below, but she, again, met his blow. They were moving slowly to start, but the more times she met his strikes, the faster he made the next one. Kyler began to make some fancy moves to try and throw Leighton off, but she never faltered. I grinned at how impeccable she looked doing it.

At one point, I heard the wooden staff connect with flesh and winced. Leighton cursed as her hand flew to her thigh, where Kyler had made contact.

Kyler stepped back, leaning on his staff. He hardly seemed phased while Leighton's shoulders moved with her deep breaths. "Excellent, Leighton." He gave her a close-lipped smile and turned to Ken. "Kendall, you're up."

Leigh and Ken switched spots. If I thought Leighton looked like a natural, then Kendall looked like a professional. Her movements were easy and swift, her footwork was evidence of Tom's teaching, and she nearly made it off the mat unharmed. But her colorful curse came when Kyler's staff connected with her shoulder.

Kyler pointed at me with his staff as Kendall stepped back into line. I glanced at Kaleb, but he wasn't looking at me. He was studying his staff, practicing his spins, and looking slightly nervous. Who knew what was going through his mind? Martial arts was one thing, but staffs and jiu-jitsu were totally different.

I stepped forward and faced Kyler, my jaw set and eyes focused. He gave me a slight nod before his first strike. When I watched him with the twins, he used the same routine. But, of course, he'd changed it up for me. Instead of striking high first, he struck low. I blocked it quickly and anticipated his next move by blocking his upper strike. His eyebrows rose in surprise for a split second before continuing his movements. I stopped each one—never missing a beat, often blocking before he'd fully made his next move.

He wasn't prepared when I struck out at him offensively, but he blocked it. Surprise flashed across his face again, but I didn't stop. I made my favorite three-combo strike, and his leading foot retreated. I held back a grin as I spun my staff and hit his with a cross, up, then stab. He swept the stab up like I'd planned, and I used another upward strike. It hit home.

His knee buckled as I caught the back of it, and he cursed.

I smirked and pulled my staff back to my side, leaning on it like he had.

He straightened and mirrored me, "Why didn't you tell me you knew staff work?"

"You never asked," I said, shrugging. I picked up my staff and returned to the line, glancing at Kaleb again, who grinned from ear to ear. I winked, and his eyes shone brighter.

I took my place next to him on the line and bumped his shoulder in encouragement. His smile faded as he looked at Kyler, who had just called him to the mat.

Kaleb took a shuddering breath and stepped onto the mat.

XXXVI
The Last of the Real Ones

Kyler started slow like he had with us, and Kaleb had a great response time. He used his breathwork properly and even seemed to anticipate Kyler's moves. It took a little longer for Kyler to get up to speed with his movements like he did with the twins and me.

The boys started grunting as each blow was met. Their jaws were set. Their concentration was unbreakable. The girls and I exchanged glances. This was either going to be really good or really bad.

I watched Kaleb with admiration, impressed by how quickly he caught on. He was a quick learner like me, but I never expected him to fight like this.

Nor did I think I would be so turned on watching him fight. He wore a cut-off shirt, showing off his muscular arms, glistening with sweat. It also gave me sneak peeks of his chest as it flexed with every movement of the staff. I felt that chest last night, but, *Damn, when did he get so fit?* I put my thumbnail in my mouth to try and conceal the smile that appeared on my face.

Ken nudged me, pursing her lips and raising her eyebrows suggestively. "Hot, isn't it?"

I grinned and nodded, watching Kaleb as he almost struck Kyler's shoulder. "Who knew Kaleb was so good?" I breathed, giving him a slow once-over.

She scoffed next to me, "I was talking about Kyler."

"Hmm. I didn't even notice," Which was true because I'd been focused on Kaleb. Ken's jaw dropped, but I just enjoyed seeing my man defend himself against a dragon in disguise.

They were both more focused now, sweat dripping down their foreheads, their staffs moving at incredible speeds. Kaleb was determined not to lose. Kyler was determined to win. I could see it in their furrowed brows. Their movements became impossible to follow.

Then I saw it. The move that would end the match.

Kyler swept his staff at Kaleb's feet while he was recovering from a high strike, taking his feet out from under him. Kaleb swore on his way down. He was silenced as his back hit the mat, knocking the wind out of him.

As a good sport, Kyler reached his hand out to help him up immediately. Kaleb groaned but took his hand and was quickly pulled to his feet. He nodded at Kyler, and his eyes met mine.

I bit my lip and used my hand as a fan dramatically. He pulled in his lips as his ears reddened, understanding what I meant. His eyes shifted to Kyler, and the gleam faded slightly when he looked back at me. But I made sure he knew what I meant as he returned to the line again.

I grabbed him by the front of his shirt and planted a kiss on his lips before he could protest. The kiss turned into a smile, and I pulled my mouth away but kept a hold of his shirt as I whispered, "That was *hot*."

He fought a smile, "The part when I fell on my ass?" His heavy breaths were hitting my lips as his eyes flickered between mine.

I shook my head, "The part where you almost kicked his." And kissed him again. It wasn't a lie. There were several moments when I thought Kaleb might get Kyler, but Kyler's impossible speed stopped the winning blow every time. I released his shirt and pulled him back in line as Leighton went up against Kyler again. "I thought you said martial arts was just a hobby," I whispered.

Kaleb shrugged, "It is. I just happen to be really good." He winked.

"I'll admit, I haven't held a staff in a few years, but it felt more familiar the longer we sparred." He glanced at me sideways and grinned, "I almost had him?"

I mirrored his grin, "You did. He's just hella fast." I turned my eyes to the mat to see Leighton jump a sweep and land a hard blow on Kyler's staff above his head. She tried my move of hitting the back of his knee, but he blocked it and tapped her shoulder, ending the match.

We each took another turn with Kyler, and after a quick water break, he paired us with each other. Since we'd all been trained in staff work and knew defense rather well, he switched to correcting our form for strikes and how to get out of being on guard if we were stuck conceding steps. Each of us had a turn with each other, Ken being the only one who could beat me, and she smacked my ass so hard with the staff that I squealed. She had to suppress a laugh. It was definitely going to leave a mark.

By dinner break, we were all exhausted and starving. We ate silently, letting our bodies recharge, and grumbled when Kyler announced it was time to go back down for hand-to-hand combat.

Kaleb seemed more apprehensive about close combat, but I told him it would be similar to his martial arts class, only more grappling than kicking. Mari, Theo, and Tom joined us, and Kyler paired us off. When he put Leigh with Mari, I couldn't help but grin to myself as her cheeks turned pink.

He paired Kendall with Theo and Kaleb with Tom, and I rolled my eyes as he pointed at me and said, "You're with me."

I gave him a sarcastic grin, "Looks like we'll make it thirteen after all, huh?" Mari and Theo chuckled under their breath, and I gave them a wink before turning to Kaleb. He was scowling at Kyler, but I grabbed his chin and made him look at me. "Tom is the best teacher. You'll catch on quickly. I'm gonna go kick his ass," I gestured towards Kyler with a nod of my head, "so you can watch him tap out, okay?"

"I'd rather make him tap out myself," he grunted.

"Don't worry. You'll get your chance." I kissed him before he could respond and stepped onto the mat that Kyler claimed. "No cheating," I told Kyler, tapping my head to be sure he understood.

"Wouldn't dream of it." The corner of his lip twitched up, but he took up his fighting stance. He made the first move. I shook my head. *Predictable.*

In two moves, I had Kyler in a headlock. I was on his back, my legs wrapped around his torso. He was struggling against my hold, so I whispered right in his ear, "You gotta stop thinking you can beat me."

"Oh, I can beat you," he grunted and used his strength to roll us over. I kept my grip on his torso, but my headlock broke. It gave him the opportunity he needed to twist me around to his front side and slide an arm under one of my legs.

But that cost him because now I had the space to lock my legs around his neck. I let him think he was deterring me by getting his arm under my leg and saying, "You have yet to prove that." Then I struck, pulling my now loose leg up over his shoulder and bringing my other one up to meet it so fast that he didn't even realize they were both there until he was struggling against them again. "Tap out," I said.

He growled, but that was the first time he tapped out immediately.

Apparently, everyone else had been watching because applause echoed in the space. I released Kyler and helped myself up, finding Mari there with a huge grin on her face.

"That was incredible! You let him think he had you, didn't you?" At my nod, she shook her head. "I don't know if there's anything I can teach you if you're that good at jiu-jitsu already. How long have you been training with Tom?"

"Six months?" I breathed heavily, "But I've always had this weird knack of learning things quickly in a very short amount of time. Kind of like a hyperfixation." I noticed Kyler listening but pressed on anyway, "I also have this weird fear of being trapped, so I have studied every way out of every hold you can think of. Some call it being competitive, but I just want to be prepared, ya know?"

Mari nodded, "Well if I can't train you in jiu-jitsu, we can always hit the weights." She winked and walked back to her mat with Leigh, who waited nervously.

To no one in particular, I said, "I think I need a different partner." Despite beating Kyler quickly, I was still catching my breath. I glanced at Kaleb, who was squaring up with Tom. He was getting the basic rundown of sparring, nodding, and mirroring the movements. Had he even seen me beat Kyler?

"Can I have a go against the champ?" Theo piped up. I turned to him and saw a huge grin on his face. "I think I've got a chance." He was practically bouncing on his toes. Kyler was taller than Theo and definitely more muscular.

I wasn't sure how he thought he could beat me if Kyler couldn't, but I shrugged and said, "Sure!" Ken switched mats with me, and I squared up against Theo. Even Mari and Leigh paused to watch. "Ready?" I grinned.

His smile disappeared, and that was the moment I knew I'd made a mistake. Theo's eyes flashed gold as he gave me what I can only describe as an evil grin. "Ready."

I swallowed thickly and gave him the signal.

Theo dropped and swept at my feet, but I jumped. That was his intention. He sprung up from his crouched position and grabbed me around the waist. The quick movement caught me by surprise, and that's all it took to drop my guard. My back met the mat as he crashed into me. I wiggled to get out of his grasp, but he pinned me by the hips with a quick mount. I positioned myself to escape, but he tucked his feet under my legs just as I tried to buck him off. His arms caged me in. I moved to swipe them out of the way, but he used his legs to flip us over. His legs were wrapped tightly around my waist. That was his mistake. It left me in the offensive position.

Or so I thought.

Before I could make my move, he released one of his legs. It wrapped around and met the other one, just like I'd done with Kyler, and that was that. I was in a headlock that was impossible to get out of. I tried the only escape I knew from that position, but his grip was too tight.

It was no use.

He had me.

I tapped out.

He released me and bounced up so fast that he offered me his hand before I'd recovered enough to sit up. He looked to Kyler as he pulled me to my feet, "How long?"

Kyler lifted his chin, "Forty-two."

"Seconds?!" Ken shrieked.

"Gosh darn it!" Theo stamped his foot. "I thought I beat my record."

My jaw dropped. This sweet man was far more dangerous than I ever expected him to be. I didn't want to know how lethal he was with weapons. Or as a dragon. "You've been playing me, Theo."

He placed a hand on his heart, his face showing mock shock. "Little ol' me? Never." He waved me away but winked. "I just don't usually get to show off like that."

I looked at Kyler, "Forty-two seconds? Really?" He nodded, and I turned back to Theo. "What's your record?"

"Thirty-seven." He smiled, showing all of his pearly whites.

"Damn," Ken and Leigh said in unison.

I squinted at him with a grin. "Against who?"

His dark complexion turned a tad darker in what I assumed was a blush. "My mate."

My eyes widened, wondering if that meant his wife or if it had a different meaning where we were from. I gave a slow nod as a grin spread across my face. "Impressive." I didn't want to go out like that, though. I felt like I'd hardly gotten a move in with him because I'd been so caught off guard. "Care to go again?"

He grinned, "Well, well. You are a 'challenge accepted' kinda girl, aren't you?"

I squared up. "That's me, alright."

He mirrored me. "Let's go girl."

Sparring went on for a few more hours. I got paired with everyone except Kaleb, who claimed he needed a little more time to practice with Tom before he fully went into sparring with us. Both Ken and Leigh were much better than I predicted, and I didn't know why it surprised me. We had the same teacher.

Theo was the only one who beat me, though Mari came very close in one match. She may have gotten distracted by something—or someone—because her grip lost its strength for half a second, which was enough for me to turn the tables on her and lock her up.

Kyler avoided putting himself against me again, probably to avoid embarrassment. He did end up trading spots with Tom a few times to teach Kaleb himself, as Kaleb had requested. Seeing them on good terms seemed strange, but I wasn't about to comment for fear of making it stop.

When we were dismissed for the night, I walked Kaleb to his door and told him I was going to shower and sleep in my own bed tonight. I didn't want another wake-up call like this morning.

"I could come join you in the shower," he said gruffly, closing the distance between us by fisting my shirt and pulling me to him.

My stomach flipped at the idea, but I knew it wasn't the best time for that. "Not tonight. Not in this house," I said, but I walked my fingers up his chest to his chin and pulled his mouth down to mine. Before my lips touched his, I whispered, "When things have settled down, I promise we will have more time to... explore."

His pupils dilated before he claimed my mouth with his. "I can't wait."

"Kaleb?" I said before pulling back too far. There was no good time to bring it up, but I supposed now was better than never. "You know he only calls me Sunshine to get under my skin, right?"

Kaleb closed his eyes and let out a hefty breath. "That guy flips from asshole to charmer and back so quickly," he said, then opened his eyes to meet mine. "Did he try to tell you he had no idea about the surprise party?"

My look of surprise spoke volumes. There was no way... "He said he told you guys not to do it," I mumbled, stepping back from Kaleb to study his face.

He pursed his lips and shook his head. "He said you needed a moment of levity or something, so he sent Mari and me to get a cake during your lesson and pulled you away after so we could get ready."

The whole thing with the mark was a ploy to hide the surprise party? But the bond was real... so he used it as a distraction until they were ready. He probably could have told me in front of everyone that he'd chosen me as his rider. Well, his dragon had. I guess they had good timing then. The question of what the mark on his hand was was still burning a hole in my skull.

"Rayleigh?" Kaleb pulled me from my thoughts. "Everything okay?"

"Yeah." I shook my head at the thoughts that were rising up. "You're right, though. He acts one way one minute and totally different the next. It's annoying, honestly." A yawn forced its way out of me, and when it finished, I said, "I'm exhausted. I'll see you in the morning."

He pulled me into a hug and kissed my forehead. "Goodnight, girlie."

I rolled my eyes. "Goodnight, goobis." And turned to walk to my room alone.

After working up a serious sweat trying to beat Theo, the shower felt incredible, but I had to admit it was nice to have a tough opponent. It was rather infuriating how fast he could move, though.

I walked out of the bathroom in my robe while brushing my hair to get one of the ridiculously comfy nightgowns. They'd grown on me. I loved the smooth silk against my skin when I slid into it.

As I turned to change in the bathroom, I noticed the gift on my desk again. I'd totally forgotten about it. For a split second, I thought about waiting, but it was only my birthday for a couple more minutes. So I crossed the room to the desk and sat down to open it. I set my hairbrush down and pulled the present into my lap.

The box wasn't very big, but it was on the heavier side. I had no idea what it could be because I hadn't told anyone here about my birthday, let alone what I wanted… I peeled off the tape holding the box shut, and opened the top flaps. I took the tissue paper off the top and sucked in a sharp breath at what lay underneath.

It can't be…

But it was.

I reached in and pulled out my snow globe.

It looked brand new. But the same. The trees and meadow were perfectly intact, and the new sparkles floated through the water to create the perfect rainy-day look.

Tears filled my eyes. I thought it'd been lost in the fire. That they hadn't thought to save an already broken snow globe. But I was never more happy to be wrong.

Something caught my finger on the bottom of the stand. I tipped it over and found a knob. That wasn't there before. Did they modify it? Or was it missing that piece initially? When I looked closer, I gasped.

A music box? Dad never mentioned it played music.

I twisted the knob until it wouldn't twist anymore and then released it. As soon as the music started playing, I covered my mouth as tears filled my eyes.

It was the song Dad used to sing to me.

The emotions that surfaced were ones I'd been holding back, keeping at bay over the last few days. With so much going on, I had barely let myself feel anything. So that's what I did. I allowed myself to feel it all. The pain of losing Mitch. Ma's story about who my real parents were. Being kidnapped and tortured. Finding out I wasn't who I thought I was. Learning my stalkers were hunting me. Kyler, Mari, Theo, Smiles, *and* the sheriff were dragons. Kaleb... everything that happened with him. It all ran through me, and when the song ended, I took a deep breath and sat up straight, wiping the tears from my face.

I set the snow globe down and searched the box to see who it was from. There. At the bottom. A note.

Written in purple ink.

> *This seemed important.*
> *I took the liberty of having it repaired.*
> *Happy Birthday Sunshine*

There was no signature. But it didn't need one.

I jumped as a knock sounded at the door.

I set the box and note by the snow globe on the desk and went to answer it. It wasn't until I had my hand on the doorknob that I realized I was still in my bathrobe. I tucked it tighter around my body and only opened the door enough for my head to pop through.

It cracked open just as Kyler lifted his hand to knock again. He played it off by putting his hand on the door frame instead. His eyes traveled from my face down to my bathrobe, and I quickly grasped the highest open point to hold it closed.

"What do you want?" I whispered to him angrily.

His eyes jumped back up to mine, flashing that fierce blue before they softened a tad back to green. "I came to apologize."

My eyebrows shot up. This was not the same guy I met last week. Or maybe it was... "For what, exactly?" I echoed my own words from our similar encounter a week ago.

Surprise flashed across his face, and he gave me a small smile. But it disappeared quickly, his gaze falling to his feet. "I didn't know calling you Sunshine was so personal," he said quietly.

I opened the door a little more, crossed my arms, and leaned my shoulder on the doorframe. "Even after all the times I asked you to stop calling me that?"

He paused, considering my question. His voice was low when he said, "I wasn't aware your dad called you that."

My heart dropped to my feet. "How do you know that?"

His eyes found mine through his eyelashes. "Kaleb's thoughts are... loud." A knowing smile crossed his face as I realized his room was directly across from Kaleb's.

Heat traveled up my neck. I didn't want the answer to the question that crossed my mind. It would just make the heat now hitting my ears even hotter. I cleared my throat. "It doesn't bother me so much anymore," I confessed. The fact that I saved his life told me enough about the friendship that was forming between us, even if I didn't like to admit it to myself. But I had to. I'm sure the bond made an impact, too, but I don't think it would have changed anything between us if it wasn't there. He lifted his gaze to mine and gave me a half smile. "But," I said, holding up a finger, "you have to stop finding ways to get under Kaleb's skin."

Kyler cocked a brow. "Under his skin? Or yours?"

I rolled my eyes. "I know better than to ask you to stop getting under mine." This bond of ours already crossed boundaries I wasn't sure I was comfortable with, but I didn't think I could do anything about it.

He set his jaw and gave me a slight nod, a sparkle of something in his eyes. "I'll do my best." Something over my shoulder caught his eye. "You opened it."

I knew what he meant. "I did." Butterflies attacked my stomach as I tried to hide the genuine smile that crept up on me. Whether he knew what it meant to me or not, he still gave me the best birthday present ever.

Before I could change my mind—before I could think twice, I did the only thing that could convey what it meant to me. I pushed off the doorframe and moved to wrap my arms around him. It was all I could do to thank him for the priceless gift he gave me. His body stiffened under my embrace, likely not expecting it, but I squeezed him anyway, trying to convey all the words I couldn't find into that hug. My head landed right under his chin, and my ear lay on his chest, where I could hear his erratic heartbeat.

I was about to let go of his rigid body when he finally relaxed, and his arms slowly wrapped around me. Where I thought I'd find a rock-solid wall of a chest, I found a soft but strong embrace. His body was warm and comfortable against mine. It felt like it had been missing from my life for a long time, and I'd finally found my way back to him. He took a deep breath and laid his chin on my head. The gesture felt familiar.

The snow globe was my most treasured possession before it got destroyed, and I thought I had lost it. Kyler not only repaired it but revealed an element I hadn't known existed. The song healed me many times in the past and let me recover from some things even now. Kyler may not have known the effect that repairing the snow globe would cause, but I wasn't ready for him to know that just yet. Deep down, though, I knew something had solidified between us at that moment.

After everything we'd been through over the last few days, I considered him a friend.

Before any other dangerous thoughts could surface, I pulled away and broke the tension. I hadn't realized any tears had fallen until I saw the stains on his shirt. I quickly wiped the evidence from my face and looked up to find him studying me. "What?" I said.

He didn't say anything at first, keeping his eyes on my face. I ran my fingers through my still-damp hair, stepping back into my room. He wiped his face clear and took another deep breath. He was keeping something from me. I could tell. He wiped away the thought when he ran a hand down his face. Instead, he said, "You wanted to know what the mark on my hand said about you." He held up his left hand with the back of it facing me.

A rush of excitement ran through me from head to toe. Giddiness and nervousness rose up. I could only nod. He was going to show me evidence of who I was—proof of my powers and what I could do.

He reached his hand out in front of me, palm up.

I lifted my hand, slowly trailing my fingers across it. Lines and shapes appeared, along with some dots sprinkled among the design. Kyler exhaled, moving the loose hairs around my face, but I kept my gaze on his hand.

"This represents my air magic?" I stared at the design, which seemed to have a lot of lines for just one symbol.

"No." My eyebrows raised in surprise as I glanced up at him, but Kyler was studying the design. I felt his free hand join mine on his exposed palm, so I looked back down. As his finger followed a line running from his thumb to the heel of his hand, I felt the urge to mimic his movement. The magnetic pull was too strong to ignore. I gave in. I followed his path along the symbol he traced, the light touch sending electricity through my veins. Kyler's voice seemed to shake when he said, "*This* represents your air magic." He followed the path of another symbol to the edge of his palm, and I followed suit, unable to stop myself. "You also have earth magic, represented here." I gasped at his words, but he held up his finger. "And," he put his finger on the last symbol and started to trace it, "this represents your fire magic." The symbol started on his palm but extended onto his middle finger and looped down where his thumb met his palm. I followed the path to the end but didn't lift my finger from his hand as I processed what he said.

"Three elements?" It wasn't possible. I remembered reading about the elementals with more than one type of magic. They were extinct. There must have been some mistake. I met Kyler's gaze and saw what I could only describe as admiration in his eyes. "What does this mean?" I whispered.

"It means," he whispered back, "you're a lot more powerful than we imagined." Holding his hand up so the patterns on his palm faced me, he confirmed, "You're an Evanian."

XXXVII
Fire N Gold

"But Evanians— they're extinct," I breathed, knowing full well I wasn't mistaken.

"Or so the history books say," Kyler shrugged. He crossed his arms over his chest and leaned his shoulder on the doorframe. "There is no way to prove that all of them were killed in the war."

Questions rolled through my head, one after the other. I thought about grabbing my notebook, wanting to write down all my questions, but then I realized my best source was standing in my doorway. I turned my gaze back to him, trying to decide where to start. "If you didn't know I was an Evanian, why did Theo say I was 'the most powerful fae in all the realms'?"

He cocked a brow at me, "He said *one* of the most powerful."

"Same thing."

He rolled his eyes but answered me. "We were told you came from a line of Ignalians, the rarest and most dangerous fae. There are few left in our realm. You were thought to be one of the last, making you *one* of the most powerful fae... if that were true." He chuckled to himself a little.

"What?" I asked incredulously, thinking this wasn't a time for laughter.

He shook his head, a smile still playing on his lips. "Theo liked to refer to you as the 'forgotten flare.'" I raised a brow, and Kyler just shrugged, continuing his train of thought, "When Tom told us he thought you were Annysian, both Theo and I were surprised. When I saw this last night, though," he held up his palm again, "it all started to make sense. Why we were sent here with little information, how Koladon and Adarachi could trace your magic…" He replaced his arm across his chest and dipped his chin briefly, looking up at me through his lashes, "The *madí* may prove that you are, indeed, *the* most powerful fae."

"What's a *madí*?" I asked quietly.

"A fancy way of saying tattoo."

"Well, it could be wrong," I offered, not wanting to think about the fact that I had a matching tattoo with Kyler.

He shook his head. "It uses the point of connection to bring the blood to the surface, reading the mark of your lineage through that. I've only been researching rider bonds since…" He trailed off.

"Since ours was made?" I guessed, to which he nodded. "So you're not familiar with it like you are everything else?"

"No. Not as much as I'd like to be."

I thought for a moment about what he said. "Why were the Evanians targeted?"

Kyler took a deep breath, letting it out slowly as he contemplated how to respond. "A long time ago, a very powerful drakalasson decided that fae with the ability to control more than one element were too powerful. He had an irrational fear that they would try to control the realm with that power, simultaneously taking over the dragons' hierarchy as well as the Fae. This shifter was in the highest ranks of the court, with direct access to the Dragon King." He took a moment to clear his throat, then went on. "He manipulated the King into starting a war against the Fae as a means to eradicate the Evanians."

A dragon—with the ability to breathe fire, fly, and magic of their own—was scared of a Fae with more than one elemental power? Sure, they're more powerful with multiple, but how could they be more dangerous than a *dragon*? *They* had more than one ability. Why didn't that make them more dangerous?

"How could a dragon be intimidated by someone like me?" The question sounded even dumber out loud.

"You *are* pretty intimidating," he mused, a sparkle of something in his eyes as I scrunched my nose at him. The glimmer vanished when he went on, "No one knows why he was so threatened, but it's rumored that something happened to him when he was younger." Kyler adjusted himself against the doorframe.

Knowing that I would have more questions, as I always did, standing in the doorway to ask them didn't seem ideal.

I glanced over my shoulder into my room, contemplating, then turned back to Kyler and stepped back. "Do you want to come in and sit?" I gestured toward the chair at the desk. Of course, my books were still scattered on the floor, but I honestly didn't care.

He lifted his eyebrows, briefly gave me a once over, and said, "You sure?"

My cheeks burned when I realized, once again, that I was still in my robe. But I nodded, "I'll put pajamas on." The blush deepened when I realized a nightgown probably wasn't any less revealing, and I opted to grab sweatpants and a sweatshirt.

When I returned, I found him sitting among my books on the floor. Apparently, we were both floor people. He was holding *Fae Magic* and had a few other books open and laid out between his legs. Deciding that this was likely the best and most interesting study session I'd get, I joined him on the ground.

"What are you looking for?" I asked, sitting cross-legged with my hands in my lap, my back against my bed.

He didn't look up when he said, "These books are magically updated by the keepers of knowledge within our realm. So I'm looking to see if there's anything new since I've been here."

I gaped at him. "I'm sorry— what?"

He glanced up at me. "Whenever new information is acquired about certain subjects, it's added to the original scrolls, which will consequently change each book made from those scrolls." He grinned at my still gaping mouth. "Pretty cool, huh?"

"That's nuts!" I said, still not fully comprehending how that could be possible. "Wait, can anyone change the information in the books? What if one of the original scrolls gets destroyed? Are they kept in a secur—"

"Woah woah woah, slow down. You'll hurt yourself," Kyler said, then muttered, "Maybe I should stick to the notebook."

I kicked his foot where it sat inches from mine. "I don't know anything, dumbass. And apparently, you're the book hoard. So I'm gaining my knowledge the best way I know how. Questions."

He sighed, knowing I was right. He probably still regretted his decision to answer things in person, but he did anyway. "Only those given special permission by the Mitera can access the scrolls. None have ever been damaged due to the magic protecting them, so I don't know what happens if one is destroyed." He set down *Fae Magic* and picked up a book I hadn't gotten to yet called *Lineage of the Elementals*.

"Mitera?" The word sounded familiar and brought back a list of words I'd tried to keep track of when I was kidnapped. "Does that have something to do with Omada or Kidemos?"

Kyler gave me a quizzical look from over the top of the book. "The Mitera is what some might call the higher being of our realm. The Kidemos and Asteri are the warriors for either species, each chosen by Mitera. Kidemos are among the drakalasson, and the Asteri are among the fae. A team of these warriors is called an Omada." He went back to flipping through the pages of the book he was holding, obviously searching for something. "The knowledge hoarders are called Nosi."

I snickered at the word, and he glanced at me sideways. I shrugged, "It sounded like you called them nosey."

His expression told me he must know some of the Nosi, but he returned to the book. "They are nosey when they're on the hunt to acquire the details of the world."

"So, you, Theo, and Mari are all part of," I swallowed thickly, "my Omada?"

Kyler nodded, eyes still tracking down the page. "As are Tom, Smiles, and Chief Bass." He flicked through a couple more pages and finally stopped, scanning the words he found from top to bottom.

"Ah-ha. 'The last *known* Evanian was a woman with child over two centuries ago. She was found by a shifter trying to hide in a crystal cove and was—" He inhaled sharply, closing his eyes before whispering, "She was bound and burned alive."

My breath caught, but something he said caught my attention. Scooting myself over to a position where I could read the book over his shoulder, I scanned the page myself, asking, "Does it say if there were any witnesses?"

Kyler cocked his head, scanning the pages again himself. "No. It doesn't look like there was any hard evidence recorded…" He trailed off, flipping to the next page. "The only information on the shifter that found the Evanian was his name: Dimitri Makis."

"Does that name mean anything to you?" I asked, studying the name on the paper and wondering why a spark of familiarity lit up deep within me.

I felt, rather than saw, Kyler's head shake in answer as I leaned over his shoulder to look at the book he was holding. It occurred to me I was leaning on him and probably invading his personal space, but he didn't seem to mind. The closeness felt comfortable—normal even. I wasn't sure I was ready to acknowledge how nice it was to have that level of comfort with him. Trying not to make a big deal, I slowly moved back to my position, propped up against the bed. "Is me being alive proof that this Dimitri didn't kill the pregnant Evanian?" I whispered, hoping that was true. The idea that anyone would kill someone who was with child was repulsive, but this shifter sounded like a monster, binding and burning her.

Kyler stared at me silently, then said, "If she truly was the last Evanian, then yes." He put down the book and squinted at nothing in particular, then something like realization dawned on his face. "Your mother was sent here for protection as well. One can only assume it was because *she* was Evanian, too. Your father, though…" He trailed off again, and something clicked into place. He straightened and looked to his left, lifting his hand in the air and shoving it into a black hole—

I screamed but covered my mouth when he gave me a look over his shoulder. He turned back to the floating hole and peered into it. When

I looked closer at where his hand had disappeared, I realized it wasn't a black hole at all, but a window to his room, hovering in the air next to him. I could see the bookshelves he was rummaging through, and the familiar scent of old books wafted into my room.

He was manipulating space again. I didn't think I'd ever get used to that.

He leaned closer to the window and finally pulled back with a book in hand. The hole disappeared. I blinked, briefly wondering what would happen if the hole closed on his hand. He cleared his throat, pulling me from my thoughts. "Your father is indeed listed as Ignalian."

"There's a list of every elemental and their powers?" Trying to wrap my head around that, I peeked at the book's cover to find a title, but his hand covered most of the name.

Kyler closed the book. "No. But your father was part of the Omada assigned to your mother's protection. Each member of an Omada is recorded for recovery purposes." He stretched his hand to his left again, the window in space there appearing long enough for him to replace the book and retract his hand before it was gone again. When his focus returned to me again, he studied me. "I wonder how they kept her powers secret," he mulled over his question while keeping his narrowed eyes on me.

"We only found out about mine because of our bond." I gestured to his hand, which still displayed the markings of my powers. "Maybe she was never claimed by a dragon."

Kyler bristled, his eyes darkening at my words. "Chosen," he bit out. "Not claimed. Chosen."

I recoiled at his harsh tone. "Aren't they one and the same?"

"No." He worked his jaw. "Kavaltis bonds are a two-way street. Your magic could have rejected me." That was something I hadn't thought of. I didn't have time to question it as Kyler continued. "Dragons who *claim* fae brand them as their doulos. The Fae doesn't have a choice," His voice was gruff, like some memory surfaced that he didn't want to face.

I didn't know what that word meant, but the way he said it made my blood run cold. "What's that?"

His distant look came back to focus on me. "In nicer terms? A slave," he growled. I swallowed the lump in my throat and opened my mouth to ask my next question, but he stood abruptly. "That's a topic for another day. It's late."

I jumped up to follow him, "Kyler, wait," grabbing his elbow as he stepped out my door and into the hallway. He stopped walking but didn't turn around. I dropped my grip on his elbow and stepped back, clasping my hands in front of me. I knew I wouldn't get any more out of him about the doulos. It seemed like a raw topic. So I went back to the reason he came to my room. "This bond of ours—" I started, then realized I had no idea how to word what I wanted to ask. I went for blunt. "Is it what's causing this magnetic pull between us?"

Kyler went utterly still. It didn't seem like he was even breathing. He turned, ever-so-slowly, to face me. When his eyes locked on mine, the breath went out of me as his blue eyes glowed like fire but didn't disappear. His voice was low when he spoke, "Yes. It's calling for the first flight."

"Oh," I breathed. The thought of flying through the air on the back of a dragon sent a thrilling sensation through my veins. But that dragon being the man standing in front of me? My brain couldn't comprehend. "I'm not sure I'm ready for that."

He nodded, his eyes flickered back to green, no longer glowing. "I feel obligated to let you know that that feeling will only grow stronger the longer we wait." He took a hesitant step toward me, and the air between us instantly felt charged. "We could go now. Get it over with."

I tilted my head, trying to be casual, but my insides were churning. "You make it sound like a chore."

"Oh, it's anything but that." His eyes danced. "It'll be the greatest thrill of your life."

Suddenly, it didn't feel like we were talking about our bond anymore. But what if his words were true, and the only way to calm the magnetic pull between us was to go flying? There wasn't really a point in delaying it. I didn't particularly love the feeling of that pull towards him, especially being with Kaleb. If all it took to ease the tension was to fly with him, then— "Alright," I said, trying to calm the bubbles in my stomach that started the second I made the decision. "Let's go."

A smirk replaced the flash of surprise I caught. His eyes trailed my wardrobe for the third time that night, and he said, "You'll have to change."

रमरर

Twenty minutes later, I was walking onto the front lawn with Kyler. He had given me an outfit he called riding leathers, which clung to every curve of my body and felt like a second skin. They were midnight blue and, surprisingly, one of the most comfortable things I'd ever worn. He made me take everything else off, jewelry and all. He didn't want me to lose anything. I hesitated when I went to take off the bracelet Kaleb gave me. Was I betraying him by sneaking out of the house with Kyler? Even if it was for the bond, I wasn't sure how he would react if he knew everything. But he would question me sneaking out with anyone. I told Kyler I wanted to let Kaleb know I was going, but he said Kaleb was sleeping and I shouldn't wake him. He'd ask too many questions.

"We won't have to fly very long for the bond to be satisfied," Kyler said as we walked outside. "We'll stick around here to keep out of view of the city." He became more stoic the closer we got to flying. He must have had something else on his mind. "I'll wait until I feel the bond solidify, then bring us back down." I nodded, not understanding what that meant but knowing I'd find out soon enough. He stopped in the middle of the lawn and turned to me. "You may want to take a few steps back." He didn't smile. In fact, he seemed somewhat nervous.

I cocked my head, "Are you okay?"

He pursed his lips, looking at the ground. "I haven't shown you my dragon yet."

"Okay? And?"

"Just," his eyes found mine, something unreadable there as he said, "don't insult him."

"You're acting like you don't control him."

He barked a laugh, "Oh, I don't. Not in his true form. We may share the same mind, but his instincts differ from mine. If you don't approve of him, he'll be able to sense it."

I bit my lip, "You're telling me that if I don't tell him he's pretty, he'll what— burn me alive?"

He shrugged, "He's done worse."

My jaw dropped. Maybe this wasn't the greatest idea for a midnight activity. I scoffed, trying to cover my nerves. "What could be worse than being burned alive?"

"Loads of things," he said, taking in my expression and lifting one corner of his mouth. "Still wanna do this?"

Knowing it was inevitable, I nodded and told myself repeatedly not to even think insulting things. Although, I couldn't imagine who would want to insult a magnificent creature like the one I'd already seen.

I backed up several feet as Kyler took a deep breath and let it out slowly.

He made eye contact with me, and I nodded in encouragement. This whole thing was turning into something way more intimate than I anticipated. His green eyes shone brightly from this distance, but they turned blue right as his body started to shift.

XXXVIII
One Hell of a Team

Kyler's form started to change. The color of his skin faded and became a scaly texture. His neck elongated, and the rest of his body began to grow.

And grow.

And *grow*...

Just as I suspected, he was bigger than Theo. Much, *much* bigger.

His front legs landed on the lawn, shaking the ground and throwing me off balance. I bent my knees and threw out my arms to steady myself as I took in the dragon before me.

Remembering what Kyler had said right before he shifted, I spoke my thoughts out loud, but it came out more of a whisper, "Incredible."

The magnificent midnight blue dragon blew a breath of smoke toward me. It smelled like strawberries.

I grinned, "Even in this form, your breath smells like smoky strawberries." I took tentative steps toward him, feeling smaller with each one.

I hope he won't stop eating those lollipops because you know what we are now. A deep, rumbling voice responded in my head, and I stumbled back a step in surprise.

That wasn't Kyler. The deep tone was there, but this voice sounded... Happier? Lighter?

"I— Sorry," I started, unsure how I felt right then. "I— Wha— Sorry," I repeated, unable to find the right words. The *predator* on the lawn tracked my short, stumbling steps like a cat tracking a mouse, its tail flickering. I caught myself, took a deep breath, and remembered, again, what Kyler said before shifting. I said, "I-I don't mean to insult you, but you sound way less scary than what Kyler prepared me for." Was it insulting not to be scared of a dragon? I planted my feet, standing tall, and eyed the not-so-scary dragon.

The dragon lowered its head to eye level, his blue eyes sparkling with something like amusement. It was a sleek diamond shape like Theo's but had three layers of horns, starting from its brow. *It is no insult. I do not need to be frightening toward you. Therefore, I am not.* The dragon spoke in my head again. Was that the only way for dragons to talk to humans in this form? *Kyler has only seen me interact with one other female in similar circumstances. It does not surprise me that he worries for your safety.* Well, that would be something I'd have to hear about some other time. The dragon's gaze took me in from head to toe, and when his eyes met mine again, he purred, *Hello, Rayleigh.* One of his eyes blinked.

"Did you just wink at me?" I squeaked out, trying to hide a grin while continuing to admire the dangerously beautiful beast from a distance.

Perhaps. But worry not, I do not wink at just anyone. He winked again, and I couldn't help but laugh at this weird, flirtatious dragon.

I shook my head in disbelief, then asked, "Why was yo— er, Kyler's breath smoky in human form?" I didn't know why I needed to know or why I even asked when there were several other things I should have asked. Perhaps it was because I needed to distract him while my mind focused on other things. Like the long, scaly neck he stretched proudly, as if he were preening in the moonlight reflecting off his scales. Or how the tail curled around his feet still flitted, or his enormous wings settled against his body as he slowly lowered himself to the ground.

The dragon huffed a warm breath my way. *I fear that is my fault.* The dragon paused, emitting a low rumble. *We share one mind, as you know, which allows me to see through his human eyes and him to see through mine. Though sometimes, I like to push through.* That would explain the color-changing eyes... *The need to be near my prized possession caused inner battles for control, and things got... heated.* Prized possession? Was he referring to me? *Because of that, my smoky scent came through. He found a delicious way to calm me down, though.*

I couldn't suppress my laugh, "Strawberry lollipops? Really?"

He nodded. *They stopped me from forcing him to shift so I could meet you.* The dragon's shoulders moved in what I could only assume was its attempt at a shrug.

"Huh." I sighed, taking in the creature before me once more. Everything made sense. All the puzzle pieces were coming together one by one, finding their place. "The strawberry is growing on me," I confessed. "I'll tell him to load up for you." I winked. The hum I felt was echoed by smoke filtering through his nose. I cleared my throat, "So... Kyler doesn't always smell like smoke?"

He will always smell that way to you, the dragon stated.

"Why?" I squinted at him, sensing he wasn't telling me something.

You'll learn soon enough. Like I said. He wasn't saying something. *For now,* the dragon seemed to sigh, *Kyler feels you'll be more comfortable if he is back in control.*

"Bold statement," I mused, crossing my arms.

Shall I tell him you disagree? The amusement was evident in his voice.

I raised an eyebrow and said, "Tell him I think *he's* the one who might be uncomfortable. I'm fine either way," I shrugged and added, with a grin, "He's probably afraid I'll insult you somehow and get burnt to a crisp."

A deep chuckle reached my ears. It wasn't in my head. Could they speak out loud? *He has seen me do worse, but I would never do such a thing to you.* I tried to hide my slight fear with a chuckling grin. *Nevertheless, you are correct. Kyler would be more comfortable in control during the flight. I shall be here if you need me, though. Just call to me.*

"And, uh... how do I do that?" He used Kyler's name as if it weren't his own. "Do you have a...different name?"

The dragon brought its head close to mine once more and locked his sparkling blue eyes with mine. The urge to step forward and back both hit me at the same moment. I did neither as he spoke, *Say 'Mosmudo.'*

The word made something inside me lift its head. "Mosmudo," I repeated. Something shifted within me again. The intensified feeling led me to the magnetic pull that started this midnight journey—the bond.

Good. the dragon said. *Call to me, and nothing can prevent me from responding to you. Not even Kyler.* I nodded, and the dragon retracted its neck, closing its eyes for a moment. When they reopened, they were a familiar bright green.

"Kyler?" I asked, raising one eyebrow.

His familiar, darker tone echoed in my head, *It's me.*

I uncrossed my arms and put them on my hips. "Didn't trust me, did you?"

Smoke poured out of his nostrils. *Can you blame me? How many colorful insults have you thrown my way?*

True. "Well, he's not you. He's a shamelessly flirtatious dragon. I dare say that I like him." I stuck my tongue out playfully as a chuckle rumbled in my chest that didn't come from Kyler or me. "He loves the lollipops. Better keep 'em coming."

Smoke poured out his nostrils. *Those are a result of his temper tantrums.*

The way he talked about his dragon as if it were a child made me raise my eyebrows. "You made it seem like he's terrifying and deadly."

He is terrifying and deadly... most of the time. In my head, however, he throws temper tantrums when he doesn't get his way or I don't let him out to meet his favorite person. The dragon's eyes rolled dramatically. *You.*

"Ha!" I barked a laugh, remembering how the dragon had put it. "He said your fights for control got heated. Did he mean in the literal sense?"

He nodded. *My body heat would rise because of it. That's why I thought I burned you when I caught you. That is, until you asked about it again.*

My jaw dropped. "You didn't know it was a rider bond?"

No. Dragons and fae haven't been co-living for several decades. We don't know any outside of our island, at least. And without access to the Kyllindro, I had no idea what a rider bond was, and he didn't confess to it right away. His long blue tail flicked around his feet as he caught my eye.

"Uh huh…" I smiled, but it slowly faded as I remembered why we were out here: me in my flight leathers and the dragon crouching on the lawn before me, waiting for me to climb on its back.

Kyler seemed to have followed my train of thought. *Come on, Sunshine. Stop stalling. Let's go for a ride.* His deep voice reverberated in my chest as I was mere feet from him now. The magnetic pull vibrated within me, too.

Taking a deep, shaky breath, I followed the path of his dark wings tucked into his side up to where they connected just above his shoulder blades. "Is that where I sit?" I asked, referring to the place where his neck met his back.

The dragon nodded. His head lowered to me again, and that hot, smoky breath landed on my face. He may have been trying to intimidate me, but I wasn't about to back down. The blue eyes may have scared me, but I wasn't afraid of the green-eyed dragon.

Knowing it was Kyler but also not, I straightened and lifted my hand, reaching for the dragon's snout. Something about his scaled face made me want to feel it. To run my hands along his scales and see if they were as cold and unyielding as I imagined.

I watched my hand travel to his nose but didn't notice his flickering eyes as I reached for him. My hand stopped millimeters from touching him. When I met his gaze, my breathing stopped. The blue color in his eyes moved like the ocean at this distance. Then, the green flicked back into place. I knew those moments when Kyler's eyes had flashed blue, it wasn't him looking at me, but this magnificent creature before me.

This *dragon.*

A beautiful and terrifying creature I never knew existed. Yes, I'd seen Theo's dragon, but somehow, this interaction made a more significant impact on me. I bonded with a dragon—*this dragon*—*Kyler's* dragon. The magnetic pull intensified even more as my hand hovered over the dragon's face, holding my gaze with his.

Kyler, or the dragon, I couldn't tell with the way his eyes flickered between blue and green, moved to close the gap I'd left between us.

Where I expected to feel that cold, rugged, and unyielding strength, I only felt smooth scales buzzing with warmth and power.

And lightning—

The minute my hand touched him, my muscles went weak, and I felt like my legs would collapse under me. I braced myself by placing my other hand on the dragon's snout, and he pushed me back up to keep me standing.

My senses were suddenly overstimulated. The lightning rushed through my body.

But where I thought it would be crippling, it wasn't.

It was *empowering*.

I could suddenly *feel* the air, though there was no breeze. The earth *shifted* beneath my feet. And that crackling, lightning energy, like fire, flowed through me.

My powers.

Kyler must have sensed it, too, because I could feel the rumble of a joyous laugh, his hot breath hitting my legs. *There she is,* his voice rang clear as day in my head, and I couldn't help the flip my stomach did amid my building power.

I let out a nervous laugh as the flow of magic continued through me, still holding myself up with both hands on the dragon's snout. My body was shaking with power. It filled every part of me, from the tip of my toes to the top of my head. It found places to settle within me, and I looked up to catch the dragon's gaze, which shone bright green. "This is insane."

The sparkle in his eyes told me he'd been waiting for this moment. The connection between us grew stronger as I stood there, Kyler still supporting me as I seemed to become the dragon—I felt his heart beating, steady breathing, and minuscule yet precise movements before they happened. So when his tail curled slowly around my torso, I shifted my hands to where it wrapped around my waist, bracing myself as he lifted me off the ground.

The gentleness with which this creature handled me told me enough about how this dragon viewed me— he'd said so earlier. I was his prized possession. He chose me. *Me.*

Yet Kyler controlled each movement. His green eyes still focused on me. So, was he or his dragon treating me with such care? I decided to believe it was the dragon because I didn't want to consider what the other option meant.

His neck twisted, following the progress of his tail, lifting me onto his back. I positioned my legs as if I were going to sit on a horse and braced myself as he lowered me to the spot right in front of his wings. My breathing was uneven, my hands shaking with power, but I felt an overwhelming sense of calm the minute I settled onto his back. His tail snaked away, and I relaxed into the spot that seemed to be made perfectly for me.

That was the moment I knew I was right where I was meant to be.

All my life had been leading up to this moment. Everything I'd been through—every death, every accident, every trip to the hospital—led to me developing my powers and sitting on the back of this magnificent creature.

Are you ready? Kyler's voice interrupted my thoughts.

There were many things I didn't know, but I somehow knew that I was, indeed, ready. I took a steadying breath and nodded once.

His facial features changed into what I could only describe as a smile. Who knew a dragon could do such a thing? He faced forward, and I felt the muscles of his back shift as his wings stretched out to either side. Against his body, the wings looked midnight blue, like his scales and the leathers he'd given me. But as soon as they were spread out and the moonlight filtered through the membrane, I gasped.

The boning structure was midnight blue, but the membrane had spots reflecting the light like diamonds. It was like the night sky was painted on his wings. "They're beautiful," I breathed.

His wingspan was much bigger than I thought it would be, but with the size of his body, it made sense. Each wing was about the length of a school bus, which, from tip to tip, was probably the same length from nose to tail of the dragon's body. The fact that I was about to go flying with this creature should have terrified me, but instead, all I felt was the thrill of adventure.

Hold tight.

It suddenly made sense why Fae were trained in—and supposedly really good at—jiu-jitsu. My ability to hold tight to something with my legs would come in handy keeping myself on the dragon. When I looked for a place to hold with my hands, I found a shortened spine at the base of his neck angled away from me like the pommel of a horse's saddle. I hadn't ridden a horse since I fell off in lessons five years ago, but it was all coming back to me now.

I twisted in my seat, searching for a place to hook my feet, and he spoke again, *Right where the wings attach. It helps anticipate their movements.*

It was indeed the perfect spot. As I settled my feet in place, a thought occurred to me. "When we're in the air, will I be able to talk to you?"

If you use our bond, he said.

Duh. *Right.*

With his wings expanded, I settled into my spot and felt him rise off his belly to stand on all fours. Then he lifted his wings and brought them down with one mighty swoop.

Nothing could have prepared me for the weightlessness I experienced on the first beat of his strong, powerful wings. I tightened my grip with my legs before he could do it again—afraid if I didn't grip hard enough, I'd slide right off—and we lifted off the ground.

As we rose higher into the air, I watched as the details of the ground became less clear, and the view of the surrounding trees turned into an eagle-eye view. I could see the house and the surrounding forest, the falls coming into view just past the house. Kyler leveled out and soared in the direction of the town's namesake.

The magic I'd felt flood my body on the ground had settled into every cell, but something else started buzzing through my body again. That magnetic pull was now becoming stronger, something more tangible. I could feel it searching for a place to reside—a permanent place within me. It felt like an invisible string. The flight was solidifying the connection between us, making the bond unyielding. Nothing could break it.

We flew high over the falls. The feel of the wind through my hair and around me was intoxicating. I closed my eyes and breathed in the fresh, cool air from high above the ground. It felt different from this height. Like it wanted to dance and sway with me. And something within me wanted to answer that call. Opening my eyes, I brought my hand up next to me and started making waves up and down, curving my hands through the air, dodging air pockets as if I wer–

I am flying, I reminded myself.

The wind made it tough to keep my eyes open, and I thought for a moment about what Tom had taught me in preparation for my powers. That was what was calling to me—the air.

The breathwork came easily. I concentrated on the magic inside me, reaching for that feeling of lightning within me, and grabbed onto it.

Once I had it in my grasp, I focused on the air around me. I wanted to do something small to start because, at this height, with too much power, I could fly off my seat and easily fall to my death. I felt the moment the magic worked. I'd tried creating a shield of air against the wind. And it *worked*.

I laughed out loud at the insanity of it. Tom had prepared me well. I'd have to fill him in because he had two more powers to train me in. He would be in over his head, but I'm sure he would be ecstatic to learn my magic had come in.

The strength of the magnetic pull overwhelmed my senses abruptly, my heart pounding as the feeling settled into my chest. It felt like a hum of power attached to that invisible string. It flowed through my entire body and snapped right into place right next to my heart. It took my breath away, and I knew Kyler felt it, too, because the dragon lifted its head to roar into the clouds. But the sound he made didn't resemble a roar at all. It was more of a whistled call of celebration reverberating through me, causing me to make my own answering call of joy.

Hold on tight, Sunshine. The difference in his voice said that Kyler was sharing control, and both he and the dragon were filled with utter happiness, which only mirrored the feeling inside of me. *We're going for a victory lap.*

A giggle escaped me at my overwhelming joy, but I did as I was told, leaning forward to bring myself closer to the dragon's neck. I went as far as hooking my elbows around the spine while still trying to concentrate on keeping the wind out of my face.

Kyler pulled in his wings and made a dive toward the falls below. I was glad I tightened my leg grip because the weightlessness returned on the dive, and I screamed this time. The concentration on my air shield vanished, and I closed my eyes to keep the wind out. His wings spread out to catch our fall, and the feeling of gravity returned. I opened my eyes to find we were gliding over the lake, a few inches from the surface. He banked right, the tip of his wing barely dipping into the surface, circling over the lake where the falls emptied.

I had a strong desire to reach out and touch the water myself, but the dragon evened out before I could. I loosened my grip but realized my mistake almost immediately as the dragon dove again. I barely had time to close my mouth and take a breath.

We submerged under the water, and the shock of the cold plunge almost made me release my grip, but I kept hold with my mouth shut for the few seconds we were under. When we resurfaced and flew out of the water, I sucked in a gulp of air.

"You asshole!" I sputtered, wiping the cold water from my face with one hand while holding tight with the other as we climbed back into the night sky.

A roar of laughter echoed across the water and rumbled beneath me. It was nice to know the dragon had the same sense of humor as Kyler. I hadn't planned on going for a swim tonight.

Use your magic to dry yourself off. Kyler said it as if that had been the plan all along, and dipping in the water wasn't just him being a jerk.

I shivered as the wind hit my cold, wet clothes and bit through to my skin. Taking a steady breath, I blew it out, intending to turn the air around me into a warm breeze. My chattering teeth must have distracted me too much because I almost blew myself off the back of the dragon. I scrambled to keep myself on with a better grip. The breeze was still cold and sharp when I settled back into my spot.

A chuckle sounded in my mind as Kyler said, *A bit gentler next time.* That gust of wind hadn't affected his flying, or maybe he was just that good at controlling his flight. I didn't trust myself to stay on the dragon if I tried again. So, instead, I pressed my body against the dragon's warmth and opted to wait until we landed before attempting to dry myself off again.

When we circled the lawn, I braced for the landing, squeezing my legs against his unyielding, scaled body. He landed much softer than I anticipated, and once he settled on the ground, I swung my legs to one side, intending to slide down. His tail caught me around the waist again, though, and the feeling of it against the madí made it buzz with life.

He lifted me tenderly off his back and set me down just as gently. He brought his head around to take me in. With the warmth of his scales gone, I now shivered where I stood, my teeth chattering and wet clothes clinging to me.

You're still wet. That was the dragon.

"I c-can't do the m-magic," I said through chattering teeth. "Too c-cold."

His blue eyes feigned disappointment before his mouth opened. I caught a brief glimpse at the sharp, pointed teeth there, but his mouth formed an O and blew a warm breeze that covered my entire torso and slowly moved down to my toes before coming back up to my head. I let out an audible sigh at the heat that rushed over and through my body, turning around so he could do the same to my back. My hair flew around my face as the warm air from behind flowed through it before traveling down my body again.

When I felt cozy and dry, I tried to face him again. *Wait,* Kyler said, *I'm shifting.*

I was intrigued about the transformation, unsure why I could watch him turn into a dragon but not shift back. But I did as I was told and waited until his deep but human voice sounded behind me, giving me the go-ahead to turn back around. He wore the same clothes he'd been in before shifting, making me wonder how they kept in one piece through the shift. I'd have to ask later. The breathlessness and joy I felt occupied my thoughts, making all others disappear as I took in Kyler's full smile, dimples and all. Damn. I was in trouble.

"That was... something. Wasn't it?" He said, a bit breathless, but his eyes communicated so much more about how he felt. His green eyes danced with a joy I'd never seen from him.

Even the water trick didn't stop me from returning his smile, genuinely and effortlessly. "It was incredible!" The bond seemed to vibrate with the happiness we both felt. He was still smiling as he stalked toward me from where he'd landed on the lawn after his shift.

I couldn't wait to tell my friends about the night I'd had, soaring through the night on the back of a dragon. The look on their faces would be incredible. And Kaleb—

Kaleb.

The reality of the situation hit me. The smile on my face slowly faded as my heart plummeted to my feet. I couldn't tell him. Anything. The incredible new life experiences I was having—I wouldn't be able to share with him because he was *human*. I wanted to tell him about my powers, what I could do, the land I was from, and that I'd just *ridden a dragon.*

Instead, I—what? Had to be content with him thinking I was an *alien?* That wasn't the life I wanted with him. To keep secrets. He was my best friend— boyfriend now. If I told him the truth, would his reaction change? Would he still be okay with what I was and who I was associated with?

Kyler stopped a few feet from me, concern crossing his face as he took in my expression. "What's wrong?"

I held his gaze, trying to gauge how he might react to my next words. Then I said, "I want to tell Kaleb the truth."

Kyler's concern turned to surprise, but only briefly before it softened, and he asked, "You're sure?"

I nodded slowly, thinking about all the possible outcomes of the conversation ahead of me but knowing I couldn't keep this from him any longer. If he decided that he couldn't handle it, I would let him go. But he deserved the truth. He deserved to know exactly what he was getting himself into at Prom, including who and what he could be dealing with. "Positive."

Kyler let out a deep breath and extended his arm to the house. "Let's go then."

It was my turn to raise my eyebrows. "He's asleep." I started toward the house anyway.

"Trust me," Kyler said as he fell into step beside me, "he'll be happy you woke him up."

Not sure I wanted to know how he knew that, I started mentally listing how I could approach this complex subject. You know, the one where I'm a powerful fae with dragon shifters for guardians, and, oh, yeah, I'm bonded to one of those dragons as their rider. I guess I could go right for the gut by saying precisely that, but I figured it would be better if I broke it down in simpler terms—easily digestible sentences.

As we climbed the steps to the front door, an overwhelming sense of *wrong* hit me.

I realized why when I saw the door had been left ajar.

I stopped in my tracks.

Kyler didn't, though. He burst through the door at incredible speed, disappearing inside.

Panic rooted me to the spot for only a second before I chased after him.

His senses probably told him precisely what was wrong and led him to whatever danger was in the house.

My body screamed as I ran, panic coursing through my veins at the thought of what could have happened.

Kyler was fast. Too fast. I lost him around several corners.

When I finally spotted him again, he stood frozen before a door.

I knew that door. My already ragged breath hitched.

When I reached Kyler, I almost crashed into him as I charged into the room.

But Kyler stopped me, wrapping both arms around me and pulling me back against his chest. I struggled against his grip as I took in the scene before me.

Kaleb was on his knees, face pale as a dagger was held to his throat. A trickle of blood ran down his bare chest from where it had broken the skin. There were bruises on his ribcage, his lip was bleeding, and a black eye was forming as his left eye swelled shut. The dagger seemed to have left its mark just below his ribs before it was held to his throat to keep him from doing anything reckless. The blood from the stab wound poured slowly onto the rug, leaving a small collection of it at his knees.

Aaidan stood behind him, grinning maniacally, revealing blood-stained teeth. "Perfect timing, princess," he spat.

Kaleb was breathing heavily, as if he'd fought back. From the looks of it, he'd gotten a few hits in before he was forced to his knees.

"Let him go!" I shrieked, still trying to break free of Kyler's grasp with every ounce of strength.

The look on Kaleb's face told me just how frightened he was, tears pooling in his eyes. "Rayleigh," His cracked voice made me want to sob. Aaidan pushed the dagger further against his throat, and Kaleb strained his neck to keep the blade from sinking in deeper.

"I wouldn't speak if I were you," Aaidan crooned, turning his gaze to me. "I was beginning to think I'd have to leave a note. You were gone for so long on your little *outing*." His eyes sparkled with mischief as they shifted between Kyler and me.

We hadn't been gone more than thirty minutes. How did he know where to find us? And how did he know Kyler and I were out of the house? Where were Theo and Mari? I pushed the questions aside. Kaleb. Kaleb was the most important thing right now. The blood flow from the shallow cut on his throat increased. His eyes met mine, a trace of panic and something else as they shifted to Kyler and then back to me: hurt. My heart sank. I was going to kill Aaidan for insinuating that anything happened with Kyler and me.

"What do you want?" I seethed, relaxing enough for Kyler's grasp to loosen slightly—a plan forming in my head. I searched for the energy within me as I tried to calm my staggering breaths.

Kyler let out a growl as Aaidan shifted his attention to him. "You have twenty-four hours."

Hurried footsteps sounded down the hall, and I assumed Mari or Theo had been made aware of the break-in, or perhaps my yelling alerted them. I focused on the task I'd given myself, concentrating on where I wanted to send the energy I now had a grip on. I kept my gaze on the dagger against Kaleb's throat.

Aaidan shrugged as if Kyler had said something to him that I had missed. "Your choice," he said. The running footsteps closed in, but it didn't matter.

They wouldn't make it in time.

I felt the energy in the room shift as Kyler's grip on me tightened again, preparing to hold me back. What he didn't know was that it was never my intention to run toward them.

But that dagger made its last cut on Kaleb's body. I released my power. The blade whipped from Aaidan's hand and landed on the floor before me. I gave him a wicked grin as he cursed, giving me a look that said he hadn't been expecting that. Kaleb relaxed only slightly with the blade gone. His face was in utter disbelief as he stared at me.

When Aaidan's shock was replaced with anger, I knew there was no stopping his next move.

The room around me constricted, and there was a rush of air before a moment of darkness.

When everything in the room around me appeared again, a scream erupted out of me, "KALEB!"

The spot where Aaidan and Kaleb had just been was empty.

He was gone.

"KALEB!" I screamed again. But my body collapsed on itself, and I was thankful for the arms that held me up. "Kaleb…" I sobbed, staring at the spot where he disappeared.

He was gone.

XXXIX
Relentless

Kaleb. My sweet, smiling, *human* Kaleb. He wouldn't survive this. That wound on his stomach and the torture that I'm sure Aaidan was about to put him through. He wouldn't be able to take it.

The strong hands that held me back loosened, and I found my strength, whipping around to face Kyler.

"*You!*" I snarled, getting right up in his face. "You let this happen!" I put both hands on his chest and shoved as hard as I could. He barely moved. "Why didn't you stop him!"

Mari and Theo came into view behind him, and Kyler grabbed my hands before I could shove him again. His voice was barely about a whisper as he said, "I couldn't—"

"Yes. You. *Could!*" I yelled, yanking my hands from his grasp and hitting his chest this time. All the joyous feelings from our flight moments ago had vanished. He could have used any of his powers to stop Aaidan from taking Kaleb, but he didn't. "You let him go! You just *stood* there!" Again and again, my fists hit his chest, my anger building as he stood there and took every hit without moving. "How could you?" I cried, my voice cracking, "I," I slammed my fists into his chest again. "Hate," Again. "You." Again and again and again.

Until the fight went out of me, and I collapsed to the floor in a heap.

Sobs racked their way through me as I folded into myself, pulling my knees to my chest.

"I'm sorry," Kyler breathed, kneeling before me. I don't know if I believed him. He released another breath, and when he spoke again, his voice was strained, "Aaidan's shield. I couldn't get past it."

Something inside made me want to believe him. To know that he wouldn't lie to me. But he claimed to be stronger than Aaidan—much stronger. He'd broken through Aaidan's shield before. Why couldn't he do it this time? The intrusive thought that he might have let him take Kaleb crossed my mind, and a monster within me awoke.

What if that was his plan the whole time? To somehow get Kaleb out of the way so he could— he could, what? Be the one to take me back to Niccodra himself? Use my powers for his own agenda? The thought made my skin crawl as I remembered what he said about the differences between claiming a fae and choosing one.

No, Kyler wouldn't do that. He said my magic could have rejected him, and it didn't. He hadn't claimed me. We were bonded. It was a mutual choice. The feeling that had coursed through me during our flight was enough evidence for me to know he wouldn't betray me like that.

It didn't stop the nagging feeling that perhaps Kyler's motives could have been something else entirely. My blood heated at the idea, but I pushed that down and tried my best to bury it deep and forget about it.

No matter how mad I was that Kyler hadn't done anything, I knew he was telling the truth. He couldn't get past Aaidan's shield. But that didn't stop me from asking myself how *I* got past it. And if the look of shock on Aaidan's face before he disappeared was any sort of clue, it meant he'd been surprised by that, too.

I took a deep breath and slowly lifted my head to Kyler. "I'm getting him back," I said through gritted teeth.

Kyler met my gaze with a fierce one, "I know." He gave me a single nod. "Theo is going to—"

"Where did he take him?" I said before he could finish.

He dropped his shoulders, his head falling with them. "The portal."

The meadow. *My meadow.* I knew that place like the back of my hand. The only thing I didn't know was where the portal was. But I knew everything else—all the hidden caves and hollow trees. Playing hide-and-seek in that place made me a master of the terrain. I would tear that place apart to find Kaleb and bring him back. And I knew the people in front of me would help.

I wiped the tears from my eyes and stood. "Let's go."

Mari stepped in my path, holding her hands up to stop me. "Rayleigh, we have to make a plan."

"I have one," I shouldered past her.

"Rayleigh, dear. Please wait!" Theo yelled after me.

I kept walking. No one was going to stop me. I knew what I needed to do. Knew the only way to get him back. To keep him safe. And it couldn't wait. He'd already been beaten within an inch of his life and stabbed with a dagger. Who knew what else they would do to him, what kind of sick torture they had in mind? My own capture flashed through my mind, and I shuddered, picking up my pace.

Mari ran up beside me in the hallway and matched my strides but didn't try to stop me. "Rayleigh, I know you feel responsible, but—"

"I don't," I said, not slowing down.

"Okay," Mari dragged out the word, glancing over her shoulder, then back to me again. "Regardless, you need to think about this. Take a minute an—"

"Kaleb doesn't have a minute!" I whirled on her. "Before they took him, they beat him to a pulp, stabbed him, and held a dagger to his throat! He could already be dead for all I know!" Hot tears slid down my face, but I ignored them, turning to continue my trek through the house.

"There would be no point in taking him hostage if they planned to kill him anyway," Kyler spoke from directly behind me. I guess he'd caught up, too.

We had just entered the kitchen when I spun toward him, "You don't get to talk." I shoved a finger in his chest. "You could have stopped that dagger, but you didn't. *I* did." Kyler's face fell, and I knew I'd hit my mark. "You were selfish. Thought you could get Kaleb out of the way—"

"What?!" He reeled back at my accusation. "No! I—"

"I said *no talking*." I shoved my finger deeper into his chest.

He grabbed my hand from his chest and leaned closer, growling, "Blame me all you want, but I would *never* sacrifice Kaleb like that." His eyes shifted back and forth between mine as our breaths mingled. Then his face softened as he whispered, "He means too much to you." Hurt laced his words.

I stared at him and realized he was probably the one person who knew just how much Kaleb meant to me. More tears welled in my eyes. Kyler may have teased and flirted with me, but that didn't mean he felt anything more towards me. He likely just got under my skin because he thought it was fun. The bond between us proved that he would protect me at all costs. I'd seen him do it. I did not doubt that protection would extend to those closest to me.

He was my friend. We were bonded. He wouldn't betray me like that.

"I'm sorry," I squeaked, not shying away from his gaze. "I just… I can't lose him."

Kyler released my hand and cupped my face instead, wiping away a tear that rolled down my cheek. "I know, Sunshine." He pulled me to his chest, one hand on the back of my head and one around my shoulders. "We'll get him back." His breath hit the top of my head as I relaxed into his embrace, returning it. "I promise."

We stayed there for a minute before someone cleared their throat. I stepped back, wiping the tears from my face.

"What do we do?" I asked softly, knowing my plan to charge into the meadow was not a plan at all but a suicide mission.

Mari stepped up next to Kyler, "We prepare for battle."

"Battle?" I exclaimed. "We don't stand a chance against two power-hungry dragons!"

She laughed, tilting her head. "Did you forget you have *five* dragons on your side?"

I pursed my lips in response. "Oh yeah…" I laughed a little, and the tension in the air dissipated. The mention of the other members of my omada made me think. I turned to Kyler again, "Have you heard from my mom and Mitch?"

Theo stepped up. "I spoke with Bastiel a few hours ago. Everything seemed to be quiet on his end." When I gave him a funny look, he realized why and corrected his mistake, "Bastiel is Chief Bass's real name."

Nodding, I released a breath. At least Mitch and Ma were safe. Who knew what would happen to them? Maybe they wouldn't have to leave if we got rid of Aaidan and Kool-Aid Man before their scheduled move. For now, I needed to focus on Kaleb and getting him out of their grasp safely.

If what Kyler said was true, they would keep him alive until we arrived. But then what? Why did they capture him? To make sure I would go with them? To scare me into leaving? Whatever the reason, it wasn't going to work out for them.

"We knew this moment would come," Theo stated, standing in front of us in the kitchen. We woke up the twins and Tom half an hour ago, although I wasn't sure how they slept through the chaos. But we informed them of what happened, and the twins were equally shocked they hadn't heard any commotion from their rooms just down the hall. "It happened a bit before we expected it to," Theo said, "but nothing ever really goes as planned, does it now?" He gave a grim smile before continuing. "Remember, their main agenda will be to capture Rayleigh." He gave a pointed look my way. "The rest of you are likely considered collateral at this point." The way he said that made my skin crawl. Was Kaleb *just* collateral? Would he die because of me? Would these people, these *friends*, die because of me? I didn't want that. I didn't want any of this. No one should sacrifice their life because of me. But I knew better than to ask them to stay behind. It would be pointless. I knew I couldn't save Kaleb by myself, and I definitely wouldn't be able to get us both out of there alive without them, either. I needed their help. "Make sure you stay with your appointed partner."

"Who's my partner?" Ken asked.

"Me, of course," Theo smiled, which Kendall mirrored, albeit a bit hesitantly. "Leighton, you'll be with Mari and Rayleigh, with Kyler." I already knew that much, but the twins looked surprised at the pairings. "Smiles will be joining us to accompany Tom." He caught Tom's eye, and he nodded in response. "We'll be flying in."

"What?!" Ken sputtered. Leigh's disbelief echoed hers, but I gave them both a grin when they noticed my lack of surprise. I hadn't been able to tell them about my flight earlier. There wasn't time.

Theo kept his smile plastered on his face. "This is what you've been training for," he said.

"We haven't learned to fly!" Leigh cried.

"Have you not?" Theo retorted. When they looked at him like he was crazy, he went on. "The jiu-jitsu training is not only to take down your opponents but strengthens your muscles to keep a good grip while riding."

While I could see the information made sense to them, it didn't surprise me when Leigh said, "Yeah, but flying is *in the air*. That's not the same!"

Theo shrugged, "Trust me when I tell you you'll be just fine."

"So you're telling me we've been doing this training just to be able to stay on a dragon?" Ken said.

"Well, no. It also helps with controlling your magic." Theo rounded the counter. "Now. Chop chop." He clapped his hands. "We haven't had a chance to show you our dragon forms, aside from Rayleigh." Every head turned to me, and my eyes met Kyler's, who gave me a tight-lipped smile. Before I could tell the twins anything else, Theo said, "We need to get the shock and awe out of the way so we can get going." He headed to the hallway with Tom, leading us to the front door. I got up and followed Kyler and Mari, the twins shadowing me.

"I was not expecting this," Leighton muttered.

Kendall did her excited whole body tense-and-shake and said through her clenched teeth, "I'm scared but thrilled at the same time."

"There's no feeling like it," I smirked as their heads twisted toward me. "Kyler took me out after dark," I confessed, and their jaws both dropped. My face fell with my next words, "It's how Aaidan got to Kaleb."

It was still unknown how exactly he'd gotten into the house unnoticed. Theo said something about a perimeter alarm going off, but he'd thought it was just Kyler and me on our flight, which Kyler had told him about before we left. Aaidan must have made his move when we triggered the alarm. The front door had been left ajar, but with Aaidan's ability to teleport, it could have just been a message to Kyler and me. He seemed to know we'd gone out, which I also had trouble understanding.

I returned my attention to the girls, knowing they expected more details. "But flying with a dragon is—" I searched for the right word, but I didn't think one would do it justice, "the most thrilling sensation I've ever experienced. It was absolutely incredible," I finished, then remembered what happened just before our flight and raised my voice so Tom could hear me when I said, "My powers finally showed up, too." Tom turned his head slightly so his ear was trained toward me. "Turns out I've got a few more things to learn. Starting with air, but now I have to add earth and fire to that list."

Tom stopped dead and turned sharply toward me with the biggest grin. "I knew it," he whispered, his eyes alight with wonder.

I raised my brows at him as the girls processed what I said and started chattering excitedly next to me. "You knew?" I countered, thinking there was no possible way.

But he nodded in response. "I knew your mother, remember?" I had forgotten that, but he continued, "Her power felt different from the others. Stronger. I thought it was because of her status." His lips parted in awe. "Evanian." He turned to look at Theo, who didn't seem surprised by the news in the slightest, which probably meant Kyler had told him. "What does this mean?"

Theo's eyes sparkled as he took me in. "It means the tides are changing, dearie." He kept his gaze on me while answering Tom's question, "And everything we know is about to change." A shiver ran through me at the promise in his tone. I didn't want to think about what that meant in the long run.

My focus right now was getting to Kaleb. Saving him. Even if he couldn't come with me to Niccodra, which it was sounding more and more like that was where this was headed. But I would do anything to bring him back safely, even if it meant going to Niccodra with the monsters who had taken him. "We're wasting time," I said, pushing past everyone to the front door.

Out on the lawn, there was no light except the moon's. I wondered if that would hinder any part of the plan we'd gone over. Theo let me make most of it due to my knowledge of the meadow, but he made some slight adjustments so that everyone playing a part would have a task.

Theo called the plan the "Distract and Snatch," to which most everyone laughed, but it stuck. I was their target, so we would use that against them, draw them out and away from wherever they were keeping Kaleb.

I fingered the bracelet Kaleb had given me, pinching the moon between my fingers as I whispered, "I'm coming for you."

Kyler warned me that wearing it wasn't a good idea because it could get caught on something and break, but I told him I didn't care. I needed to remind myself of who I was there to save. What I was there to do. Not only had these people taken Kaleb, but they were also responsible for Mitch, Dad, and Arabella. They were going to pay for that.

While grabbing the bracelet, I saw the dagger Aaidan had tried to make me stab Kaleb with back in the courtyard and snatched it, thinking that a small blade was better than nothing. It was tucked into one of the boots Kyler had given me earlier for our flight.

Kendall and Leighton stepped up to either side of where I stood and looped their arms through mine, pulling my attention from the bracelet. "We've got this," Leigh whispered.

"Yeah, he's going to be okay," Ken nudged me.

"I hope you're right." Because I didn't know what I would do if he weren't. I pulled the girls closer to me with a gentle tug, needing their comfort.

Something about the whole night seemed off to me. Aaidan's shield was stronger than expected, and Kyler couldn't penetrate it, but I could. Somehow, Aaidan had gotten into the house unnoticed, which didn't seem to bother anyone as much as I thought it should. I had a feeling in the pit of my stomach that I was missing something. It wasn't adding up. I eyed the people across the lawn and wondered how these three shifters were assigned to protect me without knowing my entire history. Either someone was lying, or Aaidan knew more than the people now spread out on the lawn, facing us.

The thoughts were sending me down an endless spiral of doom. Trying to get to the bottom of this right now was not going to happen. And trying to get inside Aaidan's head was not worth my time and effort. But the thought lingered. Obviously, there was something I wasn't seeing.

XL
Keep Your Head Up Princess

Kyler, Mari, and Theo had positioned themselves on the lawn about thirty feet from each other. Theo shifted first, from his more petite frame of a human figure to his golden dragon form in less than five seconds.

"Damn..." Ken drew out the word for the few seconds it took him to shift and settle on the ground.

The gold dragon stretched his neck toward Kendall. How were they going to communicate if he couldn't do mind communication like Kyler?

Kyler spoke Kendall's name. She looked at him, and he gestured for her to approach Theo's dragon.

I could feel her trembling as she gripped my arm. I hadn't realized how tight her grip had gotten as she watched the dragon appear. I eased my arm out of hers and gave her a little shove forward. "Go ahead, Ken." She didn't take her eyes off the beast before us but took a hesitant step forward and then another.

"Reach out your hand," Kyler said. She placed a hand over her heart to ensure it stayed there and slowly lifted her other toward the dragon. His head was now level with her on the ground, and he pushed his snout up against the palm of her hand.

Ken yipped like a dog, snatching her hand away and shaking it as if she'd been bitten. When she brought her hand back up to study it, there was a mark on it. She glanced back at me, shock written all over her face, and then her head whipped around to Theo.

When I tilted my head with my brow furrowed, Kyler answered the question I hadn't asked out loud. *He's made a temporary bond for communication purposes. It doesn't go as deep as ours.* I nodded, more to myself than to him. My mind was reeling at the incredible abilities of these creatures.

Kendall walked closer to Theo, and he lifted his head, simultaneously lowering his belly to the ground. She reached out toward his shoulder, pausing just before she touched it, and looked at Theo's face. He nodded, and she closed the distance between her hand and his hide. "This is fantastic," she breathed. I could barely hear because she'd gotten so far away from me, but the awe was evident in her voice.

I turned to Leigh, who was staring at the spot where Mari had been moments ago, but in her place was a white dragon with violet eyes. *Interesting.* I honestly thought she was going to be purple. She was smaller than Theo, but she was by no means tiny. Her head was more of a triangular shape, and the horns on her head weren't as sharp, twisting outward rather than up. There were gill-like things along her jawline that expanded out like tiny wings. Her tail was short, but it didn't look natural. It looked like it might have been damaged to that length.

Kyler spoke again, "Leighton." He made the same motion toward Mari as he had to Theo for Ken. Mari's dragon bowed her head to Leigh, low enough to come eye to eye with her.

I shimmied my arm out of her grasp, too, and pushed her to walk toward the stark white dragon. She went through the same process Ken did, but it seemed a little more intimate, so I turned to where Kyler had been waiting and saw his blue dragon gazing at me.

Come on, Sunshine. We've got a rescue mission to run. I walked over and stopped next to his shoulder, where I could have climbed onto his back if his tail hadn't already curled around me again and lifted me into position.

What's wrong? Don't want me to climb on top of you like that? I grinned as I gestured to the twins climbing on their respective dragons. I knew the question would cause ideas to form in his head, but I needed the distraction from where we were headed. To bring humor in to lighten the mood. Because I felt like I was losing myself every minute Kaleb was gone, and I couldn't let that happen.

The voice that answered was rough, *That's not quite what I imagine when I think about you crawling on top of me, Sunshine.*

I laughed out loud, letting the sound echo through the yard. Knowing he'd played along to get me to laugh, I let the comment slide and settled into my spot on his back, gripping the spine in front of me. *You wish.*

A low rumble rattled through me, and I peered at the twins across the way. Both had turned their heads at my laughter, surely wondering what was said between Kyler and me. Ken had a huge grin on her face, like she was living out her wildest dreams. Leigh, on the other hand, looked like she might pass out at any second. "You okay?" I shouted at her across the space that was now between us.

"Uh huh!" Leighton's answer was almost a whimper. She looked like she was holding on for dear life. There was no way I could prepare her for what she was about to experience. She wasn't much of a thrill seeker like Kendall, but I trusted that Mari would keep her safe.

Tom stood on the lawn, watching us all with a grim smile. "Where is Smiles?" I asked him, not knowing if he even knew.

He got delayed at the hospital, Kyler said. Odd. Why was he acting as a human doctor when we were in a dire situation?

"Don't worry," Tom said, pulling my attention from my intrusive thoughts, "We will follow as soon as he gets here." He gave a tight nod, locking eyes with me in a promise, and I lowered my head in thanks. He wasn't going to make us wait for him. They would come as backup, which alleviated the dread I was starting to feel. "Rayleigh," The tone in his voice made me meet his gaze again. "Don't depend on your powers tonight. The stress you're under may cause them to fail you in any situation." He'd said something similar yesterday. I nodded and went on, "Use your training. Use your head. Remember what I taught you."

"I will," I replied, knowing I could take someone on in hand-to-hand combat, but that wasn't my biggest concern. I knew what powers these dragons possessed and how they could control someone with a thought. Nothing I'd been told or taught gave me any indication that I could get out of a situation like that, but something in me said that nothing was impossible. I'd fight until there was no fight left in me.

When he gave a confirming nod, Kyler spread his wings. Theo and Mari followed suit, and as we lifted off the ground, I heard Leighton's shriek of terror and Kendall's squeal of delight. I would have laughed, but the reason for this flying adventure kept my joy locked down as we rose into the air. This wasn't like the fun flight I experienced earlier. This was a rescue mission.

I stared at the bracelet on my wrist, hoping they weren't hurting Kaleb any more than they already had, but deep down, I knew that wasn't true. Not if Aaidan had anything to say about it.

What was going through Kaleb's mind right now? He knew I hadn't told him the whole truth, but he had been *teleported* out of his room after being attacked by someone he'd never seen before. And his shocked face when the dagger flew out of Aaidan's hand? It was bound to raise some questions, right? I was about to show up on the back of a dragon. That would leave him speechless. What would he think then? Would he say enough is enough and walk away from the crazy world I'm only just discovering I'm from? Would he want to know more? Would he still want to be with me after all this?

Worse than all of those thoughts, though, was what if he was already gone? What if they killed him the moment they took him away? What if we weren't going to ma—

Sunshine, Kyler's deep voice was gentle when it broke through my thoughts. *We'll get there in time.*

How he knew where my mind had traveled, I didn't care. *But how do you know?*

Remember when I said his thoughts were loud?

There was no way... He said it wasn't possible unless they were closer. But a spark of hope lit up inside me at the idea. *You can* hear *him?*

A beat of silence passed before he responded with a simple, *Yes.*

That spark went out. *You hesitated.* My inner voice shook. *Why did you hesitate?*

He's okay, was all he said. That didn't help the rise of panic that started to creep in. *But you can't think about that right now. You can't let it distract you from the task at hand. We will get him out of there. I promised, remember?*

It didn't pass me by that Kyler didn't include the word "alive" at the end of that sentence. It made my breathing hitch, and my heart started racing. I ran my hands along the dragon's neck to feel its warmth. The smooth texture of the scales brought me back from the edge. Kaleb was strong. He would get through this. He had to.

Tears started forming in my eyes, but the wind whipped them away. It reminded me to try my air shield again. When I reached for my power, though, it didn't come to me. Tom was right. I couldn't rely on my magic. My anxiety was too high. I decided to keep my head down instead, avoiding the wind as we sped through the night.

We reached a height high enough to avoid wandering eyes below and leveled out to start heading the long way to the meadow.

To our right, Mari and Leighton leveled out, and to our left, Theo and Kendall.

With her wild heart soaring, I watched Ken let go of Theo's spine and spread her arms wide as she flew through the air. "Wahoo!" Her voice echoed into the night sky. She glanced over at me and had the biggest smile on her face.

This was probably better than Ken's wildest dreams. She was flying on the back of a dragon! We all were. And we were on our way to save our best friend. We weren't the damsels in distress. Not this time.

We were fae warriors, riding on the backs of dragons, running headfirst into a battle. We had no idea what we were doing, but we did know who we were saving. We could not fail.

What if someone sees us? I said, my focus falling on the world below. I knew most people were asleep at this hour, but I wondered what would happen if they stepped outside to enjoy the night sky and found three dragons among the stars.

Most of the time, they tell themselves they're seeing things, and by the time they look again, we're already gone. But if that's not the case, I'll change what they saw.

Well, that explains why I never saw a dragon. I mean, what would I have done if I had actually thought I'd seen one? It reminded me of something. *The first night I remember at your house... Did you go for a flight?*

Yes.

I saw you, didn't I?

Yes. I thought you were asleep, he paused, hesitating to go on. I knew why as soon as he asked, *Do you remember the dream you had after you went back to sleep?*

My body stiffened. The lucid dream. Where I felt like I was flying. And then falling. *Yes...* I dragged out the word in question.

It wasn't a lucid dream, he confessed. My heart started hammering against my chest. *You had asked where you were from. And instead of telling you, I wanted to show you. I created a vision for you in your mind as best I could.*

The memory of that dream came rushing back to me. The beauty of the world felt so real in my imagination. That was why I could *feel* the ground squish beneath my feet, and the sound of the birds was so clear. If Kyler created that in my head—

Then I remembered how the dream ended. And the laughter I'd heard when I woke in my bed, knowing that Kyler was laughing at me falling in the dream. *Why are you such an asshole?* I slapped the dragon's neck, but I had a feeling it didn't have the effect I was going for.

I felt his chuckle more than I heard it. *That was another question you asked.*

My eyebrows shot up. *You took that paper, too?!* I started to rethink everything about being in that house over the last week. *Was I ever truly alone?*

Yes, but I had to keep tabs in case you decided to run.

I remembered how often I thought about running that first night and thought he was wise to keep watch, but that didn't make it much better. *Alright, I guess that's fair.*

Hold tight, Kyler said. *We're diving.*

I hadn't realized we'd reached our destination until I saw the familiar break in the trees where Dad used to park. I hadn't been to the meadow since his death, and the fact that I was coming here to try and save another person I cared about gave me a sinking feeling in my stomach. Something about the whole night *still* felt off to me, but as we closed in on our final destination, that sense of dread grew, and I couldn't help but wonder what would throw me off next.

I did as Kyler said, leaning into the dragon's neck and gripping the spine in front of me as tightly as possible. He dove. My body lifted off his back briefly, but I hugged my legs tighter and pulled myself back to my seat. The weightlessness didn't end, though. We dove down, down, down until he leveled out just above the clearing off the road. Kyler landed quietly, setting one foot down at a time, Theo and Mari following suit.

I made sure Aaidan didn't see us, Kyler said, *but I didn't see Kaleb with him. Nor did I see Koladon.* Kyler lowered himself to the ground, and I swung my leg over his neck to slide down his shoulder to the ground before he could lift me off with his tail. I hadn't anticipated the height of the fall until my feet didn't hit the ground when I expected them to. As soon as they did, though, I lost my balance and fell forward.

But I didn't faceplant.

The deja vu of the situation didn't pass me by as I realized what, rather than *who* saved me.

Kyler's wing lifted me up, and I righted my feet under me.

He pulled his wing away to reveal his bright green eyes watching me. *Legs a little wobbly?*

I laughed nervously and said out loud, "To be expected after my first flight, right?"

Technically, it's your second, he said, and I could have sworn his eyes sparkled with amusement.

I studied the dragon before me. Something had changed within Kyler, and I wasn't sure if it could be explained by our bond or not. This seemed like something else.

But as I turned to see the girls still on their dragons, I was reminded why we were here. All thoughts about Kyler vanished. Replaced with thoughts on how to proceed with rescuing Kaleb.

The girls dismounted and faced me, awaiting their instructions. But the weird feeling in the pit of my stomach made me second-guess everything. I couldn't leave the rescuing to someone else. It had to be me...

I lifted my chin, "Change of plans."

XLI
Angel with a Shotgun

We'll give you a head start to the caves, Kyler grumbled after hearing the new plan. He told me the caves were where I was being held when they rescued me, and I kicked myself for not realizing that. I'd hidden in those caves so often as a kid. That's why they looked so familiar. If Koladon were keeping Kaleb anywhere, it would most definitely be there. Although it seemed pretty dumb to bring him back to the same place they tried to hold me hostage…

Shaking my head from that thought, I focused back on the plan. I needed to go to the cave alone while everyone else went to the meadow to distract Aaidan. If what my gut was telling me was true, I needed to be the one who got to Kaleb first. Alone. Theo and Kyler argued with me initially, reluctant to let me go alone, but when I told them why it would work, they stopped arguing.

Kyler would hide me with illusions while simultaneously creating a replica of me on his back to make Aaidan think we'd all come straight to him. Once they had Aaidan engaged in battle, Kyler would meet me at the caves to keep watch or pull Koladon's attention from guard duty so I could sneak in and find Kaleb.

Hopefully, by that time, Smiles and Tom would arrive, either to keep Aaidan's attention or help Kyler with Koladon if needed. But everyone else's task was to keep the attention away from me. The bond between Kyler and me gave us that line of communication so he would know if I needed him.

It was a solid plan, but I still felt like I was missing a vital piece of information. I didn't want to be suspicious of any of the people around me, but that didn't mean I couldn't be cautious. Anything could happen. That nagging feeling kept telling me I needed to get to Kaleb alone first.

I'm going to cast the illusions now. Kyler was definitely still angry with me. He'd argued the longest, his dragon breaking through at one point to voice his opinion, too. But that's why it would work so well. They'd never expect Kyler to let me out of his sight, not after everything that's happened. As I met his gaze again, I was glad he never read my mind. I had a feeling he wouldn't be too happy that I didn't trust him.

It'll feel similar to when I saw through your eyes, but you'll feel it externally.

I nodded. I wasn't sure how to prepare for what he was about to do, but planting my feet seemed like a good choice. When my eyes met his again, I nodded. The minute his power touched me, I shivered at the gentle caress.

The sensation started on the top of my head. Like electrically charged water seeping down my face, over my shoulders, and all the way down to my feet. The feeling faded a bit when it reached my toes, but I felt it settling against my skin.

I glanced down at my body and gasped.

It was there—but it wasn't. I could see the ground through my legs, but when I lifted my foot, I saw the movement before the camouflage caught up—almost like a chameleon. If I moved too fast, it wouldn't keep up. I noted that, seeing as I had planned to run through the forest.

Kyler would have to keep up this illusion and the one he planned to create on his back. He claimed that our bond didn't limit his powers to having to touch me so he could keep the illusion up as if I were an extension of himself. My eyes found the green ones before me, "So only you can see me?"

He nodded, *I will do my best to keep the illusion up until you see Kaleb.* I nodded at the hidden instruction there.

"Incredible," I heard Leigh whisper.

The blue dragon moved his head to look at his back, where I should have been sitting. The air around where I had once been started sparkling and changing, morphing into a shape until an exact replica of me sat on his back. My jaw dropped. It was flawless—like he'd studied me for a lifetime and was able to recreate each feature to absolute perfection.

Perhaps he had. I felt his gaze on me often enough over the last week that it didn't surprise me to see he'd gotten every little detail correct. Right down to the scar on my forehead, where I'd busted it open on the counter the day my dad died. With the powers he was showcasing here and over the last week, there was no telling what else Kyler was capable of.

I briefly wondered how he'd become so powerful. He seemed much more powerful than Mari or Theo. It occurred to me that I had never had a chance to ask him about his past, his heritage. I never asked him where he came from, what his life was like before coming here to protect me, or even if he had a choice in the matter.

There was so much more I had to learn about the man within the creature before me, who had created a perfect copy of me that was now sitting proudly on his back.

The mirror image of me met my gaze and blinked.

"That's terrifying," I shuddered.

"It looks just like..." Ken trailed off. I knew what she was about to say. And she wasn't wrong. I'd grown up with someone who looked exactly like me my entire life, so why did I find it creepy to have one looking back at me now? Perhaps it was the subtle differences that made it clear Arabella was not the one sitting on Kyler's back. Or the fact that I knew she was long gone.

Regardless, the "distract" part of the plan was ready at this point, meaning they needed to go and do just that.

Kyler turned his head back to me and lowered it to bring himself to my eye level. *Give us thirty seconds to make it to the meadow. Keep your communication open.* He lowered his chin, and the look those blue eyes gave me— I didn't want to know how many ways this dragon could kill me, but that look could have been one of them. *Don't do anything stupid,* he growled.

Wouldn't dream of it, I lied.

Kyler held my stare for another minute before he decided he believed me and lifted his head to turn to the other dragons. They all nodded and spread their wings. I raised my hand to wave but remembered no one except Kyler could see me, and let my arm drop back down to my side. No use shouting, either. It would give away our location.

Their wings caused a wind tunnel, almost knocking me over at the first gust. I braced myself with a wide stance and held my arms up to shield my eyes from the dirt and rocks that had started flying. I knew Kyler was shielding their ascent from this location, not wanting Aaidan to see they were nearby. They planned to circle around to make it seem like they were flying in from their house.

When they disappeared over the trees, I gave them til a count of ten, then turned on my heel and started my trek through the familiar set of trees.

There were two paths to the meadow. The one Dad always took, leading the way to the field of wildflowers, tall grass, and the twisted tree at its center. Then there was the one Arabella and I created. A secret passage to sneak away from the cave we hid in when Mitch was closing in on our location.

It had been a few years since I'd taken that path, but I found the trodden grass and the "secret" markings on the trees to lead the way. Arabella and I would hide in the cave and wait for Mitch to check every other hiding spot before taking our secret path to go back and hide in one of the places he'd already checked. It took him a few times to figure it out, but when he did, he was livid. He told us he never wanted to play hide and seek again. The Little Monster would have rather been pushed into the lake than be tricked again.

The memory made me smile. I already missed him. He'd barely been gone a few days, but it felt like a lifetime. I let myself hope that I would see him again one day, but who knew where this day would end? I didn't even know if it would be possible for me to come back and visit him if I ended up going to Niccodra.

The ground on my trek was soft and spongy from the spring rains, which made the meadow abundant with flowers this time of year. Luckily, that meant my footsteps were mostly silent as I made my way through the trees. I heard the trees above me rustle under the breeze of what I recognized as wings flying overhead.

Good. They'd made it. I was only a third of the way to the cave, but it was farther than they thought I'd be. I had to keep ahead of them in case my gut feeling was correct, and someone had betrayed me.

I turned my attention back to the path ahead. The trek through the trees reminded me of last week's walk through the glen with Kaleb. As I pushed aside the tall grass and branches growing into the path, thoughts of Kaleb rolled through my mind.

How had the boy I'd known most of my life become such an important person to me?

The boy who called me girlie—a nickname I hated but had grown to love every time he whispered it in my ear.

The young boy I clashed make-believe swords with in a fight to protect my sister, the damsel in distress, from the evil sorceress.

The boy who sucked at finding words to play Scrabble but cleared out everyone's bank in Monopoly.

The one who walked arm in arm with me around the courtyard whenever I needed to talk about something.

Who knew every part of my broken soul but looked at me like I was the most beautiful person he'd ever seen.

The one who helped me heal from the worst parts of my life.

Who brought me back from my deepest fears and anxieties.

The one who made me feel like the luckiest girl in the world every time he kissed me.

The boy who loved me for me.

Love.

The word seemed powerful but familiar. Something I knew I felt toward him as a friend, but had slowly started to develop into something *more*.

Did I love Kaleb?

Some might say dragging all your friends to save one person might mean you're in love with them. Or the cry of horror I let out when he was snatched from right beneath my nose. Or the giddy feeling I felt every time I saw him look at me as if—

A roar sounded ahead of me, pulling me from my thoughts. I stopped in my tracks. Listening. Waiting.

The ground shook as another roar sounded, followed by an ear-splitting scream. I looked up just in time to see something falling out of the sky and darted behind a tree. A dragon crashed into the trees nearby, sliding into the path I had just been on. Mari's iridescent scales reflected the moonlight as she righted herself, shaking off the dirt and debris she'd accumulated in her fall. I looked to her back where Leighton had been when I saw her last, but the spot was empty. Before I could step out from behind the tree to ask what was going on, she shot into the sky with a battle cry.

My body quaked in fear. What just happened? Where was Leighton? Was that who screamed? I stayed behind the tree for a moment and took a deep breath. What was going on?

There was one way to find out.

Kyler? I reached out, feeling for that bond—

But it wasn't there.

I couldn't sense that magnetic connection.

It was like reaching into a black hole.

My inner voice echoed as I shouted his name again, *Kyler!*

Nothing.

My breathing hitched. Something was wrong. Very, very wrong.

My blood ran cold. I could feel it. Every pulse. Every heartbeat. An overwhelming sense of dread settled into the pit of my stomach again.

I felt it then—a change inside my body. Like an electric pulse had been put out. I raised my hand to try calling to my power. As it came into view, I froze.

I could see my tanned skin. On a hand that was no longer invisible.

Kyler's illusion failed.

My head shot up to the path ahead as another roar echoed from the meadow. I saw the cave ahead—it was a hundred feet away. If Mari had lost Leighton and my illusion had failed, that meant the one on Kyler's back would, too.

I stepped out from behind the tree and broke into a run. If I was already visible, it didn't matter. Going slow wouldn't make a difference. I had to hurry. I had to make it to that cave.

Another roar, this time closer to my destination. I looked up to ensure no one else was falling from the sky, but when I saw none, I returned my focus to my goal, covering the distance to the cave in three seconds.

There was a flickering light coming from inside the entrance.

I slowed to a walk and crept along the side of the rocks that created the cave. Voices echoed from inside.

A strained voice reached my ears, and I covered my mouth to silence the gasp at the sound of Kaleb's broken voice. "She won't show," he coughed. "She's not dumb enough to fall for your trap."

Well, at least he had confidence in me.

Too bad he was wrong. I was walking straight into this trap. Whatever it was.

A voice I recognized answered, "Oh, I have no doubt she'll come. Especially when she hears this."

Kaleb's scream echoed out of the cave, causing the hairs on my neck to stand up. I bit down on the hand I used to cover my mouth.

That monster *was* torturing him. I knew it was possible, but I never imagined it would be like this.

His scream quieted as he ran out of breath but started over again just as loud. What could make someone scream like that? A sob threatened to escape, and I bit down harder on my hand, the taste of metal and salt reaching my tongue. How did Kyler expect me to sit here and lis—

"Stop it!" Another voice echoed out of the cave.

My stomach dropped to my feet.

No.

No.

That can't be—

They couldn't have—

"Stop, *please*," Ma's pleading voice said again, and my whole world seemed to drop out from beneath me as her voice confirmed what I feared most.

If Ma was in that cave, Mitch was in there, too.

That confirmed the dreadful feeling I'd had all night.

We'd been betrayed.

Kaleb's scream quieted to a whimper. His heavy breathing was loud enough to hear from where I stood outside the entrance.

"Would you like a turn?" Koladon sneered, "Or shall I bring your son back up here while we wait for Rayliana?"

He'd been torturing *all of them??* Why? What would torturing them do?

Ma's only answer was a broken plea.

Kyler said not to do anything stupid. I knew when I promised I wouldn't, it was a lie. But I wasn't sure which was more stupid: standing outside listening to the Kool-Aid Man torture my loved ones or charging in on a dragon shifter with my newly found and unreliable magic as my only weapon.

I should have brought a real weapon with me. That would have been smar—

My dagger.

I hadn't told any of my Omada I had the dagger on me. That was one of the secrets I'd kept from them, and I didn't regret it. That way, not everyone knew everything.

Except me. I made sure to have a secret weapon just in case.

One that Theo had confirmed could wound a Drakalasson. Fatally.

I pulled the dagger free from my boot and gripped it tightly. I hadn't been taught any lessons with a blade, but with the adrenaline coursing through my veins and the knowledge of who was in that cave, it didn't matter. I'd do some damage with what I knew of hand-to-hand combat. The fucking Kool-Aid man wouldn't see it coming.

Closing my eyes, I focused on my steadying breaths.

Breathe in.

I pictured the last time I saw Kaleb's face before he got teleported away. Terrified and in pain.

Breathe out.

Ma's face flashed across my vision. When she'd said goodbye to me in the hospital parking lot, eyes full of hope and sorrow.

Breathe in.

Mitch's gawking face as he realized Kyler was better looking than I had described him. His eyes shone bright as he tried to conceal his smile.

Breathe out.

My eyes snapped open, and I poised myself to round the corner into the cave.

It was time to hype myself up. This monster wasn't going to win today. He didn't get to torture my loved ones and get away with it. He may be powerful, but so was I. I knew how to fight. I knew how to hold my ground. I'd taken down some of the greatest dragon warriors with my bare hands. What's one more?

I took a step to turn into the cave.

Another roar sounded in the meadow, this one more like a call rather than a battle cry. It made me pause for a moment to look in that direction.

Whatever Koladon was saying was cut off by the noise, and I heard his footsteps as they hurried to the cave entrance.

I hurried to find cover in a nearby bush. I could still see the opening as the monster of a man appeared there. His eyes weren't on me but on the meadow.

Another roar. I followed his gaze as a dragon shot above the trees with another one hot on its tail—black and gold. The black dragon must have been Aaidan. I strained my neck, squinting my eyes to see if Ken was still on Theo's back, but the distance was too great to be sure. That alone gave me another set of chills.

Where were Leighton, Mari, and Kyler? Was there someone else for them to battle? Someone we didn't know about? Had Smiles and Tom shown up yet?

Thankfully, Koladon didn't look down from where the dragons were battling in the sky. If he had, he might have seen my head peeking out from behind the branches of the bush. I scolded myself for getting distracted and concealed myself once more within the brush.

Another roar resonated through the night sky. This one sounded like victory. I swallowed thickly, unsure who made the noise and if it was a good sign for me or a bad one. The Kool-Aid madman whipped around to the cave.

A wicked smile told me all I needed to know about that victory roar. "She's here." He shrugged off his jacket, tossing it to the side before turning back to the meadow. "I'm going to go give her a proper greeting." He stalked away from the cave without a single look over his shoulder.

There was no way it was that simple.

He guessed that I would come for my family. That I would appear at the cave to save Kaleb. That was surely why he was the one guarding it in the first place.

So, why would he leave them unguarded now?

An idea formed in my head, and I prayed it wasn't true.

Everything that happened tonight led me to this moment—to me, staring at the entrance of a cave where my loved ones were being tortured. I took a moment to replay the night's events, trying to figure out where it all went wrong.

Kyler took me on our first flight to solidify the bond. I didn't see how that could have been planned because I had made the final decision to go on my own. He'd just given me the choice, but not before telling me I was Evanian.

Us being gone, though, left Kaleb vulnerable. One of the only people I would willingly exchange my life for. Aaidan knew that weakness well.

The question that kept coming up, though, was how he had known Kyler and I were out of the house. Had he been spying from nearby and gotten lucky when we left? Or had someone told him? Theo seemed to know we were on our flight, which likely meant Mari did as well. That meant only three people knew about our outing.

When Kyler and I rushed to Kaleb's room to save him, Kyler stopped me. There didn't seem to be any danger except for the dagger held to Kaleb's throat, which *I* successfully removed while Kyler held me back and watched.

Sometime during that whole debacle, Mitch and Ma were captured too, brought to this cave alongside Kaleb to be tortured by a monster. Someone gave away their location. As far as I knew, only two people knew where they were outside Chief Bass. I didn't even know where they were. I wasn't allowed to talk to them because it might have given their location away.

Or so Theo said. He was also the one who told me they were safe.

According to Chief.

What if this entire time I'd been played? What if all these people, the monsters *and* the ones I called friends, were working together? To get me back to Niccodra. Did that mean Kendall and Leighton were in on it too? Or were they collateral, as Theo called them earlier?

Each thought sent me deeper into a burning rage as I recalled everything from the moment I met these so-called friends. It made sense. They took everything from me. They sent my family away. Cut me off from my old life. Made it seem like everyone was on my side to save me. To protect me. Kyler let Aaidan go. *Twice.* He could have killed him both times. But he didn't.

There had to be a reason.

Theo's attack on my old home didn't injure or destroy the creatures he aimed for. In fact, he *knew* they weren't injured. Was it all an act? To get rid of my home and my last ties to this world, as Ma said earlier?

I didn't want to believe any of these thoughts, but they were all there—being laid out right in front of me like the puzzle I was putting together was upside down the whole time, and I was just now seeing the big picture.

I'd been a fool.

Another roar sounded from the meadow, followed by a laugh so evil that I could only imagine it came from Koladon himself.

If this was all an act, there was no point hiding anymore.

I was going to do what I could to save my family. To save Kaleb.

On my own.

I emerged from the bush, rolled my shoulders back, and walked into the cave.

XLII
Look What You Made Me Do

The first thing I saw in the flickering light ahead were the chains suspended from the ceiling. At least they learned a chair and some ropes weren't enough.

But my hand flew to my mouth when I saw what they'd done.

Kaleb was strung up like a puppet by his wrists, his back to me. The scar I'd seen on his back before had been mutilated even further with new gashes and indecipherable wounds that peppered his back. There had to be more on his front side because a pool of blood had formed on the cave floor under his feet.

The knot that started forming in my stomach had turned to stone. These creatures were *sick*. Torturing innocent humans to lure a young girl to her capture—

Keeping my composure as best I could, I crept along the edge of the cave, keeping to the shadows, waiting for the moment that someone would pop out and confess that I had walked right into their trap.

But no one did.

Still, I clung to the walls, checking over my shoulder repeatedly to make sure the creepy Kool-Aid man wasn't coming back to box me in.

I was still several feet away from Kaleb when the view around the bend revealed Mitch and Ma. They, too, were shackled but not strung up like Kaleb. The chains were loose, letting them recover in a heap on the floor, if you could call sitting in a pool of their own blood recovering.

My eyes burned, but I bit back the tears and the urge to run to them. I wouldn't let them see me cry. Not when I was supposed to be there to rescue them.

The light filling the cave came from a crackling fire in the center. Kaleb's feet barely touched the ground, inches from the flames. I'd be surprised if his feet weren't burnt.

My gaze fell on the iron rod sticking out of the fire.

I snapped my eyes to Kaleb again. They had adjusted to the light, and I could see more of his wounds at this distance. Most of his clothing had been discarded, leaving him fully exposed to the elements in his boxers.

But I couldn't see any fresh blood from the cuts. I furrowed my brow as I chanced a step closer.

I sucked in a gasp, muffling it as best as I could with my hands.

The wounds on Kaleb's back weren't bleeding because they'd been *cauterized*. They'd closed them so he wouldn't die of blood loss.

So they could continue the torture.

I swallowed thickly as I examined the other marks on his back. He was covered in welts.

No. *Brands*.

Over and over.

On his back, his legs, and even his arms, which were stretched out wide by the chains holding him up.

Bile rose in my throat. I didn't know if I could handle seeing the rest of him. But he needed me.

I took a steadying breath to keep myself in check, but tears welled in my eyes as I took in what he'd gone through. Because of me. Because I'd been selfish and didn't want to let him go.

But I wasn't about to let him go this time, either. I was going to get him *and* my family out of there. Even if it was the last thing I did.

One more sweep of the cave told me there was no one else there, so I stepped out of the shadows against the wall and tip-toed up behind Kaleb.

I accidentally kicked a rock, and the sound made him wince, arching away from me toward the fire. The whimper of pain he let out told me he was expecting more. I halted my approach and took a deep breath, fighting the urge to throw my arms around him and tell him he was safe.

Because he wasn't. Not yet.

"Kaleb," I choked out, stepping around him so he could see it was me. He lifted his face, and my hand flew to my mouth.

They had certainly done a number on his face. He was barely recognizable. His lip was swollen and cracked, blood seeping down his chin. A bruise graced his cheekbone, splitting it with how hard they'd punched him. His left eye was sealed shut, but his right cracked open and widened in fear as he realized who stood before him.

"Ray..." He breathed, my resolve breaking when his voice cracked. "*No.* Yo—you shouldn't—"

I held up a finger to my lips, not wanting to cause him more pain. "Shh... I need to get you out of here." His shoulders were at such an odd angle that they could have been dislocated. Depending on the length of time he'd been suspended in the air, it was likely. His feet touched the ground, but only just. Based on the angle at which they were bent, there was no way he'd be able to walk out of here on his own. "Oh my god..." That might complicate things a bit. I looked back up to his face, taking a step closer to him to try and find a place to put my hands so I could get him down. But there didn't seem to be a spot where he hadn't been burned, bruised, or sliced open. I caught his half-opened eye, "Can you stand?"

"No," he coughed, blood seeping out of his mouth as he continued his uneven breathing. "He broke my ankles, so I cou—"

"Rayleigh?" Ma's terrified voice sounded from behind me. I spun to face her and saw Mitch was still passed out next to her, his shirt stained red as he lay in a heap on the ground. She pulled my attention back to her when she spoke again, voice shaking. "Sweetheart, what are you doing here?" She pushed herself to a sitting position, but the simple task drained her. She was weak. Broken. How long had she been here?

The idea that she could have been here since I last saw her made my knees quake.

I glanced back at Kaleb, "I'll be right back." His good eye blinked, confirming he understood. My heart racing, I stepped away from Kaleb and rushed to Ma, kneeling before her. "I came to save you," I whispered because I still didn't know if the others accompanying me were on my side. I examined the iron shackles around her wrists. "If I can open these, can you help me get Kaleb down?"

She nodded, albeit a bit reluctantly. "How did you get here?" She breathed.

"Kyler," I said, shoving the tip of my crystal blade into the keyhole and twisting, hoping the knowledge I'd acquired from movies wouldn't let me down with that trick.

"How did you get past the guard?" Her voice was raspy, likely from screaming the last few days. It made my heart hurt. I heard a click, and the manacle popped open, falling away from her wrist. I moved to the other one, shoving the blade in and twisting again.

"Koladon left his post to go after the others," I said. The other cuff popped open, and I stood to help her to her feet. I used my other hand to shove the blade back into my boot. "He thought I was out there with him. Kyler's little trick. I'll tell you—"

She was shaking her head as I pulled her up. "I wasn't talking about him," she whispered, standing eye level with me.

I scrunched my brow and whirled around to search the cave again but saw no sign of anyone else. My gaze fell back on her, "There was no other guard, Ma."

"I'm certain there was. He was talking to someone else," she insisted. "His voice was familiar but different..." She trailed off, her breathing uneven from her injuries.

I nodded, understanding who she must have heard. "He was probably talking to Aaidan, the one who brought Ka—"

"No!" She grabbed my arm, stopping me from walking to Kaleb. "They were both here talking to *someone else*."

I cocked my head to the side as tingling feelings worked its way through my body. If she was right— "I didn't see anyone else, Ma," I said, shaking my head. But thinking she might agree with me, I added, "I think they're working with someone else, though. Someone who knows me. They've been feeding them information that only someone on the inside could know." I turned to walk back to Kaleb, pulling Ma along behind me. "We'll worry about that later, though. Right now, we have to get Kaleb down."

In Ma's fragile condition, I knew I'd have to support his weight while she unlocked his shackles. I pulled the blade from my boot and handed it to her. "Just shove it in the keyhole and twist it a couple of times," I instructed. "It should pop open." She gave a curt nod, and I faced Kaleb, again searching for the best place to support him without injuring him further.

I looked at his face and noticed his golden brown eye had rolled back into his head. He'd passed out. Great. I winced, knowing he probably wouldn't remember what I was about to do, but it wouldn't be pleasant. "This is going to hurt," I mumbled in warning, just in case he could hear me. I gripped his ribcage and shoved my shoulder into his armpit simultaneously.

He groaned loudly, but I shushed him, hoping he wouldn't come to and scream when I pushed up to alleviate some weight from the shackle Ma was now poised to try unlocking.

She made use of the log pile next to the fire and stood precariously on top of a wobbly log. She inserted the tip of the dagger into the keyhole and wiggled it, but nothing happened.

Kaleb's weight was making my knees shake. "Twist it," I grunted.

I heard her release a breath of frustration before a pop sounded, and Kaleb's arm fell around my shoulder. Ma practically fell off the log but caught herself at the last second. She picked up her makeshift stool and placed it under his other hand. She stepped up again and grabbed onto Kaleb for support, earning another groan from him. "Sorry!" She murmured, finally grasping the other shackle.

She made quick work of the second one, and I grunted as the entirety of Kaleb's weight fell on me. I barely kept my legs locked as Ma jumped off the log, placing the dagger in her back pocket, and stepped up to his other side. She shoved her shoulder into his armpit and draped his arm around her, taking some of his weight off me.

"Well, well, well…" A new voice echoed through the cave.

My heart dropped.

I knew that voice.

Ma *should* have recognized that voice.

I peered over my shoulder to see for myself.

A tall, familiar figure stepped into the firelight out of the shadows. "Nice to see you again, Rayleigh," Doctor Smiles' familiar greeting made my skin crawl as the grin on his face spread wide.

When another shadow appeared behind him, my body went numb. "Yes. Glad you made it here safely," Chief Bass purred.

I dropped my head in defeat. I knew this was coming, but it felt like this was just the beginning.

Letting out a long breath, I lifted my chin to find Ma staring at me with horror in her eyes. The gears were turning in her head. She was going through memories from over the years, searching for any sign or clues that these two men were working against her this whole time.

She hadn't been expecting this betrayal. I hadn't been expecting *this* betrayal, but regardless, I don't think it had the shock factor they were going for.

"Might as well put down the deadweight," Chief said. "You're not going anywhere just yet."

The way he so casually called Kaleb a deadweight made me want to strangle him with my bare hands. It reminded me that I practically could, but I didn't think I could take them both. I didn't know the details of their magic and what they could do.

I sighed and locked eyes with Ma past Kaleb's limp form between us, giving her a reluctant nod. Together, we lowered him to the ground, laying him gingerly on the rocky floor away from the fire and trying to avoid the puddle of blood there. "Stay with him," I whispered, low enough so hopefully only she heard.

I righted myself and twisted to face the two men. "So, which one of you is Gustav?" I asked, confident in my accusation.

They both gave me a look before bursting into maniacal laughter. It set my teeth on edge.

Chief caught his breath first, "I'm flattered, honestly."

"Gustav has never stepped foot on this planet," Smiles chuckled, crossing his arms over his chest.

My chest tightened, but I tried not to let it show. The theory I had formed in my head was starting to crumble. I was certain the others reported to Gustav, but if neither of these two were him—

Who was he?

"Nor would he," Chief confirmed.

"But since you're so eager to know our names, I'm Stefano." He mocked a bow and then gestured to Chief, "This is Bastiel." He copied Stefano's mock bow.

I'd never heard the name Stefano before, but Bastiel— Theo had used that name earlier. My blood tingled. "Who else is working against me?"

Both men smiled, and it was anything but pleasant.

Bastiel answered, "Isn't it frustrating? Knowing something is wrong but not being able to pinpoint exactly what it is?"

That didn't answer my question at all. I focused on him, though, searching within myself for that feeling of lightning. But my powers were quiet—almost non-existent. "So, just you two betrayed me?" I guess I'd have to figure out how to take them both on after all.

"I wouldn't call it a betrayal," Stefano said, shrugging as he decided to sit on the boulder next to him. "We just chose the winning side."

That still wasn't an answer, and I was tired of waiting. "You still look like a couple of losers to me," I grinned, watching Bastiel fall for the bait and charge for me. I dipped my chin and brought my shoulders up into a shrug.

He growled as he got up into my face, "Say that agai—"

But he never got to finish that sentence. Because I snapped my head forward into his face, silencing him. The head butt hit true to mark, and Bastiel stumbled back a step or two as blood started pouring from his broken nose. In the split second it took for him to realize what happened, I reached up to his head and brought it down, bringing my knee up to meet it. The blow caused him to crumple to the ground in a heap.

Stefano jumped up in shock at the turn of events. He looked from Bastiel to me and sneered, "You *bitch!*" Then, he lunged at me. I'd angled myself away from where Ma and Kaleb were positioned on the floor, knowing that this was no spar and things might get out of hand.

When he charged at my waist, I sidestepped but wrapped both of my arms around his torso—over one shoulder and under the other. I pulled him back, twisting my body to flip his massive frame over mine. I underestimated his weight and had to use my leg to help push him further into the flip. When I flipped with him, I used that to my advantage to trap him in a mount.

The look of shock on his face told me he underestimated me—his mistake.

But he didn't let that shock last. He started to fight back. He swiped my arms from the cage around his head, reaching to wrap his own around my neck. But I leaned back and then to the side. I pulled him into a roll and loosened the grip of one of my legs. By the time he was above me, one leg was on his shoulder, and the other came up to meet it. He shoved his arm to block the choke, but I was faster. I locked my legs in place and squeezed as tight as I could.

I wasn't waiting for a tap out this time, though.

No. This was a fight for my freedom. My life. My family's lives.

I flexed my legs more, closing them tighter on his neck, and watched his face turn red as he pulled against my tight grip. He kicked his legs, trying to get some leverage, and tugged at my legs as they strangled him. He spat a breath out, trying to suck one in, but to no avail. My muscles started screaming, but I held tight. Stefano reached behind him, for what, I don't know, but it didn't matter. He was fading. The fight was going out of him. My grip started shaking, but I knew I had to keep hold. I couldn't let go. Not yet. I didn't want to kill him—though I'm sure he would have taken that chance if the roles were reversed—I just needed him to pass out.

Finally, his arms stopped flailing, and his body went still. I counted to ten, just to be sure, and then released him. I quickly untangled myself and found Ma kneeling beside Kaleb, staring at me with her mouth wide open. "Where did you learn to fight like that?"

"Tom," I breathed heavily, still wondering if he was on my side or if I'd have to fight him, too. "Come on, we have to go." I reached for her, but as her fingers grazed mine, her body was yanked away.

She screamed as she flew across the cavern. Her body slammed into the wall by Mitch with a sickening crunch, and she collapsed on the floor, unmoving.

"MA!" I shouted, making to move toward her, but my body wouldn't go. It was frozen in place.

"Tsk, tsk, tsk." A low voice came from somewhere close by. "You are a piece of work, aren't you, Rayliana?" Koladon stepped into the light. When did he get here?

"Let me go and find out," I spat.

His eyes flashed with intrigue. "You are utterly helpless right now, and yet you find it in yourself to threaten me?" He grinned, flashing pointed canines that were sharper than average. When I didn't bother to answer him, he said, "It's no matter, really. You can't beat me." The arrogance in that statement made me want to prove how wrong he was.

My body collapsed to the ground as I felt his hold on me release. Kaleb, who was mere feet from me, groaned, coming back around at the worst possible time. I crawled over to him and pulled his head into my lap. "Shh... I'm right here. I'm going to get you out of here," I lied, tears creeping in because I knew I wasn't leaving this cave with any of them. But I hoped they would leave in one piece. I glared at Koladon, who had positioned himself between me and my family. "What do you want?" I said through gritted teeth.

He smirked at my question and crouched down, bringing himself to my eye level, but kept his distance. Smart man, unfortunately. He cocked his head, "How did you take down my men?" It was a genuine question, which meant he hadn't been there to see me fight.

"They underestimated me," I ground out.

Koladon stood up and circled behind me. "And your power? Has it manifested yet?" The sound of something sliding against the rocky floor made me tense.

I wanted to turn around, to keep my eyes on my enemy, but with Kaleb's head in my lap, I had no choice. I put a bite in my words, "What's wrong? Not powerful enough to fig—"

Searing hot pain shot through my body, and I arched my back away from the source of the pain, letting out a horrific scream as the smell of my burnt flesh filled the cavern.

"Drop the sass. Answer the question." Koladon's hot breath was right by my ear as my echoing scream died, and my body all but collapsed onto Kaleb.

The burn of the hot iron rod continued to throb on my back, feeling like a fire dancing across my skin. I swallowed, trying to coat my throat enough to speak, but my answer came out a croak, "Yes." I had no idea how Kaleb endured that hot iron brand so many times. My breaths came heavier as I realized I had no idea what kind of information they were trying to torture out of him or my family. It could have been anything. If they had to sit through that over and over, I wouldn't blame them for giving up information on me, or at least I wouldn't be surprised.

"That wasn't so hard, was it?" He crooned. I glowered at the air in front of me. The same noise of something being dragged across the floor came again, and I knew he was sliding the iron rod into the fire to reheat. I wasn't sure I'd be able to endure another touch from the cursed metal. "Which elements do you control?" His question was confident, meaning he knew I had more than one.

I wondered if I could fool him. "Air and Earth," I said through gritted teeth, glaring at the wall and pretending it was him instead.

The scraping metal on the stone came again, and he was near my ear when he said, "And?" Dragging out the word, landing hard on the last letter.

A shudder worked its way through me at his proximity. Did he know I had three, or was he guessing? Would denying my third element condemn me to another branding, or would it be news to him? I decided to play a bit dumb. "That's all I know of." I braced for the pain the lie could have brought me, but it didn't come.

"Interesting." That confirmation alone should have cleared Kyler from my suspect list, but I couldn't shake the feeling. On the one hand, if Kyler had betrayed me, he would have told Koladon I knew about all three of my powers. On the other hand, perhaps Kyler hadn't had a chance to tell him what I learned.

As much as I wanted to trust that the bond between Kyler and I would keep him from betraying me, I had trouble believing all this could have happened without him, Theo, or Mari being involved.

"Have you been able to use your powers yet?" I could feel the heat of the iron rod close by, but if he didn't know about my third element, he wouldn't know the truth about that either.

"No," I tried to sound defeated, and up until this moment, I had forgotten to test my powers again. I searched for that feeling of energy in my veins, but it was nowhere to be found. Tom said not to rely on them, but damn, it would have been nice right now.

I couldn't think of why he would have asked that question. Then he said, "Good. At least we won't have to worry about putting the gonos on you." The iron rod dragged across the ground again, and I heard footsteps echo in the cave.

"The what?" My body tensed, knowing what was coming.

But his voice was far away when he spoke again. "Power dampeners. So you can't fight back." I didn't need my powers to fight back. He had to know that. I mean, his men were passed out on the floor because of my bare hands. His footsteps stopped, and my spine tingled. "Not that I'll need them with this motivation."

A scream echoed in the cave, making my blood run cold yet again.

I whipped my head around. Koladon stood over Ma, pressing the iron rod into her shoulder with a sick smile. "Stop! Please!" I shouted. "Leave her alone!"

He pulled the rod from her shoulder, and her screams died to a whimper. She stirred uncomfortably on the ground, and it took everything in me not to run over and smack the ugly smile off Koladon's face. He made no move to step away from her, though, leaning against the wall next to her instead, the iron rod at his side.

His crazed eyes landed on me. Studying me. Roving over my body. It felt like a violation. His gaze stopped at Kaleb, and I followed it to see him staring at me through a tiny slit in his eye. Pain and sorrow swam there. I had to get him out of there.

Koladon's voice echoed across the cave, "Do you love him?"

When my gaze found his, he was still staring at Kaleb. The tone in his voice made it sound like love was an abomination. The question caught me off guard, but I didn't have to think twice before I nodded, looking back at the boy before me. Kaleb's good eye leaked a tear, and

I gave him a small smile as tears formed in my eyes.

"Do you want him to live?"

I nodded again, my tears blurring my vision, but I blinked them back.

"Then you need to come with me. Willingly."

I nodded, knowing there was no other way to get what I needed. "I'll go with you." Thankfully, the tears had dispersed, so when I bent over Kaleb to give him one last kiss, they didn't splash on his face. It was a gentle kiss, but that somehow made the goodbye worse. I touched my forehead to his and whispered the words I hadn't said out loud yet, "I love you." I didn't care if it was too soon. I'd known him for so long. I meant it.

Kaleb's voice was hoarse and low from screaming, but he said, "Don't go." He paused, and when I didn't answer, he begged me, "*Please.*" More tears welled in his eye, spilling into his hairline, "You'll die."

"And if I don't go, you'll die," I said truthfully. I couldn't tell him my plan because I was sure the monster across the cavern was listening to every word exchanged. There was no way of knowing if my plan would work or if my so-called friends would be there to help if it did, but I had to try. I kissed Kaleb's forehead and sat up, slowly moving his head from my lap to the ground with my free hand, pushing myself up with the other. I turned away from his pleading face and found Ma and Mitch against the wall. "Do I get to say goodbye to them too?" I asked.

Koladon was still leaning against the wall near Ma but pushed himself off and stalked toward me with an ugly smirk. "That was a quick goodbye for someone you claim to love," he muttered, ignoring my question. He stopped as he came to stand next to Kaleb and looked down at his broken, wounded body. "Pity he can't come with us to Niccodra."

I was fuming at this point. He looked at Kaleb like a piece of meat. I opened my mouth to ask my question again, but he held up a hand.

"No need to say goodbye to them, though." He looked at me. "They're coming with us."

XLIII
Empty Heart Shaped Box

The blood drained from my face. Humans couldn't survive in Niccodra. Not for long, anyway. "No…" I breathed, unsure how to plead for their safety when I wasn't planning on going with him.

"We need some… *motivation* to keep you in line. They'll serve that purpose." I could hear the grin in his words. "Unless you promise to cooperate. Then I will leave them here to live their miserable human lives."

The lie came so easily to my lips, "I promise."

He lifted his brows in surprise. He recovered quickly and nodded. "You have two minutes."

I rushed across the cavern and knelt next to Ma, reaching to pull her close to me. When her ear was next to my mouth, I muttered, "The dagger." Then, louder so Koladon could hear, "Keep Mitch safe." She turned her body just enough in my embrace to expose the pocket where the dagger was. I slowly moved my hand to grab it, pulling it out as I released her. "I love you, Ma." I turned the hilt in my hand so the blade pressed against my forearm, knowing I would only have one chance and had to keep it concealed until it presented itself.

When I looked at Ma's face, it was filled with cold determination. She gave me a subtle nod. "I love you too, sweetheart." What she really said was, *Make it count.*

With a tight-lipped smile and nod, I turned my focus to Mitch. He was still unconscious, but from this distance, I saw the evidence of his captivity and torture. I pulled my bottom lip in to keep my emotions in check and leaned over him to kiss him on the forehead. "I love you more than the sun," I whispered.

Before any other emotions could rise, I stood quickly and walked back across the cave to where Koladon still stood over Kaleb. "Ready?" He asked, without turning to face me.

He had his back to me. It was my best chance. I flipped the blade away from my forearm. It fit perfectly in my palm. I weighed it in my hand, wondering how much force it would take to punch through flesh and bone.

Narrowing my gaze on the spot between his shoulder blades, I moved.

I drove the blade hard and fast.

It made contact with his spine.

But it stopped there.

My whole body froze. Again.

Dammit.

He didn't move, though. I heard him take a deep breath, and he let it out slowly, dropping his head. "I was really hoping you weren't going to do that," he muttered. "I suppose that means you broke your word."

Before I could think what that meant, he stepped away from the blade, and I was forced to the ground. My knees slammed into the rocky floor where he had been standing. The dagger was still poised to strike, and I realized what was happening a split second before it did. "NO!" I screamed as my arm unfroze and continued its trajectory with a force uncontrollable to me.

Straight toward Kaleb's chest.

"NOOO!" I bellowed again, pouring every ounce of strength into resisting the power shoving my arm down.

To my surprise, the dagger stopped millimeters from Kaleb's

sternum. Thinking Koladon stopped my arm to make another deal with me, I peered up at him, waiting for the terms of a new agreement.

He was staring intently but not at my face. His eyes were on the arm that had stopped short of his prey. His gaze shot to mine, brow furrowed. Sweat beaded on his temple, and that's when I knew. He hadn't stopped me.

I had.

His eyebrows knitted further together as he took me in. My arm shook. I was holding it back while *he* was still trying to force it down. "You're stronger than I predicted," he said through gritted teeth, but then his strained confusion turned to malice with a simple grin. "But not strong enough."

The force of his power returned tenfold.

I screamed as I was forced to bury the blade deep in Kaleb's chest.

His face contorted in pain for a moment as he inhaled sharply. Then, all the muscles in his face went slack. His last breath released from his lungs in slow motion.

"No!" I screamed again, staring in disbelief at his unnaturally still body.

Koladon's influence over my arm disappeared, and I ripped the dagger from Kaleb's chest, flinging it across the cavern, where I heard it clatter on the floor. I threw myself onto Kaleb as a scream of pain erupted from me. I hoped and prayed none of it was real, but as my hands roved over his face and then his chest where the dagger had been, they came away bloody.

"Kaleb," I sobbed, grabbing his face between both of my hands. "No, no, no...Kaleb, please." I scanned his unmoving eyes, "Look at me, Kaleb! Please!" My tears splashed into the flow of blood coming from his chest as I pressed my hands over it to try and stop the bleeding. "Kaleb, please! No!" He couldn't be—

"No, no, *no*." This couldn't be happening.

He couldn't be gone.

But there was no movement. His chest hadn't risen since it last fell, and his heart no longer held a beat beneath my hands.

The river of blood stopped flowing through the gaping wound in his chest.

His body had gone limp, his non-swollen eye unfocused.

Oh my god...

What have I done? The sweet boy I'd fallen in love with— he was— he was gone. Because of me.

I would never again be able to wrap my arms around him and feel the steady beat of his heart against my ear.

There would be no waking up wrapped in his arms, my head on his chest, his breath on my head.

I would never hear his contagious laugh again.

There would be no more dirty jokes.

No more teasing.

No more sweet kisses.

He was gone.

Sobs wracked my body anew as what I did sank in, and my head fell to where my arms lay on his chest.

This was my fault.

I killed Kaleb.

The dagger was in my hand.

All because I didn't want to leave him behind.

Through my sobs, I choked out, "I'm so sorry..."

If I had just gone to Niccodra—

"Shame you had to go and try to stab me in the back," Koladon said, his voice having turned away from me. I lifted my head to watch him cross the cavern to where I'd thrown the dagger. He bent to pick it up. "Such a pretty little dagger," he mused. I watched as he wiped the blood off the blade and flipped it comfortably in his hand, catching it in a hold ready to strike.

Hot tears rolled down my face as I watched him stalk over to where Mitch and Ma were still crumpled on the ground. He reached for Mitch, and I realized his intent—

"No!" I jerked up from where I was bent over Kaleb. "Don't touch him," I pleaded. I would not be the reason for another death today. "I'll go with you."

A single brow stretched toward his hairline, "Truthfully, this time?" He pointed at me with the dagger. His hand hadn't touched Mitch yet, but I didn't want to chance it. "Because I grow weary of your games."

"Yes," I snarled through my tears. "But you can't hurt anyone else."

He smiled wickedly, "Deal." He stood from where he crouched and stalked toward me.

I'd forgotten Stefano and Bastiel were there until Koladon stepped up to them and kicked them both. Hard. "Get up," he growled. "It's time to go."

Both men stood as if they hadn't been knocked out for the better part of twenty minutes. If I weren't about to be dragged away from everything I knew and loved, I probably would have paid more attention to how easily they woke up from that state.

But when they walked across the cavern and undid the chains holding Mitch in place, dragging him and Ma to their feet, my head snapped to Koladon. "No!" My voice was raw from screaming, but that didn't stop me from yelling, "You said you'd leave them here!"

He clicked his tongue, "Yes. If you cooperated. You did no such thing." He squatted in front of me and whispered, "And if what just happened here wasn't proof enough," he pointed with the dagger toward Kaleb's lifeless form behind me, and my gaze followed, "know that every threat I make is a promise." The point of the dagger touched just under my chin, and he turned my face back to his, one side of his mouth lifting. "I take deals very seriously, Rayliana, even if you don't. I would keep that in mind if I were you." I snarled at him, and he removed the dagger from my chin, knicking the skin there for good measure. He reached out toward my face as if he were going to wipe the blood away, but I snapped my teeth at him. He *laughed*. "Oh, this is going to be fun." He cocked his head to the side. "I can't wait to see the look on your fa—"

"Boss." Koladon whipped his head around to where Bastiel stood, holding Ma over his shoulder like a sack of potatoes. Blood caked his face, and a small stream of it still seeped from his nose. "There's trouble at the portal."

Koladon stood, growling, "Go." Bastiel and Stefano bowed their heads and headed toward the mouth of the cave.

If there was trouble, perhaps that meant the others were still fighting. There was a chance they were on my side and could help me. But how could Aaidan be fighting three dragons and the twins by himself—

They were next to the portal.

Shit. Who's to say more monsters hadn't come through to help fight against them? It would make sense. I mentally cursed myself for not thinking about that. And why hadn't Theo or Kyler thought that through?

But then again, maybe they had. Perhaps the only trouble at the portal was getting it open.

Koladon sighed, "Up, princess. Time to go."

I glared at him and turned to face the boy I'd killed once more. I wanted to hope that the dagger hadn't been real and it hadn't punched through his sternum straight to his heart. But as I took in his pale, lifeless face, I knew. He was gone. There was nothing I could have done. I ran my hand down his cheek and felt the cold, clammy skin. Tears filled my eyes again, and my nose started to burn. I moved the curls of his hair plastered to his face with blood and sweat, and as my fingers trailed over his still-open eye, I gently closed it. I leaned down over him, placing one last kiss on his lips as tears spilled onto his face. I pulled away and whispered, "I'll never forget you—"

Koladon yanked me back by the hair, popping my neck in several places as I was lifted off the ground. The scream I let out was cut short as a rough hand slapped over it. "No more stalling," Koladon's hot breath in my ear made me recoil. "I'm going to remove my hand from your filthy mouth and lead you out of this cave. If you fight at all, your brother will be dead before he makes it to Niccodra."

I swallowed the whimper of pain as he yanked on my hair again for emphasis, but I nodded. His rough hand left my mouth, and he threw me toward the cave entrance with the grip he had on my hair. I stumbled over my own feet, and my face hit the ground before I could catch myself. But I pushed to my knees with the bit of strength I had left and spat on the floor. A mixture of blood and saliva landed in front of me, and I reached up to touch my now bleeding lip. "You're a monster."

His rough hand gripped my elbow, pulling me to my feet with a dark chuckle. "You have yet to meet the real monster."

Those words could have meant anything. Was he referring to himself? Saying that his true monstrous side hadn't been revealed yet? Or could the dragon he shifts into be more vicious than this form? Terrifying either way.

Or he could be referring to someone else. The monster behind all of this. Gustav.

A shudder ran through me with the possibility of meeting someone worse than the man leading me out of the cave. I'd seen what he could do. The torture he liked to dish out. The cruel and wicked ways he used others to do his dirty work. If Gustav was worse than him, I wasn't sure I'd survive under his control.

The moment we stepped outside, I knew I'd lost. There were no noises of fighting. The roars of dragons had subsided, and the meadow on the other side of the tree line was quiet. The night sky was empty, aside from the stars shining brightly with the moon.

My body tingled and went numb.

This was it.

I was being led to my cage.

Their mission was to capture me, and they used every resource they could to make it happen. Would any of this have happened if I'd been more suspicious of people sooner? If I had started paying attention to the clues? Would I have seen the betrayal coming? Looking back at all the bad things that happened, it was evident that someone was watching my every move.

Around every turn, the bad guys knew where I'd be.

The mall. The studio. The grocery store. The courtyard. My house. Kyler's house.

Sure, some of those were uneventful, but I had still been followed. The creepy person in the hoodie had been there each time. He'd only disappeared after—

I cursed myself. The hooded figures stopped appearing after Mari, Theo, and Kyler revealed themselves to me as my guardians. How could I have been so stupid? How had I not seen it? And to think, I'd started considering them my friends, trusting them with my life.

I wouldn't make that mistake again.

We stepped through the treeline into the meadow. What had once been my solace, my comfort, my favorite place on earth—covered in wildflowers and tall grass and filled with memories of my life—now became the one place I never wanted to step foot in again.

But it didn't resemble the memories at all.

The grass and wildflowers had been reduced to ash and blackened earth, still smoking from the fire that had burned them away. Smoke filled my nose as the last of the embers snuffed out. A single sunflower stood at the edge of the field, flames wrapping around its petals. I watched as the fire consumed its beauty, tears tracking down my face.

The tree in the center, the one Dad used to sit against with his guitar, hadn't been damaged at all. There were no scorch marks or broken branches.

But it had changed.

The trunk had untwisted, opening the tree to a circular archway. Through the hole, where I should have been able to see the other side of the meadow, I saw nothing.

The center was a black void.

The portal.

Koladon used his grip on my elbow to shove me to the ground. I landed hard on my knees and bit back a scream of pain. He went to speak to the people lined up before him too quietly for me to hear. Kendall and Leighton were bound by their wrists and knocked out in front of two men I didn't recognize. Kyler, Theo, and Mari were nowhere to be found. Bastiel and Stefano still held Mitch and Ma over their shoulders, unconscious, barely straining at their weight.

"Update," Koladon ordered loudly from one of the men behind the twins.

"The portal went dark after the dragons went through," the unknown man replied.

The dragons. Weren't they all dragons? Where was Aaidan? Had he gone through the portal with the other three?

Koladon strode toward the portal. He studied it momentarily, stuck his hand into the black void, and wiggled his fingers. "Hmm." He stepped around the backside of the open tree, disappearing behind it.

For a moment, I thought it wouldn't work, and I let a glimmer of hope in. Perhaps if we couldn't get back, Ma and Mitch could recover here and get away somehow. But then a spark emitted from the side of the tree, swallowing my hopes of them surviving this. I watched the tree portal as the spark turned into a stream of light, flowing in a circle around the edge of the hole in the tree, spiraling into the center.

I would have thought this was incredible if I wasn't so terrified of what was to come.

A portal to another world. In a meadow I'd frequented throughout my simple, human life. The idea was truly fascinating, and I wished, for a short moment, that my twin could have been there to see it. To see the world we had come from. So we could explore the beautiful place together, find where we belonged, and thrive in a place we were always meant to be. Together.

But the thought vanished from my mind the moment Koladon reappeared. No. I didn't want Arabella to see the world this monster was dragging me into. She would have fought until she died to free the people she loved. She probably would have fought harder than I did. I was strong. I knew that. But I wasn't strong enough. Koladon had said so right before the knife drove into Kaleb's chest. Perhaps Arabella would have been stronger. She would have let him go and gone with Koladon instead of killing Kaleb.

I choked back a sob as Kaleb's face poured into my thoughts. I hated that my last memories of him were of him being held captive, first with a knife to his throat and then chained to the ceiling of a cave. Hated that the last time I'd seen his face, it was scarred and ruined, lifeless and cold.

I pushed those horrible pictures from my head and thought of the moment he kissed me in the piano room. His laughing at my shock in response to his dirty jokes. The warmth of his hands as they roamed my body in our embrace. Those were the moments I would never forget. That I would hold on to as I sat in captivity wherever I was being taken. His torture would not taint my memory of him.

With the portal up and running again, the others started to pass under the archway of the tree, disappearing into the spinning vortex of light. Bastiel went first with Ma, Stefano and Mitch close on their tails. The man behind Kendall lifted her roughly and threw her over his shoulder, Leighton's captor doing the same, and they walked toward the portal.

Koladon approached me as I watched the people I loved being taken to an unknown land. When Leighton and her captor disappeared, Koladon stood before me. "Time for a nap," he sneered, a cruel smile spreading across his face right before the back of his hand connected with my face.

XLIV
Bad Blood

Darkness.

A steady drip of water.

Cold, hard rock beneath me.

These things greeted me when I awoke.

I was in a dungeon.

There was hardly any space to breathe, let alone move, but I pushed myself to sit anyway, hissing at the pain it caused.

A rock wall pushed against my back. Bars pressed into my legs on either side as I crossed them gingerly. The darkness prevented me from seeing any other details of my cage, but it was small.

The scrape of something on the floor close by made me jolt.

"Hello?" I croaked, my voice hoarse from non-use.

A small voice answered, "Ray?"

Kendall.

Ignoring the pain, I moved toward the sound of her voice, my body screaming with every movement. "Ken? Is Leigh here?"

There was a shaky intake of breath, "Yes. She's still unconscious. That bastard hit her pretty hard."

Shit. "Is anyone else here?"

"I am," said another soft voice I recognized, but it made my jaw drop as I turned toward the sound.

"*Mari?*" The tone of my voice did not go unnoticed.

"You're surprised." It wasn't a question. "I don't blame you. I would have thought the same thing if I were you."

I was afraid to ask my next question because I wasn't sure how I would react either way. If I had been wrong about Mari, perhaps I was wrong about Kyler and Theo. But then, who could have betrayed us? "Theo? Kyler?"

She released a long breath, "I should have seen—" She stopped short.

Footsteps echoed in the distance. A faint light appeared down the hallway, illuminating enough of the dungeon for me to see some of my surroundings.

The world was blurry from the tears I cried and then being knocked out, but I could see the bars that contained me. The cell was barely big enough for me to lie down. It was connected to several other cells. To my left, Kendall leaned against the bars of the cell next to her, where Leighton lay. To my right, Mari sat with her knees pulled to her chest, staring at the place where the light came from.

Ma's unconscious form lay beyond her. "Ma," I whispered through the bars. She didn't stir. Nausea roiled in my stomach, remembering all that had happened the moments before we ended up here.

I took in the dim space behind her. The other cells were empty.

Mitch wasn't there.

Where was he?

The footsteps came closer, and a bouncing light came around a corner far to the left of my barred door.

The hand holding the torch was connected to a familiar form.

I swallowed the lump in my throat as he stalked down the hall. His dark curls poked out from the hood he was wearing.

Shadows covered his face from the flame and his hood, but I'd recognize that asshole anywhere.

Broad shoulders pulled back.

Head held high.

Each stride confident.

Kyler.

He came to a halt in front of my cell, placed the torch he held in a sconce on the frame, and reached for the keys at his belt. He sifted slowly through them.

Kyler wasn't wearing regular clothes, or at least what I considered regular. In his dark, detailed jacket, he looked like an assassin, the hood still concealing his face. I had a feeling it was to hide the smirk I knew was there, knowing he probably came to gloat with some shitty "I'm the villain" monologue or something.

He must have found the key he needed because he thrust it into the keyhole, turned the key, and swung the door open.

He leaned on the doorframe—a stance he could have trademarked.

My breathing became difficult, and the edges of my vision faded as I took in the man before me.

My hands started to shake as I looked for something around me to ground me. The rocky floor and the solid iron bars were all I could feel. My cold fingertips found a jagged spot on the floor. I pushed my palms down, scraping my hand along the cold, hard rock. The pain of it cutting into my hand cleared my vision. I openly glared at the man before me.

I thought I'd be able to handle facing him. I wanted to spit words at him like I had at Aaidan every time he'd shown up. But every nerve in my body was standing on edge, making me shake with anger and fear. I wanted to yell at him, tell him to go fuck himself, but all the words got stuck in my throat, never making it past my lips.

All except one.

"Kyler." I meant to spit his name, but it sounded more like a whispered plea.

He stepped over the threshold and bent down before me.

I couldn't smell the sweet scent of strawberries anymore. It was overpowered by the smoke that hit my nostrils.

The light of the torch illuminated the familiar smirk on his face.

When that smirk turned into a devilish grin, the whole world felt like it disappeared beneath me—swallowing me whole at the sound of his voice.

A voice I never thought I would hear again.

"Guess again, girlie."

TO BE CONTINUED…

Pronunciation Guide

NAMES
Rayliana - Ray-lee-ah-nuh
Nikylo - Nee-ky-loh
Niccodra - Nee-koh-druh
Koladon - Koh-lah-dawn
Adarachi - Ah-dah-rah-chi
Bastiel - Bah-stee-ehl
Stefano - Steh-fah-noh

ELEMENTALS
Annysian - a-nee-see-an
Evanian - eh-vah-nee-an
Omonian - oh-moh-nee-an
Ignalian - ig-nah-lee-an
Udarian - oo-dair-ee-an

DRAGONS
Lunnox - Luh-nuhx
Ravault - rah-vahlt
Parevim - pair-eh-vihm
Fyxenal - fix-ehn-ahl
Dynkoi - dihn-koy
Solina - soh-leen-ah

ISLANDS
Delgia - Del-gee-ga
Gitapodi - Gee-tah-poh-dee
Nykeraki - Ni-kehr-ah-kee
Diplopela - Dip-loh-pee-lah
Kevastisto - Keh-vahs-tees-toh
Fotypas - Foh-tee-pahs
Pipistrella - Pi-peh-streh-ya
Eliorra - Eh-lee-or-ah

OTHER
nilatís - nee-lah-tees
kidemos - ki-deh-mohs
gissa - gee-saw
asteri - ass-teh-ree
omada - oh-mah-dah
aidi - ay-dee
lochi - lo-khee
dikitís - dih-kee-tees
glykos - gleye-kohs
tavi - tah-vee
doulos - doh-lohs
kallit - kahl-leet
myados - mí-ah-dohs
kavaltis - kah-vahl-tees
madí - mah-dee
kyllindro - kil-lin-droh

Acknowledgments

Full Playlist

I honestly don't even know where to start. The people who made this book happen are irreplaceable to me, as are all the people I met along the way. This book would not have been possible without many of my biggest cheerleaders, who range from friends to family to people I met on silly little apps called Instagram and TikTok. The overwhelming joy I feel that you, the reader, even wanted to read this book makes me the happiest person on earth.

Now, let's get into the nitty-gritty details of those in my life who have been there throughout this journey. First and foremost, my little sister Jenna was the only one unfortunate (or fortunate if you ask her) enough to read the *very* first version of this story. Even with the terrible and immature writing, she still wanted book two when she was finished. I thank her for her endless support on this journey of writing and rewriting and her encouragement every single step of the way.

Second, I'd like to thank the rest of my family for believing in me and continually showing their love and support on my journey to get this book published. My parents have constantly supported me throughout my life, whether pursuing film school or randomly deciding to move across the country alone. I would not be where I am today without them pushing me to be my very best self and go where

I am supposed to be in this life.

Thirdly, the one and only Ms. Kelley is the reason this even exists in the first place. She has no idea that I'm even writing this right now, but that assignment in May of 2009 changed the course of my life, and I don't think she has any idea how her words have encouraged me even to this day. The prologue and first chapter of this book are basically the same as the assignment I wrote at seventeen, with a little bit of an upgrade. I still have that assignment. I kept it as my motivation. Ms. Kelley had a huge impact on my life, and I couldn't have done this without her original note to "keep writing."

To my three OG lollipop gals! Gosh, without Erin, Kaley, and Lauren bugging me for new chapters every day, I do not know if this book would have gotten to where it is today. They each were given a few chapters to start, with a question of whether or not they'd read more after what was given to them. They all begged for more, and sometimes, only thirty minutes would pass after sending them a chapter before I would get a text saying they needed *more*. They are *the* biggest reason this book was finished at all. Without them, I don't think I would have been able to tell Rayleigh's story. Seeing and hearing some of their reactions as they read was one of the biggest blessings.

Liana, my girl (who also is a writer, and you should check out her series The Secrets Within Me), spent hours brainstorming, doing writing sessions, and actually reading my book when she is *not* a reader. She helped me create the overall plot of my story, unafraid to say, "No, that's dumb," whenever I felt delulu about something. She also was a massive help in finding a song for each chapter— Which, if you're reading this, go to the playlist QR code above—the first letter of each chapter spells out a little surprise! (:

To Jonas, who gave me such sage advice as a huge fantasy reader and was the first person ever to say, "Your book is as good if not better than some New York Times Best Sellers." The way I melted into a puddle and cried tears of happiness at those words... I cannot express my gratitude enough. My other author friend, Lance, gave me constant advice on writing, even if he didn't mean to, and always had encouraging words for me along the way. And Gavin. My honest and brutal truther. This book may not have been his genre, but he read it anyway and gave me his honest review—even though it wasn't great, he said he still had fun reading it. I think that helped me prepare for other people who may not like this book.

To my roommates, Dom, David, and Nate, who all hyped me up and continue to do so any time I accomplish anything with this book. Dom especially, without whom the cover of this book would not exist. He sat on the floor to brainstorm what my cover should look like and helped me choreograph scenes with Kyler and Ray so I could see what would make sense. While he may not know it, he's also been a big help along the way in my writing.

To Joni, who so kindly agreed to help me with the editing process because all I wanted to do was pull my hair out and quit several times. But her big brain helped me catch the mistakes that I apparently missed in my seven rereads of this book. HA!

Alyssa, my sweet, sweet booksta girlie, helped me with sensitivity reading to ensure I represented my girls Mari and Leighton as best as possible. I may or may not have also taken some inspiration for Mari from her...

Finally, I'd like to thank all of my friends I met along the way who wanted to read my book from the minute I told them about it. My best friend Katie, who got me into buddy reading and loving talking to people about books.

My booksta besties, Bri, Johanna, Jaqueline, KJ, Natalie, Rae, and Roni, who kept asking when they could read my book. My "real life" friends, Aria, Ashleigh, Elissa, Helix, Jenny, Jessica, Jordan, Lavender, Lindsey, Lisa, Maddie, Natalie, Reina, Sadie, Stefani, Tyson, and Victoria, who bugged me whenever they saw or talked to me about reading my book.

Lastly, every single person who donated to my Kickstarter to get this book off the ground, some I've already listed, but here are the rest: Adriane, Aleena, Alexandra, Alexia, Allison, Ally, Amanda B, Amanda H, Amy, Anthony, Ben, Bianca, Britani, Brittney, Caleb O, Caleb T, Catherine, Claire, Daniel, David, Elizabeth, Elle, Emily, Gina, Izzy, Jenny, Jonathan, Julia, Juliana, Julie K, Julie P, Justin, Kailyn, Kate, Katherine, Keith, Korey, Kristin, Lauren, Leah, Lexi, Lindsey,

Madeline, Marlene, Marissa, Marta, Megan, Melissa, Michelle, Mitchell, Molly, Nicole, Nikki, Oscar, Patsy, Peggy, Randi, Samantha, Sara, Sara D, Sherrie, Sia, SJ, Sophia, Symantha, Tara, Taylor, Ted, Thea, Tiffany, Vance, and Zuzu.

Countless others encouraged me to keep writing: authors, friends, teachers, and more, none of whom I could have done this without. So, to everyone who said no, to everyone who said keep going, and to the person reading this now, thank you. Thank you, thank you, thank you.

Made in the USA
Middletown, DE
21 June 2024